A SUMMER OF NEW BEGINNINGS

LISA HOBMAN

Boldwood

First published in 2018. This edition published in Great Britain in 2024 by Boldwood Books Ltd.

Copyright © Lisa Hobman, 2018

Cover Design by Debbie Clement Design

Cover Images: Shutterstock

Every effort has been made to obtain the necessary permissions with reference to copyright material, both illustrative and quoted. We apologise for any omissions in this respect and will be pleased to make the appropriate acknowledgements in any future edition.

A CIP catalogue record for this book is available from the British Library.

Paperback ISBN 978-1-83656-727-1

Large Print ISBN 978-1-83656-728-8

Hardback ISBN 978-1-83656-726-4

Ebook ISBN 978-1-83656-729-5

Kindle ISBN 978-1-83656-730-1

Audio CD ISBN 978-1-83656-721-9

MP3 CD ISBN 978-1-83656-722-6

Digital audio download ISBN 978-1-83656-724-0

This book is printed on certified sustainable paper. Boldwood Books is dedicated to putting sustainability at the heart of our business. For more information please visit https://www.boldwoodbooks.com/about-us/sustainability/

Boldwood Books Ltd, 23 Bowerdean Street, London, SW6 3TN

www.boldwoodbooks.com

*To the braw folk of the Scottish Highlands who have welcomed me
and my family on every single visit.*

1

As she stared out of the small aeroplane window, Zara Bailey smiled. She was thousands of feet up in the air and the clouds were the thick, fluffy white of meringue. But instead of being topped with fresh, exotic fruit like that she'd had in the past five days, they were tinged with the honey-gold rays of the descending sun. The thought of food made her stomach rumble and she realised she'd been so late getting to Miami International Airport that she hadn't had the chance to grab a bite to eat.

Although she couldn't complain really. The stateside trip had consisted of an abundance of rich food, from Cuban to Mexican and everything in between. She would have to watch herself or her next trip wouldn't include that pretty bikini she had bought from her favourite designer boutique. There had been a tad more alcohol than she usually drank on a business trip but she'd got caught up in the whole atmosphere: the cocktails, the weather, the music, the people. She'd been well and truly sucked in. It was at times like this that she couldn't imagine working anywhere other than *The Bohemian* magazine.

Travelling the world had been something she had dreamed of all her life, especially when things at school had got to be too stressful. She had lived an imaginary life in atlases and travel journals, creating scrapbooks listing the places she would one day visit. She had been one of the intelligent kids – the nerds. She'd never been invited to parties with the popular crowd, nor had she gelled with the misfits. She'd been in a category apart and there had been only a few other occupants – a couple of whom had been tolerable and had become friends. Her best friend at school, and the only person she'd kept in touch with since, was Michelle Bean. Apart from their intelligence they had another thing in common: they had both been ribbed by the cool kids – Shelley for her name and Zara for her cheap, often second-hand clothes and her spectacles that had enlarged her denim-blue eyes. The two had become known as Granny Bailey and Jelly Bean.

They couldn't wait to leave.

Zara's parents had given up on trying to improve her high-school experience and had resorted to telling her, 'One day, Zara, you'll show them. One day when you're a rich and famous journalist on TV shows they'll regret ever teasing you.' She'd hoped they were right but hadn't been about to hold her breath. A couple of last-minute-deal package holidays to Spain with the family hadn't quite matched up to the dream she had and so the world had remained a mystery she was desperate to solve. It was only after university when she'd landed a job as a luxury travel writer with the prestigious magazine that 'showing them all' had looked like a possibility; although she had never been presented with the opportunity to make good on it.

Until now.

When the silver envelope had landed on the doormat of her two-bedroomed Peckham pad she had opened it with intrigue. But on seeing the invite contained therein she had stared at it in disbelief. The words:

New Malden High Sixth Form Class of 2008 Reunion

screamed at her in shiny, Arial bold font from the card and a shiver of dread manifested itself in a funny little squeak from her throat. Memories of herself and Shelley in lower sixth form, being shunned and, worse still, laughed at and taunted, returned to torment her.

Perhaps she should say she was unavailable. After all, she hated school and most of the people she had attended with, so why the hell would she want to meet up with them now, after all this time, when her life was finally on track?

Then it dawned on her twenty-seven-year-old self. She'd bloody well earned her bragging rights. And what were these events if not to show off and tell everyone how well you've done for yourself? And to have pissing contests about who'd achieved the most amazing things since leaving school? *And let's face it, I've done pretty bloody well.*

After graduating from university with a first-class degree in Journalism she had landed her job as one half of the travel-writing team at one of the UK's top mags, based in Central London. Her opposite, Dillon, was the adventure and outdoors writer – a job that she couldn't imagine doing for all the tea in China. Zara had finally got to travel the world and, not only that, she'd stayed in many of the top hotels too. She had so much of the world left to see and she was excited to discover where her job might take her next.

Maybe the reunion would be a great way to stick two fingers up at the so-called popular kids – many of whom, she expected, had amounted to a great big *nada*. It wasn't the best reason to go but it was a reason. She resolved to think about it. She had Miami to focus on. And so that was it, the invitation remained on the mantelshelf above her modern, state-of-the-art, feature electric fire whilst she went off to write about the city at the southern tip of the sunshine state.

The flat always felt chilly and impersonal when she arrived home after a trip. And seeing as the sojourns were becoming more frequent, she had pondered on finding a lodger. She had been with Josh, her boyfriend, for around a year now and even though he was wonderful it felt a little too soon to be thinking about asking him to move in. And there was no way the two of them would fit into his rented studio flat for longer than a weekend at a time. But coming home to an empty apartment was a little depressing and having someone around might just make things better. Instead of humming Eric Carmen's 'All By Myself' like Bridget Jones, she'd feel inclined to hum something happier and at least it would mean the place wouldn't feel quite so lifeless and cold. Her obvious choice of housemate was no longer a possibility seeing as Shelley had recently moved in with her boyfriend.

Zara had been so lucky to find her place and at such a great price too. It was an ex-local-authority block, which wasn't much to look at from the outside, but inside it was spacious and bright with an open-plan layout, thanks to the changes she'd made. She'd wielded a sledgehammer on more than one occasion, under the strict supervision of her dad, Carl, who was fortunately a builder by trade. It had taken quite a bit of refurbishment and there was still plenty to do – another problem with being away so much was that she never managed to finish as many jobs there as she wanted to – but her dad always insisted on working on the place whilst she was away. Now, it was beginning to look every bit the modern, independent woman's bolthole that she had hoped for. To make matters even better, estate agents had recently valued it at around fifty grand more than she'd paid so she knew she was on the right track as far as her investment was concerned.

Living alone wasn't something she'd slipped into easily. Coming from a family of three kids, two dogs and two parents all crammed into a three bedroomed local-authority house in New Malden meant that the peace and quiet of her new place was somewhat alien. Her mother, Suze, was obsessed with the royal family and every royal celebration of which there seemed to be many. This meant bunting and flags and neighbours round for frequent parties, increasing the occupants of their relatively small home tenfold. Royal memorabilia covered every possible surface and every event that had occurred since Suze had been a child herself, and Carl was incredible to put up with it, so Zara thought. He would often come home from working at some old lady's house with a token that he had been given for his collector wife.

Andrew, Zara's older brother, had followed in the footsteps of their father and was now working with him, and even though he had moved into a rented flat with his pregnant girlfriend, they seemed to spend every spare minute in the family home. Whilst her younger brother – William, a latecomer to the family – was on the verge of leaving high school and trying to figure out what to do with his life. He had a tendency to play his music too loud, which hadn't been conducive to study *or* work when Zara was at home. The quiet at her own place was sometimes welcome and she often tried to convince herself that living alone was a breath of fresh air. But in reality she knew that there was no air quite like that of the cake-aroma-filled stuff she inhaled when she visited her family.

As she wheeled her case from the entrance, along the hardwood floor towards her bedroom she tried to think of possible flat-share options. She knew there were a couple of new starters at the office in the Fashion department so perhaps that would be a good starting point. She would weigh up the pros and cons when she had more energy but right now she needed sleep.

In her peripheral vision she spotted the silver envelope on the mantel and rolled her eyes. She would have to make a decision soon. Whether that entailed an acceptance or an excuse she hadn't decided 100 per cent, so it too would have to wait until she was capable of cognitive thought.

Catching sight of herself in the decorative hall mirror, she scrunched her nose distastefully. Her chocolate-brown hair was falling in straggly tendrils from the bun she had tied in a hurry as the plane had landed and the mascara that had been rubbed around her tired, puffy eyes made her look like a goth, but she was too exhausted to shower. Procrastination was definitely the name of the game for now.

Once her case was unpacked and the dirty laundry stuffed in its basket she wandered, zombie-like, to the kitchen. She tugged open the fridge and smiled. *Bless you, Mum.* There was a stack of ready meals for one, some fresh fruit and a carton of milk. A bottle of Pinot Grigio, her absolute fave wine, was chilling on the bottom shelf. She was so hungry and the fact that she had slept through the meal service hadn't really helped much. However, it was almost one in the morning and even zapping something in the microwave seemed too much effort.

She spotted a wholemeal loaf on the counter top and decided she would make toast instead, and as she waited for it to pop up she leaned on her elbows, yawning. After managing only a couple of bites she abandoned the thought of food and surrendered to the bigger priority. Sleep.

2

Zara had left her bicycle at home today, figuring it was far too hot to make the thirty-minute journey her usual way. And seeing as parking near work in Central London was a nightmare the old rust bucket of a car would stay in its little allocated space too. She often wondered why she even had a car for the minimal number of times it saw the light of day – mainly to visit her folks every few weeks when work and social life allowed.

The Tube journey to the office was only short but she loved people-watching. London was so immensely diverse and regardless of how many times she made the trip to work she rarely saw the same people twice. Whether it was a person with bright pink hair, someone with many piercings or a brightly dressed character wearing flamboyant, Mardi Gras style clothes amongst the suited business types, the variety of Londoner on the morning commute, was vast. Today's train journey was overly warm and an odour of sweat permeated her nostrils, which was rather distracting and very unpleasant. A man in a dirty T-shirt stood close by, reading a novel in one hand and clinging onto the overhead rail with the other. He had a distinctly damp patch around his armpit and when the train jerked to a halt at her station he almost landed in her lap.

'Sorry, love,' he mumbled without even making eye contact. That was the only thing she disliked about the capital; people could be quite impersonal. She didn't bother to respond and grabbed her bag, before making her way to the exit and stepping quickly off the train.

It was only eight in the morning, but the city was already buzzing to life. Fumes from the myriad of vehicles on the packed roads burned her lungs and she coughed hard. She had only been away a few days but already her lungs had got used to the fresh sea air they had been filled with, and for a moment she missed the golden, sandy beach near the resort hotel she'd had the pleasure of staying in. Her melancholy was brief, seeing as she knew she'd be off on her travels again before long. The piece for the magazine had already been emailed in and Noah, her long-haired, Australian editor and founder of the magazine, had already gushed about her wonderful prose. He had called her into the office today for a meeting and she just knew it was going to be about her next assignment. This was the best part of her job.

She grabbed a takeout coffee from a street vendor just outside the Tube station and set off to walk to the imposing office block where *The Bohemian* was situated. The cerulean sky overhead was cloudless and the sun glinted off the windows of each of the tall buildings that surrounded her as she walked. Her back was warm from the rays that were reaching earth without much of a barrier and she questioned her choice of beverage. As she took tentative sips of the steaming liquid, she dodged other business people making their way to work; most of them sharing one side of their phone conversations as they hurried along, heads down, deep in concentration.

She arrived at the office and took the lift to the fourth floor. The small, enclosed metal box was hot and claustrophobic and she couldn't wait for the air conditioning of the office. Although many times she recalled needing to wear a cardigan as Noah set the temperature on the AC unit and she felt sure he was really a menopausal woman in disguise. Today, however, the cool air would be welcome.

There was a bizarre hush as she entered the open-plan area of the office where the casually dressed advertising agents were based. She caught the eye of Marco, one of the friends she'd made very early on in her time with the magazine. He rolled his eyes and shook his head. *Oh, great, what the hell has happened?* Why was there such a negative atmosphere around the place that was usually filled with laughter and chatter? She mouthed the words, 'What's happened?' But Marco just huffed air through puffed cheeks and shook his head again.

She glanced over to Dillon's office and saw the blinds were closed. She guessed that he and Noah had had one of their arguments. Dillon had been the other travel writer ever since the first publication and he was the longest-standing member of Noah's staff. The two men were close friends and were known for being brutally honest with each other. No doubt she'd find out the gossip later from Marco. He loved drama and the first chance he got, she felt sure he would fill her in with the gory details.

'Ah, here she is – our intrepid luxury travel writer,' Noah announced loudly as he appeared from the direction of his own office and she felt her cheeks heating as all eyes were suddenly fixed on her. 'Come on through, Zara, I have great news for you.'

* * *

She quickly forgot about Marco and Dillon and the advertising people as a buzz of excitement rippled up her spine and she followed Noah into his office.

As he closed the door she took a seat. 'I'm excited to hear what you've got for me. That last trip was absolutely wonderful. I never really associated Miami with luxury holidays but I can now concur that I was wrong. *You* were right.' She knew he liked to be buttered up and a little greasing of his ego would help keep her in his good graces.

Noah took a seat behind his desk and smoothed down his collarless, pale blue linen shirt. She had expected something 'a little different' when she had applied for this job, and as soon as she'd walked through the doors on the day of her interview, she'd realised she wasn't far from the mark with her assumptions. In spite of sending his journalists off on trips all over the world by aeroplane, Noah was very much into green living. Everything he ate was vegetarian, and everything he owned was fair trade or home-grown. She envied the lush green garden at his luxury North Cray home. She'd been in complete awe at the first summer gathering he'd held at his palatial house and hoped that one day she'd have a place where she could sit and enjoy some beautiful scenery and perhaps pluck fruit from her own trees. It wouldn't be quite as grand as Noah's, obviously. His wife was from a wealthy family and ran her own fashion business whilst their kids went to one of the best private boarding schools in London. Zara knew she'd likely never be so rich.

He wagged a finger at her and grinned. 'Ah, I knew you'd love it.' He leaned back and placed his feet up on his desk. 'So, tell me what you thought of *Puesta De Sol*.'

The restaurant recommendation had been something she had been sure to make a note of. 'Oh, Noah, it was incredible. The crab claws were to die for. And the *tamales*...'

He nodded. 'I love their gazpacho,' he said dreamily with a shake of his head. 'So fresh and aromatic. I really must go back there soon.' He suddenly clapped his hands and Zara almost jumped out of her skin. 'Now, what's next for Zara Bailey?'

She knew it was a rhetorical question as she grinned, grabbed her notebook and pen from her bag and straightened her spine. 'Yes, do tell.'

He frowned and pursed his lips. 'Now, you know we're a team here at *The Bohemian* and we have each other's back?'

She nodded, no clue where he was going with this. 'Absolutely.'

'Good... good. Well, I have a *real* challenge for you. Something for you to get your teeth into. Something different.'

Her mind began to whir with all the possibilities. Was it going to be some far-flung country in Asia or Africa? Or maybe something on a cruise ship? Her heart skipped in anticipation. 'Go on,' she insisted, eyebrows raised, body leaning slightly forward.

He held his hands up in the air and simply said, 'Scotland.'

She paused and crumpled her brow. 'I'm sorry – what? I thought you said Scotland for a moment.' A nervous giggle escaped her throat.

He grinned. 'That's because I did.'

Hmm. Okay. Scotland isn't exactly what I expected but let's see where he's going with this. She tried to smile. 'Scotland?' She nodded. 'Scot... land, okay.' She was trying to appear excited. She knew there were some very luxurious hotels in Scotland but she wasn't really sure how this would all come together. Then it dawned on her: Scotland was going to be the starting point for some amazing cruise to the Norwegian Fjords or something equally wonderful. Perhaps she would be required to stay somewhere like The Balmoral in Edinburgh before 'boarding ship' or whatever they called it. She'd seen pictures of the rooms there and they really were beautiful. In fact, she was very much aware that the stars loved the place so who might she bump into for a quote for her piece? The cast of *Outlander* maybe? *Hmm... Sam Heughan... yes, please. And Norway... excellent.* Another stunning destination she could tick off her list.

She breathed a relieved sigh. 'And then where?'

Noah frowned. 'I don't get you.'

Her palms were sweating and she almost lost the grip on her pen. 'Well, obviously you wouldn't want me to write about *Scotland.* I mean, I usually go to more far-flung places. So, where am I heading off to after *starting* in Scotland?'

He lowered his feet to the floor and linked his fingers together, resting them on the desk. 'Zara, the assignment *is* Scotland.'

She was nodding as if she had no control over her head. 'I see... I see.'

Noah now wore a serious expression and cleared his throat. 'It's like this, Zara – Dillon would be the go-to guy for this assignment but he has *today* handed in his notice. He's accepted a position with a rival magazine.' He almost curled his lip as he uttered the words. 'So, he's in the process of packing up his desk for garden leave.'

This came as a huge shock. Dillon appeared to love his job. *The Bohemian* was his life; travelling all the wild and rugged places for work was his dream job.

'Oh... I had no idea...'

Noah nodded slowly, a deep crease crumpling his forehead.

'Hmm. It was a shock to me too. But anyway, I figured as you're the other travel writer and you're a dedicated team player you'd be right up for the challenge.'

Slowly a realisation began to sink down onto her. Pushing her into her chair, and she felt herself getting lower. 'You mean... you mean you want me to travel around and stay in youth hostels and bed and breakfasts like Dillon usually does?' She swallowed hard as a little nausea washed over her. This wasn't good. The idea of sleeping in places like that not only didn't appeal to her in the slightest but it gave her the creeps. 'Don't you?' She hoped with all her heart that she was completely wrong.

Noah sat up straight. 'Even better! You're going camping!'

3

Zara stared, open-mouthed, at Noah as if he had completely lost the plot. As if his marbles were literally falling out of his ears as he spoke. She tried to wrap her head around the words he had uttered but her mind was in some kind of baffled stupor. Did he really just say *camping* to the girl who was accustomed to reviewing five-star luxury resorts for a living?

She shook her head. 'I'm sorry, Noah, but... is this a joke?' she asked hesitantly, dreading his answer. 'You seem to be getting me confused with someone who *likes* the outdoors. I mean... I like being outdoors on the beach or checking out historical places for my reports, obviously, but camping? And Scotland?' Noah was known for being a prankster; she waited for him to burst into hysterical laughter and do the whole, *'Ha, ha! Your face when I said camping! Of course, it's a joke!'* But she waited in vain.

He leaned forward and fixed her with a pitiful gaze. 'Zara, I know this isn't your usual bag. I get that. But the fact is that the whole thing is booked. Dillon knew this and he's still betrayed me; well, all of us really.' There was a sad, yet bitter, edge to his usually jovial voice. He huffed and ran his hands through his greying, floppy hair. 'And I *need* you to help me out on this. Dillon's intern simply isn't ready – in fact, I wouldn't have employed him at all, truth be told, but that's a story for another day. It's not something I would normally ask of you, but I can't let this slip just because Dillon thinks he has bigger fish to fry. We may be a relatively small publication in comparison to others, but we still need to be at the top of our game. I'm counting on you, Zara. You're my best travel writer as it is. But now Dillon is going, you're my *only* travel writer.'

She sighed deeply and an image of her petite body being crushed by a giant rucksack manifested in her mind. 'But, Noah—'

He held up his hands. 'I know. I know. But here's the thing. *Travelarium* have got wind of the fact that Dillon is leaving. I got a call from Joel at their head office today. He couldn't wait to stick his knife in. Sarcastic bastard. Anyway, they're going to try and get there first. You know they're already trying to make a name for themselves, and taking a portion of our readership would be a big bloody boost for them. This article would be a perfect inroad, believe me. They're doing the real nitty-gritty stuff; the Australian outback and the bloody camel rides in Egypt. They're making us look like we only care about the fluffy, frilly shit. But that was never my intention with *The Bohemian*. Dillon's trip was supposed to be a real nuts and bolts piece; a chance to show our readership that we take travel seriously. And that the UK is just as important to our publication as the luxury destinations are. We can't let it go. I won't, Zara.' She had never seen him like this. Obviously Dillon's shock announcement had floored him. But she wondered if there was something behind it all. Was the magazine struggling? Why was he not telling her if that was the case?

And anyway, what was wrong with fluff and frills? Life was too short to be so bothered about real life and all the crap that came with it. What was wrong with a bit of escapism?

She realised Noah was still on his rant about *Travelarium* and snapped her attention back to him. '...and the North Coast 500 route is so hot right now, Zara. It's big news and we need to get in there first. Think of the team, eh?'

Good grief, next he'll be telling me to think of the children. Talk about playing for my sympathy. She wasn't quite ready to acquiesce. Not yet. 'But surely there must be someone else better equipped and suited to doing the report. Surely, there's someone in the team, maybe in a different department, for example, who loves camping and... and all *that* stuff.'

Noah closed his eyes briefly and when he opened them, he shook his head. 'Zara, I've been let down by my best friend of God knows how many years. *You* currently have nothing assigned that can't be put off for a while. I'm sorry but I can't send anyone else. I need this to be done just right. I need your help on this. Please, Zara? You're my only hope here.'

Suddenly the image of Noah dressed all in white with donuts for hair sprang to mind and she had to bite her lip so she didn't laugh inappropriately at Noah's Princess Leia-esque plea for help. She twisted her hands in her lap. She loved her job. And if the magazine was in trouble she wanted to do all she could to help, obviously. Noah was an awesome boss and she wanted to be the reporter he needed her to be. But this was something above and beyond. She wouldn't just be stepping out of her comfort zone. She'd be climbing in a spaceship and travelling until her comfort zone was a tiny speck on a distant planet. But she knew how much Noah had done for her. He'd taken a chance on her as a newly qualified journalist and she owed him so much.

She lifted her chin. 'I need more information.'

Noah sat up straight once more, his wide-eyed expression filled with hope. 'Anything. What do you need to know? Fire away.'

She cleared her throat, forcing the real question – i.e. *Are you insane?* – back from her tongue. 'H-h-how will I be getting there?'

He nodded and took a slow, deep breath, which didn't bode well. 'Okay, so you'd be going north by train to Inverness. Then you'd pick up your bicycle and—'

'Whoa! Hang on a darn-tooting-minute, here. Bicycle? You never mentioned anything about a bloody bicycle!'

He frowned. 'I'm mentioning it now. And you like cycling. You cycle to work sometimes and you cycle at weekends. It makes perfect sense.' He shrugged as if she was daft for not realising sooner.

Her nostrils flared and the clammy feeling returned to her palms. 'I cycle for pleasure, yes, but it's mainly a necessity for work and I'm no Lance Armstrong. How am I supposed to cycle with a backpack on? And... and tents. I've never set up a tent in my life. The one and only time we went camping when I was a kid my dad and my older brother did it all. And midges. Scotland is famous for its man-eating midges. Oh, God. I don't think I can do this, Noah. I'm just not cut out—'

'Hey, hey. Breathe, Zara. It'll be a doddle. I can show you the tent stuff. You take the trip at your own pace. It'll be absolutely fine; an adventure even. And there's this stuff that everyone up in Scotland swears by that you spray on and the midges won't touch you. Honestly, I wouldn't ask if I didn't think you were capable, Zara.'

She sat in silence for a while to allow the panic to subside. And then another question occurred. A much more pressing one that she really didn't want the answer to but knew, all too well, that she needed. 'And... and why, exactly, do they call it the North Coast 500, Noah?'

A wide awkward grin spread across his face and his eyes crinkled at the corners as a blush-red hue spread from his chest up to his cheeks. 'Well, it's like this... erm... You know the famous song by the Proclaimers?'

Zara swallowed hard, knowing exactly to which song he was referring. She nodded slowly, staring at him. 'Mmm, hmm.'

He held out his hands. 'Well, at least you won't be *walking* five hundred miles, eh?'

4

After the traumatic day she'd had Zara called a meeting of her best friends, Shelley and Marco, that would take place in the Dog and Parrot round the corner from the magazine HQ. Ironically outdoors-mad Josh was away camping with his buddies but she knew he would find this latest development hysterical. She'd reluctantly worked late researching the godawful trip that was looming in her near future. She had a month to prepare. A bloody *month*. Okay, so she was already fit on account of the cycling so she didn't really need to get in shape as such. But mental preparation for her trip to hell would take far more than four sodding weeks.

Much to her dismay it turned out her trip to the Maldives to check out honeymoon destinations for the magazine had been postponed indefinitely and this pissed her off something chronic, souring her mood further. The light at the end of the tunnel had been hit with a brick apparently.

The pub was heaving and in spite of the noise Zara sat there silently staring into her overpriced Shiraz, musing that she could have bought a whole bottle at the supermarket for what she had just handed over for a single glass. Her two closest friends had tried their best to chivvy her up when she had explained what Noah had asked her to do. But nothing they said had made her feel any better. It still sucked.

'Are you going to that stupid high-school reunion, then?' Shelley asked, presumably in a bid to change the subject that had dragged Zara's mood down.

Zara shrugged. 'I don't know yet. I'm still thinking about it. What did you decide?'

Shelley scrunched her face as if tasting something bitter. 'Oh, I don't know. I've been thinking I might give it a miss. Hated that lot when I was forced to spend time with them so why would I put myself through it now by bloody choice?'

'To show them they were wrong about you? That you're happy and in love with a very dishy bloke?'

Shelley laughed. 'I don't need their approval, babe, and neither do you. Look at you. Travel journo extraordinaire. Successful, gorgeous, hunky boyfriend, need I go on?'

Zara continued the staring competition with the red liquid in her glass. 'Oh yeah. Super extraordinary now I'm going camping to bloody Scotland.' Her voice dripped with sarcasm as she shivered at the thought.

Shelley nudged her. 'Come on, Zee, it can't be that bad. Josh has been trying to get you to camp for months now and you might actually enjoy it when you get there.'

Zara raised her chin and tilted her head as she glared at her bestie with narrowed eyes. 'Want to come along, then?'

Shelley gasped and held up her hands. 'Hell no! I'm not sleeping in a bag for anybody.'

Zara pursed her lips and rolled her eyes. 'Thought as much.'

Marco chipped in. 'I just can't believe Dillon's gone and left

Noah in the lurch like that. After all those years they've been friends. Talk about being stabbed in the back by Judas.'

Shelley snorted. 'Judas didn't stab anyone in the back, you numpty.'

Marco sat up straight and frowned at her. 'Well what *did* he do, then? You know that time when they were in the Garden of Eden and he did that thing?'

Shelley's religious upbringing was about to come into play and she puffed out her chest ready to lecture him as only she could. 'Okay, for starters, it was the garden of *Gethsemane*, you plum. And secondly, it was a kiss that Judas gave Jesus, not a carving knife to his back. Good grief, didn't you listen to anything at school?'

Marco crossed his arms and huffed. 'All right, all right. Bloody show-off. And I *did* listen, actually,' he insisted, followed by a mumbled, 'Just not in religious studies...' The two women gave each other a knowing look.

Shelley cocked her head. 'Oh yeah? Why was that, then?'

Marco's cheeks coloured and he fiddled with his hair. 'Because the boys played footie outside the Humanities block so I was a little... you know... distracted.'

Zara and Shelley burst out laughing. 'Oh my God, Marco, you were crushing on boys in shorts when you should have been studying.' Zara gave him a playful shove.

A wide grin stretched his drop-dead gorgeous features and his eyes twinkled. 'So what if I was? The teacher we had was really boring and he had this awful droney, monotonous voice. Urgh, you should be thankful you didn't go to my school. It was like purgatory for teenagers.'

Zara knocked on the table. 'Hey, come on, guys, you're supposed to be commiserating with me, here,' she insisted. 'I'm in mortal peril.'

Marco guffawed loudly. 'What, of being eaten by tiny insects?'

Zara slapped his arm. 'The fear is real, Marco. I don't take too kindly to being nibbled on.'

Shelley leaned closer. 'Oh, I don't know, doesn't that depend on *who's* doing the nibbling?'

Zara couldn't help laughing at that as an image of her sexy man popped into her head. 'Yeah, okay maybe. But it's work and Josh'll be staying at home whilst I'm dodging Highland cow poo in Scottish fields, so there won't be much of *that* type of nibbling going on, will there?'

Marco leaned his head on his hands and fluttered his eyelids. 'Oh, I don't know. You might meet some handsome laird who'll sweep you off yerrrr feet and tak ye to his castle.'

'Bloody hell, that was a truly crap attempt at a Scottish accent. He does have a point though, Zee.' It still irked her that Shelley and Marco hadn't yet warmed to her boyfriend. And what made it worse was they didn't hold back in trying to find her a replacement. 'And you might get some more inspiration for your novel. All those rugged Scotsmen. When do I get to read it anyway?'

'Erm, if she gets to read it so do I,' Marco insisted.

'Neither of you are reading it so that resolves that situation,' Zara informed them bluntly.

Shelley smirked. 'The crap Scottish accent ruined it, Marco.'

He waved a dismissive hand. 'Yeah, well... Oh, bugger off to the bar. It's your round, Shells Bells.'

Shelley made a dramatic tongue-out gesture to Marco before rising from the table and sashaying off to buy more drinks.

Once she was out of earshot, Marco leaned closer to Zara to

be heard over a group of rugby players who had walked into the pub. 'Do you get the feeling the magazine is in trouble, Zee?'

Bloody hell, if Marco's noticed too I can't be imagining it. 'Erm... what makes you say that?'

He shrugged. 'With Dillon's shock departure. You being forced to go to Scotland under duress. And Abbie from Accounts was in tears this morning too. There's just this weird atmosphere. No one's saying anything and Noah's walking round like a bear with a sore arse.'

Zara sighed and nodded. 'Yeah, I know what you mean. It does feel a bit strange. I'm hoping it's just an ego thing where Dillon's concerned. Maybe he feels he's not being challenged any more. And there's no law against moving jobs. Like they say, all's fair in love and business.'

Marco scrunched his brow. '*War*, Zee. All's fair in love and *war*.'

She raised her eyebrows. 'Okay, *Shelley*.' She laughed. 'But you said it yourself about the atmosphere. Pretty *war*-ish to me.'

Marco sighed. 'Ugh, this is just too depressing. Let's change the subject, eh?'

'Okay, let's. So how do I get out of this camping trip without letting Noah down big style?'

Marco huffed. 'Oh, honey, I think that ship has sailed. I think you're going and I think you know it. So, anyway, do you want me and Shells to come shopping with you for camping gear?'

Zara shook her head. Although she loved them dearly, she knew, from past experience, that the two of them would only make matters worse and that the outing would drag on longer than necessary. Besides, she was in the perfect situation to find everything she needed, seeing as Josh managed an outdoor clothing and accessories shop. She'd simply wait until he could fit her in for some very personal shopping. 'Nah, it's okay. I think I need to put on my big-girl knickers and do this alone.'

He grinned. 'Oh, you're so brave. And you never know, this might all be a ruse to get you into one of the places the stars go to holiday.'

If only, Zara thought. 'Not with my luck.'

Shelley returned with a tray of drinks that she placed carefully on the table. 'So, when are we off shopping for camping gear, Zee? I'm guessing sooner rather than later. Oh, and you'll need bloody comfy shoes, that's for certain. I discovered, to my horror, that hiking in normal trainers just doesn't cut it. When Jake took me walking last summer I thought my feet were going to drop off at the end. Had to soak them for days after. And you need a good rucksack. One that you can get everything in but that isn't too heavy. And you need a breathable one too or your back will be all sweaty. Yuck.'

'Bloody hell, Shells, let the woman get a word in, will you? She doesn't want us to go shopping with her,' Marco informed Shelley in his inimitable bitchy way.

Shelley flopped into a chair. 'Seriously? You'd deny your best friends the chance to help you?' She stuck out her lip like a petulant child.

Zara cringed and took a large gulp of her wine before speaking. 'I think I can probably get everything I need from Josh's store. And I need to get used to the fact that I'll be out there, alone, in the wilderness, all by myself. Might as well start as I'm being forced to go on.'

Marco snorted. 'God, you're being so bloody melodramatic. It's a camping trip, you're not being sent to the bloody front line. Honestly, Zara, you're such a wuss.'

'Oh yeah, and you'd be so-o-o brave out there camping all alone, wouldn't you?'

'Yes, Shelley, I would be brave. Because it's a bloody holiday, not a concentration camp. I think you're overthinking it. I really do. And anyway, it's me you should be feeling sorry for. I might end up living in a bloody tent for real.'

Both women turned their attention on him simultaneously. 'What do you mean by that?' Zara asked, concern for her friend now taking over the worries about midges and blisters.

Marco huffed. 'The guy who owns my flat has decided to sell. I've got a month left to find something. I... I didn't want to say anything because I thought I'd find somewhere relatively easily – I mean, I'm the perfect housemate. And I know what you two interfering old biddies are like when you're worried about me,' he said, a teasing tone to his voice.

'Oh my God, Marco. You should've said something. Jake and I have a spare room if—'

'*Really*, Shells? And listen to you two shagging all hours of the day and night? Ugh, no chance.' He was laughing but Zara could sense a hint of sadness in his expression.

'Move in with me!' Zara blurted. 'It's the perfect solution! I've been thinking that it would be good to get a lodger and at least I know you, warts and all. It would be fun.'

'Really?' Marco's brow crumpled in disbelief. 'You mean it?'

Shelley folded her arms and feigned annoyance. 'Oh, so you won't listen to me and Jake shagging but you'll listen to Zara singing out of tune in the shower?'

Marco mirrored her stance. 'Honey, at least Zara showers *alone*.'

Shelley shrugged. 'Fair point.'

'But, Zee, what about Josh? Won't he want to move in?'

Zara shook her head. 'I don't think he's ready for that yet. We haven't talked about it but if something like that happens in the future, we'll deal with it then. At least you'll have a home in the meantime, eh?'

Marco clapped his hands and did a little chair dance. 'Thank you so much, honey. You've *literally* saved my life.'

Shelley snorted. 'Now who's being a drama queen?'

Marco scowled at Shelley and a sense of relief washed over Zara. At least now she wouldn't return home from Scotland to an empty home with no one to rant at. 'So, are you in?'

'Hell, yes, I'm bloody in. Girls' nights here we come!' Marco lurched forward and hugged Zara tight. 'When can I move in?'

'Whenever the heck you like!'

5

Zara was rudely awoken by her Florence and the Machine ringtone and, with closed eyes, she reached out to grab her phone.

'Hello?' she croaked.

'Hello there, gorgeous. Have you missed me?'

Zara sat up and grinned. 'Hey, Josh. I really have missed you. When did you get back?'

'Oh, not until late last night so I didn't want to bother you. How are you doing? I didn't really understand your text. Something about hating Noah and being eaten alive?' He chuckled.

She sighed. 'Ugh... yes, he's given me a terrible assignment and I can't get out of it.'

'Define terrible.'

'Five hundred miles of cycling and bloody camping.' She knew her despondency shone through in her monotonous tone.

'Really? Don't tell me he's sending you on the NC500?'

Zara scowled. 'How did you figure that out? And yes.'

'Oh, Zara, it's a fantastic route. The scenery, the fresh air. Honestly, it's bloody awesome!'

'Says the man who'd happily live in a tent permanently.'

'Yeah, I know but, wow. I'm actually jealous of this assignment. That's a first, eh?'

It was true. Josh was outdoors obsessed. Whether it was rock climbing, white-water rafting, camping – you name it, he loved it. Zara often wondered what the hell he was doing with someone so outdoors averse.

'And you know what this means? You can come to the shop and I'll kit you out. I can't wait to see you in some sexy walking boots and combat pants,' he said huskily.

She couldn't help giggling at the mental image he'd just created. 'Oh, yes, so *very* sexy.'

'Oh, it will be, you just wait. And you never know, if it's quiet we could sneak into one of the fitting rooms.'

'Josh! I'm not having sex with you in a bloody fitting room.'

'Spoilsport. Anyway, movie and a takeaway at yours tonight?'

'Sounds good. Can't wait.'

'It's a date, then. See you later, gorgeous.'

Zara cuddled up on the sofa with Josh but couldn't help the twinge of guilt that tugged at her. Marco had chosen the same day to move in and, knowing Josh was coming round, he had exiled himself to his new room, insisting it was absolutely fine.

They were on to their second bottle of wine and the film had finished. Josh turned to her and stroked her cheek with his thumb. 'God, I've missed you. We need to try and organise our time better so that our trips away coincide in future.'

He leaned close and brushed her lips with his. She slipped her hands into his shaggy, dirty-blond hair and deepened the kiss as heat rose from within her and her desire for him grew. Josh was simply gorgeous, in that tall, rugged surfer way. Originally from the north east of England, he had a sexy-as-hell accent that she could listen to all day and never tire of it. He was muscular and lean on account of all the climbing he did, and his eyes were sometimes blue but sometimes green depending on the light.

He pulled away from her and rubbed his nose down the length of hers. 'I want you naked now, Bailey.' He grinned.

Her stomach flipped and she began unbuttoning her shirt under his watchful, lust-filled gaze. Once her shirt was open he swiped off his T-shirt and quickly unzipped and slipped off his jeans and boxers. Zara could feel her pupils dilating as she took in the epitome of masculinity before her and she reached up to drag her nails lightly down his toned abdomen.

'Ooh! Hi, Josh, it's fine, thanks; I don't need a parking space for my bike. Been working out, have you? Very nice,' Marco said as he appeared in the living room.

'Shit... fuck...' Josh, now as red as the pillar boxes on the street, immediately crouched to grab his clothes and cover his manhood.

Zara burst into a fit of nervous giggles. 'Whoops! Sorry about that, Marco. I guess we need to remember that I don't live alone any more.'

'Yeah, sorry, mate, got a bit carried away there,' Josh squeaked in a strangled tone as he dragged his clothes onto his body.

Marco was still cheekily appraising Josh's physique as he walked through to the kitchen. 'Oh, don't mind me, lovebirds.'

Once the new lodger had disappeared back to his room,

Josh flopped down onto the couch. 'Ugh, talk about coitus interruptus.'

Zara, who was now re-buttoned into her shirt, cringed. 'I'm really sorry about that. I suppose we should have taken things to the bedroom a bit earlier.'

'Never mind. Anyway, I should go. Work tomorrow. Hey, why don't you come along and we'll see what we can do about sorting your camping gear?'

Zara pouted. 'If I must.'

'Well, you have to do it sometime and there's no time like the present. Or tomorrow, seeing as the shop's shut at this time of night.' He grinned.

'I suppose.'

He walked to the door and pulled her along behind him. 'Oh, your enthusiasm is so overwhelming, Bailey.' He bent to kiss her again and she almost melted into him. He rested his forehead on hers. 'Kiss me like that and I'll not make it home. See you tomorrow?'

'See you tomorrow,' she replied with a protruding bottom lip.

* * *

The following day she walked into the huge shop and was immediately overwhelmed by the number of displays before her. Thank goodness she had Josh to help with this, otherwise she might be tempted to run away and emigrate.

'Hi there, you look a little lost. My name's Josh, I'm the manager – can I help at all?'

She turned to see her very handsome man standing there in his uniform of polo shirt and cargo shorts. The muscles on his arms stretched the banding round his biceps and his dirty-blond hair had that just-got-out-of-bed sexiness to it.

She smiled widely at his silly game and fluttered her eyelashes. 'Oh yes, kind sir, I'm a completely lost damsel in distress. I need... camping stuff?'

Josh chuckled. 'Yup, oddly enough most people who come in here are looking for exactly the same.' He stepped forward and, after surreptitiously glancing around him, he wrapped her in his arms and kissed her, making her legs weaken. Once he pulled away he stepped back as one of his staff appeared. He cleared his throat and scratched his head, as if to prove he was innocent of any possible insinuation of wrongdoing. 'Oh, Sam, can you unpack that order of waterproof coats in the back, please?'

'Okay, boss.' The spotty teen saluted him.

'So, gorgeous, are you feeling any happier about your trip?'

She sighed. 'Not really, no.'

He gestured for her to follow him. 'I still can't believe you've never been camping,' he said, shaking his head.

'Well, I went camping as a kid but since then, with the nature of my job, I've got rather used to the finer things in life, I suppose. Being out in a field in the middle of nowhere just fills me with dread.'

He shrugged. 'Think of it as an adventure. Getting back to nature. Taking some time out for yourself away from the stresses and strains of work and your sex-mad boyfriend.' He chuckled.

Zara rolled her eyes. 'You sound like Noah. Apart from the sex-mad bit, of course. Do you know, I really don't see why he couldn't go instead? It's so much more his kind of thing.'

Josh clapped his hands and then rubbed them together. 'Right, no point being all sulky, eh? Regardless of how cute you are when you pout. You know you've come to the right place and you know I'm the right person to help, so let's go get you kitted out, gorgeous.'

She followed Josh through the store and watched as he piled items up in his arms, feeling relieved that the company credit card was going to be getting a battering and not her own. He explained the need for each item he picked up and kept talking about travelling light. She explained she would be picking up a mountain bike in Inverness and that it had already got paniers fitted. He seemed to think that was a good thing and proceeded to talk about sleeping-bag weights and how many seasons they were suitable for.

He placed the huge, gathered pile on the floor by a display of tents and pulled a tiny package from a shelf. 'This little thing is like dynamite.' His eyes widened and he looked like a kid in a sweet shop.

She was a little bewildered as to why explosives were stored near the tents and, more to the point, why the hell *she* needed them. She stepped backwards and glanced round to see if anyone else was within striking distance. Thankfully the area was clear.

Josh pulled at the package and suddenly out sprang a bundle of canvas, which miraculously turned into a tent before her eyes and landed, ready erected, on the floor before her. She felt very foolish as his meaning of dynamite became very clear and was thankful she hadn't decided to question him on it before. Her stupidity would remain her own secret.

Josh waved his hands excitedly at the bright green pod. 'So, madam, there you go. A few pegs at the end of the guy ropes and you're ready to sleep. Built-in ground sheet. Nice and compact. Lightweight too. Three thousand hydrostatic head. Roomy enough for you and your backpack. Little porch that comes out enough for you to sit in the doorway of the tent and cook just outside. And all for two hundred quid.'

She had no idea of the meaning of some of what he'd said but he seemed enthusiastic enough and she trusted him, so she figured if he, the expert, was happy then so was she. Next it was on to clothing.

She was instructed to sit down by the fitting room whilst Josh walked around the shop pulling things from rails and flung them over his arm. The scene reminded her of a less glamorous *Pretty Woman* and she wished she were on Rodeo Drive instead of in a camping shop in South London.

Her self-proclaimed personal shopper returned about five minutes later. 'Now, Scotland can be wet, as you know. So you need waterproof trousers and a jacket as well as comfortable footwear that still lets you cycle as well as walk. I'll go and grab some suitable boots while you try on these clothes. Bear in mind the trousers need to be stretchy enough for you to cycle but not baggy enough that they could get trapped in the chain on the bike. Seeing as I don't know the age or condition of the bike they've sorted for you, I brought legging-type trousers that wick the water away and are quick drying. There are also some light-weight long-sleeved tops too because... well... midges.' He plonked the pile of clothing inside the fitting room. 'Obviously if you need any help undressing, I'm more than happy to assist.' He did a silly wiggle with his eyebrows and marched off in the direction of the footwear section. He was such a knowledgeable person and she was quite impressed. She had never seen him in his work domain before and couldn't help the pride she felt for her man.

Ten minutes later Zara was standing before a full-length mirror in all of her outdoor regalia, complete with a backpack that would fit all the essentials she would need. The backpack looked as though it would probably fit half of her apartment, but Josh had insisted she only take what she needed and no more. *No make-up or nice going-out clothes, then,* she grumbled inwardly, knowing that she'd also have to get used to letting her hair dry naturally unless she found a campsite with a really good shower block and hairdryers that worked.

'Well, I think you look incredibly sexy,' Josh told her from his position by the fitting room where he leaned against the wall, muscular arms folded.

She rolled her eyes at him and made a very unladylike snorting noise. 'Well, you *would* say that – I'm your girlfriend.' She stared at her reflection. The face still belonged to her, but the attire was completely different from what she was used to. She didn't know what to say so said nothing.

'In fact,' he whispered conspiratorially, 'if you've got the time we could have a little *meeting* up in my office.'

Her focus snapped to him and she felt her cheeks colouring, as she fought her threatening smile. 'Josh,' she hissed as she glanced round. 'I've told you that's not happening at your workplace,' she informed him again, even though she secretly liked the fact he fancied her so much.

He held up his hands and feigned professionalism once again. 'Please forgive me, madam. I don't usually come on to customers.'

She laughed. 'I should bloody hope you don't.'

He stepped a little closer and his cologne infiltrated her nostrils. He smelled divine and her heart skipped a little. 'You know I only have eyes for my little roving reporter, don't you?'

Gazing up into his eyes, she almost threw caution to the wind and dragged him into the fitting room with her. 'Yes, Josh, I know that.'

'Good. Now, the next time I see you, you can do me a strip-tease with what you've bought.'

This time her laugh bubbled up from her boots. 'Oh yes, I can imagine how that would look if Marco walked in again. Maybe we should go to your place instead?'

Josh scrunched his nose. 'Nah, your bedroom will work just fine.' She knew his place was tiny from the minimal visits she'd made to the studio flat. His kitchen wasn't really conducive to romantic meals and his neighbours were quite loud, but she often wondered if he got fed up with coming to her place all the time. She'd need to ask him.

'Okay, well, I think that's everything you're going to need. I'll take the gear to the cash desk for you. And when you're done there, I'll give you a hand to get it all to the car.'

'That'd be great. Thank you.' With one of his signature sexy smiles Josh bent to pick up the pile of gear that had accumulated outside the fitting room and Zara slipped behind the door to get changed. As she clicked the bolt in place, she let out a long huff of air. *Bloody hell, he really is gorgeous. How lucky am I?*

Once the gear was loaded into Zara's car, she slammed the boot shut and turned her attention back on Josh.

A little electricity crackled in the air between them and the urge to fling herself at him, lips first, bubbled towards the surface but she stomped on it before it had time to manifest. It was just a shame that she wouldn't be seeing him later to let off some of the steam she'd accumulated at seeing him in his role of boss man. Who knew camping store managers could be so damned sexy?

'Right, well, I'll be off, then. When will I see you?'

He glanced round to check that the coast was clear and slipped his arms round her. 'Tomorrow night?' He leaned down and whispered in her ear, 'You could be waiting for me in your room wearing nothing but your walking boots.'

In spite of the ridiculous suggestion, a shiver travelled her spine and everything south of her waistline throbbed. 'Hmm... It could be arranged.'

He squeezed her bottom and stepped away as a car pulled into the car park. 'See you tomorrow, then, gorgeous.'

She watched him retreat towards the shop once more and climbed into her car to head home. The fact that he had been so helpful and she'd loved seeing him in his element gave her more reasons to adore him and she smiled for the whole journey back to her flat.

6

Zara was relieved that Marco was there when she arrived home. It was nice not coming back to an empty flat. He was in his room surrounded by more boxes and she did wonder where the heck he was going to put everything. He had so much baggage and that was only taking into consideration the physical kind.

Once the last box was unpacked and the bookshelves in his room were piled high with enough paperbacks to fill a shop, Marco flopped down on the couch beside her. He'd already thanked her with a couple of bottles of Prosecco that had been chilled and she'd taken the liberty of opening one.

She handed him a glass and tucked her legs around her on the seat. 'Cheers, roomy!' she announced, clinking her glass into his.

'Honestly, Zee, you have no idea how grateful I am for this. It's going to be so much fun.'

She nudged him. 'So long as you don't keep me awake with your snoring, we'll be fine.'

'Cheeky. I think you'll find it's you who sounds like a pig in your sleep.' She feigned horror but then they both laughed. Marco glanced over at the pile of new purchases in the corner of the living room. 'So, I see you've got your stuff for the camping trip, then. I bet that cost a pretty bloody penny.'

Zara nodded as she swallowed the fizzy liquid. 'It sure did. But the way I look at it is, *Noah* wants me to go, *I* don't have the gear so *he* gets to pay. After all, the lot will be going online to be sold when I get back. I can guarantee this trip will put me off camping for life.'

'You never know. You might find a new passion for the outdoors. Josh will be whisking you off to the middle of nowhere for romantic sojourns *à la tent* before you know it.'

Zara grinned and tugged at a thread on the hem of her yoga pants. 'Camping and romance are two diametrically opposed words, Marco. You of all people should know that. And even Josh can't change my opinion on the matter. I'm not cut out for all that sleeping under the stars business. It's just not me.'

Marco gave one of his well-known eye rolls. 'Why not? People change, honey. And this is the twenty-first century. Women can do whatever they want, you know.'

'I know that. I just don't see me ever getting to the stage where I look forward to something like camping.'

'Well, I think you need to get tougher, missy. Josh would clearly love to take you on a trip that doesn't involve a bed and breakfast.'

She slapped his leg lightly. 'Since when have you been in Josh's corner?'

'I'm in no one's corner but yours, Zara Bear. But really... I mean, what do you two have in common apart from the mutual desire to rip each other's clothes off?'

She scowled at his harsh words although she knew there

was a little truth to them too. 'Haven't you ever heard of opposites attracting?'

'Obviously. I just… I don't want you to get hurt that's all.'

She nudged him. 'Good grief, is this the shape of things to
come with our *girlie* chats? 'Cause if it is, I think I'm going to
kick you out.'

'Consider the subject closed.' He mimicked locking his
mouth and throwing away an invisible key.

After feeling quite excited about a night in with Josh she had
felt a little disappointed when he had texted to suggest a night
out instead. He'd seemed a little strange the night before when
she'd texted him. He wasn't usually one for single-word
responses but Saturday night had consisted of just that.

Sunday went by in a blur and all too soon Zara stood in
front of her full-length mirror scrutinising her appearance as
Marco sat on her bed observing.

'You look sexy AF, *chica*, so stop frowning, will you?'

She huffed. 'I get the feeling something isn't right, though,
Marco. I don't know… He was great at the shop but then last
night things just… changed. Maybe he's going off me?' She
smoothed down the slate-grey, satin halter-neck top that she
had slipped on with her black skinny jeans and high-heeled
peep-toes. 'We're going to that new bar on Peckham High
Street but I want to look sexy. Do I look like I'm trying too
hard?'

Marco snorted and collapsed back onto the pillows. 'Oh my
God, just go and have fun, will you? He can barely keep his
hands off you, so I think you're overreacting. You're gorgeous
and a lovely person. He's bloody lucky to have you. He may not

be my favourite of your boyfriends but he is nice to look at. Although so was Harry...'

Zara threw him a disgusted look. 'Hey, I know Harry was your favourite. You don't have to remind me. And it wasn't my fault things didn't work out with him. He just wasn't my type in the end.'

Marco sat up and laughed with incredulity. 'Yeah, because handsome and rich are terrible qualities in a man. In fact, *I* hope to avoid them.'

'Ahem, you forgot dull as ditch water. He could send me to sleep with his monotone voice, Marco. I want someone to make me laugh, not put me in a coma. And Josh has all the best qualities.'

'Urgh, some people are so damned picky. I still can't believe you didn't even sleep with the man. Did you actually *look* at his body? I mean, come on, Zee, you could've bounced pennies off that bum.'

Zara laughed out loud. 'And that's a quality we all should look for, is it?'

'Damn bloody right it is.' He grinned. 'It's the first thing I like to check.'

She shook her head but couldn't help giggling. 'Incorrigible, Marco, that's what you are.' She turned back to the mirror. 'Anyway, this outfit, yes or no?'

'Hell yes. Bloody go and wow him with your curves and remind him why he loves you.' She paused at his words. The 'L' word hadn't really been mentioned, even though she knew *she* felt it. She forced a laugh. 'Yes... Yes, I'll do just that.'

He huffed. 'You almost convinced me there, Zara Bear.'

She shrugged. 'Do you think he *does* love me?'

His brow crumpled and he didn't speak right away. 'What's not to love?'

She turned to face him as her stomach knotted. 'You didn't exactly answer my question.'

Marco climbed off the bed and walked towards her with what she felt was a very fake grin on his face. He placed a hand on each shoulder. 'Zara, stop overthinking. I don't know what's got into you. What's with all this insecurity? He adores you, it's so obvious.'

'Then why hasn't he told me he loves me? It's been a year.'

He shook his head. 'Take it from me, darling, men are arse-holes. Most of them don't know how to order a coffee, let alone express an emotion. Give him time. Or dump his arse. I'll support you either way.' He grinned.

She slapped his arm playfully. 'Hey!' She was stopped from saying anything further as the doorbell rang. 'Shit! It's seven thirty already?'

'It would appear so. Want me to give him the big-brother talk?'

Zara slapped his arm again. 'You'll do no such thing. Now go to your room, Marco Bianchi!'

'You're such a mean cow,' he informed her with a smile as he left her room.

Trying to push down her doubts, Zara took a deep breath and opened the door. Josh stood there looking absolutely gorgeous in a blue shirt and dark blue jeans. A wide, sexy smile spread across his face. 'Wow. You look amazing.'

She felt a flush of warmth rise from her chest to her cheeks. 'Thanks. So do you.'

He held out his arm for her to link hers with. 'Come on, then, gorgeous, let's go and paint old Peckham town crimson, shall we?'

She shouted goodbye to Marco and hurriedly closed the

door behind her before he could appear to make any inappropriate comments.

* * *

The evening was going well and Zara had relaxed greatly by her third drink. Josh seemed to be back to his normal self, making her laugh.

He couldn't seem to take his eyes off her, which was very reassuring. 'I must say you look totally different in that outfit than the ones I had you wearing yesterday. Although, both looks are equally sexy.'

She tucked her hair behind her ear, suddenly very self-aware. 'I'd hardly call walking gear sexy, Josh, you weirdo.'

'Oh, I don't know. I think you're the kind of woman who'd make a tea towel look sexy.'

She almost choked on her drink. 'Well, if I was *just* wearing a tea towel—'

He leaned forward enthusiastically. 'We could always get one and try it out,' he said with that silly eyebrow wiggle.

She laughed. She really had been worrying over nothing. 'You have a way with words, that's for sure.'

He laughed heartily and grabbed his jacket, hastily placing it over his lap. 'Ahem... yes... okay, as we're in a public place let's have a change of subject whilst I try to stop imagining the tea towel scenario. Although I don't really want to, if I'm honest. Okay, shut up, Josh!' He took a deep breath and Zara tried to stop the fit of giggles that threatened to erupt, even though it felt good to laugh.

Finally he seemed calm again. 'So, are you getting excited about your trip yet? How long is it now?' he asked with a knowing grin.

She scrunched her nose. 'I don't think I'll ever be ready. It's around three weeks until I go, which is three weeks too soon.'

He cringed and hissed in through his teeth. 'You're still not happy about it, then?'

'Absolutely not. It's just not my thing at all. I'm not made for the great outdoors. I'm made for the luxury indoors,' she replied with a giggle.

He shook his head. 'You see, I don't get that. I can't get enough of the fresh air and open spaces. That's why I studied Marine Biology at uni. I absolutely adore all things to do with the outdoors. Give me a rock face to climb, an ocean to dive or a vast area to trek and I'm in my element. I don't need the luxuries of million-thread-count sheets or fluffy pillows.'

Zara felt a little indignant. 'I don't need those things either. I just prefer them.'

Josh leaned forward with a determined look in his eyes. 'I know. But... what about nature? What about breathing clean air and seeing the most wonderful scenery when you wake up of a morning?'

'I like to see a white sandy beach with a lounger on it when I wake up of a morning! That's scenery to me,' she informed him bluntly.

He sighed, clearly becoming frustrated. 'Good grief, Zara, where's your sense of adventure? Don't you want to see more than just the designer fittings of a five-star hotel?'

'Look, Josh, I think we ascertained long ago that we have different ideals when it comes to holidays. Can't we just leave it at that? I travel all over the world for my job. I do see places. I go on tours. I don't just sit by the pool, you know.' Why was she explaining herself?

'But you go on the *touristy* tours. You don't get out there to see the *real* people, the *real* places.'

Her nostrils flared and she spoke through gritted teeth. 'No, because many of the places I go to aren't *safe* for people to just go roaming off willy-nilly, that's why. I like to stay alive. I like to know I'm not going to get kidnapped or robbed.'

'But in that case you're not really living, are you?' As soon as the words fell from his lips he closed his eyes briefly, as if realising he'd overstepped the line.

Zara came to the conclusion that the night had been a mistake after all. 'Look, it's getting late; I think I'd better be going home. Thank you for a lovely evening, Josh.'

She stood to leave the table and he stood too. He held out his arm towards her but didn't make contact. 'Hey, gorgeous, I'm sorry, please don't go. I hate fighting with you. I promise I'll shut up now.'

She had been aware for a while that he had the ability to open his mouth and jam his foot straight in there and she had once found it quite sweet; disarming even. But now, especially with his strange behaviour, her patience was wearing thin.

She forced a smile. 'I really am tired.'

His shoulders slumped and he nodded in defeat. 'Well, at least let me walk you home, then.' She shrugged and turned to leave with Josh following close behind as they left the bar.

They walked in silence for a while and Zara's mind whirred with possible things to say to ease the tension that had built between them. She didn't want to lose him, but their differences were becoming scarily unavoidable and the last thing she wanted was to invest more of her life in a relationship that was ultimately going nowhere. There were *opposites attracting* and then there was just *completely opposite*. Maybe they were too different. Maybe Marco had been right when he said their relationship revolved around sex. Well, he hadn't exactly said it but she knew for a fact he thought it.

Eventually Josh grabbed her hand and tugged her to a standstill. 'Hey, I know I've been an arse. I don't know what came over me. The only excuse is that I've got a lot on my mind right now. You know I'm quite a fun bloke really. And I'm not in the least bit judgemental. But I've definitely come across that way tonight, which pisses me off. To be honest... I'm not sleeping and I talk utter shit when I'm tired. And it makes me a bit rambly. Like I can't stop myself. But I genuinely didn't mean to go all ape-shit on you about your likes and dislikes. I was way too... gung-ho back there. No wonder I've pissed you off.'

The genuine disappointment in his eyes tugged at her heart. 'You're not sleeping? What's going on, Josh? Is it anything I've done?'

He laughed. 'Not at all. It's just... work stuff... Nothing you can help with. It'll all be fine, I promise. I just... I wish I could be more like you, you know? You have this air of confidence about you. Like with this camping thing. You know it's your job and you're taking it on the chin even though you really don't want to. You haven't point-blank refused. You're strong. So much stronger than I am, that's for sure. You know what you like and you stick to your guns. I guess you're a very strong, independent woman. I don't have courage like that. So I guess I'm... I'm a little envious.' The sadness returned.

Zara gazed up with incredulity into the handsome face before her and her heart melted a little. Maybe Marco was right. Maybe he was just struggling to share his emotions. Obviously something was happening at work to make him doubt himself. And it was true that people usually took out their frustrations on those closest to them. Then there was the whole thing about him studying Marine Biology at uni. This was new information to her. She wondered why he was working in a camping shop when he was clearly qualified for something completely different.

She sighed. 'You have nothing to be envious of, Josh. I'm scared to death of making this trip. Any confidence you see in me is all bravado, I can assure you. But... I worry about us. That we're two very different people and I'm not sure how it will work going forward.' *But I want it to. I really want it to.*

He reached out and gently stroked her cheek with his thumb, sending a flush of heat where he had touched. 'It's been a year, though, Zara. We've been great so far, haven't we? And they do say opposites attract, don't they? And you know I'm very, very attracted to you.' His voice had softened to a whisper and her brain was screaming: *They do say that, he's right. They do!* 'So what do you say? Are you willing to put this evening behind us? Just put it down to silly male pride and insecurity? I promise I'll do better next time.' He tilted the corner of his mouth into a half-smile and that was it. She was done for.

Without giving her a chance to respond, he lowered his face until his lips brushed hers and her eyes fluttered closed. She took delight in the familiar feeling of his soft mouth against hers and realised it didn't matter how different they were on the surface, deep down this was love and she knew it for a fact.

7

Much to her surprise Josh had invited her for dinner at his flat the following weekend, and Zara seemed to float through the week in spite of the obvious tense atmosphere in the office. Noah was trying his best to hide the hurt he was feeling over his best friend's betrayal, yet he was acting rather like someone who'd just put their life savings on a three-legged horse and lost. To say his staff was walking on eggshells was an under-statement. Zara, on the other hand, was immune to the stress. She had a date with Josh to look forward to. This was the first time he was going to cook for her at his own place. The tiny flat was usually just a stop off on their way to a gig or for Josh to collect undies or a toothbrush. But he had decided he was going to show off his culinary skills.

Good-looking, decent job, can cook... bloody hell, what did I do to deserve this?

* * *

'So after all this time it turns out he can cook, too, eh?' Marco asked with a twinkle in his eyes as Zara applied lip gloss. 'The dark horse.'

'Well, I don't know yet. It might be beans on toast or a takeout for all I know.' Zara sincerely hoped she was wrong.

'Has he been texting every day this week?'

A smile crept slowly across her face as she made eye contact with Marco's reflection in the mirror. 'You noticed, then?' She had been relieved to see that Josh's messages were back to normal now. No more single-word answers.

He chuckled. 'Well, I noticed you were smiling again. And that there were lots of buzzes when notifications came through at the beginning of the week and then it all went quiet but you were still checking your phone every five seconds. I'm guessing you turned it to silent to hide the amount of communication that's been going on; although I don't know why. I think it's marvellous.'

Still smiling, Zara continued to get ready. 'I just didn't want it driving you mad, that's all.'

'So is tonight the night the "L" word comes to play?' He wiggled his eyebrows suggestively.

She gasped. 'Oh, Marco! I hadn't thought of that! Oh, I hope so. I really hope so.'

'Well, you're going to his home for a whole evening. He's cooking. He's bloody gorgeous. So are you. You're clearly crazy about each other.' He stated the facts as if the conclusion to the evening was going to be a proposal rather than a simple expression of love.

'I'm going with no preconceived ideas. I'm just going to enjoy myself. End of.'

Marco walked over to the window and peered out. 'Ooh, I

think your cab's here, Zee. You should be going. You don't want to keep the hunk of love waiting.'

'Trying to get rid of me, are you?' she asked with a grin as she collected her bag.

'Well, obviously I am. I'm going to binge watch *Ghost Adventures* and get my Zak fix. Then I'm going to put some music on and dance round in my undies.'

She rolled her eyes and bent to kiss his head where he'd flopped onto the sofa armed with the remote control. 'Don't be having nightmares. And close the curtains when you're dancing or you'll give the neighbours nightmares.'

'Cheek! And as if I could have nightmares about the man of my dreams! Never!'

* * *

Ten minutes after Zara climbed into the cab it pulled up at the address she had given and she climbed out, handing the cash to the driver as she left. Josh lived in a studio apartment at the top of a Victorian semi-detached house in quite a pleasant street. It had a tidy front garden dotted with pots of flowers and shrubs, which she guessed was cared for by the old lady on the ground floor, seeing as she owned the building.

Nervously, she walked up the gravel path, clutching the bottle of Pinot Noir she'd bought especially, and pressed the doorbell. As if he had been waiting behind the door it sprang open and there stood Josh, dark jeans, tight grey T-shirt and bare feet. The smell of his aftershave infiltrated her nostrils and for a moment she was ready to dive straight into bed if he made the suggestion.

For once, he was far more restrained than she, and he simply looked her up and down with an assessing gaze and said, 'Wow. Look at you.' He held out his hand and she slipped hers into it. He glanced down the street and tugged her forwards. 'Come on in before you get a better offer.'

She followed him up the stairs to his flat. Once inside, he pulled her into his arms and surprised her with a passionate kiss, stealing her breath and her willpower to behave. His tongue slipped gently between her lips and her legs almost gave way.

He pulled away and gazed lustfully into her eyes. 'I'm so tempted to say sod the food and to whisk you straight to the bedroom,' he whispered huskily.

Please just do it. Whisk away. She smiled and cleared her throat. 'Ah... b-but it smells like you've been busy in the kitchen and it'd be a shame to waste it.'

He closed his eyes for a split second as if to compose his thoughts. 'True. Very true. Come on, I hope you like Spanish food.'

'Oh, I do. What are we having?' Her stomach growled.

'I made tapas to start and paella for main course,' he replied proudly.

'Wow, not just a handsome face, then?'

He smiled and stepped towards her again. 'Flattery will get you *everywhere*, Miss Bailey.' He took the bottle of wine from her hand. 'But first, let's have a glass of wine and chat, eh?' He took her hand and led her into the open-plan lounge. It was very clean and tidy as always. The main area was L-shaped with the couch at one side and the kitchen round the other arm of the L. It was simply decorated in blue and grey, with the feel of a seaside holiday cottage. A wall of glass bricks and a sliding screen separated the living area from the bedroom and a shower room was positioned in one corner, by the main entrance. As studios went it wasn't a bad size really. The ceilings were high and the cornice was a beautiful original feature, as was the small fireplace. The flat had once been the servants' quarters of the original house, Josh had told her on her very first, albeit brief, visit.

'This is such a lovely place, you know, Josh. We should spend more time here.'

'Ah, thank you.' He cringed and shrugged. 'It's just so small. And it's only temporary really. When I moved in a couple of years ago the space was plenty but now... erm... anyway the rent's low so I'm saving up to buy my own place... eventually. Have a seat and I'll go and get us some drinks.'

She absently wondered why, all of a sudden, the place was too small. News of his intention to buy a new place was something he'd never mentioned before. Then it dawned on her that he might be about to ask her to live with him. He'd need a bigger place if that were to happen. Her heart leapt and she sat on the navy-blue sofa for a moment to gather herself together. Whilst Josh was opening the wine, she stood again to look at the photos lined up on the shelves surrounding the TV. Josh and his parents, who still lived up north. Josh and his younger brother, who was pretty much a younger carbon copy. Josh and Zara at some fancy-dress party – all familiar photographs that brought a smile to her face. But a new addition was most intriguing. A multi-aperture frame filled with photos of a young boy with mousy brown hair and the same blue eyes as Josh. The photos showed the boy at varying ages from about five years to possibly nine or ten. Her intrigue was piqued. Did he have an even *younger* brother perhaps? And if so, how come he had never mentioned this before?

Josh appeared at the corner of the unit. 'Ah,' was all he said.

Her smile faded at his reaction and she began to wonder what the hell was going on. He had gone very pale and the expression on his face was one of fear. 'Erm, sorry, I didn't intend to be so nosy. I just— who's the cute little boy?' she asked as her stomach knotted and confusion fogged her mind.

'I thought I'd moved them all...' he mumbled to himself.

'All of what? Josh, what's going—?'

'Look, you'd better sit down. I clearly haven't thought all of this through.'

Her heart skipped as worry niggled at the back of her mind. 'Thought *what* through?' She walked over and sat down.

Josh joined her and handed her a glass of red wine. His hand shook as he took a sip of his own and glanced back at the unit where the photos were. 'That's Caleb. The boy. It's Caleb.'

Zara nodded slowly, still not having a clue what was wrong with Josh. 'Caleb? And who is Caleb?'

Josh swallowed hard and closed his eyes briefly. 'He's... he's my son.'

Zara gasped in spite of herself. 'What?' Her eyes widened and her heart almost leapt from her chest.

'I should probably have mentioned this last week when things kicked off with his mum but... I couldn't get my head around it all. It was too much. And I didn't know how to explain.'

She stood quickly and glared at him. 'Well, how about you bloody *try*?' Zara was aware her voice was raised but she didn't care. All she wanted to know was how the hell he had kept this fact from her for all this time.

'Look... I know this looks bad... so bad, but I was so caught up in... in *you*. And I was scared to lose you. I was going to tell you ages ago but there never seemed to be an apt moment and we were having such a good time together that I didn't want to ruin everything.'

'It's been a bloody year, Josh. You've hidden this from me for

a whole year. How could you not tell me? I don't understand.'
Her insides roiled. It was a kind of betrayal – an omission of the
truth was still a lie, after all.

'Because... because it's a difficult and painful story to tell
but I realise I owe you that much. If you're going to continue to
be in my life after this, which I hope you are, then you deserve
to know the truth.'

Zara took a long gulp of her wine, almost spilling the
contents of the glass as her hands shook. She sat once again.
'Okay, go on.'

Josh nodded and sat gingerly beside her as if he was scared
she'd bolt. 'Okay... I was at high school when I met Katie,
Caleb's mother.' He glanced down at his glass. 'We were head
over heels in love. I'm talking totally smitten. But her parents
were so ridiculously strict. We had to sneak about to even get
five minutes together. Her older brother used to hang around to
keep an eye on us at school, which made things very tricky, as
you can imagine. But... I genuinely did love her,' he said wistfully. 'She was so beautiful. Inside and out.'

He glanced up at Zara and shook his head. 'S-sorry. Erm...
anyway, her dad was Australian and when his mother died he
flew out to her funeral and stayed for a few weeks. Luckily for
us Katie's brother became otherwise occupied and for the first
time we were free to see each other. That was when we became
physical. It was a kind of natural step really. I had no intentions
of ever leaving her, you see. She was my soulmate. Or so I
thought back then.' He paused and gulped down more Dutch
courage. 'But she got pregnant. We were kids. But I knew we
could make it work. I really thought we could. Until her father
found out. I thought he was going to kill me. But instead he did
something worse.'

Zara frowned. 'What could possibly be worse?'

Josh swallowed and ran his free hand through his hair. 'He took Katie to Australia to live. The whole family. Gone. Including my baby.' His voice cracked and Zara was torn between wanting to punch him and wanting to hug him. He inhaled and continued. 'I wanted to protest, fight for her... for us and our baby to stay together, but that bastard was determined he'd stop that from ever happening. My parents looked into it all and, after a long spell of research, they sat me down and explained it would be best if I let them go. That it was best for the baby not to have to deal with his father being on the other side of the world. That I should let him go and accept that I was powerless at that point in time. But that eventually, when he was old enough, he'd want to know me. I really struggled with that. I was too young to realise that what they were saying was true and I hated them for it. We all went through a really rough patch and I rebelled a fair bit. But eventually things settled down. Katie managed to get a message to me through a mutual friend here in the UK when Caleb was born. There was no photo. I had no other information. I couldn't hold him. It literally broke me.' Josh's eyes twinkled with unshed tears and he cleared his throat and forced a smile. 'Shit, sorry. You'll be running under the next bus if I carry on.'

Trying to keep her own emotions in check, Zara shook her head. 'Just... just go on, okay?'

'Okay... so... about five years passed and then out of the blue a letter arrived at my parents' house. There were all these photos of a little boy. *My* little boy, Caleb. Golden skin, such a cute face and smiling eyes. Turns out Katie's dad had passed away and she realised then that Caleb had a right to know his own father. Because I was nothing like hers. He was a tyrant. Possessive and controlling. I just wanted what was best for my son. And that's why I had given him up. Although I never stopped hoping and loving him. And now, I send him birthday cards and letters. Then at Christmas I get to speak to him over Skype. It's bloody incredible.' He clenched his jaw. 'I just wish... I just wish I could reach out and touch him, you know?'

Zara's lip trembled and she nodded, unable and unwilling to speak in case her emotions got the better of her. And they were so incredibly mixed up she really didn't know what she felt.

'Anyway, last week my mum and dad had the most amazing news.'

Aware she was about to hear the answer to why Josh had been behaving strangely, she guessed that whatever it was might be bad news for her. 'Oh? What news?'

'He's coming to the UK next week, Zara. He'll be *here*. Katie's visiting family and friends and has asked if she can bring Caleb to meet me.' His tear-filled eyes lit up and the huge smile on his face spoke volumes. The happiness radiating from him was a tangible entity in its own right.

Her own eyes stung and she chewed the inside of her cheek. 'Oh, wow! That's incredible.' She did her best to sound enthusiastic but there was still a niggle of hurt and betrayal at the back of her mind. This was clearly something he wanted desperately. 'Yeah. I'm so excited. I don't know how long they're staying but Katie has promised I can see him lots whilst they're here. Saying goodbye will be so hard but I'm not focusing on that right now. I'm staying positive. I have a *ten-year-old son*, Zara. Shit!'

She held out her hands, unsure how to deal with it all. 'You sure do.'

Josh's smile disappeared. 'This was why I invited you tonight. I was supposed to cook you dinner and ply you with wine and kisses before I told you the truth. I was in such a rush before you got here that I forgot to move the latest frame full of pictures that Katie sent me.'

Was the talk of plying her with alcohol and kisses supposed to be funny? Because she wasn't laughing.

He stared at her for a few moments as if awaiting her response, but when none came he placed down his glass and took her hand. 'Look, I know this is all a hell of a lot to take in. And I know that you and I are going to have more talking to do about this, but I really hope this doesn't change things. I really care about you. I think we have something special here. What do you think?' The former sadness and then joy had now been replaced by hope in his eyes.

She had no idea what to say. Of course it changed things but she just wasn't sure how. His son lived in Australia so it wasn't as if things would be impacted too much. Katie had clearly moved on if she had managed to stay away for so long. And the truth was Zara really, *really* wanted a future with Josh. He was almost a perfect package. She had gone from hoping he was about to tell her he loved her, to then thinking he was going to ask her to live with him, to finally discovering he had a ten-year-old son and a former true love. Talk about a rollercoaster ride of emotions. She really needed time to process it all.

She tried to imagine life without Josh in it but the brief moment she envisaged that reality her chest ached and she wanted to scream. Okay, so he had a child and an ex but so many men did, and women too. And most people got on just fine in those situations so why would this be any different? She adored him. And, okay, he'd kind of lied to her but he'd had his reasons, hadn't he? And he'd been going to tell her tonight, it just happened that she had found the photos and forced the issue. Her inner dialogue continued with both the angel and the devil on opposing shoulders almost coming to blows over what her next step should be.

'Zara?' Josh's voice was tinged with worry now.

She turned to face him. His crumpled brow and teary eyes made him appear so utterly bereft. Without thinking, she launched herself into his arms and kissed him passionately. All the confusion and questions manifested in a heated exchange that went so much further than she had anticipated. Not that she really had planned any of this. But before she knew it she was naked and tangled in Josh's arms in his bed, gasping in ecstasy as he kissed and touched every inch of her sensitive flesh. As he moved above her, his breathing heavy and his eyes filled with hunger, he smiled and she was done for. This sensitive, funny, passionate man had so many facets and a heart of gold and she was on the verge of letting go and just telling him exactly how she felt regardless of this new side to him. Tumbling incoherently and willingly into something scary and unknown but exhilarating at the same time. All she had to do was give in. And when he smiled down at her in the heat of that moment she lost her grip.

8

On Monday evening, Marco called a meeting of the besties and Zara arrived twenty minutes late. She dashed in and sat at the usual table where she was greeted by knowing grins from Shelley and Marco.

'I'm so sorry I'm late, guys. I was just about to leave work when this huge bouquet arrived. Look at the size of the thing.' She held out the fragrant and oversized bunch of roses.

'Let me guess – Noah's feeling guilty and these are an apology?' Marco winked at Shelley.

'Oh yeah, he's feeling *so* guilty he's talking about me doing more of these horrible camping trips. He's got absolutely no chance. No, of course, my lovely flowers are from Josh.' She beamed as she placed them on the spare seat.

'Has he bloody proposed or something, Bailey?' Shelley asked, arms folded across her ample bosom.

Zara felt heat flush her cheeks and she couldn't help smiling. She shrugged. 'No, nothing like that. Not just yet. But it certainly feels like something big.'

Marco clapped his hands together excitedly. 'I knew it! He told you he loves you finally, didn't he?'

Zara paused and wondered whether to mention the small matter of Josh's surprise admission. But these were her best friends so how could she not?

She inhaled deeply and summoned up the courage. 'Not exactly that either, Marco.'

'So what's with the cheesy grin and the flowers? He either cooks like bloody Jamie Oliver or the food was crap and the flowers are an apology for almost poisoning you. So which is it?'

'We didn't exactly eat much.' She tucked her hair behind her ears and chewed on her lip. 'There's one small new bit of information though.' She held her breath and waited for the assumptions to fly. And fly they did.

Marco's eyes lit up. 'He's bi?'

Zara scoffed. 'No!'

Shelley placed a hand on each of her own cheeks. 'Oh my God, he's married.'

Zara rolled her eyes. 'No, he's not married. But... it's almost as complicated as that.'

'Divorced? Gay? Come on, Zee, just spill it.' Marco was leaning forward so much Zara expected him to fall from his seat and bash his chin on the table.

'No... he... erm... he has a ten-year-old son.'

Marco's gasp was almost theatrical. 'What?'

Shelley's eyes almost popped out of her head. 'Bloody hell! How old was he when it was born? *Twelve?*'

'He was seventeen. It's a heartbreaking story. To put it bluntly the girl's dad whisked her off to Australia and the baby was born there. Josh has never met him, but...'

Marco and Shelley glanced worriedly at one another. 'But

he's going out to visit soon?'

Zara cringed. 'Not quite. The mother, Katie, is bringing the boy, Caleb, here. To England.'

Shelley's expression changed to one of sadness. 'Oh no. When?'

'Next week. But don't be like that. It's not a big deal. I'm fine with it. I'm looking forward to meeting Caleb. Josh says he doesn't want to lose me so I'm not going to start getting worked up about something that's out of my control.'

Marco reached out and took her hand. 'But you really love him, sweetie. I'm worried for you.'

Zara shrugged off the comments and her friends' worried gazes that were now fixed on her. 'Come on, you two. Good grief. It'll all be fine. I'm telling you, he really cares about me. He said so. We really care for each other and we want this to *be* something. Neither of us is going to do anything to spoil that.'

'But this is his child, Zara.' Shelley only used her full name when she was being extremely serious. 'That's something you can't just shrug off as *no big deal*. I think you should maybe back off a little until they've gone back to Aus.'

Zara was pissed off at her friends' apparent lack of support. 'Back off? Why should I back off? We've been together a year. It's not like we've only just met and I can just dump him, Shelley. I love the man, warts and all.'

Marco sighed. 'You just likened his son to a wart, Zara Bear. I hardly think that's a good start, honey. And why has he only told you about this now if he's known all this time?'

Zara sighed and shook her head. 'Because it's broken his heart for all this time, that's why. There's no wonder he daren't tell me he loves me. He's got issues about commitment, seeing as his would-be father-in-law took his child and the love of his life away.' Her voice was raised and she hated that she had to justify everything.

Marco lifted his hands to his cheeks. 'He said she was the love of his life?'

'That's all you took from what I just said? Jeez, Marco. Both of you, you're being ridiculous about this. I'm a bloody grown woman, not some teenager with a sodding crush. Give me some credit for maturity, will you?'

'Zara, honey, Marco and I are just worried for you. We're your best friends.'

The flush she had felt earlier was nothing compared to the raging furnace beneath her skin now. She stood up and grabbed her bouquet. 'Well, why aren't you bloody acting like it, then?' Shelley gasped so loud it was a wonder the whole pub didn't fall silent.

'Zara, please! Don't go. Oh, *Dio, le si spezzerà il cuore,*' Marco said, shaking his head.

Shelley stood too. 'Yes, come on, stay and have a few drinks, please? Don't leave like this. You know we love you and only want you to be happy.'

She glanced down at her two best friends in the world and slumped into the chair again. 'Fine. But you have to stop worrying about me. It *will* all work out, I promise.'

Marco sighed in what appeared to be relief. He shook his head. *'Le ultime parole famose.'*

Things were being blown out of all proportion. Marco was speaking Italian; Shelley was using her full name.

Zara forced a laugh of incredulity. 'Pah! You two are hilarious. Anyone would think I'd agreed to adopt the bloody kid. Seriously, you're worrying over nothing. It's all going to be fine. I'm telling you. I'm a grown woman. Now, I fancy some shots. Who's with me?'

* * *

Zara left the pub soon after downing a couple of shots at the intervention-style drinks session with her two friends. Marco decided to stay a while longer whilst Zara hurried home to put her flowers in a vase. The fragrance filled the room and she couldn't help smiling every time she saw them. But her friends' words had worried her. The situation was so much more complicated than she could've ever expected and she was terrified of having her heart broken too. She wouldn't mention that to Marco when he got home later though. No, she was better staying quiet just now. The last thing she needed was an Italian drama queen wrapping himself round her ankles whenever she went to meet Josh.

She carried the bouquet through to her bedroom and placed the vase on top of her tall chest of drawers before flopping down onto the bed. Of course, they had been right to worry. Up to now the feelings in this relationship had seemed a little one-sided. That was what made this all so scary. She loved Josh, but what if he still loved Katie? Deep down she knew there was every chance her heart was in danger. But she would have to trust him. He'd said the right things. Well, most of the right things. If only he'd told her he loved her. But he did say he wanted her in his life and that he cared for her. She just had to have faith that he meant every single word.

As she lay there her phone vibrated. She reached for it.

> Hey sexy. I can't stop thinking about you. Want to come over? J x

Butterflies danced excitedly in her stomach and she hit reply.

> Rather busy lying on my bed thinking about you just now, sorry. Z x

An almost immediate reply arrived.

> Funnily enough I have a bed too. You could come over and lie on it whilst you think about me. But the best bit is… I'll be there too. We could even get in the bed and see what happened… J x

She giggled and chewed on her lip.

> I think we both know what would happen if we did that.

There was a long pause and she wondered if he had got bored. But eventually a reply came.

> See you at mine in fifteen. You can just wear the flowers if you like ;-) J x

We haven't even talked things through yet. My immediate response was to dive into bed with him. There's so much I need to know about how this will affect us. I must be completely mad. I shouldn't have slept with him right after his revelation for starters. And I most definitely shouldn't be so bloody drawn to him. But…

* * *

Thirty minutes later Zara's cab pulled up outside Josh's place and she climbed out. The butterflies from earlier were dancing a merry jig inside her and she was shaking. But was it from lust or the fear that she was falling head over heels into the abyss?

After Josh's message she'd showered and changed. Put on

some of her sexier undies – nothing slutty, just pretty – grabbed a bottle of Pinot Noir from the wine rack in the kitchen and left a note for Marco telling him she'd be home late... or not at all.

Josh opened the door and she almost passed out with lust. His muscular, shirtless torso greeted her – of course, it was attached to the rest of him but it was that particular area she noticed first. When her hungry gaze reached his eyes she found him grinning.

'Well, well, Miss Bailey. You've practically undressed me with your eyes so how about you come in and do the job properly?'

She stepped over the threshold and he scooped her into his arms, his mouth on hers as he carried her up the stairs to his flat. Once inside he let her feet drop to the floor and with one hand he took the wine bottle from her vice-like grip – she blamed the nervous excitement – and the other hand slipped down to squeeze her bottom through the satin fabric of her floaty skirt. At that precise moment, in a haze of lust, she decided to hell with her friends' worries. Josh was who she wanted and she'd do whatever she could to feel like this for as long as it could possibly go on. She wouldn't think about forever. Nope. That would be utterly crazy at this point. It was something she absolutely *wouldn't* do, she told herself as he led her through the flat, placed the unopened wine on the coffee table and then, with her hand still in his, he pulled her towards his bedroom. She repeated her mantra over and over as he removed each item of her clothing slowly, seductively, until he devoured her naked flesh with both his gaze and his body.

* * *

The following morning was a Tuesday and Zara was woken in Josh's bed by the alarm on her phone. After a moment of panic she remembered she'd had the foresight to pack some work clothes. She stretched out to feel for him but he wasn't there. She could hear talking through the flimsy sliding screen and decided she ought to get up. She spied a checked shirt over the chair in the corner and grinned. She'd always wanted to do that thing where the girl walks around in just her man's shirt. There seemed no time like the present so she grabbed the shirt and slipped it on. For decency she put on her panties, too, just in case anyone turned up unexpectedly.

She found Josh in the kitchen on the phone. His hair was damp from the shower and he had a towel draped round his bare shoulders. He wore board shorts that showed off his shapely calf muscles and she paused at the door to admire the view for just a few moments more.

'I see. Okay, well, it's a bit short notice. But, of course, I'll do what I can. Thanks for letting me know anyway. Speak to you soon. Yeah... you too. Bye.' He hung up and turned towards her. 'Hey, good morning, gorgeous. Did you sleep well?'

She sidled over to him and slipped her arms round his waist. 'Mmm. I certainly did. You?'

He leaned forward and placed a tender kiss on her lips. 'Extremely well. I could get used to waking up to your naked body wrapped around me.'

She felt heat rise in her cheeks and was suddenly very self-conscious. She pulled away and tucked her hair behind her ears.

He frowned and tilted his head. 'What did I say wrong?'

She shrugged. 'Nothing... it's just...'

He smiled in that heart-melting way he had. 'Come on, just say it.'

'I'm just worried there's a bit of a pattern developing here.'

'Pattern?' He shrugged. 'What pattern?'

'Well, you told me about your son and I dived into bed with you when really we still have things to talk about. I don't want us to get used to papering over any cracks in our relationship with sex.'

He laughed and his shoulders bounced up and down. 'Zara, sweetheart, you have to admit there are worse ways to deal with relationship crap.' He stepped closer and slipped one arm round her. 'And you also have to admit we're pretty bloody awesome at the papering part,' he said huskily.

She shook her head, a little annoyed that he wasn't taking her seriously. 'No, you know what I mean. I'm not... I don't...'

He tilted her chin so she would make eye contact. 'Hey, I don't think we paper over things with sex. Not at all. I just... I struggle to say how I feel out loud and so sex is... it's a kind of expression of how I feel inside. What we have is good, Zara. I don't want to lose it. So if you need to talk more, we talk more. But just to be clear, the sex I have with you, it means something, okay? Obviously I can't get enough of you in that department. I think the three times last night proved that. But... what I'm inarticulately trying to say is that...' he swallowed '...I haven't felt this way about anyone since... well, since Katie. And I don't want to mess it up. So if I'm expecting too much of you over this thing with Caleb, or if I'm not dealing with it how you want me to, then just say, okay? Because I don't want to do anything to spoil this. I like us.'

It was an 'L' word. But it still wasn't the one she'd hoped for. He'd as good as said it. And even in the absence of the hallowed word itself her heart beat faster and she was suddenly overcome with emotion. She forced it down deep lest it be set free and give her away. Instead she nodded and smiled. 'Me too.

Very much.'

9

It turned out the phone call Josh had received had been from his mother. She had heard from Katie and was calling Josh with news that his son and ex would be arriving earlier than originally planned. Zara reminded herself that she was absolutely fine about the whole thing and Josh enthused about the day trips the three of them could take. Zara smiled sweetly and nodded but deep inside she was beginning to worry that perhaps she wasn't quite ready to meet Josh's son. Wouldn't it be like meeting a stepchild for the first time? She'd seen films about such scenarios where the kid was a delight when everyone was around but then as soon as they turned their backs the stepmum got it. Okay, so comparing herself to a stepmum was probably a little OTT. But it still niggled at the back of her mind.

Josh beamed as he spoke about his son. 'Yeah, apparently he loves all things to do with science. So he must take after me a bit, eh? I thought we could take him to the Natural History Museum. I used to love places like that when I was a kid.'

'Look... Josh, I think maybe you should spend time with

Caleb on your own. Don't you? I mean, this is all very new for both of you and I don't want him to feel intimidated by you bringing me along.'

Josh's excited smile disappeared. 'But I thought you'd want to meet him.'

'Oh, I do, Josh, absolutely. I just think... he's coming all this way to see his dad. Not his dad and his dad's girlfriend. I just don't want to impose. This is a really big deal for you. For both of you.'

He reached out and took her hand. 'But I don't want you to feel left out. Like I said before, you're important to me too.'

She smiled and squeezed his hand. 'And I'm so happy you feel that way. But I want you to make the most of seeing him. After all, he's not going to be here for long. You need to make every single moment count.'

Josh was silent for what felt like an age but eventually he leaned and placed a kiss on her forehead. 'Thank you. Maybe you're right. I just l...' He cleared his throat. 'I appreciate how thoughtful and understanding you are.'

'I know you do.'

* * *

Zara was spending her time researching her impending trip north as it loomed ever closer. She had agreed to see Josh on Thursday evening seeing as Katie and Caleb would be up in Newcastle visiting friends and family initially. But she'd continued to tell Josh that he should concentrate on spending time with Caleb alone and see her properly when they had left to return home; eventually, albeit reluctantly, he had agreed.

Thursday night was going to be the last time she saw him for a short while so she wanted to make the most of things.

Marco had a hot date, meaning she had her flat all to herself, so she was planning a romantic meal followed by... well, whatever happened next.

Marco had given her some of his favourite Italian recipes and she had prepared home-made pasta with the little gadget her roomy had brought when he moved in. Josh couldn't fail to be impressed.

He arrived on time and looked decidedly nervous as he stood there in the doorway. He had a bottle of wine in one hand and a small box of chocolates in the other. 'I thought I'd bring these seeing as you already had flowers,' he said as he crossed the threshold.

'We can enjoy those later. I made Italian.'

'You made the Italian do what?' Josh laughed. 'Jeez, that was such a shit joke. I'm so fucking nervous, Zara. What's wrong with me? I feel like we're on our first date or something.'

She laughed. 'I know exactly what you mean. I've been a wreck all day. How daft are we?'

'Get this bottle opened, eh? I reckon we both need a bit of Dutch courage tonight.'

She opened the bottle as Josh took a couple of wine glasses down from the cupboard. 'So, are you excited about tomorrow?'

Josh closed his eyes and shook his head. 'Hey, look, why don't we forget about Caleb, Katie and all that just for tonight, eh? Let's make this about us.'

Relief flooded her veins and she stepped closer to him, slipping her arms round him and tiptoeing to meet his lips with hers. Their exchange became heated and soon enough Josh had her pressed against the counter top as his hands roamed her body.

He stopped and pulled away. 'I know you're worried about us making everything about sex but right now... I just want—'

'So do I.' She grabbed his hand and led him to the bedroom.

There was something a little different about how he made love to her. She couldn't help feeling that he was trying to prove something. He worshipped her with his tongue and with his mouth; teasing and tasting her as if this would be the last time. And then it dawned on her that it might be.

* * *

After the first meeting with Caleb, Josh telephoned, oozing enthusiasm and praise of the little boy. 'He's a really smart kid. I mean, I know I'm biased, but he really is. He told me all about the marine life where he lives. They're not far from the Great Barrier Reef. Imagine that! I can't believe he loves the ocean as much as I do. And he really looks like me. Poor kid. My mum said he's the spitting image of me when I was his age. And she's right. When you compare photos it's like we're the same person. Except he's got tanned skin and the photos of me as a kid show me as so pale I'm almost blue.' He laughed heartily and Zara smiled. He sounded so very happy and excited.

'So... ahem... how is Caleb's mum?'

There was a silent pause. 'Oh, she's fine. Jet-lagged obviously. Says it's strange to be back in the UK. She doesn't miss the weather. Typical it should chuck it down all day today. Oh, you should have seen Caleb's face when he opened his presents. That microscope you suggested was a hit. Thank you for that.'

So he wasn't going to talk about Katie. Maybe that was a good thing. 'Well, I'm glad it's all going well for you.'

'Thanks, gorgeous. Hey, I can't wait to see you. Maybe we

can sneak in a meeting? I don't think I can wait two weeks. And before we know it, you'll be off on your travels.'

She was relieved he wanted to see her but decided to stand firm. 'Like I said, your focus should be on Caleb. I don't want to detract from that. But I promise as soon as he goes home I'll be right there.'

'Hmm... if you insist on keeping away I might just have to come and break into your apartment.' He chuckled.

'Don't forget I have a Marco. He's not a dog but, I'm telling you, he can be a lot worse.' She laughed as the image of Marco humping Josh's leg came to mind.

'What's so funny?'

Zara tried to quell her amusement. 'Oh, just my stupid sense of humour. Listen, I should go. Up early tomorrow. Unlike some of us, who get to play football and go to museums for the next two weeks, there are those of us who have to go in to work to earn a crust.'

'Yeah, well, you can always ditch work and come with us.'

'Night, Josh, lo—' *Oh, shit, that was bloody close.* 'Lovely to hear from you.' She hung up before any comments could be made about her ridiculous almost-confession. It had begun to trip from her tongue and she'd felt this way for so long, it felt natural to say it. But now wasn't the time.

Four days later she was sitting eating breakfast with Marco when out of the blue he asked, 'Josh hasn't been in touch for a couple of days, has he?'

Zara sighed. 'No, but only because I insisted he focused on his son. I'm regretting it, to be honest. I miss him like mad. I don't know what to do.' She placed her spoon down and stared into her yogurt and berries as if the answer might miraculously appear there. An image of the berries forming words in the bowl sprang to mind. *They'd no doubt spell out 'Get a life, loser' or something equally scathing.*

'Maybe you should just give in and call him? Ask him out for a quick drink. I'm sure he's missing you just as much. Honestly, if I see you scroll through those bloody selfies you took once more I'm going to go over to his place and drag him here by his bed hair.'

Zara cringed and put down the phone that had become somewhat of a hand accessory. The post-coital, silly bed selfies were really sweet. Cheesy but lovely. But looking at them only made her miss him more.

'What the fuck is wrong with me, Marco? I've pretty much loved him since the day I met him but I daren't tell him in case it leads me to find out that he doesn't feel the same. It's pathetic. And not normal.' She huffed.

Marco grinned. 'Well, Zara Bear, you've never been normal. I mean, you put ketchup on everything. You drift off into your head all the time and let's face it; *I'm* your best friend. So I think the whole normal thing is a ship long since sailed, honey.'

She couldn't help giggling. 'Sod off. And I don't put ketchup in yogurt.' She tilted up her bowl as if to prove a point. But then she did begin to wonder what that would actually taste like...

'Oh my God, you're considering it, aren't you? See! Case in point! Not a shred of normality in you, girl.'

* * *

After stewing on the idea of calling Josh for the majority of her working day *and* being faced with an ever-increasing to-do list, thanks to the recent departure of her colleague, Dillon, Zara couldn't focus. As soon as the clock hands ticked round to five o'clock, she grabbed her bag and dashed towards the exit. She was owed some time and she was damn well going to take it.

She had just reached the door when Noah's voice stopped her. 'Zara! Before you leave I have the details through about your bike hire for the NC500. Do you want to come in and we can go through it?' he called from the doorway of his office.

With her back towards him, she sighed and rolled her eyes. *A bike is a bike, surely?* But, as obedient as ever, she turned and walked slowly towards her boss. 'Look, Noah, would you mind awfully if I take a rain check? I'm shattered and I have somewhere to be tonight.'

Not used to people saying no, he looked a little stunned. His eyebrows were raised and the slow nod of his head told Zara he wasn't keen on it. 'Oh. Right. But it's vitally important you get the right bike. We need to send some more details. Dillon, of course, had his own titanium-framed bike that cost him over four thousand quid...' His nostrils flared at the mention of his new arch nemesis.

'I totally understand, and I promise I'll give it my full attention tomorrow, okay?'

'Sure. Sure. Enjoy your *afternoon*.' He stressed the word as if to make a point that she was some kind of part-timer. But Zara chose not to bite.

'Great. Bye, Noah.' She dashed once again for the door. It was raining hard and the fact that she had chosen the Tube again today became a huge relief. She couldn't cycle over to Josh's house in this bloody weather. Turning up looking like a drowned rat wouldn't do.

* * *

Once off the train at the right stop, Zara put up her brolly and set off walking to Josh's little flat. As she walked the rain became heavier and the wind whipped up so much that her umbrella turned inside out and broke.

'Oh, shit!' She wrestled with it for a while but to no avail. Eventually she stuffed the mangled metal and plastic into a dustbin and began to jog. She knew very well she was going to look like a drowned rat when she finally got to Josh's but at least she'd get to see him. Maybe she'd even get to meet Caleb too.

She rounded the corner of his street and the rain was coming horizontally straight at her. She lowered her head and stared at the pavement as she walked quickly, too out of breath to jog any more.

She was freezing cold, in her flimsy little suit and heels and wished she'd given this surprise visit a bit more thought. She reached the point in the road where she knew she needed to cross and lifted her chin to check for traffic.

Something caught her eye and she fixed her gaze on Josh's building. A couple stood on the steps under a large stripy umbrella. It looked like a nice sturdy one, unlike the ridiculous excuse for a rain cover she'd just had to ditch. The umbrella lowered and she saw that Josh was its owner. The dark-haired woman with him was presumably Katie.

She stepped forward and lifted her arm to wave but stopped when Josh slipped his arm round the waist of the woman and pulled her into his arms. What happened next broke her heart. His companion tilted her chin up to meet Josh's lowered face. And then he kissed her. But it wasn't the kiss of two long-lost friends. It was the kiss of two people still head over heels in love.

10

Tears streamed down her face as she turned and walked back in the direction of the Tube station. Thankfully the heavy downpour went some way to disguising her heartbreak.

'Zara! Stop!' a familiar voice called from behind her. 'Please! Let me explain!' She ignored Josh's pleas and kept walking, head down against the torrent. There was nothing to explain. He was a cheating, lying bastard. End of. He'd lied about having a son – or, rather, he'd lied by omission about that – and he'd lied about wanting a future with her. How the hell could she trust him now regardless of whatever stupid excuse he chose to present?

Eventually he caught up with her, grabbed her arm and pulled her to a stop. 'Zara, please—'

'Please what, Josh? Please forgive you for kissing your ex? Or for not telling me about your son? Or for forgetting to tell me you're still in love with his mother?'

Josh swiped his wet hair from his forehead. 'I didn't mean for this to happen. Honestly... I...'

With a trembling lip Zara asked, 'Was what I just witnessed

the *only* thing that's happened between you since she's been back?'

He closed his eyes and tilted his head back. 'Zara, please—'

'I'll take that as a no then, shall I?'

'Please just come back to the flat. Let me explain. It's all so damned complicated. There's history and then there's Caleb.'

Her heart squeezed in her chest at what was happening. They only had a year of history but it had been the best year of her life and all she wanted was more of it. More of him – especially his heart, seeing as he had hers. But, like the rain, her dreams of a future with the man she loved were falling to the ground round her feet, only to be stepped on and washed away.

'There's nothing to explain, Josh. I get it. I loved you with all my heart. But you never felt the same. If you had this wouldn't have happened. But do you know what hurts the most? It's that you could have just been honest and told me we were over. Yes, it would've still hurt like hell, but it would have saved me this humiliation.'

He stepped towards her and cupped her cheek in his palm. 'Don't leave like this, Zara, please. Let's just talk.'

She shook her head. 'No. You had a chance to talk and chose not to take it. Please don't try to contact me again, Josh. Goodbye.' And with her final words she turned and walked towards the station. The fight was gone from her. The rain couldn't soak her any more than it already had and she was past caring about how she looked. She just wanted to go home and be with people who actually cared for her. At least she had that chance.

11

Since having her heart broken, Zara's days had involved cycle training and lots of it. For endurance purposes she had been cycling in all weathers, figuring she had to be prepared for every eventuality. She'd also spent time online researching places she could visit for the article. Some of them looked lovely but she would still rather be going somewhere warm. Shelley had bought her a kind of warts-and-all guide book that had scared the crap out of her with its real-life advice of what to do and absolutely what *not* to do. It had taken her mind off Josh, but she couldn't say she'd enjoyed it and it hadn't exactly helped reduce the dread of her impending trip north.

At work Noah had continually commended her for her efforts and praised her for her abundance of team spirit; he'd even given her several days off to train, which had been a big help. Although what would've been even more helpful would have been for him to have called the whole thing off entirely.

Shelley and Marco had rallied round her after Josh had been caught cheating. Neither one had said, 'I told you so,' and she was grateful for that fact. Her fragile and bruised heart still ached for all the things that might have been, but she was relieved that he hadn't made any lame attempts to contact her. The last thing she needed was to be reminded of all the things she'd lost thanks to his lies and stupidity. And only now was she becoming resigned to the fact that time away in Scotland would be the thing to drag her back from the edge of the precipice she had been teetering on. She certainly hoped so.

The day of Zara's travel arrived way too quickly for her comfort. And soon she found herself standing on the platform at London Euston at 11 p.m. with her compact camping gear in tow. Her mood was solemn and her bags weren't the only things that weighed heavy.

Shelley rubbed her hands up and down Zara's arms. 'Aww, come on, Zee. It's only ten days. You've been away longer for work in the past, sweetie.'

'She's right, pumpkin. It'll fly by,' her mum agreed, cupping her face. 'You'll be home before you know it. Are you going to give Queenie a kiss? She'll miss you.' Her mum pouted and held up the shaking Yorkshire terrier.

Zara tried not to gag at the prospect, even though she adored the ancient pooch. 'Erm, thanks, Mum, but no. I'm covered in midge repellent and it might poison her.' *Or, more to the point, the dog's breath might poison me.*

Marco stepped forward. 'You never know, Zara Bear, you might meet some handsome man in a sexy kilt,' he said dreamily. 'And I want to know if it's true about their underwear.' He winked.

Zara laughed and hugged him. 'Hmm. We'll see. No wild parties while I'm away, you hear me?'

He saluted. 'Aye, aye, Cap'n.'

Her dad held her at arm's length. 'Now, you listen to me. Anybody, and I mean *anybody*, tries to fleece you, tries to have their way with you, or tries *anything*, you tell 'em I know people, right? Scary people. And you take names, darlin', right? I won't stand for my girl being hurt again. I'm still thinking I should go round to that Josh's house and take him down a peg or two.'

The scariest person her dad knew was Merv, the toothless alcoholic who spent most of his life in the King's Head pub down the road from her parents' house. Only he was scary for totally different reasons from the ones her dad was insinuating – most of them connected to his wild-eyed appearance.

'Dad, I love you, but you really don't need to do that. I'm moving on. I'm a strong, independent woman, you know?' She forced a smile.

Her dad grappled her into a bear hug and for a brief moment she was ten again. He meant the world to her and his hugs could ease most ills.

Shelley tugged her sleeve. 'And make sure you don't miss your bloody train home, okay? I figure, sod it, we'll go to that damned school reunion and we'll show 'em how good we turned out,' she insisted in a wobbly voice.

Marco whispered loudly through gritted teeth. 'Shells, stop getting upset. You'll make Zee upset too. You know how soppy she can be.'

Zara whacked him. 'Oy!'

The station master called for boarding and she gave one last hug to everyone. This was the first time she'd been seen off by her friends and family, which made it apparent that they were all worried.

It really didn't help.

* * *

Once she had waved to her leaving party, Zara was shown to her first-class sleeper cabin by an attendant who also took her breakfast order. The space was compact but clean, with a single bed, a hide-away sink and a little hanging space. Once she had closed the door, she placed her backpack in the corner of the room and decided she was too tired to walk up to the lounge car. She doubted that she would sleep thanks to the nerves jangling throughout her body, but vowed to at least try. Once her face was washed and her teeth were brushed, she stripped from her clothing and grabbed her old T-shirt from the backpack to sleep in. The thermals she'd bought would be saved for the tent. With the lights out, she snuggled down under the duvet and closed her eyes.

Instead of being irritating as she'd imagined, the clickety-clack of the train on the rails had a soporific effect and, before she could worry too much about the days to come, she drifted into slumber.

When she woke the following morning she was surprised at how refreshed she felt. Perhaps train sleeping was the cure for her recent insomnia? She washed and dressed just in time for the light knock on the door by the attendant who delivered her breakfast tray. She lifted the blind and, as she ate, she watched the last few miles of her picturesque journey pass by the window. Rugged plains and jagged, rocky hills were preceded by calm rivers and lakes. Little houses that looked like models sat out in clusters and she wondered what the people therein were doing. Preparing for work or for school probably. For the first time in ages she felt quite relaxed; or perhaps it was resolved. Either way, the worry that had plagued her since Noah's announcement about the trip was gone.

She pulled her itinerary from a side pocket in her bag and checked the details of her bike hire as she munched on a warm croissant, brushing the flakes of pastry away and then feeling a little guilty as they fell on the freshly vacuumed floor.

She was going to cycle approximately fifty to sixty miles per day, which sounded horrendous. But she reminded herself that once she got moving she really could motor and that was on her own bone-shaker. The bike she was being loaned was constructed from titanium, which, she was assured, was lightweight and tough. She had watched tutorial after tutorial on bike care and repair but in all honesty the information hadn't really sunk in. She just hoped she wouldn't really need any of it.

Armed with sandwiches, chocolate and water she had bought, Zara made her way to the bike shop with a riot of butterflies dancing the Harlem Shuffle inside her. Her nerves were totally unfounded, however, as the people at the shop were really helpful. She was given full instructions on how best to load the panniers and tent rack, meaning only her clothes and things she needed quick access to would stay in the backpack. The staff at Highland Trax waved her off with the assurance that they were happy to help if she had any major issues, so to call if she needed to, and she set off on her newly acquired two wheels, in the direction of the first stop.

The first day was supposed to be a fairly easy ride of sixty or so miles on smooth, flat ground. The words of the woman who had assisted her at the bike shop sprang to mind. *'It sounds monstrous but, believe me, when you get going, the time and the miles will fly by.'*

Hmm. I wish you were here doing this for me, she huffed to herself as she pedalled.

Her destination for the end of her first day was a little place called Lochcarron in Wester Ross. Considering she was starting on the right-hand side of the country and aiming to be way across the *other* side by the end of the day, she wondered if she'd even survive day one. It was daunting to say the least.

The road took her out of Inverness towards Contin with a slight diversion to avoid heavy traffic on the main trunk road. Once she was away from the city fumes she began to enjoy the scenery a little more. Surrounded by trees, with a small loch on her left and the sun shining down on her, Zara began to relax again. Maybe this trip wouldn't be so bad after all? Within half an hour she had to make a stop. Her bottom was numb and her back ached.

She climbed off the bike and glared at it. 'So, my silver nemesis, you're trying to kill me, are you? You dickhead. It's been... what, thirty-five minutes and I have *arse* calluses. How is that even possible?' She huffed as she held the inanimate object with as few fingers as possible, staring at it with disdain. 'I don't want to be here. And I certainly don't want to be here riding *you*.' Realising she was already on the verge of insanity, she glanced round the lay-by. No one else was there, thankfully. Then her attention turned to the loch before her and her breath caught. She took out her phone to snap some images – purely for business purposes, she insisted to herself; it wasn't that she actually *liked* the place.

The loch's surface was still and smooth like a mirror and the mountains opposite appeared to dip down into the loch as an upside-down version of themselves. It really was quite spectacular. She had expected to see murky brown watery depths but instead the shade was a simply darker version of the sky overhead. *Okay, so it's pretty. I'll admit that much. But it's not Egypt.*

Back on the bike she had now nicknamed *Silver Dickhead*, she cycled along the shore of the Black Water with its pretty single-storey houses and village post office; then onward still. The roads were fairly flat, which made cycling less stressful, and the scant vehicles that passed by were courteous enough. Before she knew it, she was greeted with another stunning loch. She had heard that there were lots of them in Scotland and, of course, she'd seen them on the map, but hadn't quite grasped how frequently she would skirt them in reality.

Another stop was necessary… purely for photos… it was nothing to do with Silver Dickhead trying to cut her in half – *well, the piece would be useless without accompanying images, wouldn't it?* As she travelled she memorised the stunning places and the array of vivid colours. Sights and smells became fixed in her mind so that when she stopped she could type up a few notes on her tablet. She was grateful that Josh had recommended buying a solar gadget charger as she was sure she'd make good use of it.

Josh… She sighed. *I wonder if he's with Katie…*

Buzzards circled overhead and she found herself smiling as she watched them catching thermals. When she reached the next village she was tired but not exhausted. She found a quiet spot beside yet another body of water and ate her lunch and massaged her sore extremities surrounded by nothing but the gentle swoosh of the breeze and the birdsong overhead.

Once she'd refuelled herself, she dropped a quick text to her friends and family to assure them that all was well so far, but with very little signal it took a while to send. She was in no great rush and got on Silver Dickhead once more.

* * *

Lochcarron was stunning with its view of the distant mountains and a wonderful, peaceful tranquillity. The journey, including various loo breaks, drink stops and photo opportunities, had taken around seven hours. Longer than she had originally anticipated, but she had taken it steady, knowing very well that this was a very new experience and she shouldn't push herself too hard on the first day. But a real sense of achievement settled over her as she rode into the little campsite that would be her home for the night.

Thankfully the tent pitched easily and, before she knew it, she was sitting by it on a comfy little foldaway pad, overlooking the calm loch, eating another sandwich and watching the sky over the mountainous backdrop go from light blue to pink to orange and then to navy-blue.

The little pinpricks of light overhead twinkled and as she stargazed she thought about home. What would her family be doing now? And what would Marco and Shelley be doing without her there to referee their conversations?

At around eleven, when she could fight her tiredness no more, she climbed into the canvas enclosure, removed her boots and slipped, fully clothed, into her sleeping bag.

12

Day two began with a bacon sandwich from a little van on the campsite. It was almost the best thing she had ever eaten. And on realising that she chastised herself. *Of all the places you've been and all the exotic fare you've eaten this simply cannot be the best thing you've tasted. Come on, Zara, get a bloody grip.*

Once washed and dressed she tried to pack up the tent. She fought with it for around five minutes trying to remember how the hell it fitted into the tiny pouch but in the end stuffed it in as best she could. It didn't resemble, in any way, the package she had purchased and she hoped it didn't make life difficult at tonight's stop. She logged onto her tablet and typed up notes on her first day's experiences whilst they were still fresh in her mind, and then eventually she was ready to embark upon another day of cycling.

After checking her itinerary and map she loaded up the Silver Dickhead, straddled it and left the campsite. Today would be over sixty miles and she would encounter some very steep climbs. One of which was the notorious Bealach na Bà, or Pass of the Cattle, which was apparently a gazillion miles above sea level – well, just over two thousand feet in reality but it might as well have been a gazillion miles. And as per the instructions on her itinerary she stopped at the village shop and stocked up on water and food. *It's a good excuse to eat choco-late. The calories are blooming necessary!*

The Tarmac before her meandered away like a curly line drawn by a child and disappeared round mountainous corners painted grey by the igneous rock it was composed of. Round every turn another view presented itself proudly, as if trying to convince her that it was the best yet. She hadn't wanted to be impressed but was failing to remain ambivalent about her surroundings. Suddenly all the things that Josh had said about the outdoors made a little more sense.

As she cycled she sang in her head to take her mind off the aching in her muscles. Song of choice for this leg was 'I'm Gonna Be (500 Miles)' by The Proclaimers. It seemed apt and it was catchy enough to help her keep up a good cycling rhythm. Although after ten minutes of cycling uphill some of the lyrics had changed to swear words and there had been several unkind references to Silver Dickhead.

'Why can't you be motorised, eh, SD? Why can't you make this easier for me? But more to the point, why the hell do I keep talking to you? Ugh!'

She inhaled deeply and, instead of exhaust fumes and cigarette smoke, cool, fresh, clean air filled her lungs. The sky above was blue but there was just enough cloud to cover the sun's rays. *Better for cycling,* she surmised. Every so often she was passed by vehicles with bikes strapped to the roof. And she'd expected to envy the people in their safe, little, fast-moving, metal boxes; but what surprised her was a little dash of sympathy that she felt for them. Okay, they had air condi-tioning and would get to their destinations faster but they couldn't enjoy the fragrance of the trees and the slight salty tang to the air. *Poor people.*

The feeling was short-lived.

The road climbed higher and higher and her heart pounded, not only with the exertion but the fact that the road fell away steeply to her left, rather unnervingly so. She had to make several stops and at one point got off to push.

'Come on, Bailey,' she said aloud, past caring who might hear. And with a wobbly voice she sang, 'I will not cry for five hundred miles,' as her legs throbbed and nausea overtook her. 'And you, you dickhead of a bike, I want you to know I hate you. There. Now you know.'

By the time she reached the Bealach na Bà viewpoint her legs were painfully tight and aching, she was sweating profusely and she was breathing heavily. 'How the hell did I think cycling round bloody Peckham Rye Common would prepare me for *this*?'

One of the cars that had passed her was there, its occupants now standing in the fresh air, snapping photographs of the vista that lay before them. Although she was absolutely shattered she took out her phone and snapped some of her own. A strange feeling of euphoria at her achievement made tears well in her eyes and she had to wipe them away. The view really was spectacular. *There's that word again.* The sky was clearer now and you could see all the way to Skye in the distance and even further beyond. She paused and just stood, silently taking it all in. *Breathtaking... absolutely breathtaking.* Every person at the viewpoint in that moment was evidently feeling the same. A contented silence fell over the strangers.

She glanced to her left through the fog of tears and a man with a strong German accent informed her, 'I come to Scotland many times. This view. It gets me at my heart every single occasion.' He patted his chest and Zara thought she could see tears glinting in his eyes too. She nodded and smiled, unable to form words. *Wow, so it isn't just me feeling emotional, then.*

After munching on a chocolate bar as she enjoyed the scenery, she climbed back on the bike ready to make the descent to Applecross. The name alone sounded idyllic and she found her stomach fluttering in excited anticipation of her arrival. The fact that it was downhill all the way pleased her even more.

'Come on, Silver Dickhead, we've got this bit!' she yelled as she set off, freewheeling. But within seconds she was wide-eyed and screaming like a lunatic, trying to get her feet back on the pedals. 'O-o-o-oh my Go-o-o-o-o-o-o-od! I'm going to di-i-i-i-i-i-i-i-i-ie!' Silver Dickhead clearly was getting its own back for her verbal abuse as she hurtled down the road towards death and the little village in the distance. 'I want my mu-u-u-u-u-u-um!' she shouted, thankful that no one was around to witness the terror ride she was now unable to disembark. There was a reason she never went on scary rides at the fair.

Thankfully she managed to find the pedals again and pulled over to catch her breath and give the bike a swift kick before climbing on once more and finishing the descent at a more appropriate speed. A row of white cottages lined Shore Street, which faced the Inner Sound; their views over to Raasay must have been a wonderful sight to wake up to every morning. Once again Zara was taken aback by the clarity of the water and was so tempted to take off her shoes and dip her toes in.

She noticed one of the cottages had a 'To Let' sign in the window. It was a double-fronted building with two dormer windows creating an upstairs space. She wandered over and read the poster that showed images of the inside. She could imagine sitting by the front window on her laptop, finishing the novel she had always wanted to complete but never had the time. These days the incomplete story was confined to the memory stick that accompanied her everywhere, *just in case.*

Being an author had always been a dream of hers. But she knew it was something that would likely only happen when she perhaps retired. There were not enough hours in the day in her current life, let alone hours she could set aside to write for pleasure. *Maybe one day...*

Another hilly road took her along the stunning coastline and she made a couple of stops to take pictures and make notes and then continued along the peninsula round to another picturesque village called Shieldaig. By this time she was craving coffee and so she stopped off at a coffee shop that faced Loch Torridon. It was called The Coffee Shack but in no way did it look shack-like. It was a very modern building with large windows that made the most of the view. An old wooden door was attached to the side of the building with the name painted on it. She made her way inside and ordered a coffee to take out. The man behind the counter was very welcoming and friendly. He wore a badge with the name 'Jim'.

'Let me guess, you're doing the North Coast 500?' Jim said as he made her drink.

She smiled. 'Under duress, yes.'

'Oh? That's not usually the response I get.'

'Yes, well, I work for a magazine in London and I'm here writing an article on the route because the original journalist left, meaning it was down to me.' She rolled her eyes but kept her smile in place.

Jim smiled in return and raised his eyebrows. 'Oh, right. I'm familiar with London. Lived there for a while when I was first married. But I guess the pull of home was too strong. I couldn't stay away.'

'So you and your wife relocated?'

He nodded. 'Aye, eventually. This place... well, the Highlands in general... it gets under your skin.'

She was still a little bewildered at the prospect of anyone leaving the convenience of London, but couldn't deny she was warming to the Highlands. 'I bet it's a great place to bring up children,' she said, noticing a photo of the man and a blonde woman with two children behind the counter.

He turned and glanced at the point her gaze had fallen and grinned. 'Oh, that it is. My wee ones love the beach.'

'Can I ask a question?'

'Fire away,' Jim said as he placed her coffee before her on the counter.

'Why is it called the Coffee *Shack* when it's not exactly a shack?'

He chuckled. 'Before you leave, nip through to the little hallway where the toilets are. You'll see the photos that show the old building. Believe me; the word shack definitely fitted its original form. We bought it as the shack and ran it as a business for a while but we've expanded it quite a bit, as you'll see.'

Wow, so people do choose to make lives for themselves here, regardless of the remote location, she mused. She paid for her coffee and, as suggested, she went to look at the photos. The little shed-like building that had stood on the spot years before bore no resemblance to the current one, but it was incredibly cute. The door that was fixed to the side of the modern exterior was the original old door and she thought how sweet that they had kept it. She could see immediately why the man had bought it, even at the small size it had been. He had clearly made a wonderful life for himself and his young family. It intrigued her and she made a mental note to write something about it in her article; even if it was only to point future north coasters to The Coffee Shack for refreshments and a warm welcome.

13

The second night's sleep was fitful to say the least. Clearly her first-day exhaustion had helped lull her off the night before but that wasn't the case this time. She tossed and turned and almost tied herself in knots in the sleeping bag. She even dreamed that someone had stolen Silver Dickhead. Of course they hadn't, much to her dismay.

After breakfast Zara was back on the road again pretty quick. Her porridge had been surprisingly palatable and she hoped it would give her the energy she needed for the morning's route. The first stop on the seventy-five-mile trip was to be Gairloch – a place she had read about and was keen to explore. Rumour had it, Gairloch was where rock star, Nick Dacre, from Sonic Idols had escaped to live incognito during the band's hiatus. She wondered if she might pass him on the street in some terrible disguise like a false nose and glasses. She loved Nick Dacre but scouring the people she passed was fruitless. Obviously his disguises were much better than she gave him credit for.

The day was a little cooler and there was a mist hanging over towards the coastline, but her view of Loch Maree was uninterrupted. A flat road that meant less abuse for Silver Dickhead was bordered on either side by a rugged mountain backdrop and a pallet of colours that ranged from grey to purple to green and brown. A bank of Christmas trees lined the road as she travelled further and she wondered if anyone had ever been tempted to come along at night and decorate them for a giggle. It was the kind of thing Marco and Shelley would do. She wondered what they were doing and if Marco had rearranged her furniture whilst she'd been away. Admittedly it had only been a few days, but she knew what he was capable of.

She pulled over and fired off a text.

> Hey you guys. Have I mentioned how I am selling my bike when I get home? Well I am. I have blisters on my arse! ON MY ARSE! Anyway, I hope you miss me as much as I miss you. Z xx

Once she arrived at Gairloch the sun was beating down on the sea and a sense of nervous excitement gripped Zara. She was booked on to a dolphin watching cruise and the prospect of seeing the sea mammals at close range made her giddy. *Josh would be so proud,* she thought sadly. Life jackets were handed out and the skipper made the necessary checks before they set off out to sea.

Once out in the open water, it wasn't long before a pod of dolphins joined their boat, as if escorting them on their sailing expedition. Zara had never seen dolphins in the wild and tears welled in her eyes as she watched them leaping out of the water and flopping back down again. Their skin was smooth and silvery and she longed to reach out and touch one to see what the texture was really like. They were playing and performing for their human observers and Zara stood there with a hand over her heart as she giggled through tear-fogged eyes. It was magical. There was no other word for it. She managed to snap a few shots on her phone and the grin on her face remained fixed in place for ages.

'Isn't this magical?' one of the passengers said in an American accent as they watched. Zara turned to see an elderly lady smiling at her.

'Oh, it really is. It's wonderful.'

'I live so far inland, in Kansas, that I never get to see the sea. My husband and I are here celebrating our anniversary and this has just made the trip even more special.'

'Oh, wow. You've travelled such a long way. Why did you choose Scotland and not somewhere warmer?' Zara could think of lots of amazing places she had visited that would suit such an occasion better.

The woman smiled. 'Ever since I was a teenager I've been obsessed with Scotland. Highlanders really, so romantic. My darling husband booked this trip as a surprise. We've been married forty years and this is the first time I've been out of the USA. I'd relocate over here in a heartbeat if I could bring my family and friends with me,' she said wistfully.

There was a variety of accents on the boat now she really listened and she was taken aback by how many people had made this their holiday destination when she had been so reluctant to come. She was beginning to really question her opinions.

The boat sailed past a small clump of rocks jutting out of the sea and the skipper, a marine biologist, went on to explain about the seal-breeding colonies that surround the coastline. The closest Zara had ever been to a seal was the stuffed one that lay on her bed. It had been a souvenir from Margate when they had gone on a family holiday. These seals weren't quite so clean-looking. But they had the cutest stubby faces and lay there on their sides – the skipper called it *hauling out*, but Zara couldn't help giggling at the similarity to a phrase used on her dad's favourite US cop show. *The seals are hauling ass – I must remember to tell my dad. He'll think it's hilarious.*

As they bobbed along the skipper talked to them about the conservation of the wildlife and the importance of recycling plastics – or, better still, not using plastics at all. Mid-sentence he pointed to the sky. Overhead a white-tailed eagle was hovering, its beady eyes trained on the water. It was searching for lunch and at the thought of food Zara's own belly grumbled. The trip had been a memorable one and she had loved chatting to the other occupants of the boat about their holiday experiences. It seemed she was the only one to have such negative feelings about camping. She decided she needed to be more open-minded.

The view of the little seaside village on the way back was like something from a postcard – and probably was. She snapped a few more shots of the row of white buildings edging the harbour and vowed to frame some of them for her walls at home. If something good was to come from this trip it might as well be artwork.

* * *

Once back on dry land she thanked the skipper and waved goodbye to her fellow passengers before deciding on lunch at a seaside-themed café just by the boat-trip booking office. She was greeted by a very friendly woman with an unfamiliar accent.

'Hi there. What can I get you today?'

'I'll have the seafood risotto, please. Everything sounds so delicious I was struggling to choose.'

'Ah, well, you can thank my husband for the selection. He buys all the ingredients locally. Not a fried Mars bar in sight.' The woman laughed.

'Can I ask where you're from? You have an intriguing accent.'

'I'm from Czech Republic. Prague to be exact.'

'Oh, wow. How did you end up living in Scotland?'

'I met my husband when he visited my country. He was on holiday and made me laugh a lot. And he was very handsome. He came back two months later so he could ask me out again. I moved to Scotland in 2012 and we get married.' She shrugged as if it was the most natural thing ever.

'Prague is so beautiful though. Don't you miss it?'

'Sometimes. But I love my husband and we have our daughter and our business so I'm busy, busy in my wonderful Scotland life.' She laughed. 'I'll go get your coffee.' She smiled widely and walked away, singing to herself.

The meal was divine and all locally sourced, which seemed to make it taste all the more delicious. Zara sat and lazily drank coffee, irrespective of her schedule, as she watched the world go by and let her food settle before setting off again.

A little bit of mobile signal served up a picture message from Shelley and Marco pouting sadly with a huge jug of cocktails and a message that said:

We miss you so much we're drowning our sorrows but we can assure you we're not enjoying the Margaritas one bit.

The afternoon was going to be a difficult one. Over fifty miles of cycling and sitting on Silver Dickhead lay ahead before Zara would reach her next stop at Ullapool. Perhaps she would need to find a pub with live music for the evening to cheer her up. She decided she would try to do just that but at that precise moment she needed all her focus to be on the road ahead.

As she was about to set off her phone rang. It was a bit of a shock to hear her Florence and the Machine ringtone as she had been making do with text messages due to poor signal. She hadn't yet removed Josh's number from her phone and seeing his name flash up on the screen sent her into a tailspin.

'H-hello?' She was hesitant and she was aware that it was clear in her tone of voice.

'Zara? Hey, it's me... Josh. I just wanted to check that you're okay. You know... see how you're getting on up north. And... to tell you that I miss you.'

She sighed heavily. 'Josh, please, that's not fair. You were the one who ruined things. You can't just call me out of the blue and say things like that.'

'I know. I know, I'm sorry. I just... I wasn't ready to let you go. It's crazy, I know. I just... Look, I meant everything I said about wanting you in my life. I really did want that.'

She didn't want to acknowledge the little spark of hope that had ignited inside her because deep down she knew it was pointless. '*Did* being the operative word though. Are you still seeing Katie?' There was a long pause, which acted as the confirmation he didn't actually say.

'Things are just so complicated, Zara. I'm so mixed up about everything. I just don't know what I really want any more.'

Zara closed her eyes and willed herself not to get upset. Nothing had changed. Josh simply wanted his cake and to eat it too. Well, she wouldn't be any part of this little game. She deserved so much more than someone who cheated with his ex the moment her back was turned.

'Look, Josh, I think you *do* know what you want. And I think it's the new life you planned with your son and your ex. And I don't factor into that. I can't forgive you for cheating on me when you'd assured me that nothing was going to change between us. But I'm not going to ask you to choose because the decision has been made. I've made it. We're over, Josh. We were over the moment you jumped into bed with Katie. And I think you know that.'

He sighed now. 'I just wanted to hear your voice. Things had been going so well between us when everything happened. It threw me for a loop. I just wanted to know that you're okay. Are you really? I don't just mean with your trip and camping and stuff. I mean... well, you know...'

She inhaled deeply to steady her breathing and prickled with annoyance. Did he think he'd made such an impact on her that she'd never recover? *Conceited much?*

Forcing a brightness to her voice that she simply didn't feel internally, she said, 'I'm absolutely fine. It's not as if my love for you was reciprocated, was it? So I've had to get over you,' she lied. 'And I don't need you checking on me. Okay? I'm a tough woman, not some damsel in distress. And you have your son to think about. Just go and make plans and have a wonderful happy life with him, okay?' Her voice broke in spite of her determination to remain tough.

'But... can I call you again? Just to make sure things are okay?'

Her resolve was firm. 'No. You don't need to. And to be honest I'd rather you didn't. It won't help either of us to move on, will it? And like I said, I'm absolutely fine.'

Another long silence ensued. 'Okay. I understand. Just please take care. I'm so sorry about how things turned out. I genuinely mean that. If things were different... well... If you ever need anything you know where I am.'

'Yes, in the arms of another woman is where you'll be. I have people I can call on who won't take me for a fool. Bye, Josh.' Before he could speak again she hit the 'end call' button and stared at her phone. A growl of exasperation, anger and sadness left her throat. What had been the point in his call? Was he deliberately trying to make her miss him? And if so, why would he be so damned cruel? She hadn't taken him for that type of man.

* * *

The rugged coastline lay out before her like something otherworldly. She remembered watching TV shows with her dad as a child, shows like *Doctor Who* that used remote locations to represent other planets. This could have been taken right from one of those shoots.

Onwards along the road that snaked its way, hugging the western coastline, dipping and rising again just as suddenly. She couldn't appreciate the view as much on this stretch of her journey. She needed her wits about her to take notice of the bends and hills that sprang up on her with less than a moment's notice.

Her legs burned and her heart pounded as tiredness began to set in. She found yet another lay-by and pulled in for a break. It was a location with another spectacular view. The high vantage point was such that she felt as though she were literally on top of the world. She took off her helmet and ran a hand through her knotted hair and took a long drink of water from the bottle mounted on the bike frame. Then she took out her phone and snapped several shots, making sure to note down as much detail about the location as she could for her article.

Standing a little distance away in the parking area was a man in a very sharp, well-fitted suit. He was standing by his four-wheel-drive vehicle, staring out at the landscape before them; his shoulders slumped as if the weight of the world were pressing him down. Zara wondered for a moment why anyone dressed in such inappropriate clothing would be in this remote location. As if he felt her watching him, he turned his head and met her eyes. She smiled. From what she could see at the distance he was handsome and clean-cut. More her type than Josh had been. He would look right at home in the financial districts of London but here in the Highlands he looked as out of place as she felt.

He smiled stiffly in response and nodded an acknowledgment but turned away quickly as his phone rang. 'Yes, I'm on my way home… No, it hasn't been great for me either but this is something I have to do… I know you don't understand but… Look, I can't really talk now. I don't want to air my dirty laundry in public when someone's listening.' He glanced over at Zara again and she felt her cheeks flame with embarrassment. Did he really think she was listening? Okay, so she'd heard what he was saying but it wasn't deliberate.

He hung up his call and stood there again, this time his head hung and his hands rested on his hips. He had a defeated air to his demeanour. She pretended to search her backpack in the hope he would see she wasn't actually paying attention to him. He sighed and rubbed his hands roughly over his face, glancing sideways at her again as if he was waiting for her to leave. But she wasn't quite ready and, anyway, it was a public highway. Did he think he owned the bloody place?

Plucking up courage from somewhere, she turned to face the handsome businessman. 'Excuse me; I just wanted to say that I wasn't listening in. Well, not on purpose anyway. But we're the only two people standing here so it was a bit hard not to hear. But I wanted you to know I wasn't intent on being nosy.'

Mr Smart Suit turned to face her and scrunched his brow. 'Sure, whatever.' His tone was dismissive and a little acerbic – unnecessarily so, she thought.

She wasn't sure why it bothered her so much but for some reason it did. 'I mean, I don't go deliberately listening in on phone calls. Not usually. I'm a journalist so I think I'm inherently inquisitive, but I don't make a habit of such things.' *Oh God. I'm waffling like a loony at a total stranger in a lay-by.* In a bid to make herself appear less bizarre, she continued, 'Lovely spot, this, isn't it?'

He gave her a befuddled look and shook his head. 'I suppose it is.'

Regardless of his sexy-as-hell accent, his monotone response was the hint she needed. 'Well, I suppose I should be on my way. This magazine piece isn't going to write itself, I guess. Have a lovely day.'

The man snorted. 'Not likely.'

Instead of leaving well alone as her gut was insisting she did, she inhaled deeply in an over-exaggerated manner and gestured out at the stunning vista of mountains, trees and water. 'But just look at that view and that bright blue sky. I mean, I didn't even *want* to be up here but, honestly, how can anyone be in a bad mood today when they look at that?'

He huffed. 'Look, I don't mean to be rude but I've just returned from my second funeral in as many weeks, one relative and one dear friend, and I have a hellish time ahead of me, so I'm not really in the mood to be happy or to enjoy pretty views with total strangers I meet in lay-bys. So please excuse me if I don't share your enthusiasm.'

His attitude stung and Zara clamped her mouth shut. She really would have to stop trying to fix things that weren't hers to mend. 'I'm very sorry for your loss… es… *losses*. Please forgive me for interfering. I'll leave you to it.' She clambered onto her bike and pushed off, trying not to be affected by the man's unfriendly nature. He was the least amenable person she had encountered on the trip so far. Good thing she wasn't likely to see him again.

As she cycled a car pulled up alongside her and she tried to stay focused on the road in spite of the fear that knotted her stomach. *You hear about people being dragged into cars. Please just let them pass.*

'Excuse me!'

She glanced to the side to find handsome Mr Smart Suit shouting to her through the passenger window from his position in the driver's seat.

'What?' She huffed as she pedalled faster in a bid to escape.

'Look, I wanted to apologise. I'm not usually an arse like that. It's been a crap few days and I shouldn't have been so snappy.' She didn't reply. She just continued to pedal. 'And you were right. That view back there... one of the best.'

She glanced at him again and he smiled but she was still rather wary so she returned her attention to the road.

'I just wanted to say sorry,' he called again.

'Well, you've said it now. You can be on your way.' She was aware that she was feeding him a taste of his own medicine and that it was a tad unkind considering what he'd just told her, but she was on an isolated stretch of road and was feeling uneasy.

'Okay... well, have a good journey.' She heard the motor of his window and he suddenly sped away.

'Not likely. Have you seen what I'm riding?' she shouted after the car. 'No offence, SD, but you're not a bloody sports car, are you?'

* * *

By the time she reached the coastal town of Ullapool she wanted to collapse and cry, but she wasn't sure in which order. She found a quiet spot up from the harbour and struggled off her bike. She removed her helmet and slumped onto the grass, resting her head in her hands and her elbows on her knees. She was exhausted, emotional and still sore. Angry tears cascaded down her face and she let them, unsure which was pissing her off the most: the aching, the loneliness or the fact that she was crying to begin with. Another cyclist pulled into the lay-by and she wiped at her face, desperate not to look like a wimp.

'Hi, are you okay?' the man asked. She guessed he was from Yorkshire by the accent. *This place really is a melting pot.*

She nodded. 'Yes, thank you. I'm just tired.'

He nodded. 'Aye, I get you. I was bloody knackered the first time I did this ride.'

'You've done it before?'

'Oh aye. And I wasn't as fit back then either. I thought a bit of cycling round't park'd be enough training. I was wrong.' He laughed and his words resonated with her as she cast her mind back to her nice little rides round the common. 'Anyroad, you'll get used to it. Just keep going, lass. Don't let the buggers eat you alive, though, eh? I looked like a bloody dot-to-dot puzzle when I got home first time. I brought better midge repellent this time.'

'I haven't really had much of an issue, to be honest.'

His eyes widened. 'Pfft, it'll come. Take it easy.' He waved and cycled off into the distance.

Suddenly feeling homesick, she pulled out her mobile and dialled her parents' number.

'Hello?' Her mum's familiar sing-song voice filled her with relief and she had to bite back tears.

'Mum, it's me, Zara. How are you all?'

'Oh, sweetie, it's so good to hear your voice. Hang on... Everybody! Zara's on the phone! I'll put you on speaker phone, darling.' There was a clink and suddenly her whole family shouted 'Hello!' simultaneously.

Hot tears streamed down her face and for a moment she struggled to speak. 'I'm... I'm... not great today, truth be told. I'm so tired. And I feel... I feel quite lonely.' Her voice wobbled and she swallowed, trying to force her emotion down but failing miserably – literally.

'Oh, sweetheart, it's just the tiredness talking. You're doing so bloody well. We're so proud of you.' Her mum's voice wobbled too.

'Hey, princess, have you had any trouble? Do I need to be sorting anyone out?'

Zara giggled. 'No, Dad, honestly. Everyone so far has been lovely. Very friendly.'

'Have you had any of that haggis shit yet?' There was a loud whack and her younger brother Will shouted, 'Ow! Mu-u-um! What did you hit me for?'

'William Bailey, you do not swear.'

He sighed in that typical teenager fashion and huffed. 'Sorry. So, have you then, Zee?'

Zara was laughing by this point. 'Well, Wills, all I can say is don't knock it 'til you've tried it, mate. You'd be surprised.'

'Ugh! They make it from sheep eyes and all sorts, you know.'

Zara's laughter increased. 'They do not! I'm not on an episode of *I'm a Celebrity Get Me Out of Here*, you know. I'm not being forced to eat weird stuff. The food has been really good so far.'

'Ah, but I bet you miss your mum's Sunday dinners, eh?' her dad chimed in.

'You lot are acting like I've been away months.'

'Well, it does feel like a long time, darling. We can't wait for you to come home.'

Zara sighed. 'Yeah, me too. But my work needs me. I'll be home before you know it.'

'See, that's my smiley girl. I knew you'd be all right. You just needed to hear your family's voices.'

'I think I did, Mum. Anyway, better go. Love you all.'

'Love you!' came the response in unison and she hung up. She felt so much better just for that brief chat with the people who grounded her. She wiped her eyes and checked her itinerary for the campsite details and set off once again.

* * *

Once she had checked into the site and her tent was set up, Zara sat on the picnic bench right beside where she had pitched. Once again, the view of the water spread out before her like a huge living canvas. She brewed up some coffee on her little foldaway stove and relaxed, eyes closed for a moment.

'Hiya. Are you cycling the NC500?' A voice with a Geordie accent dragged her from her trance-like state. She blinked her eyes open and looked up, shielding her eyes from the sun. A woman clad in bike leathers stood over her, her dark hair tied in a ponytail.

Zara squinted and adjusted her hand. 'Erm, hi. Yes, I am.'

The woman nodded and squatted beside her. 'Thought so. Look, me and my friends are touring the Highlands on our motorbikes. We're here for the night and thought we'd head into town; find a pub with some live music. We thought we'd invite you. We saw you arrive and presume you're on your own, seeing as we didn't see anyone else turn up with you. Us girls have got to stick together, eh?'

Zara glanced over to the group of five women who were sitting outside a cluster of tents. Their bikes were lined up beyond, all shiny and silver with huge chunky tyres. The women waved and so Zara waved back. 'That's really nice of you. But I don't want to impose.'

'We insist. You get yourself freshened up. I've stayed here before and the showers here are really good. We'll have a bite to eat and then we'll set off. Carrie's doing a barbecue, if you fancy a burger. Although I must warn you, she's a veggie so there's no meat.' She rolled her eyes. 'But anyway, if you can't stomach meat substitute just come over anyway.'

Zara smiled. The thought of a veggie burger that she didn't have to cook *or* buy sounded fantastic. 'Deal. Thanks again.'

'No problem. Oh, I'm Joan; the one with the blonde hair is Carrie.' Joan held out her hand and Zara shook it.

'I'm Zara.'

'Good to meet you, Zara. I'll introduce you to the rest of the gang when you come over. Now go get a nice long soak under that hot water, lass. You look like you deserve it.' Joan stood and walked back over to her group of friends.

14

Joan had been right about the showers. As Zara stood under the pounding hot cascade she could have fallen asleep on her feet. It was only the promise of food that dragged her back to reality. She dried and rifled through her bag for dry clothing.

'Hmm, what should I wear tonight? Leggings and a base layer, or maybe a base layer and leggings just to change it up? Ooh, I know... *leggings and a base layer*.' She huffed and looked forward to the day her outfits could be varied again and not weight dependent. She dropped her towel and washbag back at her tent before making her way over to the gang of biker women.

'Ah, here she is. We thought you'd washed away.' Joan laughed.

'Oh yes, I know, sorry about that. You were so right. Those showers are incredible.'

'They are. Anyway, grab a burger and I'll introduce you to the rest of the gang. Not that we're an actual gang. Don't be thinking that. It's not like *Daughters of Anarchy* or anything.' She burst out laughing and Zara joined in. She tried to picture the group of women before her on the hit US TV show. Somehow it didn't quite work.

'Zara, I'd like you to meet Carrie – she's the one who cooked for us tonight.' Zara nodded and smiled at the blonde woman. 'Next to her is her wife, Melody.' Melody was dark-haired and olive-skinned. 'Then this here is Claire.' Claire was petite with chestnut hair and sparkly eyes. 'I'm Joan, obviously, this is Jan and, finally, this here is Sally.' Jan was around forty and had fiery red hair whilst Sally was tall and slim with short mousy hair. Everyone seemed incredibly friendly and Zara immediately felt right at home with them.

'So, tell me how you all came to be up here on your motorcycles. Is it a regular thing you do?' Zara asked, intrigued.

'We get together as often as we can and usually have one week a year where we go off and tour somewhere new. But this is our second time doing the NC500,' Jan informed her.

'And the great thing is, it gives us a break from the men in our lives.' Sally laughed. 'Well, with the exception of Carrie and Melody. But they don't seem to mind spending so much time together.'

It was Melody's turn to laugh now. 'Yes, they keep telling us we're still in the honeymoon phase but we've been married since 2014 and we were together around five years before that.'

Joan rolled her eyes. 'I get the feeling they'll never tire of each other, those two. It's sickeningly sweet.' She grinned and nudged Carrie with her shoulder.

'Right, ladies, I don't know about you but I'm ready for checking out some proper Scottish music,' Jan yelled and followed this with a whoop.

The others clinked beer bottles together and Zara wolfed down the delicious bean burger she'd been munching on. She could've eaten another but didn't want to be the party pooper.

* * *

The group walked into Ullapool and it didn't take long to find a pub with a live band playing bouncy music that had Zara nodding along before they even walked in the door. The pub was alive with an almost tangible buzz as the group entered. They shared wide-eyed glances, each grinning like the Cheshire Cat as they made their way to the bar. People clapped and whooped along with the musicians, who were clearly enjoying themselves. The band on stage were a three-piece comprising a fiddler, an accordion player and a guitarist who could make his guitar sound like a variety of instruments, including a drum. A gathered throng at the front, close to the small, raised platform being used as a stage, were twirling each other round in time with the music as the rest of the crowd watched and clapped along.

Zara couldn't help the grin that spread across her face as she soaked up the atmosphere and watched the packed pub full of enthusiastic dancers and singers enjoying themselves.

Joan nudged her. 'Bloody brilliant, eh, pet?'

Zara nodded emphatically. 'Oh yes, it's incredible. What an atmosphere.'

Before she could even take a drink out of the glass she was passed by Carrie, an elderly man grabbed her by the hand and swept her to the makeshift dance floor.

She squealed and laughed before shouting over the music, 'I've no idea what I'm doing!'

The man leaned a little closer and replied, '*Dinnae fash*, lass, just follow my lead!'

She tried her best as the man – who was spritely to say the least – swung her round and twirled her this way and that. The result was that she almost looked as if she could dance. At the end she was thoroughly out of breath but grinning like an idiot. She hugged the man and thanked him.

'You *didnae* do too bad, lassie. You're a natural,' he told her.

When she got back to her new friends they applauded her and she was enveloped in a group hug as they told her how fantastic her dancing had been. Her ego was boosted even if they were just being kind. The band announced a short interval and within a few minutes the pub was filled with the sound of more contemporary music coming over the sound system.

'So, what's your story, Zara?' Melody asked, her head tilted to the side.

Zara shrugged, still a little out of breath. 'My story? I don't really have one.'

'How come you ended up all the way up here on your tod? You sound like you're a long way from home.'

Zara explained to the intrigued group the whys and wherefores of her trip to the Highlands and somehow managed to mention Josh in the scheme of it all – not just the fact that he had been the sales person to ensure she got the correct kit.

Sally shook her head. 'Well, he sounds like an idiot, honey, and to be honest you're better off out of it. It all sounds too complicated and love shouldn't be like that. You need to look for a man who knows his own mind before he decides to drag some poor unsuspecting woman into his drama.'

Zara smiled briefly. 'Nah, I think I need to just swear off men. I was better off before when I was without one.'

'Damn right,' Carrie chipped in.

'That doesn't mean she wants a *woman* instead, Caz.' Joan laughed.

'No, I know that, you daft bat. I just mean she doesn't need a man. That's all I'm getting at. I mean, look at what she's doing.

She's all alone in the Scottish Highlands on a bloody *pushbike*. She's a rock star!'

Joan nodded. 'Carrie does have a point there. You are brave. And you must be bloody strong-willed, Zara. I don't think I'd have agreed to it. Probably would have lost my job instead. And I don't mean just because you're female. I think anyone who does something like the NC500 on their own must be either mad or have a will of bloody iron.'

'I think stubborn probably covers it,' Zara said with a cringe.

'Well, I'm going to give you my mobile number. We're going home tomorrow but I'm sure the rest of the lasses would love to hear from you. You know, to find out how you get on.'

'And to know you're safe,' Jan added. Zara was overcome with emotion. This small group of women who were, to all intents and purposes, strangers had included her in their evening when she was feeling homesick. They had bolstered her, made her laugh and ultimately made her forget that she was hundreds of miles away from everything and everyone she loved.

The night ended in lots of singing and more dancing and Zara eventually climbed into bed with a smile on her face and a heart that felt lighter than it had in weeks.

15

The following morning, after she had typed up her notes on her tablet that had charged overnight, she joined the Daughters of Anarchy, as they had now become ironically known, for a breakfast of Carrie's special porridge and honey. That woman could cook and Zara was going to really miss her food. The friends sat around chatting and laughing just as they had the night before and Zara was once again reminded of how accepting they had been.

Once she was showered and dressed it was time to wrestle with the tent again. Only this time she had an audience. She just got it twisted into the right size and shape when someone shouted, 'Yeah! Go, Zara!' and it pinged out again, meaning she had to start over. She forced down a scream and string of expletives as she ended up cramming it back into the bag any which way it would fit, and in the process she inadvertently tripped over the bike and chuntered at it again as if it were a living being. *Yup, losing it.*

Once she was packed up ready to leave she went to say her

goodbyes. Each of her new friends hugged her and reminded her what an amazing thing she was doing and how strong she was. Mobile numbers were swapped and assurances made that they would all keep in touch. Joan even tried to convince her that she should buy a motorbike and join them on their next jaunt.

Zara laughed. 'I don't exactly have a lot of balance on Silver Dickhead so I'm not sure handing me something bigger with an engine is a great idea.'

Laughter erupted. 'I can't believe you named your bike something so derogatory. It's hilarious.'

'And apt,' Zara pointed out. More hugs ensued and she said goodbye before mounting SD once more.

* * *

With her faith in humanity firmly restored Zara set off on the next leg of her journey. An approximately seventy-mile coastal trek lay ahead of her. It would include the Kylesku Bridge and would then take her on to the day's destination, Kinlochbervie. She was relieved that her companions had been sensible about the amount they drank as cycling this route with a hangover would have been an added nightmare.

Thanks to the many hills on this particular part of the route, Zara made the most of the stops along the way. The road took her through the Highlands geopark. Who knew that rocks could be so fascinating? There were explanation boards on some of the stops and she made notes again to include in her article. The way she was going she might need the whole magazine to showcase what she had experienced – this in itself was a massive surprise to her and it was only day four of her cycle.

Her dad was a Kiss fan and her song for the day was aptly

'Rock and Roll All Nite'. Although, she didn't know all the words so just mumbled and sang the tune in the bits she couldn't remember. She did, however, make sure to sing extra loud on the choruses, seeing as she was on the road alone; she decided it was probably a good thing she was taking the trip solo as no one would want to put up with her cater-wauling.

Thirty-five or so miles in – although it felt like a hundred – the singing hadn't helped her tiredness. She was more out of breath than ever so she stopped for a break and a bite to eat at a pretty fishing village. A mixture of whitewashed and granite buildings lined the water and she found a little bistro that served food and hot drinks. The view from the window was once again one that she would treasure. The early afternoon sunlight glinted on the water as it rippled with the slightest breeze.

'Are you all by yourself, hen?' the waitress asked as she placed down the steaming mug with an aroma that made Zara's mouth water.

'I am, yes. North Coast 500 for a work project.' She'd expected that she might have been fed up of explaining herself by now, but it hadn't happened yet.

'Aye, we get lots of folks doing the same. Rarely do we get a woman on her own though. You're a brave wee soul.' That seemed to be the general consensus of opinion about her trip.

Zara shrugged. 'I don't mind it really. I can go at my own pace without annoying anyone.' She smiled.

The woman leaned forwards. 'Aye, well, here you go. A wee piece of flapjack for your next snack stop. Full of syrup and oats so not great for the waistline but essential for energy.'

The flapjack smelled tantalising and looked delicious with its golden-brown colour that was slightly darker at the edges, just how she liked baked goods. 'Oh, wow, thank you so much. What do I owe—?'

'*Och*, nothing, hen. On the house. I own the place so it's no bother.'

Zara smiled warmly, once again surprised by the kindness of strangers. 'Thank you. I'll look forward to eating it.'

Once she was refuelled and had typed up more notes on her tablet, she packed her things into her backpack and left, waving another thank you to the owner, who smiled and wished her lots of luck and good weather. She glanced at her watch and realised she had perhaps stayed a little too long in the comfort of the bistro with its friendly owner and welcoming atmosphere. *Par for the course, I suppose, when everyone is so relaxed. It rubs off on you...*

* * *

Tackling more miles of rugged coastline that afternoon, Zara couldn't wait to climb into her bed for a rest. At one point she pulled over onto a rough patch of grass and just stood, staring out at the white sandy beach beneath her, catching her breath. Could she maybe get down there? It would possibly put her even further behind schedule but it would be worth it. She fastened the lock round her bike and laid it on the grass before locating a very narrow path that descended through craggy rocks and finally reached the dazzlingly clean sand.

She sat on one of the rocks and inhaled a deep breath, trying to calm her erratic heartbeat that was pounding from the descent. She had taken her map with her so she could figure out which of the beaches she was on; that way she could take photos and add it in to her article. She pulled the map out and examined the knotted spaghetti of road networks that circumvented the coastline and turned the map every which way but couldn't quite figure out which beach it was. A man walking his dog was throwing a tennis ball from a long plastic catapult and she jogged over to him.

'Excuse me! Could you tell me which beach this is, please?' she asked, out of breath as she reached him.

'Aye, it's the beach by Clashnessie. Pretty, eh?' The man smiled.

'It's gorgeous. Thank you for your help.' She jogged back to where she had left her helmet and the map and scrutinised it once again. She wasn't exactly off her route but she was behind schedule. To add insult to injury she had a stitch in her side so sat a few moments longer waiting for the pain to ease. A sudden, unexpected gust of sea breeze whipped the map out of her hand and took it flying across the rocks.

'Shit! Shit, shit-shitty-shit!' She clambered after it but it kept fluttering off as the wind increased. When she eventually grabbed it, the map was torn and wet from where it had landed in a rock pool. Why the hell hadn't she brought a spare one? *Stupid Zara.* Her stitch had worsened from running and she had difficulty clambering back up the rocks to Silver Dickhead. Thankfully... or not... it was still there. She took off the lock and tried to cycle but the pain in her side grew worse so she got off and walked steadily for a few hundred yards until it became far too dangerous to go any further on the hairpin bend that lay ahead.

She stopped again on another smaller grass verge and doubled over, willing the pain to subside. After what felt like an age, she lifted her wrist to find that her schedule had run away from her. She needed to get back on the road if she was going to reach her designated campsite before darkness fell. She pulled out her phone to check for signal in case she had to give in and call for help.

Nothing. Nada. Zilch.

'Ugh, you're well and truly on your own now,' she informed herself aloud – she had discovered during her trip that talking to herself made her feel less lonely and that fact alone was worrying. With a huff and a wince she climbed back on the bike and chuntered at it, 'I bet if you could you'd be laughing at me right now, wouldn't you? Yeah, well, you're *can't*... so... piss off. Oh God, I'm doing it again. I'm talking to a bloody bike.' She began to pedal steadily, trying not to over-exert herself, whilst also being very much aware that her map was next to useless until it dried out *and* that finding her campsite was going to be tricky.

Several miles on and the roads had quietened to nothing. It was an eerie feeling to be the only person on the winding road and nerves began to dance in her stomach. *Just keep going. Just keep going,* she repeated over and over in her head. *But what if it's appendicitis? I could die out here all by myself. Oh God, this isn't helping.*

She began to sing Nina Simone's 'Feeling Good', hoping the positivity would rub off on her. But instead she realised she sounded rather like a cow giving birth on account of the pain. She passed more beaches, although the light was fading and she seriously regretted being bewitched by the one she had stopped at to get a closer look. *Stick to the bloody schedule, you idiot.* After around an hour and a half, not a single vehicle passing her, she was resigned to the fact that she was entirely alone. It was a sobering thought. All the pretty views in the world weren't worth feeling this isolated. It was a feeling she had never really experienced back home and being out in the eerie dimming light of early evening simply compounded the sense of melancholy that had descended upon her.

Her side was still aching, but it had eased a little, which was a blessing considering that she was just about to embark upon yet another hill. She reached down and flicked the switch for her lights, hoping that she would be able to see better in the failing light, but, more importantly, she would *be* seen.

There was a loud popping sound and her bike ground to a halt in spite of her hard pedalling.

'Please, no. Not a puncture. Please, for fuck's sake, no!' she yelled at the inanimate object. 'How the hell do I repair a puncture in this light? Or bloody lack of it. Oh God, I hate you, Noah!' If her boss had been there at that precise moment she would have knocked him out. She checked her phone again and, not only was there no signal, but the battery was dying. She had forgotten to plug it into the solar charger as she cycled. 'Shi-i-i-it!' she screamed like a banshee into the open space before her.

She glanced round but couldn't see much at all now the light was pretty much non-existent. *What the hell should I do?* She couldn't see any buildings. All there was to her left was a huge expanse of what she hoped was just grass. She wheeled the bike over the bumpy ground and found a spot that was as level as possible. It would have to do. She would have to set up camp for the night and then figure things out in the morning. *Good thing there are no bloody trespass laws in Scotland.* She was grateful her conversations with friends prior to the trip had dished up that little gem.

As she laid down her bike she felt the first spots of rain. 'I don't fucking believe this! Can this day get any worse?' A bright flash of lightning was followed by a deafening crash of thunder. And a hysterical laugh left Zara's throat.

'God, if you're up there, is this your idea of a bloody joke? Because I don't reckon much to your sense of humour!' she yelled at the sky. 'So please, please, for the love of *Mike*, just stop it now!' Her cries were absorbed by the sound of the rain pounding at the ground as she yanked the canvas out of its bag and tried her best to wrestle it in to place. Just then the mocking worm in her ear began to sing 'It's Raining Men' and she really wished for once that it were.

16

Setting her tent up in the pitch black wasn't exactly Zara's idea of fun. But having the rain lashing down whilst she did so put the crap icing on the shit cake. *Why, oh, why aren't there more hotels in this godforsaken part of the country? Or bed and breakfasts? Or even a bloody barn to shelter in, for goodness' sake?* This was officially the worst night of her life and she prayed, as she shivered in her soggy clothing, that Noah would somehow miraculously contact her and call the whole thing off early; tell her she'd done her bit for the good of the magazine. Even breaking up with Josh had been less horrendous and *that* was saying something.

After the hurried, slapdash way she'd erected her tent she wasn't sure it would even last the night. She wasn't entirely sure *she* would either. She'd tried so hard to catch up on time and had failed miserably and her lack of dry map and daylight meant she had no clue where she was. In the end, the field where she'd set up camp could've been filled with rampant bulls for all she knew. But with the way she was feeling she would simply accept her fate if it was. The fact that her waterproof jacket was bright red didn't exactly help in the bull scenario, but at least it was dark now; so, *so* dark and silent, apart from the rain lashing at the tent from every angle. She was sure that it was even raining upwards at one point; it wouldn't have surprised her. Nothing would have at that moment.

Sitting there, shivering and shaking with a combination of cold and fear, she was swamped by an oppressive feeling of loneliness. Her heart ached and, admittedly not for the first time since being an adult, she longed for the warm, familiar embrace of her mum. She closed her eyes and imagined her laugh, loud and cackling, and for a moment she smiled fondly. What would they all be doing now, her family? *Watching some typically British comedy, no doubt.* Reruns of *The Royle Family* being their favourite. She wished she were there, too; curled up on the squashy old sofa, giggling along next to her dad, with their old Yorkie, Queenie, in her lap. That old dog had been in the family for as long as Zara could remember but she kept on going. She was toothless and smelly but adorable nonetheless.

Zara became aware that tears were adding to the overall dampness of her cheeks and she swiped them away angrily. What was the point of getting all emotional? The way she saw it, in spite of her recent – albeit short-lived – enjoyment, this trip was something to *endure* and then she could go home and forget all about this wretched place and the awful experience.

* * *

Sleep must have taken her at some point, as she awoke with a start to find herself in a very uncomfortable position, scrunched in one little corner of her minute, temporary abode. She rubbed her sore eyes and felt at her clothing. Thankfully

Josh had been right about something: the clothes did dry quickly.

From the silence of her surroundings she was grateful to note that the torrential downpour of the night before had ceased. Her stomach growled and she fumbled around in her backpack for the piece of flapjack bestowed upon her by the lovely bistro owner at Lochinver. She hadn't eaten since lunchtime the day before and would need to find somewhere to eat pretty soon else die of starvation and be eaten by cattle; only to be found months later by some oafish farmer, who'd no doubt comment on her excellent attire, which would still be in perfect condition, of course. *Bloody hell, Bailey, you're such a drama queen sometimes,* Marco's voice crept into her mind, and she smiled in spite of her solemn mood.

She grappled her body out of the sleeping bag and opened the zip on her tent. She stuck out first a leg; if that didn't get ripped off by a wild animal she would risk the rest of her limbs. When nothing tried to eat her she clambered free of the confines of the small space and stood.

'Ahem. Good morning.'

Zara almost jumped off the ground and she twisted round to find a man standing there, hair in disarray as if he'd just woken up, arms folded and a scowl of disapproval on his unshaven face.

'Oh, erm... good morning. Can I help you?' she asked boldly, standing her ground and hoping to God he wasn't an axe murderer. There was something eerily familiar about him and she racked her brain, trying to decide if she had seen his photo on *Crimestoppers*.

'I think it's *me* that should be asking *you* that question,' the man replied gruffly. He had a fairly mild Scottish accent, unlike most of the people she had encountered up to now in these parts, and his voice sounded familiar, too, which increased the feeling of dread that was building. He wore dark green overalls that would've looked more appropriate on some old, fat, ruddy-cheeked man. Instead this man was broad and muscular, dark-haired with dark, brown eyes and was probably in his late twenties or early thirties. *Quite handsome in an oafish, farm worker/axe murderer type of way.* Not that she found him attractive, obviously. She had sworn off even looking at men after what had happened with Josh. She even would have ignored Brad Pitt if he'd stood before her naked at that precise moment; or at least that was what she insisted on telling herself.

After remembering how the Daughters of Anarchy bulled her up, she snorted at his intimation that *he* could somehow help *her*. 'Not likely. Thanks, though.' She scrunched her nose up at him. What the hell was his problem anyway?

'Okay, so maybe you wouldn't mind explaining why you're wild camping on private property, then?'

Frustration got the better of her and she mirrored his defensive stance. 'I don't think that's any of your damn business, actually. Now sod off and leave me alone. I have a schedule to stick to and standing here arguing with *you* isn't helping me get on.'

He stared at her for a moment and then he seemed to smirk before letting the mercurial mask fall into place once again. 'It's every bit my business, actually.'

Anger built further and after the night she'd had she wasn't going to take rubbish from some glorified shit-shoveller.

She snidely tilted her head to one side, stuck out her bottom lip and asked in a mocking tone, 'Going to tell your boss on me, are you?' She was aware at how patronising and utterly out of character she was behaving but she was past the point of caring. 'Well, go ahead. Believe me, you can't make things any worse right now. I've had the shittiest night of my damned life, which consisted of a puncture, getting lost, being terrified in case my appendix burst or I was raped, mugged or murdered in the middle of nowhere, getting rained on and soaked to the skin, struggling to put up a tent in the pitch dark and having no food.' Her voice was getting louder and more high-pitched as she ranted. 'And to add insult to injury I didn't even want to make this stupid effing trip in the first place. So you go ahead, report me to the landowner and have him get the police. At least if they arrest me I'll get to sleep on a half-decent bed and have a hot bloody meal.'

Her heart pounded and her chest heaved as she took out her frustration on this complete stranger. To make matters worse, hot tears were streaming down her face and her nose was uber snotty. She knew for a fact that she already looked a sight with her unwashed, ratty bed hair and lack of make-up but now she was puffy-faced, too, no doubt.

The man huffed. 'I'll help you pack up your tent, then you can come up to the house with me.'

She yelled, 'I don't need your bloody help, thank you very much. I'm a strong, independent woman. And I'll come with you quietly so there's no need for you to keep your beady eye on me. There'll be no need for a pigging citizen's arrest!' Her etiquette had completely flown out of the non-existent window now.

He shrugged with nonchalance. 'I doubt you do anything quietly, but fair enough.' He folded his arms across his chest and stood there watching, in spite of her demand, as she went about gathering her things and shoving the tent into its minuscule pouch. It was so much easier when the damned things were dry. She had to keep pausing to swipe away the damp trails that insisted on trickling down her flushed cheeks. The tears were now part embarrassment, part anger and part self-pity. And all the while she could feel his eyes on her; mocking her; pitying her maybe too. *Poor little southerner trying to be all outdoorsy and failing miserably. Yeah, well, I'd rather be in some swish Caribbean resort, thank you very much. In fact, I'd rather be anywhere right now than this bloody dump.*

Sulkily she hauled her backpack on and clipped the chest strap closed before lifting her useless bike from the sodden ground. 'Right, I'm done. Take me to your leader,' she sneered.

Without speaking the man turned and headed off up the field to a quad bike and trailer that was parked by a low stone wall that circled a cemetery – good thing she hadn't noticed *that* particular feature last night. She followed obediently, silently cursing the man for not offering to carry the bike, whilst simultaneously knowing she would've refused help anyway.

When she looked to her left her breath caught. The sun had made a dramatic appearance and what she could see of the landscape now left her lost for words. There was a rugged limestone pavement that led to the water's edge where there lay a tiny, deserted beach with pale golden sand and crystal-clear, azure-blue water that glinted in the early morning light. It was by far the most stunning sight she had ever woken up to and she stopped to take it in for a moment.

'Come on! Stick the bike in the trailer. You'll have to hop on the back of me,' the man called out to her, pulling her from the daydream in which she was toes deep in warm sand, inhaling fresh, salty air.

She chuntered, 'Keep your bloody hair on,' under her breath as she stomped over and lifted her lightweight bike onto the small open-topped wooden trailer, and then reluctantly she clambered onto the back of the man's quad. She sat there awkwardly, unsure as to how she would stay on the damn thing.

'You'll need to put your arms round me or you'll fall off,' he informed her, a hint of frustration straining his voice.

Of course, I will. Stupid arse. Ugh, why did I not just run away? Because I can hardly bloody leave my wrecked bike here, can I? Let alone run at all, that's why. Her inner dialogue rampaged around her head and she gripped the man's waist tightly. It was all a little too intimate for her liking.

After a few uncomfortable, bouncy minutes crossing rough terrain, her captor, as she had now begun to think of him, pulled the noisy beast of a vehicle to a halt in the cobbled courtyard of a farmhouse. *Here we go,* she thought. *Let the bollocking begin.* She wondered what the farmer would be like. Would he be the type to have a soft spot for damsels in distress? She hoped so. Maybe if she cried in front of him he would take pity on her and not call the police after all. She could try it, perhaps.

'Follow me,' the gruff man instructed, but offered no help to get her down from the quad. *Charming.* Once she had dismounted and righted herself after almost toppling backwards – *stupid effing backpack* – she followed him inside and fully expected the farmer to be there, ready to read the Riot Act.

The kitchen was warm and there was a smell of fresh bread that carried through the air and made her stomach growl. There was an open fire and a black and white Border collie curled up on the rug before it. The dog yawned and stretched before making its way towards the man, tail wagging and tongue lolling out.

'Hiya, Bess,' the man said affectionately as he bent to

scratch the dog behind its ears. 'I wondered where you'd got to. Now be nice to our visitor.'

As if following his instructions obediently, the dog walked over and sniffed at Zara, but she froze. Why had he told the dog to be nice? Was it a vicious monster of a canine that would take her fingers off if she attempted to stroke it? But Bess nudged her hand and gave it a lick.

Zara's body flooded with relief and she reached out to pet the animal. 'Hello, Bess, you're lovely, aren't you?' She glanced round the large but cosy room. It was fairly traditionally decorated with wooden units and a free-standing old range cooker. There wasn't any sign of the farmer and she began to think maybe she'd had a lucky reprieve. Her reluctant companion was certainly making himself at home around the place and that made her wonder if perhaps he was the farmer's son.

He nodded to the large pine table in the centre of the room. 'Have a seat, eh?'

She removed her backpack and let it drop to the floor with a thud and did as she was told, closely followed by the beautiful black and white dog. 'Look, can we just get this over with? I really wasn't kidding when I said I had a tight schedule.'

He nodded. 'You're doing the North Coast 500,' he said without turning to face her. It was more of a statement than a question.

'Yes. I got waylaid yesterday thanks to a puncture. I... I don't suppose you or your boss have a repair kit?' She cringed, very much aware that he had no obligation to help her.

He placed a mug of steaming coffee before her on the table. 'I'll have to ask him. Hang on.' He shouted towards a closed door. 'Lachlan! Have you got a bike puncture kit?' Then with a brief grin at her he shouted again, 'Aye, but you'll have to wait as I'm attending to a trespasser!'

17

On realising she had presumed *all* the wrong things about the man and the farm, Zara covered her eyes with one hand. 'Oh God. Of course, it's *your* farm.'

He sat opposite her and chuckled. 'Aye, it is.'

'I'm sorry. I just presumed... I mean... You're quite young and I always think of farmers being older.'

He raised his eyebrows. 'I'm not that young. I'm thirty-one and it's not unheard of for people my age to run farms. You're stereotyping and judgemental.' He gulped down a mouthful of his coffee.

'And you're stroppy and annoying,' she snapped.

'That's not what you said the other day. I actually thought you were quite nice back then.'

She scrunched her face whilst simultaneously scrutinising his. What the hell was he talking about? And where the hell did she know him from? 'I beg your pardon?'

He narrowed his eyes. 'In the lay-by. You were all concerned about my lack of enthusiasm for the bloody view.'

She gasped. 'You! I might have known someone like *you*

would get all uppity about someone being on your bloody land.' She folded her arms across her chest.

He froze and fixed her with a glare. 'I might remind you that as you were *illegally* camping on *my land* you're answerable to *me*, so you might want to hold off with the insults.'

She closed her eyes briefly, summoning up the courage to speak to him rationally. 'Look, I'm sorry, okay? This trip hasn't exactly been something I've been looking forward to. In fact, I'm here under utter duress. Last night was really scary and I didn't realise I was on private property. I don't even know where I am – all I know is that I *was* aiming for Kinlochbervie. But I got totally lost and just needed a place to stay, that's all. And *actually* I was told there were no trespass laws in Scotland.'

The man, now known to be called Lachlan even though he hadn't formally introduced himself, heaved a frustrated sigh. 'Bloody urban myths. Try telling the writers of the Scottish trespass *law* that it doesn't exist, see how you get on!' He rubbed his chin. 'Except you can't... because it was written in 1865 so they're all dead now.' Zara fought a giggle but he waved his hand in frustration. 'But that's beside my point – the fact remains there *is* a law. You can't just set up on land wherever you please. You could disrupt livestock, damage property, get yourself injured or goodness knows what else. So next time you decide to embark upon such a mission, make sure you do your homework first, okay?'

Zara huffed and curled her lip. 'What are you, a bloody lawyer?'

He fixed her with a firm stare and rested his hands on his hips. 'Aye, I am *if* you must know. Although... my speciality was family law but nevertheless...'

Zara opened her mouth to speak but was rather dumb-founded that someone so well trained was working on a bloody farm when he could earn fantastic money and live in whichever city he damn well wanted.

Eventually she asked, 'You're *really* a lawyer?'

He scowled. 'Well, it's hardly something I'd lie about, is it?'

'But you're working on a farm,' she stated plainly, hearing the disbelief in her own voice.

'I *own* the place. I don't just work here, remember? And it's a croft actually.'

'Oh, right, a croft, yes, sorry. So... you work remotely from here for a law firm?'

He crumpled his brow and it was clear his patience was waning further. 'What? No, no. I just run the croft now. I had to give up my practice. Well, not *had* to... I chose to give it up.'

She was utterly intrigued and ideas for articles for *The Bohemian* began to rattle around her mind. *High-powered lawyer gives it all in to run a Highland farm... erm... croft.* 'Stress, was it?' Her question was way too personal and she realised as soon as it was too late to suck the words back in.

He scoffed. 'Not at all. My father was terminally ill and I had to make a choice. Come home and take over or sell the place I grew up in, that my father had built from nothing. I chose the former. He passed away recently and I was on the way back from meeting his solicitor at the will reading when I encountered you in that lay-by.'

Her heart softened a little for the brusque man. 'I'm so sorry. And gosh, that's very noble.'

He rolled his eyes. 'Hardly. I used to love being here when I was a kid. When I went away for university I just got dazzled by the city and pace of life, not to mention its convenience. Coming home has been... well, it's different. It's the kind of place that never really leaves you. It's part of who I am and always will be. It's in my blood, I suppose.' He shook his head and briefly closed his eyes. 'Anyway, I haven't got time to sit here chatting all day. I'll go find that puncture kit. There's porridge on the stove and a clean bowl beside it. Help yourself. Then you can be on your way and back to your *schedule*.' He seemed to find a little amusement in that word. 'Oh, and by the way, you're just outside Scourie so you're not exactly off your route as such.'

He possibly realised he had divulged quite a lot of personal information to her as a total stranger and had somewhat shut down now. He left the room and she heard the entrance door slam.

She got up and went to fill up a bowl with porridge as he had invited her to do and squeezed a little honey on the top. Bess sat beside her, staring up with her tongue lolling out the side and a string of drool dangling from the corner of her mouth.

'Euw, Bess. You can't have this. It's people food. You're a dog. Don't you have a bone to chew on?' As if she understood, the dog glanced towards her bed and then back at Zara, still evidently desperate for some porridge. 'Come on, I'm off to sit down and eat. I'm starving. You can come and drool over here.' She walked back to the place she had been sitting earlier and sat down again.

Lachlan seemed to be gone ages and Zara was beginning to worry that he couldn't find the puncture repair kit after all. She washed her bowl in the large pot sink and hunted round for a tea towel. Once the bowl was dried, she wandered over to the dresser beside the fireplace where lots of photos proudly sat. She presumed the ones of the small boy were Lachlan as a child and the man who looked incredibly similar to how Lachlan looked now must have been his dad. There was only one photo of the older man with a woman and it was quite old and stained brown with age. *His mother perhaps?* A little further along was a more recent one of the old man in a hospital bed. Lachlan was sitting beside him and they were holding hands. What struck her was that they were both laughing. The love they had for each other was so clear in their eyes. The photo told a story of a father and son with a wonderful relationship. A father who doted on his son and a son who would clearly do anything for his father. Her heart ached a little for Lachlan's loss.

'Right, you're all done.' Lachlan's voice snatched her back from her daydream and she spun round, feeling guilty for snooping.

'Oh, sorry, I was just... erm—'

'Being nosy? Aye, I figured. Look, I know you're not one to accept help, you being a strong, independent woman and all, but I've repaired your puncture. Don't go shouting at me, okay?'

She sighed and smiled. 'Ugh, I've not made a very good first impression, have I? I'm sorry. I'm not usually quite so loud and neurotic.' Lachlan didn't speak; he just stood there, his piercing eyes fixed on her. She blushed under the weight of his gaze. 'Okay, I think I've maybe outstayed my welcome. I should go.'

As if he was snapping out of a trance, Lachlan began to speak again. 'Lachy. My friends call me Lachy. And there's no rush. I thought you might appreciate a freshen up. You can use the bathroom at the top of the stairs if you'd like a shower. I have an en-suite one so I don't use it really. There are clean towels set out and some fancy shower stuff.'

'Ooh, ready for guests at all times, are we?' Zara had no idea why she made that question sound so sleazy. In fact, she really was questioning her mental state after the last day or so.

'Something like that. Anyway, I'll make some fresh coffee

and you can have a cup when you're done, if you like. Unless you're desperate to get back on the road?'

She snorted. 'Oh, believe me, the only thing I'm *desperate* for is my own bed and clothing that doesn't rustle when I walk.'

Lachy laughed and his face changed completely. He really was incredibly handsome... *if* you liked farmers. But she reminded herself that her male embargo was still in place so noticing a handsome man was a waste of her precious time.

She stood and made her way to the stairs and as she reached the bottom step she glanced back over her shoulder. She hadn't told him her name, had she? She'd been so hung up on being pissed off that it had slipped her mind.

'Erm, Lachy... my name is Zara. I forgot to mention it before, you know, when I was—'

He grinned. 'Ranting like a lunatic? Aye. Well, it's nice to meet you, Zara. I'll get the coffee on.'

She made her way upstairs to use the bathroom, making sure to lock the door just in case. After all, she didn't know him from Adam and appearances could be so deceptive. She'd learned that the hard way.

* * *

Zara had to admit that after the previous day's shenanigans the shower and porridge had been incredibly welcome, and she almost felt human again. Once dried and dressed, she combed through her knotted locks and made her way back down to the kitchen. As promised, Lachy had made fresh coffee.

He rubbed the back of his neck and looked everywhere but directly at her. He pointed to a pile of aluminium foil on the table. 'Look, I... erm dried out your map on the range. It's a wee bit crumpled but you should still be able to use it. And I made you a sandwich to take with you. That way you can just eat and not worry about looking for somewhere. It's home-made bread so I apologise if it's a little overdone. I put an apple and a chunk of tablet in there too. The sugar will give you a boost.'

A little overwhelmed by the man's kindness, Zara was unsure what to say and stood silently for a moment searching for something that wouldn't sound trite, like calling him a domestic goddess or something equally condescending. 'Tablet? Like headache tablets?'

Lachy smiled that same gloriously handsome smile from earlier. 'No, it's a wee bit like fudge. Only better.' He raised his eyebrows as he spoke and Zara's heart skipped a little.

Good grief, I need to get a bloody grip, I do.

'You didn't have to go to so much trouble, you know. I *was* illegally camping on your land, after all. I don't exactly feel as *in trouble* as I should.' She smiled warmly, hoping that his first impressions of her had been forgotten somewhat.

'Aye, I know but... Well, you're doing a brave thing, cycling that route all by yourself. And I don't mean that to sound patronising. It's a fact. And a wee bit of kindness never goes amiss, does it?'

Yep. She had totally underestimated this man in her angry state. He was a decent bloke. Not an oafish shit-shoveller. She cringed at her earlier assumptions. 'I guess not. And I really do appreciate it.'

They shared a smile but then an awkward silence descended again and something a little like sadness washed over Zara.

'So anyway, why *are* you out here if you don't want to be?'

Zara sighed. 'It's a long and boring story involving me being guilted into writing an article on the NC500 for the magazine I work for. Let's just say I usually write about luxury hotels in far-flung places, so this is a little different for me.'

'And you're really hating it?' He looked disappointed.

'Not as much as I expected, to be honest. Yes, yesterday was hell. Or certainly felt like it. Silver Dickhead getting a puncture really didn't help.'

'Silver...?'

She cringed. 'Yes, I named the bike Silver Dickhead... SD for short. We have a love-hate relationship. It loves making me uncomfortable and I *hate* it. But there have been some lovely highlights.' She smiled and dropped her gaze for a brief moment. 'I think this has been one of them.' Another moment passed between them and she wondered if he might laugh at her comment. But he didn't. Instead he smiled and nodded.

Lachy cleared his throat. 'Look, I know you don't really want to stray from your route too much, but if you get a craving for hot chocolate you really should head to Balnakeil. There's a chocolate shop there called Cocoa Mountain. Seriously the *best* hot chocolate I've *ever* tasted and I happen to be quite the connoisseur.' He grinned before taking a drink of his coffee.

'Balnakeil. Cocoa Mountain. Duly noted. I happen to adore hot chocolate too.'

'Aye, well, you've not tasted anything like it. Believe me. Better than se— erm anything.' His cheeks coloured bright red and he stood from the table. Bess dutifully rose and skipped around. 'Ah, you'll be wanting to help me check on the sheep, eh, Bess?'

Zara pulled her lips between her teeth in a bid to stifle the giggle at his almost slip-up. *Hot chocolate that's better than sex? Might just be worth the detour.*

18

Lachlan walked Zara out to her bike and stood there awkwardly as she loaded the panniers onto the back and examined the tyres.

'Thanks again, Lachy. You really have been incredibly gracious, considering my imposition.'

He shrugged. 'Nah, it's not every day I get to help a *strong independent woman*. I was thinking your name might be Beyoncé until you introduced yourself officially.' His eyes twinkled with mirth.

Zara sighed and covered her beetroot-red face with a hand. 'Ugh, I can't believe I said that out loud. You can blame the bulling up I had from a group of lady bikers I met the day before yesterday.'

He threw back his head and laughed, his shoulders shaking. His laugh was gravelly and sexy and the fact that she took notice of that annoyed her.

He held his hands up and continued. 'Hey, I'm all for feminism. Don't get me wrong. And to be honest, I think the fact that you're camping in the middle of nowhere and not running for the airport is evidence of your will and independence.' He patted the bike. 'Look after your passenger, eh, Silver Dickhead.'

She couldn't help smiling now and that little twinge of sadness resurfaced. 'Well, thank you, Lachy. You've been amazing. I'll be sure to mention you in my article.'

'Oh no, I wouldn't do that if I were you. I don't want to be overrun with women looking for a husband or anything,' he joked. 'I'm better keeping my light under its bushel.'

She stepped towards him and was reaching up to kiss his cheek when he enveloped her in an unexpected hug. He smelled fresh and clean, not as she might have expected. She hugged him back and closed her eyes. The warmth of his embrace comforted her and she realised she really did need to stop being so damned judgemental.

He released her and stepped back. 'Take care of yourself, okay?' He rummaged in his pocket and pulled out a business card. 'Here, it's got my mobile number on. And my email. Not that you'll need them, you know. But... just in case. I'm not suggesting you'll need to be rescued or anything though, don't take it to—'

'Thank you,' she said, taking the card from his fingers. 'I appreciate it. And no, I won't take it the wrong way.' She glanced down at the card and read aloud. '"Lachlan Grant, Scouriemore Croft, Lairg." I didn't realise farmers had business cards.'

He nodded. 'Erm... *crofters* and, aye, we have to have a means of contact and such for the sales. Plus I think I'm just used to having business cards. Old habits die hard, I guess.'

'Crofters, yes, sorry. Right, well, I'll be on my way. Thanks again, Lachy. I'll remember this.'

'Oh and... erm... better text first rather than call. I'm usually driving the quad and I don't answer unknown numbers anyway.' She nodded her understanding and he continued, 'Well, bye just now. And watch out for those sharp bends, eh? And don't be talking to your bike too much. They call it insanity, you know.'

Zara mounted SD and set off. At the end of the track she paused and looked back over her shoulder to find Lachlan still standing there. He raised his hand in a wave and she reciprocated before focusing on the road and leaving the croft.

She had calculated that she was only fifteen miles behind her schedule and, after hearing Lachy talk about the orgasm-inducing hot chocolate on offer at Balnakeil, she decided she would make the detour. After all, it was those kinds of places that would be of interest to people reading her article. Places to eat were definitely a priority in her mind – but maybe that was simply because she had an increased appetite with all the exercise. Whatever the reason, the thought of hot chocolate plagued her mind and she knew it was an itch she would absolutely be scratching.

The little craft village at Balnakeil was intriguing and made up of a collection of small buildings that had previously formed an old warning station for nuclear attacks built in the fifties when the cold war was at its peak. These days the buildings had been transformed into bookshops and craft shops. Some had colourful artwork painted on their exteriors and each was unique. She locked up her bike and removed her helmet before wandering round each little outlet. Handmade glass, wooden artefacts and ceramics of every conceivable colour and design adorned the shelves in the little shops. She wanted to buy something from every single place but knew she was sadly limited on baggage space.

In the quirky artist's studio she immediately fell in love with a miniature painting of Scourie Bay and she had to purchase it. It would be a reminder of the kindness she had been shown and the beautiful scenery that greeted her at every turn in the road. In spite of the horrible day she'd had only yesterday, she really was warming to the Highlands and could at least appreciate why people loved it so much – even if it wasn't a place she could live.

She thanked the artist and walked along the curved path, following the signposts for Cocoa Mountain. The aroma that infiltrated her nostrils when she opened the door was sweet and tantalising. Her mouth watered as she stood before the glass cases that were filled with delectable-looking pieces of chocolate heaven. She peered up at the drinks menu and the variety of hot chocolates on offer seemed too good to be true. Which should she choose? They all sounded amazing. After much deliberation she chose one and ordered it. She took a seat by the window overlooking the complex and was soon presented with a mug drizzled with melted chocolate round the edges and fresh cream dolloped on the top. She closed her eyes and took a sip. The liquid was velvety smooth and as the dark sweetness hit her taste buds she had to stifle a groan of sheer pleasure. *Lachy was right. This is divine.* She took out her tablet and tried to put down in words a vivid enough description of the drink so that readers of the article would want to visit and try it for themselves. *No one should miss out on this,* she surmised.

Trying to savour the mug of indulgence, she drank it slowly and languorously; enjoying every single mouthful as if it were the first. But all too soon it was gone. She was on the verge of ordering another when a group of cyclists walked in, dragging her back to reality and the cycle ahead of her.

As she walked back to where she had left her bike she tried to take in as much of the place as she could before she had to leave. She took photos on her newly charged phone – another reason to be thankful to Lachy – and smiled as she mounted her titanium steed once more.

* * *

Zara's next stop was a funny little place named Smoo Cave. It sounded like somewhere you would find an old dragon hiding out. She managed to tag along on a tour that was just about to leave as she arrived, and joining a group of other intrigued visitors, they wondered what on earth they were about to see. A narrow path led from the car park where she left her bike and wound its way down towards the wide opening in the rocks that faced the sea.

Zara snapped photo after photo, all the time grinning and gasping along with the other members of the group as the guide regaled them with stories of the cave's past. It was an eerie, yet simultaneously wonderful, place to see and another place she would no doubt remember for a long time to come.

Cycling along with 'Puff the Magic Dragon' playing in her mind, Zara eventually arrived at Tongue. The campsite was located with a fantastic view of Ben Loyal in the distance. She had made up her time but it had been hard going. Once her tent was set up, she sat beside it and tucked into the home-made bread and pâté that Lachlan had packed for her. He had been quite self-deprecating about his bread, but it was delicious. Fresh and crusty. There wasn't much that could better home-made bread. The tablet melted on her tongue and she relished the grainy consistency. It was different from fudge and possibly sweeter but, wow, it was so good.

As the sun began to set she climbed into the tent and decided that after she'd made some notes, she would make the most of the peace and quiet and get to sleep early. Sleep came easily and she dreamed of hot chocolate, dragons and wide-mouthed caves. And of handsome Scottish men who could cook *and* fix bicycles.

19

After an *almost* refreshing night of sleep Zara woke feeling positive. She was over halfway round the route, which meant she would be going home soon. That also meant she would be going to her high-school reunion, which didn't fill her with as much glee, but text messages from Shelley had revealed she was quite excited about the event now, so Zara hoped her enthusiasm would rub off on her.

Every time she was in an area where the signal peaked she received a barrage of texts from Shelley, Marco and her family. They all had encouraging messages and said how much they missed her. Contact from Noah had been scarce and she just knew that it was because he was scared of her backlash. She was past the point of hating him now though. Aside from a few glitches the trip hadn't been as horrific as she had expected. She still wanted to give him a piece of her mind, simply for his lack of contact. But it would wait.

Today's journey would take her to Lairg. She had been advised to take the smaller roads as the main route was known for heavy traffic and she really didn't fancy battling with that on

SD. After packing away her tent for what felt like the millionth time and making a complete mess of it for the same number, she set off. There was a brief stop at a little bakery where she grabbed a buttered scone and a cup of tea for breakfast, which she enjoyed whilst drinking in the view before her.

* * *

The scenery was more and more breathtaking with every new turn she made and Zara was beginning to think that Lachlan was right about this too: Scotland really *was* the place where you could find yourself; the place that got under your skin and into your heart. She had never before in her life been emotionally affected by hills and trees. Possibly because she lived in a fast-paced city with every conceivable thing she could need or want at her fingertips. Who would have ever thought that a beautiful landscape could bring a tear to her eye?

The people she had met along the way had chosen to come to Scotland. And then there was Lachlan, who was clearly affected by the place. He'd chosen to come *home*, after all. His words had rattled around her head in the hours since she'd left his croft. And he was so incredibly sweet and quite sexy. Although, she reminded herself, the last thing she had needed was another brush with romance, so it was a good thing that he was behind her.

Jeez, no. No more men. Not after what happened with Josh. Ugh, Josh... She hadn't thought about him for a while and it'd been rather nice not to have been reminded of how hurt she'd felt. But he had cheated on her and there was no coming back from that. So she would have to keep moving forward and eventually she'd stop remembering how good she'd had it with him for a brief time. She just hoped that 'eventually' would happen sooner rather than later.

A loud crack echoed through the air and birds scattered from their branches. Then she heard what she thought was gunfire and shouting coming from over a hill to her right and her heart began to pound. *Shit. I thought this was a fairly safe place. Guns and trouble in London were just par for the shitty course these days, but the Scottish Highlands?* She continued cycling as the gunfire got louder. Her heart almost jumped out of her chest as she made her legs work harder. It was a distinct possibility that within seconds the gang of thugs could be over the hill and she'd be in plain sight. *Fuck! Oh God. Oh God, what do I do? There's nowhere I can hide.* Her legs burned with the effort of pushing the pedals so hard, as fast as she could, up what was now a steep incline. Her chest heaved. *If I keep pedalling… If I push harder, I can get away. They won't see me.* Fear gripped her stomach and twisted it in knots. Her eyes began to well with tears and her knuckles turned white. More gunfire. More shouting. More pounding of blood through her veins until she felt light-headed.

Her front tyre hit something and before she knew it she was flying through the air in slow motion, like something from a car-chase movie. The floor became the sky and vice versa. She let out a piercing scream and impacted with the ground with a thud and then blackness…

* * *

'*Fuck*. Is she dead?'

'Don't say that, Tosh. *Jesus*, man.'

'But she's no moving, Rab. She went with a *muckle* thud. She might be dead.'

'Na, mate, that wee backpack will have taken the impact.'

'Aye, but landing on it *cannae* be good for her spine, eh? If she's no dead she might be paralysed.'

'Fuck's sake, Tosh, I hope the poor wee lass *cannae* hear your death knell.'

Another voice, this time out of breath. 'Help's on the way. They said to check her breathing. But not to move her.'

'We think she's dead, Angus.'

'No, wait... I can see her chest moving up and doon. Aye... aye, she's breathing.'

'Thank fuck for that. Any of the guys doctors or nurses, do you *ken*?'

A new voice chimed in. 'Erm... what about Lurch? He's some big-wig bloke, eh?'

'Nah, you tube! He's an accountant, not a fucking doctor.'

'Close enough for me. Hey! Lurch, over here!'

Footsteps approached in the distance, crunching on the gravel road. 'What's going on?'

'Come over here quick, you tube!'

'Aye, all right, keep your bloody kilt on!'

Zara blinked open her eyes. Her head throbbed and it felt as though every fibre in her body were doing the same. When she focused she realised she was surrounded by a group of men in Highland bonnets and tartan sashes. White linen shirts covered in dirt could just be seen under the coarse, woolly fabric. There was a distinct eighteenth-century appearance to the men but the bizarre thing was that their swords appeared to be made of... *wood. What the—?*

A strange realisation dawned on her.

She gasped and widened her eyes. *Shit! I've somehow gone back in bloody time. Like that woman on* Outlander. *How the hell?* Her breathing rate increased and she began to hyperventilate.

This can't be happening. Outlander *isn't real. I didn't touch a big bloody stone. I must be dreaming. I remember the gunfire...*

Oh, shit, am I dead?

One of the bearded Scotsmen laughed. 'No, lassie, you're not dead.'

Okay, so I said that last part out loud.

'You had a wee fall off your bike, that's all. But you're awake and talking. Just try and slow your breathing, eh?'

At least he was being kind and not trying to rape or pillage her like the character from the TV show. She scrunched her aching brow. 'But your clothing...'

Beardy man glanced down and, as something akin to realisation hit him, chuckled. 'Re-enactment group. Let me guess, you thought you'd done a "Claire"?'

She opened and closed her mouth, trying to make sense of his words. 'A... a what?'

He glanced at his gathered friends for their assistance. 'You know, Claire Fraser or whatever she was called, you *know*? *Outlander?* Don't tell me none of yous Jessies have watched it. Gone back through time, oooooh.' He waved his fingers around.

'Oh no... Silver Dickhead—?' she mumbled and the bearded man looked a little hurt.

'Charming,' he chuntered.

'Leave her be, man. She's probably got concussion,' another one of the men, a younger one, insisted. 'Anway, here's Lurch.'

Another man peered down at her but he was silhouetted against the sky so she couldn't see his face. 'Oh, bloody hell, you again.' He leaned back slightly and she saw the features that accompanied the familiar-sounding voice.

She snorted but managed a wee smile. 'I could say the same thing, Lachlan.'

'Aye, well, we'll have to stop meeting like this, eh?'

'Look, Lurch, I told them you're an accountant not a bloody doctor, but the stubborn tubes *wouldnae* listen.'

Without taking his eyes off Zara, Lachlan said, 'Lawyer. Not accountant. And I really wish you'd stop calling me Lurch, guys. We're not in school any more and I'm neither exceedingly tall nor grotesque.'

Beardy man chimed in, 'Not looked in a mirror today, eh?' The rest of the men laughed.

Lachlan rolled his eyes and shook his head but smiled down at Zara. 'How are you feeling?'

Zara's mouth was dry and she was a little overwhelmed with her almost dip into the eighteenth century and the shock that accompanied the whole incident. 'Erm... My head aches and I feel a bit queasy but I think I'm okay.'

'Can you wiggle your fingers and toes?' She nodded. 'Any pain when you do?' She shook her head. 'Probably a mild concussion. I've had it when I played rugby at university. It's not pleasant but you'll probably be okay.'

A siren could be heard and a car with a green flashing light arrived. Zara heard one of the toy soldiers, as she'd decided to call them, talking to the doctor. 'Hi, doc. She's over here. Bit fuzzy-headed but seems okay. She's already insulted me.'

The doctor arrived beside her. 'Hi, I'm Dr Mackay. I'll give you a check over. Can you tell me your name?'

'Zara... erm Zara Bailey.' He proceeded to ask her facts about the date, what she had for breakfast and who was the prime minister. Then he shone a light in her eyes and asked her to follow it. Other checks followed – he was certainly thorough – and he finally gave his diagnosis.

'You've a mild concussion. I'm afraid you shouldn't really get back on the road for a day or two. And to be honest you shouldn't be alone. Perhaps I can contact the medical centre at Thurso and see if they can sort you a bed. Leave it with me.' He stood to leave and disappointment sank like a heavy weight on Zara's shoulders. More delays. More hassle. Just when things were starting to feel okay.

'Erm, Doc, does it have to be a hospital stay? Or could she maybe stay with someone... you know, not medically qualified as such?' Lachy asked.

'I didn't think she'd know anyone. One of your... erm... band of merry men said she was cycling the NC500. Guessing she doesn't have friends here or she wouldn't be cycling alone.'

'Aye, you're right but... I've met Zara before. She camped on my land the night before last. I'd be happy to take her in for a couple of days to make sure she's okay, if it'd help.'

'Well, only if you're sure.' He pulled a leaflet out of his bag. 'Here are the signs to look for with concussion. If anything changes you must contact me immediately, okay?'

Lachy nodded. 'Sure thing, Doc. No worries.' He walked back over to Zara. 'Is that okay with you? You're welcome to stay with me. I know going to Thurso will take you off the officially recommended cycle route and I guessed you'd not want that.'

Zara's eyes began to sting. 'I don't want you to put yourself out again because of me. I—'

'Hey, don't cry, it's really not a problem. I think you should heed the doctor. And I'm okay to work around you. I'm the boss, after all.'

'Hey, she can always stay with me,' beardy man insisted.

'I've a spare room at mine,' the guy known as Tosh added.

'Thank you, everyone, but I think Lachlan's place will be fine.'

'Aye, if he doesn't bore you to death with accountant speak.' The men laughed as they dispersed.

'Bloody lawyer. How many times?' He shook his head again. He helped her to her feet and she went a little dizzy and wobbled. 'Whoa. Take it easy. Come on, I'll help you to my car.'

She glanced down at his thick calves where they protruded from the bottom of his kilt. How had she never noticed how sexy those were before? He had gorgeous, manly legs and she'd heard things about kilts and undies... She snapped herself out of her daydream. 'Oh God, I feel so bad. I'm stopping you from your acting thingy.'

'Re-enactment. And it was only a run-through really. I'm not even sure if it's me, to be honest. My neighbour got me involved as they needed more men but I... oh, I don't know.'

She smiled. 'Well, the outfit suits you.'

He laughed. 'Cheeky. Don't you be taking the piss or I'll put salt in your porridge instead of honey.'

'No, I really mean it. You look... erm... authentic.'

'I bet you got the fright of your life when you woke up surrounded by that set of ugly munters, eh?'

Zara giggled as she remembered her immediate reaction. 'Just a little. Not the ugly part, I mean. But the clothing scared the crap out of me. I honestly thought I'd somehow travelled back in bloody time.'

'No way. Seriously? That's hilarious!' Lachy had to stop walking to laugh and Zara, whilst she felt incredibly silly, couldn't help but join in.

Suddenly a thought occurred to her as they approached what she presumed to be Lachy's car. A rugged, mud-covered four-wheel-drive complete with a trailer. 'Shit! Silver Dickhead! I asked one of the men earlier but...'

Lachy stopped and turned to face her. He cringed and sucked air in through his teeth. 'Yeah, about that. It's in a bit of a state, I'm afraid. A tractor kind of... erm... ran over it.'

20

When she heard the news about her wrecked bike, Zara's eyes widened. 'What? Oh my God! What am I going to do? Where is it?'

Lachy pointed to the trailer. 'Tosh loaded it and your bags up already. It's not roadworthy, I'm afraid.'

She glanced over the side of the trailer at the twisted hunk of metal and suddenly wanted to cry. 'Oh no, I'm so sorry, SD,' she whispered. But then her heart rate increased as panic set in and she gripped her hair. 'But... it was an expensive bike and it was on loan. And... the North Coast 500. And my school reunion.'

Lachy held up his hand. 'I know. I know. Look, I'm sure if we contact them they'll be fine. They must have insurance for things like this.'

She knew there was insurance, but it didn't take the sting away. 'That's not the point. This is a disaster of epic proportions. How the hell do I explain—? What do I say to—?'

Lachy placed one large hand on each of her shoulders. 'Look, there's no point stressing about it. Let's get you back to mine and get you settled, eh? We can sort the rest out tomorrow. Try not to worry.'

She gazed up at him; his face was kind and reassuring. She nodded. 'You're right. Not a lot I can do right now. I just feel so stupid.'

He smiled and she could tell he was going to tease her. 'Well, you *did* think you'd travelled back in time, so I'm not 100 per cent sure of your mental state but... Look, these things happen. It was an accident. And it wasn't your fault the tractor ran over it. It's a narrow road and it was a choice between avoiding you *or* avoiding the bike. I'd like to think he chose wisely.'

'Ugh, I don't know. Maybe he should've chosen the other way.'

He helped her into the car and closed her door. Once he was seated behind the steering wheel he started the engine and Florence and the Machine blared out of the speakers at full blast. Her favourite song too.

'Oh, I love "Delilah".' She smiled and, for the first time in the last couple of hours, calmness washed over her.

'Aye, I do like a bit of Flo and the Machine. Especially this track. Gets me right here.' He patted his chest.

She knew exactly what he meant. It was such an uplifting song; empowering even. It was the kind of song you listened to when you were feeling low and couldn't help dancing to it. Although she couldn't exactly imagine Lachy dancing round the kitchen in his underwear as she'd tended to do before her lodger moved in. Now it seemed that Marco had taken over that particular baton, as she had discovered when she'd arrived home late and found him waving his arms and singing 'Bohemian Rhapsody' at the top of his voice wearing only his designer fitted boxers. He had all the operatic parts off pat, but the crazy thing was he hadn't even cared when he'd realised he had a gobsmacked audience of one. In fact, he had tried to encourage her to join in.

Lachy set off in the direction of his croft and they both sang along in mumbled tones to the track until it had finished, neither wanting to really let go for fear of embarrassment.

'So, school reunion, eh? I hate those bloody things. I can't believe you actually want to go to one,' Lachy said out of the blue.

Zara scrunched her nose. 'My best friend, Shelley, is suddenly desperate to go and show everyone what we've achieved. And I think I'd like to show them, too, in a way.'

'Seriously? Why does that even matter? And this *them* you speak of, I gather you weren't keen on them when you were at school so why go to the trouble of attending an event you don't want to attend just so you can show *them* how well you've done? Isn't that what social media is for?'

She laughed. He did have a point. 'Yeah, I don't really go on that much, to be honest, except for work. And if I did I wouldn't be friends with any of *that* lot. They used to call me and Shelley names and we were excluded from everything fun. We had our own little group.'

'I bet you were the brainy bunch or something.'

'Now who's being cheeky?'

'I can just tell you're intelligent. It's not an insult. I mean, you work for a well-known travel magazine. So in spite of your penchant for time travel, I'm guessing you're quite bright.' He was grinning at her again. Her stomach flipped.

Stop it, Bailey. Stop noticing how attractive he is.

They pulled up outside the croft and Zara felt happy to be there again. The house was a pretty, stone detached building. Quite sizeable but not overly large. It was homely and its isolation wasn't intimidating as she might have expected. She hadn't really taken much notice of the exterior the last time she was there, so now she was having a good look at the typical Highland architecture. It was more function over attractiveness, but in being so it was more appealing. Like someone who was beautiful but didn't go bragging about their looks.

Lachy came round and opened her door. He held out his hand to help her down, and rather than insist that she could manage, she accepted his help. The feel of his strong hand on hers made her arm tingle and she snatched it away as soon as her feet hit the floor.

They entered the house and were greeted by Bess, whose whole body was wagging excitedly. Zara bent to stroke her, but a spell of dizziness took her again and she grabbed a chair to steady herself.

She felt Lachy's hand on her arm. 'Hey, are you okay? Come on, I'll help you into the lounge and I'll go and get you some painkillers, eh?'

She nodded, trying not to think of the nausea bubbling up from her stomach. Lachy led her into a room off the kitchen at the opposite side to the staircase and helped her to a leather couch. The room was cosy and had an inglenook fireplace. It was a little dated but the couch was more modern. She wondered if he had brought that along when he'd moved home again.

Once she was seated Lachy asked, 'Will you be okay whilst I go get some wood for the fire and get you those tablets?'

'Absolutely fine. Thank you.'

He nodded. 'Bess will stay and keep you company. Oh, and if she tries to get on the sofa, don't let her. Bloody little madam. I swear she thinks she's human.'

Of course, as soon as Lachy left the room Bess cheekily hopped up beside Zara and snuggled into her side.

'Hey, you'll get me in trouble, you little tyke,' Zara informed the dog, but stroked her fur regardless. How could she not? Bess was adorable.

Lachy appeared again moments later. 'Ahem, I see you're a soft touch with the animals, then.'

Zara cringed. 'But she's so cute. I couldn't resist.'

He grinned and shook his head as he handed her a glass of water and two tablets. 'Here you go. Just paracetamol. You're not allergic, are you?'

She took the pills and swallowed them as she shook her head no.

'Look, I was going to give the bike place a call. I know one of the owners from way back. Thought I might be able to sweet-talk them for you.'

'No! No, I need to fess up. I can't have you doing that for me. I mean, it *was* an accident, after all.'

He sighed. 'God, you're stubborn. But whatever. Anyway, the guest room's ready for you. Although I should warn you that I'll be coming in to check on you in the night, so you'd better not sleep naked if you want to save your dignity.'

Zara gasped and felt her cheeks warming – the ones on her face, that was. 'Why would you be doing that? It's creepy.'

'Look, you heard the doctor. Sleep can be a problem with concussion. I need to make sure you're still alive. How would it look if I wound up with a dead cyclist in my spare room?'

'Erm... okay, fair enough. Nice to know it's purely selfish on your part,' she huffed.

'Oh, totally selfish.' He grinned again and left the room and Zara proceeded to call her friends to let them know what had happened.

* * *

Lachy

Two in the morning.

He'd be getting up for real soon but right at that second he was hovering over the young woman in his spare room. Her face was turned to the side and her elbow bent so that her fingertips touched her chin. She was beautiful. Something about her drew him in even though he knew it was pointless. She'd be leaving soon enough and he'd go back to tending sheep and advising his local friends and neighbours on boundary disputes and encroaching trees. He didn't miss law. In fact, he wasn't given the chance to miss it, considering how many legal matters he'd assisted on since coming home. He didn't mind. Not really. It beat what he had left behind anyway.

When he had first qualified as a lawyer, he'd had amazing ambition. He was going to sail to the top and make his father and mother proud. The silly thing was they were proud of him regardless. His dad had told him so when he'd returned to save the croft from ruin when his father was gravely ill.

'Lachlan Grant, with every breath I have left I want to make sure you know how much it means to me that you've come home. Your mother, God rest her soul, would feel the same. She missed you so much when you left for studies.'

Lachy had gripped his father's wizened hand, the paper-thin skin crumpling beneath his touch. 'I should never have gone away, Dad,' he had sobbed.

'I'll have none of that, Lachlan. You've helped so many people. Done so much good. And I want you to know that when I pass on you have my blessing to sell this old place. Go and make your own life. You're a lawyer now and a damn good one too. So as long as that makes you happy, son, you keep on keeping on, you hear me?'

It had been that particular conversation that had made the decision to come home to Scourie for good so much easier. Knowing what the law firm had planned and knowing the good he had been doing up to now wasn't going to be good any more had spurred him on.

He remembered telling Saskia he was leaving to go back to the croft. 'You're throwing your whole education, future and us away because of a little on-the-side working? Are you mad?' She had flicked her jet-black hair over her shoulder and regarded him with utter disdain. 'Don't bother asking me to come with you, Lachlan. I'm not prepared to throw everything away like that. Not to live in the middle of a field covered in sheep dung. It was nice whilst it lasted.' It had lasted three years until she had left him standing in his office surrounded by boxes as he'd packed, a sense of unexpected relief settling over him.

She was wrong about the firm, of course. The 'on-the-side working' had involved some pretty serious money laundering and Lachy wasn't willing to throw away his reputation on a job that was no longer fulfilling, nor taking him down the path he had originally intended. He wasn't prepared to defile his parents' image of their son. Not for money. Not for prestige and most certainly not for some hard, ice-cold woman whose world rotated round a sun made of possessions and wealth.

In the stillness of the dark room he could hear the faint sound of Zara's inhalations and exhalations and the cute little squeak that came from either her nose or throat – it was hard to tell. But she was alive and that was the main thing. Concussion was so unpredictable and he couldn't let anything happen to her. He wasn't sure where the protective streak had emerged from but emerge it had. In the slim shaft of moonlight coming through the window he could see her chocolate-brown hair fanned out on the pillow round her, the ends curled naturally but only ever so slightly.

He had never watched anyone sleep on purpose before and realised that if she awoke she'd think him pervy or creepy for doing so. But he was mesmerised. She looked so relaxed and calm – different from the last couple of times he had encountered her – and he wanted to memorise the way she looked. He had already admitted to himself that he was attracted to her, but doubted that a city type like her – as Saskia had been – would be in the slightest bit interested in someone like him; well, at least not the current version anyway. He didn't have anything to offer someone who was simply passing through. In a matter of days she would be out of his life for good and the thought caused a twinge of sadness that he didn't wish to acknowledge. But he couldn't help wondering if something or someone had put her in his path on purpose, considering the number of times they had coincidentally been thrust together.

She murmured in her sleep, something that sounded like *Josh* or *Joseph*. No doubt there was some clean-cut, handsome banking executive waiting for her to return home to him; to their plush London apartment with all the mod cons. All the cons he had left behind when he'd returned home to Scourie.

Realising he was fantasising about an unattainable stranger, he shook his head and tiptoed from the room. Back in his own bed he lay awake trying not to think about the fact that, when he had seen Zara lying there on the ground, injured and bewildered, he had wanted to hold her and comfort her. And then when she had been upset about the wrecked bike, how he had longed to feel the closeness of the woman before him who was so fiery and passionate, not frozen to the core.

21

Thankfully Zara had slept well enough not to notice her host popping in to her bedroom throughout the night. And the following morning she had showered and dressed early ready to make the call to the bike shop. When she descended to the kitchen Lachy was already sitting at the table eating a bowl of porridge.

'Afternoon,' he joked.

She glanced at the clock and was relieved to see it was only nine o'clock. 'Funny.'

'Help yourself to porridge. I've to go and check on the sheep. I think Bess might want to stay with you.' He nodded to the dog, who was patiently waiting at Zara's feet, whole body wagging as usual. 'I think she likes you.'

'Is it okay if I take her down to that little stretch of beach maybe? I could do with just relaxing today, I think. Especially after I've called the bike shop.' Her shoulders slumped as she imagined how the conversation would go.

'Oh aye, she loves it down there. Take her tennis ball. You'll have a friend for life. Oh, and I found this. I'm presuming it's yours?' He held up her bright pink memory stick.

'Oh, shit! Yes, where did you find that?'

'It was just on the floor in the hallway. Guessing you dropped it. Pink's not my colour. Well, not *that* particular shade anyway.' He grinned.

She tucked her hair behind her ears and tried to figure out what explanation she could give. She went with the truth. 'It's my novel; I'd have been gutted if I lost that.'

He raised his eyebrows. 'Novel, eh? What's it about?'

Her cheeks reached the point of near spontaneous combustion. 'Oh... erm... it's a kind of gritty romance story, I suppose. Quite dramatic in a *Wuthering Heights* kind of way. It all takes place during one summer and everything changes for the main protagonist. Her life is thrown into chaos.'

'Great. I love a good book. I'm not into romance but I like the sound of the gritty part so if you need someone to read—'

'Oh God, no!' She gasped as she walked over to pour coffee.

He laughed. 'Okay, okay. So how far done is it? Your novel?'

She spooned porridge into a bowl and added honey. 'Oh, I don't really know,' she lied. 'Well, that's not entirely true. Actually it's just about finished but I'm struggling with the ending.'

As she sat across the table from Lachy, he folded his arms across his chest and tilted his head inquisitively, his eyes crinkled at the corners as he smiled. His teeth were a little crooked but white and his biceps were huge.

She realised she was staring when he started speaking again. 'What made you start writing a book?'

'I just love stories. Creating worlds and characters. Controlling their lives. Living vicariously, too, I suppose.'

He chuckled. 'Ah, so you *are* a control freak, eh? I knew it.'

'I guess I must be.' She laughed too. 'But there's something magical about losing yourself in a book. I can lose hours if a story grips me. I wanted to see if *I* could create that reaction in readers.'

'I'm sure your articles have that effect.'

She scrunched her nose. 'Oh, I don't know about that.' She felt her cheeks warming. He seemed to have the effect of a teenage crush on her and she had no clue why. 'But anyway, if it paid the bills I'd rather be a novelist. It's a bit of a dream though. Probably won't ever happen.'

He leaned forwards, his gaze fixed firmly on her. 'You know, you really light up when you talk about writing. In my opinion you should do what you love. Your passion will shine through that way. And if you're passionate you'll excel.'

'In an ideal world I would. But... well, we don't live in an ideal world, do we?'

'No. That's true. But we have to make the best of the world we *do* live in. And I still think you should make time for your passion.' He stood from the table. 'Anyway, the offer stands if you want someone to read it. And you might be here a few days so if you fancy working on your story just let me know. I can get you my laptop.'

She shook her head vehemently. 'A few days? No-o-o-o, I'll be on my way tomorrow, I reckon. Even if I'm heading home on the train. I... I don't want to impose.'

'See what the bike people and your boss say, eh? You're really not imposing. As you can see, I'm not exactly cramped for space.' He placed his bowl in the sink, drained his coffee cup and grabbed his fleece from the chair. 'See you later. Oh, and don't bother trying to lock the door when you go out. You'll not find a key.'

* * *

'Two more bloody days, Bess,' Zara huffed as she threw the tennis ball for her new canine friend. 'I can't believe there were no suitable bikes available to send right away. It's a bloody bike-hire place. And, okay, so it's peak season, but surely they have spares? Although I suppose they could've refused to send a bike at all.' The dog ran off up the slip of beach, tongue lolling out as she chased the ball. 'I honestly thought Noah would've just asked me to go home. But no-o-o-o, *"This article's going to be so good, Zara, you're doing such a brilliant job."* Pah! Doesn't matter to him that I could've died several times.' She paused and looked round to make sure no one was witnessing her ranty monologue. Thankfully she was still alone apart from the dog. She gazed out at the still water and inhaled the fresh, cool air. How come she always felt so much calmer when she did that? She turned and glanced up the hill to where the farmhouse stood with its pretty view and sighed. What was the point of getting wound up? There was nothing she could do until the bike arrived. *Whoa, I'm not worried or stressed? Bloody hell, what do they put in the water around here?*

Bess appeared at her side again and dropped the ball at her feet. 'You've got the right idea, Bess. Just chilling out and doing what you love, eh?' Perhaps that was what she should do for the couple of days she was stranded? Lachy's offer of his laptop echoed inside her head. She might just have to take him up on it.

She gazed across the water to the mountains that stretched up from the water's edge and she imagined what it would be like to climb right to the top. She guessed this vista from up there would be spectacular. It was a shame, she mused, that she wouldn't be here long enough to find out. Sheep meandered round her, munching at the verdant grass, too busy to notice the interloper admiring the view. The air was fresh and in spite of the sunshine there was a coastal nip to the breeze. Every so often her companion would drop the ball at her feet and she dutifully threw it, sometimes crouching to nuzzle the dog's fur. As she watched the billowy white clouds overhead casting shadows on the ground and the striations in the rocks over the inlet, a flash of inspiration hit. Her eyes widened and her heart skipped. The ending of her novel had appeared as a flash of inspiration and it was all because of this view; this incredible landscape before her. She called Bess and dashed back to the croft to wait for Lachy.

Lachy appeared back home around lunchtime looking dishevelled and incredibly sexy in a rugged, dirty kind of way. His overalls were slipped down and tied round his waist and he wore a black T-shirt that contoured to his muscular abdomen.

'How are you feeling? Did you get sorted?' he asked in that lilting, gentle Scottish accent as he washed his hands at the pot sink.

She relayed the details of the conversations she'd had that morning with the bike-hire place and work. 'So I wondered... could I take you up on the offer to borrow your laptop?'

He smiled, apparently happy that she had asked. 'Absolutely. Who am I to stand in the way of the next Emily Brontë? It's in the desk drawer by the window in the lounge. You can set it up there and enjoy the view of the beach whilst you're writing. Might just be the inspiration you need, eh?'

It had been that view that had sparked this urgent need to put fingers to keyboard and she had to stop herself from squealing with excitement. 'Fantastic, thank you.' Giddily she jumped up from the table and went through to the lounge, closely followed by Bess. The laptop was a top-of-the-line model and worked at lightning speed once turned on. She inserted her memory stick and pulled up the file. Butterflies fluttered in her stomach as her words appeared before her on the screen. It had been a long while since she had worked on the book in earnest and she had to familiarise herself with the last chapters she had written. Bess sat under the desk, resting her chin on Zara's feet and keeping them toasty warm.

About an hour later Lachy approached her with a bowl of home-made soup and a chunk of that delicious bread. 'How are you getting on?'

She grinned from ear to ear. 'Really, *really* good. I can't tell you how amazing it feels to be writing again. I mean, yes, I write for work and I do love my job but... *this* is what I've wanted to do for so long. Thank you.' She smiled up at him and hoped the sincerity of her gratitude shone through.

He gazed down at her and seemed transfixed for a moment before clearing his throat. 'Hey, don't thank me. You're the multi-talented one. I've put a beef stew in the range so it'll be ready about six. I'll leave you to it.' He hurried away and closed the door.

* * *

The hours ran away with her and by the time Lachy called Zara through to the kitchen for dinner she was exhausted but filled with a sense of accomplishment. She had figured out where the plot of her novel was going astray and had typed up the miracu-lous end scene. Now all she needed to do was proofread it and check for any obvious plot holes. It would be completely finished by the end of her stay at the croft – something she'd never dreamed would happen so soon.

She walked through and was hit with a delicious aroma that made her mouth water.

'Wow, that smells incredible.' She took a seat in the place she had been using since she'd arrived. Bess was lying dutifully in her basket but kept her eyes trained on Zara in case any morsels landed on the floor.

'Aye, I'm not a bad cook, I suppose. But that's what living alone will do, eh?'

Zara huffed. 'Oh, I don't know about that. I enjoy cooking but until Marco moved in there were lots of ready meals for one at home. Or takeaways.'

'Is your boyfriend a good cook, then?' Lachy asked without making eye contact.

'Oh no, Marco isn't my boyfriend.' She giggled at the prospect. 'I'm not really his type, if you know what I mean?'

'Ah, he's gay?'

'As the day is long. It's a shame really as he'd probably make a pretty good boyfriend.'

'So what does your *actual* boyfriend think about you being up here all by yourself?'

She smiled with a tinge of sadness as she thought about Josh's last call. 'Currently single, I'm afraid. I was seeing someone. Josh. We were together for a year and I thought it was love but I scared him off back to the arms of his ex.'

Lachy tilted his head and frowned. 'Oh, I doubt that. I'm pretty sure if he went back to his ex it was all his *own* doing, not yours.'

'Hmm. Well, whatever it was he broke my heart, just before I set off to come to Scotland actually.'

'Well, you didn't deserve to be treated that way. No one does.'

She was unwilling to bring the mood down and tried to

turn the topic round to him. 'What about you? Don't you get lonely up here by yourself?'

Lachy chewed thoughtfully for a few moments. 'I don't have the time to feel lonely really. Too much to do around the place. My last girlfriend wasn't too keen on the prospect of moving up here so it ended just before I left the city. I think the whole thing had run its course anyway, if I'm honest.'

'That's a shame. I bet you miss her. After all, people need people.'

He shrugged. 'Not really. She was a very dramatic person. You know the kind: everything had to be about her and if it wasn't, she'd make it so. I didn't get much say in anything. Well, not if I wanted a peaceful life.' He laughed. 'I think moving home was the right decision and the timing couldn't have been better.' He cringed and placed his fork down. 'Shit, I didn't mean that to sound like I was happy my dad was ill.'

Zara reached out but couldn't quite touch his hand. 'Hey, I didn't think that at all.' A companionable silence descended for a while as they both tucked into the meal.

Lachy reached over and topped up Zara's wine glass. 'So, how come you didn't refuse to come here if it's not your usual type of assignment? I know you're hating it.'

'Noah, my boss, he's very persuasive. Or should I say he's very good at laying guilt on thick?' She took a sip of the fruity red wine and pondered his words. 'You know, I haven't hated it up here. Not really. I mean, the scenery has been spectacular.'

'It's like I said, the place gets under your skin. The people too. Honestly, I can't imagine living in a city again. Life can be over so fast, why would I want to rush through it with my head down when I can breathe in and look up?'

'I'm beginning to understand that now. I've only been up here a few days in the great scheme of things but already the thought of being in the midst of the hustle and bustle fills me with dread. It's like your life and mine are polar opposites.' She smiled.

Lachy frowned and placed his glass down. 'Yet I wonder which of us is happier.'

A strange, heavy silence settled on the room as Zara contemplated Lachy's words. She had never really questioned her happiness before. But then again London was all she had ever known. This whole experience had thrown her for a loop. She was still shocked at how a sense of belonging had rooted within her and, even though she had been angry, irritated, frustrated and on the verge of packing it all in, the thought of leaving the Highlands made her incredibly sad.

She decided to try and lighten the mood. 'I could just have done without the accident, the puncture and getting lost.'

He smiled and his face lit up again. 'I suppose they were a tad inconvenient.'

'Just a bit.'

'I still can't believe you thought you'd travelled back in time.' His shoulders began to shake again. 'Honestly, I wish Tosh had snapped a picture of you. He says you were all cute with dirt on your cheeks and a look of sheer horror on your face.'

She laughed along. 'Well, you've some room to talk. At least I wasn't playing dress-up with a bunch of other adults carrying wooden swords.'

'Fair point, fair point. I don't even know how they roped me in to doing the damn re-enactment thing. I blame Tosh. Known him since school when he was a wee munchkin of a lad.'

'So why were they calling you Lurch?'

He rolled his eyes. 'Oh God, I forgot you'd heard that. Another remnant of school. I was the tallest one in my class and for some reason one of the teachers called me it *one bloody time* and it stuck. The similarity to my actual name didn't bloody help any.'

'Ugh, kids can be so cruel. I had awful nicknames too, but it was worse for my best friend, Shelley.'

'How so?'

'Well, her name was... *is* Michelle Bean. So you can imagine what the kids used to call her.'

Lachy pulled his lips between his teeth and tried not to laugh but instead made a snorting kind of noise. 'I'm sorry, I know I shouldn't laugh. I blame the wine.'

'Yes, and thanks to my plastic National Health specs I was Granny Bailey.'

Lachy stopped trying to hold back his laughter. 'Oh God, that's brilliant. Jelly Bean and Granny Bailey.' He reached across the table and held out his hand. 'Pleased to meet you, Granny, the name's Lurch.'

She took his hand and shook it. 'Hello, young man,' she replied in a silly, old-lady voice.

Once their laughter had subsided Lachy fixed his attention on her again. 'So, what will you do with your book once it's finished?'

She shrugged. 'Oh, nothing. I don't think it's good enough to actually publish. It was more of a challenge for me really. I just don't seem to have the time with work.'

'You know, one thing I learned when I was working in the city, you've got to make time to do the things you enjoy, like I said before. Make time for yourself. You deserve it. We all do.'

She knew he was right. Since she had embarked upon this trip she had begun to reassess her work-life balance and had come to the conclusion that there really *wasn't* one. She was either at work in the office, on assignment in some foreign country or planning for one or the other. There were a couple of brief meet-ups a month with her best friends and a trip home to see her family as often as she could but there really wasn't time for the thing she was passionate about. Perhaps she needed to make some changes now after feeling such a buzz over writing again?

'I must admit, this place makes me understand why you think that way. I guess in the city everything is so impersonal and moves at such a fast pace. But everything is so convenient so you don't need to make an effort for things like you do up here. I mean back home I have everything I need on my doorstep and I suppose I take it for granted. I have my close friends but they have their own lives. Shelley will be getting married and having kids soon and Marco... well, Marco's a law unto himself.' She glanced round the homely kitchen and imagined her mum standing at the range making her famous stew and dumplings. 'My mum and dad would love to live somewhere like this. I think Dad would love to work on the land instead of in the building trade. I could really imagine him as a farmer.'

Lachy huffed out through puffed cheeks. 'It's no picnic, that's for sure. But I do go to bed every night feeling a good kind of tired, you know? Not a mental exhaustion like my work in the city. This is an honest to goodness, physical tiredness. But it's really hard. I wouldn't be doing it if I didn't love it.'

'It's like you said, there's a lot to be said for doing something you're passionate about, I suppose.'

'You got that right.'

22

After dinner Lachy and Zara sat in the lounge watching the flames dancing in the fireplace and Bess spread herself out as close as she could to the grate without burning her nose. There was something very relaxing and familiar about the whole scenario and Zara had to remind herself that her bike would be arriving after two more sleeps and she would then be back on the road and heading home.

Much of what Lachy had said was true. She *did* love her job, but it left little in the way of time for her to do the one thing she had always wanted to pursue. Maybe she wasn't good enough to be a novelist, but how would she know if she never tried? Making a huge change was terrifying and she wasn't sure she was as brave as Lachy had been when he'd left the city to return to the family croft.

She guessed it was the romance of the location that was playing with her mind *and* her heart. She hoped that when she left Scourie in a couple of days she would forget about the feeling of belonging she had begun to experience. After all, Lachy wasn't looking for a lodger.

The soporific effect of the wine was becoming difficult to fight and Zara was considering taking herself off to bed when Lachy spoke.

'Do you think you'll ever return?'

'To Scotland? Or... or to *here* specifically?' she asked.

He turned to look at her. 'To here.' There was a strange intensity to his gaze that she couldn't decipher. Was he inviting her to visit?

She shrugged. 'Maybe. Who knows what Noah will have me doing next? Trekking in bloody Antarctica or something. I wouldn't put it past him.'

'I don't mean for work necessarily. What I mean is... It's just...' His inability to put into words what he wanted to say was endearing. She was seeing a softer side to the brusque man she had first encountered. 'Well, you'd be welcome. Here, I mean. If you wanted to come back.'

She smiled and her heart fluttered. 'Thank you. That's really nice of you. I thought you'd maybe have had enough of me.'

He shrugged and glanced down at his wine glass. 'It's been kind of nice having some company.'

A twinge of sadness knotted her stomach again. Getting back to her normal, fast-paced life would be strange. But good... wouldn't it?

She stood from the sofa. 'Well, I'm bushed. Time for bed, I think. Thank you for a lovely evening.'

Like a true gent Lachy stood too and he was only inches away from her. 'Thank you. It's been good to just sit and eat a proper meal and to talk to another person. It's been a while. I spent a lot of time at my dad's bedside when he was ill and then, since he died, I've spent too much time here alone. You're right about people needing people. I think I'd forgotten that until... well, until these last few days.'

Zara had the urge to hug him but then her eyes drifted to his lips as they parted slightly and the urge changed. *No,* she told herself, *don't go getting attached. You know it'll end badly and you'll get hurt.* She swallowed and snatched herself from the brink of a huge mistake. Instead she stepped back and turned towards the door.

As she began to walk away he reached out and touched her arm. It was the lightest contact but she felt her wrist tingle where his fingertips had met her skin. 'Goodnight, Zara.'

'Goodnight, Lachy,' she whispered.

* * *

The next morning when Zara came down to the kitchen Lachy was nowhere to be seen. Bess greeted her in her usual smiley manner and skipped round her feet as she walked towards the stove. There was a pot of fresh coffee brewing and porridge in the large pan, as always, so she helped herself. As she sat chatting to Bess as if they were old friends Lachy came bursting in from the lounge.

'It's bloody brilliant!'

She scrunched her brow. 'What's brilliant?'

'Your book. You have a serious talent, Zara. It's incredible. I've never read anything like it. It *needs* to be published.'

She wasn't sure whether to be horrified that he'd invaded her privacy or delighted that he'd had such a positive reaction to her prose; even if the book *was* on *his* laptop. The former emotion won.

She glared at him. 'You *read* it?'

He sat opposite her at the table, an expression of wild

happiness on his handsome face like she'd never seen on him before. 'I'm sorry, I know I shouldn't have read it without asking your permission. But you left it open on my laptop and I was just going to read the first couple of paragraphs. I'll be honest, I wasn't expecting to enjoy it. Romance isn't really my thing but... it's not *just* romance, is it? It's dark and edgy. Gritty, like you said. It's got real passion, Zara. The story gripped me and I couldn't stop reading. I think a publisher would snap it up. You need to submit it.'

She pushed herself up from the table, anger bubbling up from within. 'I appreciate your enthusiasm, Lachy, but it's *my* private work. You shouldn't have read it at all. It's an invasion of my privacy. If I had known you were going to do that I would never have agreed to use your laptop. Is that why you read it? Did you feel you had the *right* because it was on your computer?'

He frowned, opening and closing his mouth as if her reaction was a huge surprise to him. 'I... no... I didn't mean to invade your privacy. I just... it's really good, Zara,' he repeated, as if doing so would make her feel less violated.

She didn't care that his expression had turned from one of excitement to one of confused hurt or that the flush of his cheeks had paled and regret was now visible in his eyes.

She slammed her spoon down on the wood of the table. 'I'm going for a walk. I'll thank you not to go through my things again.' She stormed out before he could speak and Bess, as usual, followed close behind.

Zara sat on the sand and looked out at the water. The sunlight glinted like tiny light bulbs bobbing on the surface as the breeze caused little ripples. Overhead a couple of birds caught thermals and floated, dipping and looping. So peaceful. So uncomplicated.

How dare he read it? How bloody dare he? But... did he mean what he said? Or was he just being nice? Or did he think it was utterly crap but said it was good to cover up the guilt he felt for reading it in the first place?

She sighed heavily and, as if she sensed her mood, Bess placed a paw on her arm. 'Oh, Bess, I'm going to miss you when I leave.' Saying the words out loud caused a ball of emotion to tighten her throat and her eyes began to sting. 'I think I'll miss your owner, too, but don't tell him I said so, okay? I bet he'll be glad to see the back of me. Especially over that reaction to him reading my stupid book.'

By the time she had returned to the house Lachlan had gone. She had no idea where or how long he would be, but she had calmed down and realised that her overreaction could have just caused her to lose a friend. Because that was what Lachy had become. It might have been fast but he'd been there for her when she'd been vulnerable and needed someone. He'd taken her in when she'd had nowhere to stay. And how had she repaid him? By being a snappy, childish bitch. Instead of focusing on the fact that the *first person* to read her book – an intelligent person to boot – had loved it, she had focused on him reading it without permission. He'd read an open document on his *own* bloody laptop. In truth he could've kept quiet about reading it and she'd have been none the wiser. The fact that he loved the book so much that he was excited to discuss it should have been the wonderful thing to cling to in all this. She needed to make amends pretty damned quick.

She riffled through his fridge, freezer and cupboards hunting for ingredients. *Lasagne, I can't go far wrong with lasagne,* she thought as she piled up the necessary items. Bess watched her every move with a tilted head and a string of drool hanging from her mouth.

'Ugh, Bess, you're no lady, are you?' Zara laughed as she ruffled the dog's fur. 'Right, I need to make this special meal for your human. Does he like lasagne?' she asked the black and white canine, who simply licked her lips. 'I'll take that as a yes.'

Two hours later Lachy appeared. Zara was sitting at the table facing the door and stood as soon as he walked in.

'I wanted to—'

'Lachy, I'm—'

He gestured in his typical gentlemanly way. 'You first.'

She held up her hands. 'Look, I'm sorry. I totally overreacted and it was ridiculous. You've been so good to me and you didn't deserve me going off on you like that. I totally understand if you want me to take my tent and camp somewhere out there until the new bike arrives. But I made you lasagne. Think of it as an apology lasagne. Now, I'm no expert chef. No one will be renaming me Nigella Lawson any time soon. And I think the cheese is burned. And I may have overdone it with the herbs, so you might not even want to eat it, but I had to do something to—'

She hadn't even realised he had walked towards her but when his lips touched hers she gasped in a breath. His hand slipped into her hair and she parted her lips as she gripped his shirt. The kiss was intense and desire flooded her body like wildfire. His tongue caressed hers and her knees weakened.

When he pulled away he rested his forehead on hers. 'Well, that certainly quietened you down.' He smiled. 'I had to do it because you really weren't selling that apology lasagne. It was sounding more like *revenge* lasagne with every sentence.'

She touched her lips. 'You kissed me.'

He stroked her cheek with the soft pad of his thumb. 'I believe I did, yes. I've wanted to do it since that day you stood outside your tent with wild hair and crazy eyes professing to be a strong, independent woman. Now come on, feed me, woman. How bad can this lasagne be?'

23

Zara served up two plates of the lasagne but she couldn't eat. The feel of Lachy's lips pressed against hers remained and she couldn't shake the sadness that was weighing heavily on her shoulders.

'Well, for all the talking-down you gave it, that lasagne was bloody delicious,' Lachy said as he pushed away his empty plate. 'You've hardly touched yours.' He frowned.

She shook her head but didn't meet his gaze. 'No, I'm not really that hungry.'

'Bloody hell, did my kiss put you off your food?' He laughed.

She lifted her chin and was greeted by his handsome smiling face, tilted inquisitively to one side. 'Why did you kiss me, Lachy?'

He leaned forward and rested his elbows on the table. 'Because you were insanely gorgeous when you were fretting over your cooking skills. And like I said, I've wanted to kiss you for a while now.' His smile disappeared and he straightened up. 'I'm sorry if I overstepped the mark. I... I didn't mean to upset you. I know there are boundaries and I kind of lost myself there for a minute.'

She shook her head. 'You didn't upset me... I just don't really understand what the point was.'

His brow crumpled. 'Point? I'm attracted to you, isn't that obvious? I saw an opportunity to kiss you and I took it.'

'But I'm leaving tomorrow. You and me... well, there *is* no you and me. I live at the other end of the UK and you live in the middle of nowhere. Our lives are completely different.'

He grinned but his eyes contradicted the gesture. 'Jeez, Zara, it's not like I proposed marriage, for goodness' sake.'

'I know that. I just— I don't usually kiss people unless it means something. And now I'm confused.'

He stood from the table. 'Look, you're reading too much into this. I kissed you. Maybe I shouldn't have. I'm sorry. I don't usually do things like that either. But... I'm drawn to you. You're the complete opposite of every woman I've known and, even though you do my head in with your bloody stubborn ways, I'm attracted to you. I hoped maybe you might be attracted to me too but clearly I put you off your food.' He forced a laugh. 'So let's just put it down to experience, eh? Like you said, you'll be gone tomorrow and so I suppose that's why I took the chance.' He ran his hands through the shaggy strands of his hair and his T-shirt rose up to show the bottom of his toned abdomen. She tried not to notice but failed. He huffed the air from his lungs. 'I'm off to shower. I'm sorry if I made you uncomfortable, Zara. It was honestly never my intention. I just happen to think you're a beautiful, intelligent woman and I really wanted to kiss you. I hope you can forgive me.' With a haunted expression of regret he turned and left the room.

Zara sat there and closed her eyes for a moment. She lifted her fingers to her lips and remembered the feeling of Lachy's hand in her hair. The kiss had been incredible but she could tell he had held back a little. If he could turn her blood to liquid fire when he was holding back, what could he do when he wasn't?

She had fallen fast for Josh; she had trusted him and he had betrayed her so easily at the first opportunity. She wasn't willing to make that mistake again but to feel *that* heat that Lachy created was intense. The desire that burned within her made her want him. Even if it was for just one night. It could never be anything more, after all. The physical distance between them was too vast.

Even though she wasn't a risk-taker, the urge to break free of her self-restraint was almost overpowering. He was a handsome, muscular man and he'd taken a risk to kiss her. But she had to admit she wanted more. Just for one night she wanted to let go and know what it felt like to give in to lust.

She stood from the table and climbed the stairs.

As she walked into Lachy's bedroom she could hear the hum of the en-suite shower and the pounding of the water, but it was only slightly louder than the hammering of her heart against her ribcage. Outside the closed bathroom door she took a deep breath and removed her clothes, throwing them onto a chair in the corner.

It was now or never.

She reached for the handle and turned it. If it was locked, she would grab her clothes and run as fast as she could for the spare room. But it wasn't. She pushed the door open and stepped inside. Through the steamed-up door she could make out the shape of Lachy's firm, naked body and she swallowed hard. *I've gone completely mad.* But she didn't stop. The old floor creaked and Lachy turned to face her through the glass.

He wiped the condensation away and opened his mouth to speak. 'Zara?'

She inhaled a shaking breath. 'If... if I join you in there would you promise me not to read anything into it?' Her voice trembled with the fear he would reject her. But instead he pushed open the door and held out his hand. She took it and stepped inside.

As soon as the water heated her skin Lachy's mouth was on hers. His tongue slipped over hers and one hand slid down her wet skin to the curve of her bottom. He squeezed and pulled her closer, his arousal pressing into her belly. She smoothed her hands up his chest and into his hair as his kiss grew more urgent. He lifted his hand and toyed with her breast as she moaned at the pleasure and desire coursing through her veins. She didn't care that this was out of character. She didn't care that it was just no-strings-attached sex. She'd never had that before and, my God, it felt good. To be touched and explored by an almost stranger was exciting and exhilarating and she couldn't get enough.

Lachy's mouth moved to her neck, where he nibbled and sucked. 'Can I take you to bed?' he whispered huskily.

'Yes,' was her simple reply.

He slipped his hands under her bottom and lifted her effortlessly. She wrapped her legs round his waist and he pushed the glass door open with his foot before carrying her out of the shower room and over to the bed at the opposite side of the room. The chilled air made her shiver and every nerve ending stood to attention.

He placed her down gently and kneeled between her thighs as he devoured her with his gaze. He didn't need to speak. His eyes portrayed everything he was feeling and she had never wanted a man as much as she wanted him right then. He lowered himself down and kissed her deeply once again as she let her fingertips trail down the damp skin of his back. He lifted her so she wrapped her legs round him again.

'You're not going to regret this, are you?' he whispered as he fixed his penetrating gaze on her.

'No,' she whispered and he smiled.

'Good, because I want you *so much*, Zara.'

'I want you too,' she breathed in reply.

He placed her down again, reached over to the bedside table and took something from the drawer. She closed her eyes; for some reason she couldn't watch as he sheathed himself. It felt a little too intimate in spite of what they were about to do.

The next thing she knew he was connected to her in the most glorious way, moving slowly as he breathed hotly into the crook of her neck. He kissed her everywhere his lips would reach and his fingers caressed and teased the places his mouth couldn't.

He moved so that he could look into her eyes and she tried not to read what she saw there. She needed this closeness; to feel desired and wanted. She needed to lose herself in sensation and passion just for one night.

Pleasure, deep and languorous, began to build within her and she arched her back, gasping as Lachy moved over her and in her. No words were spoken. They weren't needed. And as she soared with her climax he joined her, holding her tightly until she relaxed and a sated haze settled over their intertwined bodies.

24

Zara had slipped out of Lachy's bed in the early hours of the morning and gone back to the spare room. And the next morning she had showered and dressed in her cycling gear in preparation for the day ahead. When she stopped to make coffee she became acutely aware that she had been busying herself to stop her thoughts from deafening her. She didn't want to think about the night before; yet, simultaneously, it was *all* she wanted to think about.

Lachy hadn't appeared yet and she hoped he wasn't avoiding her. Bess was following her around as if she knew something was amiss. But then again she guessed that Bess was a particularly sensitive creature. Leaving her behind was going to be tough; that was one thing she had let herself admit to. She seemed to have an affinity with the beautiful black and white dog.

At around nine o'clock there was a knock at the door and, in the absence of Lachy, she went to answer it.

A guy in the uniform from the bike shop stood there with a big smile on his face, holding a clipboard. 'Miss Bailey?'

She nodded. 'Yes, that's me.'

'It's good to see you up and about after what happened. That must have been awful.'

She felt that familiar heat enter her cheeks and she cringed. 'I'm just so very sorry about the bike.'

'Hey, don't worry. Bikes can be replaced. People can't. Could you sign here for the replacement and point me in the direction of the invalid and I'll take it away?'

She signed the form on the clipboard and gestured towards the barn adjoining the house. 'Silver D... erm the wrecked bike is in there. Just inside the doorway. Do you need any help?'

He waved a hand dismissively. 'Nope, you're fine. I'll go get it and I'll be on my way. Take it easy, okay? And enjoy the rest of your route.' He jogged back to the van and wheeled the replacement bike over to the door, propping it up against the wall. 'It's virtually the same as before but a different colour so the transition should be straightforward.' Then he waved goodbye and collected the damaged one from the barn. He had to carry it because of the buckled wheels and twisted frame and Zara almost whimpered at the pitiful sight of it. Then the man loaded SD into his van and drove away.

And that was it. No complication, no hassle, no stress. Just a replacement bike and no questions. She was relieved to say the least.

Once she'd closed the door she walked over to make more coffee and Lachy appeared. He slipped his arms round her waist and kissed her neck. A shiver of desire travelled her spine and she closed her eyes before pulling away.

'Coffee?' she asked without looking at him.

'Sure. You're dressed to go already?' Disappointment was evident in his voice.

'The guy has just been and delivered the replacement bike. I should probably make an early start.'

'Right. Of course.'

'I'm all packed and ready to go. I hope you don't mind but I pinched a bit of flapjack and some bread and butter for the road. I'm going to miss your home-made bread.'

'And I'm going to miss you,' he whispered.

She turned to face him. He stood there in jeans and a grey T-shirt. His hands were in his pockets and his sad smile made her heart lurch. 'Lachy...'

'I know. I'm not allowed to say things like that. Blah, blah. But it's true, Zara, so now you know.'

She sighed. 'You've been so good to me. I really appreciate everything,' she said in an effort to change the subject.

He nodded. 'Yeah. I know you do. And you're welcome. I... erm I got you a gift.'

'Oh, Lachy—'

'Don't go getting annoyed. It's nothing major. I have a friend who makes things. And after all that talk about your passion for writing I just... Well, I think you should definitely pursue it. You should be free to do the thing that makes you happy. And anyway, I just thought I'd get you a gift to remind you of this place. But do me a favour; don't open it until you get to wher-ever you're going next. I'll just get embarrassed and you'll just get annoyed at me for being sentimental.' He shrugged as he opened a drawer in the old dresser and took out a small gift bag. He handed it over to her and she took it.

'Thank you,' she whispered.

He nodded. 'Look, I'm going to go check on... erm... stuff in the yard.' He cleared his throat and could no longer appear to make eye contact. 'I'll see you before you leave.' He turned and rushed out of the door before Zara could say anything further.

She went upstairs and made sure she had collected everything she had brought, including her memory stick, and had one final glance round the pretty room. Another twinge of sadness tugged at her stomach as she closed the door. As she passed Lachy's room she noticed that the door was ajar. She stepped inside and gazed at the bed. It was neatly made now and the pale blue duvet cover showed no evidence of what had happened but she could still feel the way Lachy's limbs had tangled with hers as she'd lain in his arms only hours before.

The bedside clock said it was almost ten and she knew she'd need to leave soon so she made her way down the stairs once more. Lachy was back and sitting at the kitchen table. Bess sat at his feet with her head resting on his knee. The dog gave one brief wag of her tail as Zara entered the room.

'Well, that's me – all ready to go.' Her throat tightened as she spoke and she mentally chastised herself for feeling anything other than relief that the trip was nearly over and she'd soon be home in London ready to get back to normal life.

Lachy stood and walked over to her. 'Well, it's been great having you here, Zara. It'll be strangely quiet when you've gone.'

She nodded and swallowed, willing her voice not to sound strained. 'Thank you for everything, Lachy. You've been... well... the perfect host.'

'Can I at least hug you before you walk out of my life forever?' He smiled but his eyes remained sad.

She flung her arms round his neck and inhaled the scent of him one last time. 'Take care.'

He rested his face in the crook of her neck and mumbled: 'You too. No more time travel or run-ins with tractors, okay?' He laughed but it sounded forced.

She nodded. Then she crouched to say goodbye to Bess.

'Bye bye, my little friend. I'll miss you so much.' Her voice wobbled and as if the dog knew exactly what she was feeling she placed her paw on Zara's leg. Zara bent forward and sank her face into the dog's fur where a few tears could escape, hopefully unnoticed. Bess licked her cheek and whined before lying down on the stone floor.

'Goodbye, Zara. Be free and be fine,' Lachy said as he hugged her once more. The lyrics from Florence and the Machine's 'Delilah' echoed around her head and she held on tight for a few more moments. 'And do what you love. *Never* think you're not good enough. Because you're *more* than good enough,' he whispered. He kissed her cheek and stepped away. 'Come on, Bess. Let's go to the beach, eh?' The dog stood as if waiting for Zara to accompany them and when Lachy walked away she paused, unsure what to do.

'Go on, Bess. Go on,' Zara said as she gestured towards the door and eventually the dog ran after her owner.

Through the fog of tears Zara loaded up the new bike and clipped on her helmet. She had never expected leaving this place to be so damned hard. As she climbed onto the bike and glanced towards the beach once more, she saw Lachy standing with his back towards her, head down, with Bess beside him, and a heavy wave of sadness washed over her.

In spite of what she had tried to convince herself of, she knew deep down that this was going to be the hardest goodbye.

* * *

Lachy

How the hell was it possible that one stubborn, opinionated, strong, independent woman could shake the foundations of his life so rapidly? Lachy had no clue. In the three years he had spent with Saskia he had never felt such a strong connection when they were in bed together. So how the hell could it happen with someone who was – to all intents and purposes – a stranger? And why couldn't he wave goodbye?

He stood there on the strip of sand with his back facing his home and the woman who had somehow tugged at his heart, leaving her mark after such a small number of days. The thought of waking the next morning and Zara being gone made his chest ache. How was he supposed to carry on as normal after that brief interlude of sunshine and fire?

The water lapped at the pebbles that scattered the edge of the sand and he focused on the familiar sound. A necessary distraction for the reality he couldn't affect. She was leaving and taking a tiny sliver of his heart with her. How the hell had he allowed that to happen so fast and so unabashedly? Deep down he knew he'd been powerless to stop it. She was like a comet passing through the atmosphere of his life. Beautiful but all too fast.

He hadn't taken her number. There had been no point. As she had quite rightly said they were living at opposite ends of the country, living completely different lifestyles. So like a comet he would have to enjoy the memory of her even though it was unlikely she would appear in his sky again.

* * *

When she had cycled for thirty minutes, long enough to create plenty of distance between herself and Scourie, Zara stopped and took out the little gift bag Lachy had given her. Inside was the most beautiful keyring she had ever seen. Hanging from the ring was a laptop charm and a cute dog charm that looked just like Bess. In addition to these was a silver disc that she thought was blank until she turned it over. But on the reverse it simply said:

Zara
Be free and be fine
Lachy x

25

She cycled right past the turning that led to Balnakeil. The hot-chocolate place reminded her of Lachy and she didn't need to think about him. She needed to get on with her assignment and *then* she needed to go home and get on with her life. At least, that was what she kept telling herself.

It was strange to be back on the road again. To be all alone after having company for a few days. Whenever she thought about Bess, she had to swallow that familiar lump of emotion that tightened her throat. *Bloody hell, Bailey, she's just a dog, for goodness' sake.* And even though she repeated that over and over like a mantra she knew it wasn't exactly true. Bess was just one small part of a strange-shaped hole that had formed in her heart since she'd left Scourie. She could only hope that time would heal it.

She had one brief stop to eat the home-made bread and flapjack that she had taken from the croft and then, after cycling around fifty-five miles during the day, she arrived in Tongue. She was back at the same site she had stayed in only a few days before but at least this meant she was back on track.

She resolved to have an early night and eat whatever she could buy from the little shop. There were no notes to type up as this part of her journey had been covered already. Tomorrow she would set off for Lairg and then she would be on the home straight.

As she sat beside her tent her phone pinged and she grappled for it. Could it be Lachy? She eagerly swiped at the screen.

> Hey Zee! We miss you. Don't go getting addicted to fresh air! Shelley & Marco <3

A ridiculous photo of the pouting pair accompanied the message and Zara wondered how the hell a multi-media message had managed to come through. She drank the mini bottle of Shiraz she had purchased from the shop; the taste of it took her back to the dinner she had eaten with Lachy when they had got to know each other a little and she smiled at the memory of their conversations. She reached into her bag and took out her memory stick. Unsure as to why, she felt a connection to him when she held it in her hand.

She climbed into her tent when the temperature began to drop and pretty soon she drifted off to sleep.

* * *

The following day was a particularly early start but she was determined to make up as many miles as she could even though she knew she would still be finished a day or so behind the original schedule. The replacement bike wasn't right, however. She had got used to Silver Dickhead and it had eventually stopped being quite so uncomfortable. *Blue Bollocks* – as she had named this one, purely because if she'd been male *that* was what it would've given her – was like starting over. The trouble was she had no choice; it would have to do. And as she cycled towards the day's destination she welcomed the cool rain that soaked her skin. Even with the dramatic covering of dark clouds the scene that surrounded her was magnificent.

She passed the site of her accident and the incident with the re-enacters and smiled to herself as she recalled Lachy teasing her about the time travel thing. She wondered what he would be doing now. Would he be out on his quad bike tending to his sheep? Or maybe in the kitchen making bread to replace what she had taken? She imagined him at the sink, glancing at her over his shoulder with that handsome smile he'd seemed to save for when they had been alone.

Then her thoughts ran away with her and she remembered the feel of his lips on her skin. His fingers teasing and touching her. Being with him had been different. Maybe even better than with Josh. There had been no expectations. Just pleasure. She shivered as she recalled the way his body had fitted so perfectly with hers. But that didn't mean anything. It was just sex. It was *meant* to be that way. It was how the human body was made. There was no one perfect person for every individual. No soulmate crap. She'd let go of that illusion a long time ago. But she missed him.

She had to focus on something else.

Riffling through her memory, she tried to find a song that would replace the aching sadness that had taken hold of her. But every song she came up with somehow brought her back to Lachy. Especially 'Delilah'. She settled on letting it play in her mind as background music for her journey and for that moment accepted that she missed Lachy *now* but it would pass.

It had to.

She cycled through a varied landscape and decided to stop and take both notes *on* and photos *of* a little ruined castle she encountered. The texture of the clouds behind the crumbling stones created a powerful image that she hoped would translate onto paper, but she doubted it. None of the photos she had taken so far went any length towards creating the atmosphere she had experienced by being there in the moment. She wished she could be there when the aurora borealis lit up the sky in a multitude of waving colours. And that was something else she had learned about herself. She'd never imagined she would enjoy isolation or solitude, but she had experienced some incredible things by going through the very situations she'd thought she hated.

After a brief stop at a mini supermarket for her evening provisions she finally arrived in Lairg. The campsite had beautiful views over Loch Shin and a games room that she thought she might try out for research purposes. Pool had always been her game at university and she hadn't played in a while so wasn't sure if she still had it. She set up her tent and her solar charger. The little gadget had been an absolute lifesaver as far as her work was concerned.

The tent was erected in minutes. It had become second nature even though she'd had a brief reprieve, she only wished it were the same with packing it away. Her first stop was the shower block. Cycling all those miles a day was hard work and both her muscles *and* her nose appreciated what the hot water did for her body. Once towel-dried and dressed she made her way to the games room, but was sad to find no one else around. It was early. She threw a few darts and hit the white ball round the pool table for a while but then decided to return to the tent and eat. The packet pasta salad she had bought was nice enough, but it was no home-cooked Lachy meal, that was for sure. A man who could cook was incredibly attractive *and* good in bed was far too good to be true. *Although, he did invade my privacy... But if that was his only fault...*

Later on she watched a group of people wander into the games room. They were together in a large tent and she guessed from the car stickers that they were doing the NC500 too. *Might be good to do a bit of an interview...*

The people seemed friendly when she introduced herself. Three couples in their late thirties. She asked them why they had chosen the route.

'I just love the fresh air,' said one of the men, very athletic-looking and wearing outdoorsy clothes. 'My work's city-based in Leeds and so I come up here to escape the fumes and breathe a little. Both literally *and* figuratively. I can let go of the stress here.'

'So you've travelled this route before?' she asked with intrigue.

'Oh yes. We come and do the 500 every couple of years but we visit the Highlands annually just for the scenery. If I had my way we'd relocate up here but Henry's job won't allow it just yet,' the man's partner said.

They played pool and she drank a bottle of beer with them. It struck her how similar some of them were to her. Busy city types who had taken a break from the hustle and bustle of city life. And it surprised her how many of them wished they could relocate.

'Now if I was you, with your job, I'd be up here like a shot working remotely or freelance or something,' one of the other men, a guy called Rich, told her. 'You have the perfect job to live somewhere incredible and have the best of both worlds.'

She shook her head. 'Oh no. I think I'd miss the city too much. The inconvenience of everything here. The... the...' She scrambled around her mind for what she had once known without a doubt.

Rich pointed his beer bottle at her and laughed. 'See! Even you're getting addicted to this place! To say you didn't want to come here, you're really going to have a hard time saying good-bye, I reckon.'

She worried that he had a point.

Nope. She was a city girl. Big city, bars, shops, cars, fumes... lots of people rushing... Lots of shops though... and bars...

She decided to quit whilst she was ahead – who was she kidding? 'Well, folks, I'm back on the road tomorrow so I'm going to call it a night. Thanks for chatting. You've been really helpful. I have all your email addresses so I can let you know when the article goes live.'

She bid them all goodnight and wandered out into the dusky evening to go back to her tent. The air was warm and there was a smell of heather and greenery. She could hear the calm chatter of the campsite occupants and nothing much else. The sky overhead was a pinpricked navy-blue canopy exposing tiny dots of light and the moon lit up her way just enough to help her get back.

26

Zara awoke to a rainy morning and much to her surprise, the weather matched her mood. This was going to be her last day of cycling. She had decided to combine the two final days into one due to her delays. Tonight, if all went well she'd be in Inverness, find a cheap hotel and chill out. She could consolidate her notes and eat a good meal before travelling home. Noah had booked an open-ended return rail ticket and even though she was keen to see her family and friends she needed to sleep in a bed and rest, and was looking forward to doing just that.

Her usual morning routine ensued: she battled with the tent, cursed and swore under her breath but ultimately managed to get it in the bag with less hassle than usual. *Bloody typical.* In no time she was on the road again. She waved at the group she had chatted to the night before as they sat outside their tent eating bacon sandwiches – the smell of which made her stomach growl in jealousy. Once again she was surrounded by lush green trees and scant traffic. *Sheer bliss.* The rain had cleared and the sky above was blue but there was a slight chill to the air, which made cycling a little more comfortable.

The group she had met had recommended a place called the Storehouse so she made that her destination. She'd been told to try the scones and she wasn't one to argue where such things were concerned. Once she had chained up the bike, aka BB, she walked inside. Baked goods and their sweet, delectable aromas enticed her and, after all the exercise she'd had recently, she threw caution to the wind as far as her diet was concerned. She went to the counter and ordered a scone with fresh cream and jam and a coffee and went to sit at a table that looked out onto the Cromarty Firth. She could certainly see why her new friends had suggested the place.

All too soon the scone was devoured and she went to the counter to purchase another for later. Then she had a stroll round the deli and collected a few small gifts for Marco and Shelley, her mum and her dad and some tablet for her brothers. She wandered by the water's edge and took a selfie with a giant blue anchor that had been placed by the shore like a majestic sculpture. She made notes about the café and the scones – it had to be done. And then she was on her way again.

* * *

She had mixed emotions as she cycled towards the Highland Trax shop in Inverness; SD was gone and she'd soon be parting ways with its replacement. It was bizarre how she appeared to have formed an attachment to the thing that was involved in much of her trauma over the preceding days, but in some ways she would remember the first bike fondly... Well, perhaps once her bottom was back to normal.

The city was buzzing with people on their way home from

work, everyone rushing, chatting, carrying shopping bags and briefcases. It was like a much more compact version of London only this city was a stone's throw from some of the best views she had ever witnessed. She glanced up at the old clock tower and was a little shocked to find that she had a matter of minutes before the bike shop closed.

Thankfully she was lucky to arrive just in time and, as much as she had surprised herself by enjoying the trip, it was a relief to hand the bike over to the staff. There were definitely more comfortable and less strenuous ways to travel.

The man who had delivered her replacement bike was there to greet her. 'Ah, Miss Bailey, how are you doing?'

'Hi. Great, thanks. Relieved to be back on two feet, I think.'

He nodded. 'Aye, it's been quite an adventure for you, eh?'

She laughed. 'Oh yes, you could say that.'

He held up his finger. 'Oh, hang on there a minute, would you? We had a letter dropped in for you earlier today actually.'

Zara frowned. 'A letter?'

'Yes. One sec.' He disappeared into the back office and returned moments later clutching the thick cream-coloured envelope. 'There you go. Dropped in by one of the hotel staff in person.' He raised his eyebrows.

The envelope was embossed with a fancy logo from a swanky hotel in Inverness. She opened it and read.

Dear Miss Bailey,

We will be delighted to welcome you this evening to stay in our Grand Suite. Payment has been made in full and dinner is booked for 8 p.m.

Yours sincerely,

Hugo McTavish

Manager

She smiled and shook her head. *Noah's on one serious guilt trip.* She thanked the shop staff and waved goodbye. Once outside she dropped Noah a quick text to thank him for the booking but she didn't expect a reply. She knew what he was like when he was feeling bad and after the time she'd had he must have been feeling terrible.

As she had been informed that dinner was booked for eight that evening and the hotel was apparently quite upper class, Zara dived into the closest dress shop she could find. She was very much aware that cycling clothes weren't really appropriate for fine dining, but was also aware that she had less than thirty minutes before the shop closed to find clothes, shoes and undies, which wasn't exactly a long time. She dashed round the store and picked up a black dress, black bra and panties, a pair of ballet pumps and some make-up. She arrived at the checkout with five minutes to spare, feeling quite impressed with herself. *At least in a fancy hotel there'll be nice toiletries,* she surmised.

She made her way across Inverness to the address of the hotel and gasped as she walked up the long driveway. It was a white-painted Victorian building in beautiful grounds – not the kind of place she would have expected Noah to book. *Bloody hell, he really is on a guilt trip.*

Inside, the marble-tiled floor glistened under the chandeliers in the reception area and just beyond the main desk she could see plush leather sofas to either side of a stone fireplace. A tartan carpet in deep burgundy and green covered the floor in the sitting area and Zara couldn't help smiling at how cosy it looked.

A smartly dressed young man stood behind the desk – his waistcoat matched the carpet she could see – and he greeted her with a warm smile.

'Good evening, madam. How may I help you?'

She smoothed down her dishevelled locks and cleared her throat, suddenly feeling very underdressed. 'Ahem… hi, yes, my name is Zara Bailey. I believe there's a room booked here for me.' She handed him the letter she had received in the bike shop.

He typed into the computer. 'Ah, yes, Miss Bailey. You're in our Grand Suite this evening. It's through the door to the left and up the stairs or the elevator to the third floor. Would you like help with your bags?'

She cringed as she looked down at her minimal luggage. 'Oh, that's okay. I think I can manage.'

'Very well.' He smiled again. 'Dinner is booked for eight and your guest will join you then.'

'My guest?' Confusion took over as she tried to figure out why Noah would come all this way. It was one major bloody guilt trip if he had. 'Do you have the name of my guest at all?' The man scrunched his brow and she replayed what she had just asked. 'Oh, erm… this has been booked as a surprise for me by a friend. I just don't know *which* friend.' *Nope, that doesn't really help you to not look like a prostitute, Bailey.* She suddenly felt like Julia Roberts' character in *Pretty Woman* when she arrived at the Regent Beverly Wilshire.

He glanced at the screen again. 'I'm afraid I don't have the name. And I didn't handle the call, so I can't really help. It's all just booked in your name. I can call my colleague if—'

She felt that awful tell-tale heat rise in her face and just wanted to get to her room. 'Oh no, that won't be necessary. I have a good idea who it is. I've been cycling the North Coast 500, you see, and this is their way of congratulating me for not dying,' she said, feeling the need to explain. She dashed for the elevator – well, she *had* just cycled almost five hundred miles so the stairs were an absolute no-no.

As she rode upwards to her floor it dawned on her that maybe... and it was a long shot... but maybe this was all Lachlan's doing. Maybe he missed her and had decided to surprise her? Her stomach flipped as she thought about that possibility, as minuscule as it was. The nervousness in her stomach turned to butterflies doing the fandango as she imagined him walking into the fancy restaurant in a kilt. Of course, he probably wouldn't *do* that but if he did... Those calves... His thighs under that kilt... The elevator pinged and the doors opened. She walked along the corridor and located her suite, stuck the key card into the slot and the door opened.

She stepped into a beautifully decorated hallway with a thick carpet that sank underfoot as she trod further into the suite. A bathroom lay straight ahead with his and hers marble sinks and a roll-top bath big enough for two. Round the corner was a walk-in shower cubicle too. As expected, expensive toiletries graced the surfaces in readiness, along with thick fluffy bathrobes and towels. *Oh God, I could move into this bathroom alone.*

She came out of the bathroom and walked into the main area of the suite. Shimmering fleur-de-lys wallpaper covered the bed-head wall – the bed-head itself was a sumptuous burgundy velvet. A plush leather couch, much like the ones in the reception area, sat in the bay window overlooking the grounds and the biggest bed she had ever seen was situated to make the best of the view.

She walked round open-mouthed and excitement built once again. *This wouldn't be Noah. This has to be Lachy.* But if it was Lachy he was being very presumptuous. Unless all he expected was to dine with her and leave? *That* would be acceptable. How would she feel seeing him again? She closed her eyes and let the image of him walking towards her unfold. *That handsome smile on his face and that stubble on his angular jaw.* The short amount of time they had spent together had felt sexually charged and she knew if it was him she wouldn't be able to resist him. But this was such a grand gesture for someone she'd had no-strings-attached sex with, wasn't it? Had it meant more to him? She wasn't ready to admit that there was a good chance it had meant more to her... Not yet. Even though deep down...

'Oh, for fuck's sake, this isn't helping me. I need to shower. In fact, no, I need to have a long soak in that massive tub,' she said to the empty room, as if doing so would dislodge the images and feelings coursing through her. Pissed off with herself, she stomped through to the bathroom and turned on the taps in the tub. Whatever happened she was leaving tomorrow to go back to London, so even if Lachy did turn out to be her 'guest' for the evening nothing could come of it. She couldn't allow herself to feel something for someone who lived so far away.

Zara poured vanilla-scented bath oil into the water, stripped her tight-fitting bike clothes from her body and stepped in. As she sank down she immediately began to relax. The cocoon of steam enveloped her like a hug and she exhaled some of the tension she had been holding onto. She closed her eyes and thought back to some of the sights and experiences she'd had during her trip. The eagles, the dolphins, the seals... Bess' little face as Zara mounted her bike to leave... Lachy standing with his back towards her as if he couldn't wave good-bye. Tears over-spilled her eyes and trickled down her cheeks. Lachy had been right – in spite of her original reluctance to come to Scotland, she would be leaving a little piece of her heart in the Highlands.

But more specifically in Scourie.

Once the water turned cold, she stepped out of the bath and into the shower cubicle to wash her hair. But all the while images of Bess and Lachy whirred around her mind and the hope that he would be the one that arrived at eight took up roots in her heart. *Please let it be him...*

She remembered the business card Lachy had given her. Maybe she should just bite the bullet and call him? Or at the least send him a text. That way, depending on his response, she would be put out of her misery... or maybe not, but at least she'd know. She rifled through her backpack but there was no sign of the card. Realising she had put it in her pocket with the gift he had given her, she looked there but it was gone. *Shit.* It must have fallen out when she took the gift out to open it. With no way to contact him, she resigned herself to the fact she would just have to wait and see if he showed up.

Thankfully the hairdryer in the room was better than the one she owned at home so once she had finished drying her hair and getting dressed, she looked almost like herself once more. She brushed lip gloss over her lips and checked the clock on her phone. It was almost time. She grabbed her wallet and key card, slipped into her new ballet pumps and left the room.

The dining room was as luxurious as the rest of the place only this time the decoration was burgundy and gold. The setting, with its subdued lighting and candles, was very romantic – striking Noah out of the equation completely. He would have booked her a youth hostel and taken her to a vegan restaurant probably. This place just wasn't his style.

The maître d' showed her to a table for two but no one else

was there yet. Other couples were seated enjoying the atmosphere, holding hands across the linen tablecloths as piano music floated through the air from hidden speakers. A waiter smiled as he carried an ice bucket towards her complete with a bottle of what looked like champagne. She presumed he would bypass her and deliver it to one of the other sickeningly happy couples, but instead he placed the bucket on its stand right by her table.

'Oh, I think you must have the wrong—'

'It's okay, madam. This was pre-ordered and paid for.' She thanked him and he walked away.

She sat twisting her fingers in her lap and trying to discreetly look at the clock situated on the wall above a loved-up couple. But the woman seemed to think she was trying to flirt with her man and kept scowling at her, so she stopped. He was late. Whoever *he* was. *Maybe Lachy had second thoughts? Maybe it's not Lachy? Maybe it's a bloody prank by Marco and Shelley? Oh God, that would be awful – surely they wouldn't do that? Maybe it is Noah after all. He isn't known for his timekeeping.* If her so-called *guest* didn't arrive in the next five minutes—

She was planning her exit strategy when a large hand rested on her shoulder and squeezed as someone bent to kiss her neck.

'God, I've missed you, Zara, so, *so* much,' he whispered and her stomach leapt.

'Josh? What the *hell* are you doing here?'

27

Josh took the seat opposite her and smoothed down his tie. He looked handsome in a suit, but she had no clue what to say to him *or* why he had done this after their last phone conversation.

He glanced round and lowered his voice. 'Look, I know this is all a bit—'

'Weird? Stalkery? You pick an adjective,' she hissed. 'Why the hell didn't you let me know this was all your doing? Instead of all the ridiculous cloak and dagger stuff.'

He held out his hands and shrugged. 'But who else could it have been, Zara? Unless you've met someone else in the last... what... *week*?'

Uncomfortable at his words and unwilling to address them, she simply replied, 'You didn't answer my question.'

He sighed and pleaded with her with his eyes. 'Because I knew you wouldn't come, Zara. Not after we spoke on the phone.'

'Well, if that was the case, why go to all this trouble?'

He reached across the table and tried to take her hand, but she angrily snatched it away and he balked at her reaction. 'Like I said on the phone, I'm not ready to let you go.'

Exasperated, she huffed air through puffed cheeks. 'But you *did* let me go, Josh. You slept with your ex. I caught you kissing her, for goodness' sake. So what's changed?' It was a rhetorical question, seeing as she knew nothing had.

'I just want you in my life. I can't stop thinking about you. About *us* and what we had together.'

This was not how she'd expected her night to go. She inwardly rolled her eyes at herself for even hoping that it might be Lachy who had engineered the evening. Disappointment tugged at her insides, knotting around the poor excited butterflies that had danced there only minutes before. 'Josh, I loved you. I did. But you made your choice and I've had to deal with the aftermath of that. And now I'm trying to move on. You just have to let me. And, anyway, what about Caleb? And what about Katie? What the hell would she think if she knew you were here? I'm presuming she has no clue.' Her voice was a little louder and a little wobblier than she intended.

Josh glanced round the room again with a fake smile plastered on his face. 'Look, let's go up to the room and talk properly, eh? We can order room service. Take the champers with us.'

She was happy to leave the dining room now that people were staring. But she wasn't sure that she wanted to be in a bedroom with Josh. But the alternative was the bar and more observers.

She stood and glared down at him. 'Well, I'm not sleeping with you, in case that's what you were planning,' she spat before turning and stomping away.

Once inside the suite she slumped onto the sofa and Josh followed her in, carrying the champagne and two glasses.

'Here, this'll help.' He smiled as he handed her a glass that was half liquid, half bubbles.

She took it but didn't drink any; instead she placed it on the floor. 'Josh, why are you here? Just tell me the truth. Is it for sex?'

His brow crumpled. 'No, Zara. I'm not that kind of man. I thought you knew me better. I wanted to spoil you. I felt that you deserved this after what you'd been through. The accident and everything. Slumming it in some grotty farmhouse while you got over a concussion. And don't worry, I'll send a thank you in some form to the bloke who rescued my girl.' He grinned as he took a sip of his drink.

'How do you know about all that?' *And why the hell are you still calling me your girl when you cheated on me? And how dare you presume that Lachy's house was a slum?* In spite of her anger, none of the internal conversation manifested in reality.

He swallowed, placed his drink on the little side table beside the sofa and sat. 'Your flatmate, Marcus? I called at your place and asked after you. I thought you'd be home but—'

'You know very well his name is Marco. And why the hell were you at my flat?'

He rolled his eyes, but the smile remained in place. 'Like I said, I wasn't ready to let you go. Zara, we had something special. I loved what we had and I don't want to lose that,' he whispered as he leaned closer and she caught the scent of that delicious aftershave he wore. He moved towards her until his lips were almost touching hers...

She pulled back. 'Whoa! Hang on a damned minute, Josh. I asked you about Katie and Caleb. I want the truth.'

He sighed and rubbed his hands over his face. 'Caleb is awesome. He's such a bright kid. I can't wait to get to know him even better.' He lowered his chin and brushed an imaginary thread off his trousers. 'Me and Katie... that was just a silly mistake. I think I got caught up in the past for a while. But... I've figured out that the past is the past for a reason. I realised on that day that you witnessed... well, me being a total prick, that it's *you*. You're the one I want, Zara. You're the one I care about.' He reached out and took her hand and sincerity shone from his eyes. 'It's *you* who I love.'

She gasped. He'd said it. He'd said the words she'd been desperate to hear for the longest time. Tears of confusion prickled at her eyes. What the hell did she do now? *People make mistakes,* she told herself. She'd made a huge one herself with Lachy... although, it hadn't felt that way at the time. But Lachy hadn't done all the things that Josh had done to welcome her back from her journey. *He* hadn't been the one to surprise her with a lavish hotel. And *he* hadn't been the one to tell her he loved her.

'Zara, *please*.' Josh squeezed her hand, bringing her back to the present. 'Please say you'll at least think about us. I can't imagine not having you in my life. You have to admit that, before my idiotic regression to seventeen, we were *so* good together.'

She shook her head. 'But, Josh—'

'Don't say no. Not now. Look, I'll leave. I'll give you space. I know that's what you need. And I'll do anything I can to make things right.' He stood from the sofa. 'Enjoy being here. Relax. I'll go and find somewhere else to stay but please say you'll think about what I've said, okay? Because I meant every word. I love you.'

She gazed up at him as he spoke. She wanted to believe his words. She wanted to trust him, but he would have to earn that trust again, if she decided to give him another chance. And it was still a big *if*.

'So will you think about it, Zara?' he asked again. His eyes were clouded with worry, sadness and regret.

She closed her eyes and thought back to some of the fun times they had shared. The laughs, the silly little fights followed by incredible make-up sex. But then the image of him kissing Katie appeared to assault her frontal lobe and she snapped her eyes open.

'I know I'll have to earn your trust again. And we can take things slow. I just... I can't lose you.' His voice cracked and his lip trembled. She'd never seen him like this and it knotted her insides.

She nodded as she wiped away the stray tears that had sneakily escaped her eyes. 'Look, Josh, I'll think about it. But know that I'm making no promises. You hurt me so much and it will take me a long time to recover from that. But I did love you. So, yes, I'll think about things and I'll see you back in London.'

A huge handsome grin spread across his face and he bent to place a chaste kiss on her lips. 'Thank you. Thank you so much. Now enjoy your last night in the country that you hate and then come home where you belong.'

He turned and left her sitting there wondering if she'd completely lost her mind.

* * *

Twenty minutes later she had drunk half the bottle of champagne and was sitting alone on the luxurious bed explaining to a panicked Noah why she had thanked him for a hotel room he hadn't booked. After that she had the same conversation with Shelley and Marco on speakerphone, seeing as Noah had contacted them amid worries Zara had been kidnapped by some pervy millionaire to be used as a sex slave. And she thought *she* had a vivid imagination.

Once she had finished her calls and everyone was calm again, she began to look through the photos she'd taken during her trip. She'd caught some sneaky, candid ones of Lachy and Bess and seeing them made her heart twinge with sadness all over again. She closed the album on her phone and flicked to the contacts list. Had she by some miracle saved Lachlan's number there without remembering? Or had he maybe input it for her? She scrolled but there was nothing. She frantically searched her possessions again but there was definitely no sign of his card.

She wondered if hearing his voice again might help in the huge decision she had to make about her future with Josh. But it was a moot point. She could scramble around the Internet, searching for him there. But what was the use? That one night had been amazing. Why not just keep it as a fond memory? File it away under the heading 'lovely things to think about when I'm low' and just move on.

She clicked back on the photos and looked at the one of Lachy crouching down on the beach with Bess that she had taken when he hadn't realised. His smile lit up his already handsome face. His hair was all tousled with the breeze coming in off the water. Behind him the distant hills arched towards a vivid blue sky. It was a picture of something close to perfection. She felt a pang she could only assimilate with homesickness, yet it wasn't for London. Realising she was being utterly ridiculous, she threw the phone down on the bed and flicked on the TV.

Hours later she awoke to see some bizarre film on the screen that she had no interest in, so she switched it off, stripped out of her clothes and climbed under the heavy, sumptuous duvet. But as soon as she drifted off she returned, in her dreams, to the little stone croft with the beautiful black and white dog and her handsome, kind human...

28

After breakfast Zara made her way into town and purchased some comfy clothes to travel home in. Noah was going to have a field day when he got her expenses bill. She changed in the fitting room with the permission of the shop staff and immediately felt better. Linen trousers and a T-shirt were better for travelling in than cycling leggings and a base layer. She also purchased some slip-on trainer shoes that she could easily take off on the train seeing as she was booked into first class and had more room to herself.

The railway station was buzzing with business people and holiday-makers alike as she boarded the train that would take her to Edinburgh where she would change for London Euston. She had already messaged her family and best friends over breakfast to let them know she would be home around seven that evening and expected the same group would be there to welcome her.

Home. That special four-letter word. She should be feeling excited and relieved about the journey, so why did she feel so deflated and sad instead? She took her seat in first class and pulled out the novel she had purchased in the station, knowing full well that she probably wouldn't be able to concentrate. It was going to be a very long day and she figured she might as well try to sleep at some point. Although, knowing how tired she was from all the fresh air, she doubted it would take much effort to drift off.

Various people embarked and disembarked the train during the journey and the scenery changed before her very eyes. Gone were the mountains and lochs and instead were industrial towns, factories and houses. Zara kept on checking her phone. No messages. Well, except for the silly ones she kept receiving from Shelley and Marco. Shelley was dress shopping for the reunion and Marco was joining in. In one of the messages he had offered to be her date for the school event as Shelley was taking Jake. She'd accepted on the proviso that he didn't wear a dress and upstage her – his legs were far better. And at least if it was awful she and Marco could just escape and go home.

The event was in three days and she hadn't a clue what she would wear *or* if she even wanted to go. The previous eleven days had been tough but enlightening in ways she'd simply never expected and the desire to brag about her wonderful life seemed less important. She was definitely changed now. She felt stronger; more empowered. She didn't need anyone's approval any more. Not after what she had achieved. But perhaps she'd feel differently when she arrived back home to her real life? She certainly hoped this bizarre heaviness inside her would lift.

Just before seven in the evening her final train pulled into Euston and she gathered her belongings. As she was walking towards the exit her phone pinged. Eagerly she took it out but once again her hopes were dashed.

It was Josh.

> Hi Zara. I hope you slept well in your fancy hotel room. There was nothing I wanted more than to climb into that bed with you and show you how much you mean to me and how sorry I am for what I put you through. But I'm trying hard to give you the space I know you need. I hope you're still thinking about us and remembering the good times. And I hope I can see you when you arrive home. Even if it's just for a drink and a chat. Remember I love you.
> J xx

She closed her eyes and remembered how emotional he had been when he had apologised. He wasn't the type of man to show such strong feelings, so he must have been sincere. She had a lot more thinking to do, but she knew she missed him like crazy even though he'd trampled on her heart and her trust.

* * *

Pretty soon all thoughts of Josh and Lachlan were shoved to the back of her mind as she was enveloped in a familiar group hug. Her parents, brothers and best friends were there just as she'd expected. For some reason being surrounded by so much love brought her emotions bubbling to the surface and she sobbed into whoever was closest.

'Aww, bless her. Poor darlin's all tired out, aren't you, petal?' her mum said as she kissed the side of her head.

Zara nodded. 'Yeah, I think that's it,' she lied. She knew very well what the problem was. And it wasn't to do with tiredness. Not really.

Marco grabbed her tight. 'I've missed you and your inability to make decent coffee. Oh, and I have a nice bottle of Pinot Noir breathing at home for us. Shells and Jake are coming too, aren't you, Shells?'

Shelley was next to grapple her into a bear hug. 'Don't listen to him. Your coffee's not that bad. And, yes, Jake will be there when we get to yours.' She pulled away and peered into Zara's eyes. 'That's if you're up for company? I know you've been stressed on that awful trip.'

Zara sniffed and smiled. 'It really hasn't been awful. And I'm happy to have company, it's fine. Although I may need to crash early. I'm bushed.'

She glanced up and spotted her dad waiting patiently to hug her. She walked over to him and he pulled her close. 'How you doing, Princess? Do I need to duff anyone up?'

She frowned. 'I'm fine, Dad. You definitely don't need to duff anyone up.'

He tilted her chin up. 'You're crying. But it's not tiredness. I know you. Some*thing* or some*one* has hurt you.'

She shook her head and buried her face in his shoulder. 'No, it's nothing like that, Dad. I think I really am just tired and glad to be home.'

He kissed the top of her head. 'Well, you let me know if someone needs sortin', okay?'

She adored her dad and the way he wanted to protect her. But he was the least violent person she knew, in spite of his assertions to the contrary. Once she had kissed her parents and brothers and said her goodbyes with a promise to come for Sunday lunch, she climbed into Shelley's car.

'Come on. Spill it, Zee. Something's up. You're different.' Shelley had always been perceptive so there was no point in making things up.

Zara shrugged. 'I think the trip just affected me more than I expected.'

Marco twisted in his seat. 'In what way? Was it that bad? What about the farmer you stayed with? Was he a minger?' He bombarded her with questions as if he was interrogating her.

Shelley huffed. 'Bloody hell, Marco, let the girl answer... But anyway, Zee, what *he* said.'

Zara couldn't help giggling at the familiar banter between her two friends. 'He was a *crofter*.' She smiled as she remembered Lachy correcting her. 'And it wasn't *bad* at all. In fact... it was quite... awesome.'

A stunned silence fell in the car. Her friends were clearly gobsmacked – which was a first. 'So you enjoyed getting a sore arse and being eaten alive by midges?'

She laughed again. 'I didn't actually get bitten much. Josh had recommended some really good repellent so—'

'Oh God, speaking of Josh. I was shocked when he came round looking for you. I told him you were going to be delayed because you'd been in an accident, which seemed to spur him on more. I still can't believe he booked that posh hotel and came up there though. He seems to want you back really badly, Zee.' Marco cringed as he told her.

Zara sighed. 'Hmm. He said as much. He told me he loves me.'

'What?' her friends yelled in unison.

'I know. All that time I waited for him to say the three little words and he waits until *after* he's bloody cheated.'

'Well, I hope you told him to take a running jump onto the Jubilee Line,' Marco huffed.

'Did he seem sincere, Zee?' Shelley asked.

Zara rested her head back. 'He seemed to be. But he hurt me so much and I won't play second fiddle to his ex.'

Marco grabbed her hand. 'Damn right you won't. You deserve someone who puts *you* first. Doesn't she, Shelley?'

'Bloody right she does,' Shelley concurred from the front.

* * *

They arrived back at Zara's home and her friends helped her inside with her minimal luggage. Jake arrived just as they were pouring wine and Marco got a few big bags of crisps from the kitchen. They all sat in the living room in their usual spots.

Zara glanced round the place. It was so strange to be back. It wasn't even that she had been away for a long time. In fact, she hadn't felt *this* strange when she had been away longer and further afield. Shelley was right. Something had changed in her.

Shelley snuggled up to Jake on the sofa as she asked, 'So, this guy who took you in after your near-death experience. What was he like?'

Zara envied Jake and Shelley's relationship. It was so natural. Effortless but in a good way. There was no pretence. Both could just be utterly themselves and the other loved them in spite of *and* because of that fact.

Zara smiled. 'His name was Lachlan. Lachy for short. He was sweet and kind. He made me laugh too. It was really good of him to take me in, considering the first time he met me I was uber nosy about his circumstances and the second I was illegally camped on his land.'

Marco sat up straight. 'You met him *twice* before the accident?'

'Yes. The accident was the third time I met him. He was wearing a kilt, too, Marco. You'd have loved that.'

Marco placed a hand over his heart. 'Did he have thick calves?'

Zara laughed and nodded and Marco pretended to pass out, and then from his reclined position on the floor he said, 'Is he gay, by any chance? Oh, please tell me he's gay and you got photos.'

At that point Zara's cheeks flamed and she tried to turn away and feign interest in something else. 'Was there much mail whilst I was away?'

Shelley leaned forward. 'Hang on a minute. You didn't answer Marco's question and *why* are you glowing like a beacon?'

Ugh, perceptive as always. 'He's not gay. There. Now you know,' Zara huffed.

Marco sat upright again. 'And *how*, pray tell, do you know that for a fact? Married to a woman, was he?' he asked with a tilt of his head.

'No. He wasn't married. If he was...' She decided to own her decision and straightened her spine. 'If he was married or with someone I wouldn't have slept with him.'

There was a sharp intake of breath so loud that Zara expected the room to implode. She waited for the fallout.

'So *that's* why you were so upset to be home. You really like him, don't you?' Shelley's voice was soft and filled with concern.

Zara smiled but her eyes began to sting as she nodded. Talking about Lachy made her realise just how much she missed him and, what was worse, that it was unlikely that she'd ever see him again. It wasn't as if she would bump into him on the high street. And she wouldn't be going to Scotland again any time soon.

Shelley and Marco leapt from their places and hugged her. She was sure it was just exhaustion and that she would feel better after sleeping in her own bed, but she let the tears flow and allowed her friends to do what they did best.

'Did he feel the same about you?' Marco asked.

Zara shrugged. 'Honestly, I don't know. I think it was maybe just a one-night thing. No strings attached. That's what *I* intended, anyway. I didn't *want* to feel anything. I just wanted to feel sexy and desirable. And he really made me feel all those things. But then it was over. And now... I don't know how I feel apart from sad and miserable. But why do I feel like this, for goodness' sake? I hardly know the man. And we didn't exactly get off to the best start. And I don't want to have a stupid long-distance relationship. But all I can think about is his smile and how good he was to me. How he made me feel. And his little house and Bess the dog.' She sobbed and her body shook even though she knew how crazy she must sound *and* look. She'd been with Josh for a year and hadn't cried so much when he'd cheated on her as she had over the man she knew even less and a place she'd never wanted to visit in the first place.

Once she had calmed down she wiped her face on the mountain of tissues that Jake had awkwardly passed over to her and she laughed. 'You know how there's jet lag? Is there such a thing as *train* lag? Or *bike* lag? Because I'm telling you right now, it exists. It should be acknowledged because it's the only possible reason for me feeling this way. And that's what I'm putting all this down to. This temporary lapse in sanity is simply *bike lag.*'

'Oh, well, that's easy! I know the cure for bike lag!' Marco chimed in.

Shelley rolled her eyes but grinned. 'This should be good.'

Marco disappeared into the kitchen and returned moments later with a massive box of chocolates and another bottle of wine. 'Tadaaaaa!'

29

Noah was overly gushy about her article when she presented it to him. 'Zara, this is sheer brilliance. You've not only captured the setting but the people. I can picture everything from the colour of the skies to the sound of the water lapping at the sand on the beaches. Just... *amazing.*'

Okay, Noah, calm yourself there. A bit over the top, aren't we? She smiled as he continued.

'You've really encapsulated the Highlands. If *this* doesn't sell thousands of magazines, then I honestly don't know what's wrong with the world.' He leaned in conspiratorially. 'I'd go so far as to say it's better than *anything* Dillon ever produced for the magazine. I mean, don't get me wrong, he was a good writer, but this... You've really captured the human aspect of the trip too. Your difficulties will be the reader's difficulties.'

She smiled and thanked him but inwardly rolled her eyes and screamed *Pah!* at him. His enthusiasm felt incredibly contrived and she seriously doubted that she had produced anything like the type of article Dillon would have, but she had given it her best shot.

'And don't even get me started on the images. I mean, to say they were taken on a phone is just... incredible! Look at the colours. The depth of field. You really have excelled yourself, Zara. And I'm not just saying that.' *Yeah, you probably are, but go ahead and polish my ego a little more; I'll let you after what you made me do.*

To be fair to Noah, the photos *had* reproduced well and she decided to leave it up to him to select which ones accompanied the piece. In truth she didn't want to look back and be reminded of what she had left behind.

'Right, Miss Bailey, I think you deserve to take the rest of this week off.' *One and a half days? Gee, thanks, boss.* 'Go and relax. The hard work is done and you should be proud of what you've achieved. You've overcome your fears and doubts and have produced such a wonderful piece. I'm so very proud of you.' *Ugh, pass me a bucket.*

She plastered on an expression of what she hoped appeared to be gratitude and not nausea. 'Thank you, Noah. I have a high-school reunion to attend at the weekend so I should really shop for something to wear, I suppose.'

'Well, you'll certainly have lots of wonderful stories to share now. These things are always pissing contests, in my experience. Who earns the most, who's the most successful, which couples actually stood the test of time.' He shivered. 'As much as I hate them, it really is a good way of getting one up on those who doubted we would ever amount to much, eh? I wouldn't think that there'll be anyone in that room quite so able to wow people as you, Zara.'

'Hmm. We'll see. See you Monday.'

She left the office and took the Tube into the city. People rushed all round her, heads down, no eye contact. She was jostled by ignorant civilians too hell-bent on continuing their conversations on mobile phones to be courteous enough to lower their elbows for a split second. By the time she reached her favourite shopping centre she was annoyed, sweaty and exhausted.

Instead of shopping she grabbed a take-out coffee from a concession stand and hopped on a train at the closest Tube station to head home. She hadn't the energy for shopping any more. *Surely there must be something in my wardrobe that will suffice? It's one bloody evening, for goodness' sake.*

As she sat on the Tube in an overground station her phone rang. It was her mum. 'Hi, sweetie, how are you settling in back at home?'

Zara laughed. 'Mum, I was only away a matter of days, remember? I'm fine. Home is home.'

'Oh yes, darling, I know, but it only takes a few days to change a person forever.' Her words were strangely insightful.

'True. But I'm fine, Mum. Honest. It's good to be home.'

'And you're definitely coming for lunch on Sunday, aren't you? It'll be so special.'

'I'll be there, Mum. I can't wait.'

'Great. Right, darling, I have to go. I'm helping Mrs Murton build a flat-pack bookcase. It'll be like the blind literally leading the blind, bless her.' Mrs Murton was their long-suffering neighbour who had put up with many years of footballs appearing in her garden, stereos being played too loudly and shouting matches between siblings. Now she was in her eighties her sight wasn't what it was and the Baileys had adopted her as a kind of grandmother figure.

'Sounds like fun. Watch out for your toes,' Zara told her with a laugh, remembering when they'd helped Mrs Murton move her bed into the living room and the result had been a broken toe for her mum.

'I think I'll borrow your brother's steel-toe-capped boots!
Bye, love!'

* * *

Marco cooked his delicious *pappardelle al salmone* for dinner on
Thursday evening and whilst he was at work on Friday Zara
spent the time reading through her novel and remembering
Lachy's reaction to her prose. Maybe he was right and she
should actually submit it somewhere and see what happened?
She spent a couple of hours preparing a submission letter to go
with her manuscript. She still wasn't sure she would be brave
enough to send it, but it felt good to know that the book was
complete and that she had achieved something pretty fantastic
all for herself.

She could now visualise the jacket of the novel too. An
image of a rugged setting much like the places she had visited
in the Highlands, with the heroine of the story standing alone
and gazing longingly off into the distance. *How wonderful it
would be to realise that dream.* For some reason, since her return
from the North Coast 500 trip Zara's passion for writing had
increased tenfold. Many more story ideas had manifested
themselves and she now had notes scribbled on every possible
blank page she came across. It was as if someone had released a
dam in her mind and the words were a deluge that had to
escape. Her heart raced as she typed, her fingers struggling to
keep up.

She kept the keyring Lachy had given her close by and
smiled every time she caught sight of it in her peripheral vision.
More ideas flowed. A story of a man and woman who met for a
brief moment in time but shared something beautiful that they
would cling to forever.

A knock on the door snapped her from her writing frenzy and she hoped to goodness it wasn't anyone important. Her hair was tied in a messy bun and she wore yoga pants and a scruffy old Kiss T-shirt that used to belong to her dad.

She pulled open the door to see a huge bouquet of flowers hiding the face of the delivery man.

Josh peeped out from behind the colourful spray. 'Hi, gorgeous.'

'Josh? You didn't message to say you were coming.' She folded her arms across her braless chest.

'You look as beautiful as ever, don't worry. I wasn't even sure you'd be in but seeing as I have the day off, I thought I'd chance it. I brought coffee from your favourite place too. Caramel Machiatto.' He held out a tray with two large, lidded paper cups.

'You'd better come in.'

He followed her into the living room and sat down. 'Here, take this and put them in some water, eh?' he instructed. 'What have you been up to?'

She took the flowers and walked over to the kitchen. 'Oh, nothing much. A bit of writing.'

'So did you finally finish your novel?'

'Yes, yes, I did. Turns out the Highlands were quite inspirational.'

'Is this it open on your laptop?' he asked as he crossed to the dining table.

She walked over and closed the lid so he couldn't pry. 'Yes. Look, I'm going to go and change my top,' she told him. 'I won't be a minute.' Once inside the safety of her room she rested her head back against the door. There had been a time that having him in her apartment meant steamy sex, butterflies and passion; but now she wasn't sure how she felt. She slipped on her bra and a clean, newer T-shirt and walked back through to where he sat sipping his coffee.

'Why are you here, Josh?'

'I wanted to see you. To see if you'd had any more thoughts about us.'

She heaved a sigh. 'You said you'd give me space.'

He nodded and cringed. 'I did say that, didn't I? Shit. Zara, I'm sorry. But I miss you. So, so much. I want to be able to hold you and kiss you again. If you'd just let me—'

She held up her hands. 'Look, the flowers are beautiful. And I appreciate the coffee, but I need time to think. And I need to not see you as I'm doing that. You blur the edges, Josh. You confuse me.'

He stood and walked to stand only inches in front of her. 'I understand. I really do.' He slipped his hand into her hair. 'And I wish I could turn back the clock and undo what I did. But please know that I would do anything to change things. Anything.' He lowered his face and brushed his lips against hers; that familiar feeling of him washing over her as she closed her eyes and let the kiss happen.

Suddenly he stopped and pulled away. 'Sorry. God, I'm an idiot. I'll go. And I'll be waiting, Zara. You can count on that.'

He walked away and out of the apartment, leaving her standing there feeling even more confused than ever. Alone with space to think again, Zara sat back at the laptop and began to type.

* * *

On his return from work Marco brought her coffee and snacks. He even brought dinner to her from the kitchen. He knew better than to read over her shoulder. Instead he sustained her energy by providing the things she was unwilling to break off for. It was exhilarating.

She felt free and she felt fine.

That night Marco played 'Delilah' by Florence and the Machine on his phone with the little portable speaker plugged in and they danced round the apartment, arms flailing and wide, wild smiles on their faces. Marco in his boxers and Zara in her pyjamas. But the whole time, in her mind, Lachy was dancing with her too.

30

The day of the reunion rolled round and, in light of her non-existent shopping trip, Zara raided her wardrobe for something to wear. She settled on a plum-coloured dress and matching shoes that she had purchased for a media awards ceremony she had attended with Noah a couple of years before.

Marco offered to be, not just her date, but her pretend *boyfriend* for the night if she wanted to show off her hunky partner. 'I mean, I don't really *look* gay as such so no one would know.'

She smiled and kissed his cheek. 'No, but you *do* have a roving eye. So I'm thinking we just say we're friends and then you can be free to flirt with whomever you choose. How's that?'

He sulked. 'But I wanted to pretend to be straight for a night. It'd be a giggle.'

She snorted. 'I can assure you it's not even *close* to being a giggle for me right now.'

He rested his arm loosely round her shoulders and stared at her reflection in the mirror as she applied make-up. 'Ah, honey,

I do feel for you. Maybe you should just bite the bullet and forgive him?'

She scowled at her best friend. 'Since when are you all for forgiving the man who cheated on me?'

He shrugged. 'Since I've seen how sad you are now that you're back home. I don't want you running off back to the Highlands to that farmer, so Josh is a safer option.' He grinned.

She shook her head vehemently. 'Running off to Lachy? Not a chance. I've had enough of bloody rejection for one year, thank you very much. I'll stick to being melancholy and liking him from a safe distance.'

Marco sighed. 'I suppose six hundred and fifty miles could be classed as a safe distance.'

There was a knock on the main door and Shelley shouted through from the hallway after letting herself in. 'Hey, you guys! We're here. We brought wine to start the night off properly. The cab will be here in twenty minutes so get a move on!'

Zara and Marco walked through to the kitchen to find Shelley and Jake chatting there. The wine was already poured.

'I want to make a toast,' Shelley announced. 'Here's to being yourself and thinking fuck 'em all.' She held her glass aloft.

The others chimed in unison with, 'Fuck 'em all!'

* * *

Being in a room full of people she vaguely recognised was bizarre to say the least. She perused the high-school photo board and she wore the obligatory name badge. She stood against the wall as Marco went off to chat to someone across the room who had been making eyes at him since they arrived.

Before giving him permission to abandon her she had

laughed. 'It took you all of five minutes to prove my point, Marco.'

Shelley had left Jake at the bar and arrived moments later by Zara's side carrying a glass of punch. 'Look at you, you're being all-wallflower when you should be all-centrepiece.'

'Ooh, very profound. Ugh, this is just mind-bogglingly boring, Shells. I'd rather be at the pub with you, Marco and Jake.'

'Nope. Come on. Time to get your boast on. Stephanie Watson is over there. Remember her?'

'The gorgeous one that all the boys adored but who was a total bitch?'

'Yup. She's all wrinkly from too much sun and looks a bit like a leather handbag. She runs a hotel in Spain with her husband and can't seem to stop bragging about it. Come and say hello.' Shelley winked, grabbed her wrist and dragged her across the room.

'Stephanie, look who I found! It's Zara Bailey!' Shelley announced as they arrived before a rather orange-faced woman who looked ten years their senior.

'Zara! It's so lovely to see you! You look... erm... lovely,' Stephanie said as she eyed her up and down with disdain. She had always hated Zara at school and it appeared time had changed nothing.

'Hi, Stephanie. You're looking *well*. How are you?'

'Oh, not too bad. Well, considering I'm rushed off my feet running a very successful boutique hotel in Spain. I don't get much time for myself, you know how it is.' She flicked her indubitably bleached blonde hair over her shoulder.

Shelley leaned closer. 'Ooh, it's a *boutique* hotel now. It was *just* a hotel before you joined the conversation,' she whispered discreetly. 'A teensy bit threatened, me thinks.'

Zara smiled and nodded. 'That sounds lovely, Stephanie.'

'Oh, it is. Francis, my husband, he's a lot older than me, you know, but he's very business savvy. But all the wealthy ones are, aren't they? He calls me his young strumpet.' She giggled.

'Well, there's something to be proud of,' Shelley whispered again.

'So, what is it that *you* do now, Zara?' Stephanie asked as she glanced round the room, clearly not interested in the answer.

'I'm a journalist with a travel magazine.'

'Mmm hmm,' Stephanie mumbled.

Before Zara could speak Shelley interrupted, 'Yes, she travels all round the world visiting luxury hotels and writing articles in *The Bohemian* for—'

Stephanie was suddenly all ears. 'Ooh! You mean a *proper* journalist? Not some crappy rag? Oooh, you should come and do an article on *Pasión del Castillo!*' She patted her hair. 'We run a very luxurious establishment. Perfect for your magazine, what was it again – *The Behemoth?*' She grinned maniacally.

Zara and Shelley exchanged amused glances. '*The Bohemian.* I'll mention your hotel to my editor. Although we're incredibly busy doing cruises and the hotels around the Red Sea just now.'

Stephanie turned on the charm. 'Yes, but you'd do an article about a dear friend's luxury hotel, wouldn't you?'

Clearly at the end of her bullshit tether, Shelley butted in again. 'Stephanie, you hated *both* of us at school. In fact, I distinctly remember it being *you* who started the whole "Jelly Bean and Granny Bailey" thing.'

Stephanie's cheeks were probably flushed bright pink, but it was hard to tell under the oak-coloured-fence stain. 'Oh, I don't think that was me, love. I think it was David Bilton. Yeah, I remember *him* saying it first. You probably just overheard me telling people how mean it was that they called you those names.'

Shelley had had a fair bit to drink by this point and she evidently wasn't in the mood for such bollocks. She turned to Zara and exclaimed, 'Did she really just do that? She did, didn't she? She just chucked her childhood sweetheart under the bus!' Then her focus was returned to the vision of orange before them. 'Stephanie, there's as much chance of you being in *The Bohemian* as there is of Meghan and Prince Harry staying at your hotel. Come on, Zee. Let's go get another drink.'

As they walked away Zara felt a smidge of guilt. 'That was a bit harsh, wasn't it?'

'Pfft! You should have heard her earlier. She was being a total bitch about the glasses you used to wear and even worse about your clothes until I told her you were still my best friend and that you were here this evening.'

'Oh. Charming.'

Shelley gasped. 'Oh God, I think Marco has well and truly pulled.'

Zara turned in the direction Shelley was looking to find Marco snogging Toby Hunt just outside the fire doors.

'I remember having a massive crush on Toby. We had History together. He was so good-looking and shy,' Shelley said dreamily.

'Not so shy any more!' Zara said and they giggled.

As they wandered towards the bar she recognised more faces and overheard conversations in which cars, jobs and families were mentioned. Everywhere she turned was the one-upmanship-slash-pissing contests both Lachy and Noah had commented on prior to the event. She couldn't be bothered any more. She was ready to leave.

'Oh, hi! Zara, isn't it?' a tall, handsome man asked as Shelley went to find Jake.

She scrunched her brow. 'Yes, but I'm so sorry, I don't remember—'

He held out his hand. 'Yeah, I do look different now. I'm Patrick O'Shea. We had English together. I was rather over-weight and a bit geeky. You were one of the only kids who acknowledged me back then. I'm glad I've bumped into you. Gives me a chance to say thank you for making school less shitty.'

She shook his hand as the original Patrick – nicknamed Fatrick by the delightful Stephanie Watsons of the school – sprang to mind. 'Oh, my word! It *is* you. You look incredible. How are you? What have you been up to?'

He shrugged and a genuinely warm smile spread across his slender, sculpted face. 'Well, I actually moved away quite a while ago. I own a couple of bike-hire shops in Inverness with my partner, Sophie. I say partner, but we're getting married later this year.'

She inhaled sharply. 'Oh God, you're *kidding*? It's not Highland Trax, is it? Like the one on Church Street in Inverness?'

He frowned but his smile remained in place. 'It is. How do you know?'

She groaned and covered her eyes. Peeping through her fingers, she admitted, 'I don't believe this. I've just returned from doing the North Coast 500 and the bike my magazine hired was from your shop.'

His eyes widened and he laughed. 'Oh, *my* word! You're not the journalist from *The Bohemian* who had a run-in with a trac-tor, are you?'

She cringed and nodded. 'I'm *so* sorry but, yes, that was me.'

'Oh, shit! Are you okay though? You didn't sustain any permanent damage, did you?'

'Only to your bike.' She felt terrible.

'Hey, please don't worry. We were all really concerned when we heard. I was away visiting suppliers when I was informed. I didn't think for a minute it would be someone I knew!'

'Ugh, well, now you know who to invoice for the damage.'

He laughed again. 'I'll do no such thing. I'm just relieved that you're okay. I'm so glad I've seen you. I wasn't even going to come tonight. Not my kind of thing, seeing as everyone at school hated me and the feeling was *completely* mutual, current company excepted, of course. So how was the NC500? It's incredible, isn't it? We've cycled it a few times now.'

She sighed and a wistful feeling took over her. 'It is. Absolutely wonderful. The strange thing was I did it under duress. It really wasn't my kind of thing. But now... I really miss the fresh air and the stunning views.'

He raised his eyebrows. 'It's got you, hasn't it? Honestly, the Highlands get under your skin. There's something that pulls you back, just you wait and see. It really does stay with you.'

She nodded. 'It certainly does. But I fell in love with it so fast, which I absolutely wasn't expecting. So many incredible places and vistas.'

'Yes, and the beaches. Seriously, there's no need to go abroad when you've got stretches of clean sand with hardly anyone to bother you.'

She remembered that feeling of standing on the sand during her trip and how she had thought exactly the same thing. 'I wasn't sure I'd manage it at first. Some of the hills are killers. And I'm not the best cyclist in the world. I'm not a regular at the gym or anything so I was dreading it.'

'You're not alone there. Exercise of any kind was hell for me when I was a kid. When I met Sophie at university in the High-lands and it turned out she was a real outdoorsy kind I decided to make some changes. We were friends for ages first, but things just blossomed. And that was before I lost all the weight. I've got the Highlands to thank for that. The place found a little space in my heart and filled it. I adore it. The fact that Sophie's Scottish and mad about the Highlands too just ices the cake really.'

'Why did you go to uni all the way up there?'

He chuckled. 'Oh, I wanted to get as far away from London as I could without going abroad. My memories of school weren't exactly happy ones.'

'So why did you decide to come here tonight?' she asked with journalistic intrigue.

'In all honesty, I wanted to come and show them all I've made something of myself but when I arrived and saw everyone again as adults the threat was gone. The need to prove myself was gone too. They're not doing the kind of things I'm doing, but that doesn't mean they're better or worse than me. Just different. And I accept that even if *they* can't. I'm happy with my life and I don't need anything from this lot to make that so. How about you?'

She grinned. 'Exactly the same.' She pondered for a moment. 'What you said about the Highlands filling a space in your heart, I totally get that.'

'Well, maybe you'll relocate too someday. What's stopping you?'

She huffed through puffed cheeks. 'The fear of failing. Of not being able to do what I love. Of being alone, I guess.'

'What do you want to do with your life? Are you happy being a journalist?'

She nodded. 'Oh yes. I love my job. But... I think maybe

travelling so much is making it difficult for me to put down proper roots. And I can't help feeling that I'm missing something.'

'You've the perfect job to be freelance, you know. There are lots of newspapers and magazines where staff can work remotely.' He had a good point.

'I suppose so. And that would be really great...'

He tilted his head. 'I sense a "but".'

'Hmm... you see, what I really want to do is... Ugh, it'll sound so far-fetched and stupid.'

He grinned. 'More stupid than a fat kid ending up owning a bike shop and cycling round the Highlands for fun?'

She smiled and took a deep breath. 'Okay... okay... I want to be a novelist. I want to see my books on shelves in shops. I want to tell my own stories, not just those belonging to other people. I've actually written a book already, in my limited spare time, but I'd love to write more.' She couldn't believe she had so readily admitted it aloud to someone she hadn't seen for years.

His eyes widened and he pursed his lips. 'I'm impressed. You should and could totally do that. Rent a little croft somewhere with good Internet. Get a dog. Be a freelance journalist and in your spare time write those bestsellers.'

'You make it sound so easy.'

His expression changed to one of serious sincerity. 'Zara. You have *one* life. Make it so that you're free to be the thing you want to be more than anything. You might not end up a millionaire, but you'll certainly be happy. And that's what life's all about, isn't it? Being happy.'

He was right on so many points but there was no way she could simply up and leave everything and everyone. And not on a whim like this. Not after one trip to the Highlands. It was crazy to even consider it... wasn't it?

Patrick held out a business card. 'Here, my number and my email are on there. If you decide to visit Scotland again you should come and stay with us. I'll get Sophie to work on you. You'll be packing London in for good in no time.'

She reached up to hug him. 'Thank you, Patrick. I'm so glad I've seen you. It's a small world, eh?'

'It sure is. Now go and fight for your ultimate dream. It's totally doable. Time to make some changes.' He glanced round the room. 'Well, I think I'm done with this place. Time to move on for good, I reckon. So long, Zara.'

Patrick hugged her again and she watched as he walked towards the door without so much as a backward glance at what was, to all intents and purposes, his past.

31

The next morning Zara awoke with a thick pounding head to find a pint of water and two headache pills on her bedside table. There was also a note from Marco.

> *Zara Bear,*
>
> *Thought you might need these. We drank a LOT when we got home.*
>
> *I've gone to meet gorgeous Toby for coffee. Wish me luck. Enjoy lunch at your folks.*
>
> *Love you,*
>
> *M x*

She dragged herself out of bed, took the pills and went to shower. The marching band in her head was slowly being replaced with words that echoed Patrick's from the night before about changes. Although as her earworm from her Highland travels was back the words came in the form of 'Changes', the David Bowie song, another of her dad's favourites, and the lyrics she had known since she was a girl now resonated deep within her.

* * *

The front door to her parents' was locked when she arrived later on that day. It was rare but not unheard of, thanks to a number of opportunistic burglaries in the area. She pressed the doorbell button and could just make out the opening bars of 'God Save the Queen' as it alerted the occupants to her arrival.

Her younger brother, Will, opened the door and before actually greeting her he shouted over his shoulder at the top of his lungs, 'Mu-u-u-um! It's her! She's he-e-e-ere!' He then turned to her with a grin and said, 'Better come in, sis.'

As she stepped into the living room she almost jumped out of her skin as party poppers exploded and The Proclaimers' 'I'm Gonna Be (500 Miles)' blared at full volume from her dad's stereo system.

Her mum, dad, brothers, Shelley, Jake, Marco and even poor Toby sang to her at the top of their voices with big cheesy grins in place, but every time the word 'walk' came up they changed it to 'ride'. Zara stood there watching and laughing at the scene before her as the group jumped up and down singing in terrible fake Scottish accents.

'What the heck are you doing, you barmy bunch?' she shouted over the music.

Her dad, out of breath, walked over to her side and hugged her with one arm. 'We wanted you to have a proper homecoming, sweetheart. But we thought we'd wait 'til you'd caught your breath a bit.'

She beamed at her family and friends. 'Well, this is brilliant. *Ridiculous*, but brilliant.'

'We got you gifts too!' her mum announced, still dancing.

'Aw, you guys didn't have to go to so much trouble, you know. It was only a work trip.'

'Yeah, but we know how much you were dreading it, so we planned this for when you got back.'

The song ended and was soon followed by Queen's 'Bicycle Race'. Her mum informed her, 'Will and Andy made the track list for you on Spotify. They're all biker tunes. "King of the Road", "Born to Be Wild", "Bat Out of Hell", and stuff like that. Genius, eh?'

Zara laughed, her shoulders shaking and tears forming. 'You do remember it was a bicycle, not a motorbike, don't you?'

Andy huffed. 'Yeah, but you try finding songs about cycling. All we got was Queen, which is okay, and bloody Mungo Jerry. It's not exactly rock and roll, is it? So we had to use a bit of artistic licence.'

She hugged him. 'Well, I absolutely love it. Thank you so much.'

'Anyway, love; instead of a Sunday roast we've done a buffet. I hope that's okay?'

'Ooh, is the food biker themed too?'

Her mum rolled her eyes. 'Oh, good Lord, no. Even I have limits, love.' She laughed.

'Well, that'll be perfect, Mum, thank you.'

Her parents went to sort out the food and she was joined by Shelley, Marco and their respective partners. 'We clubbed together and got you something.' Marco handed her an envelope.

She opened it and pulled out a voucher for a weekend at a spa hotel of her choice. Shelley winked at her. 'There's one in the Highlands. You know, in case you fancied a return trip.'

Marco told her, 'The voucher's good for a year so there's no rush.'

Zara hugged them both. 'That's so sweet of you. Thank you. But I think I might use it a bit closer to home if you don't mind.'

'Up to you,' Marco said, 'but the Highland retreat is the one with the best reviews.' He grinned.

'I'll bear it in mind.'

'I bought you a prezzie too,' Will said as he handed her a long, wrapped, rectangular gift.

Once again, she ripped off the paper and pulled out the surprise. 'Haemorrhoid cream? Seriously?'

Will burst out laughing. 'Well, I heard that those thin bike saddles can take a bit of recovering from so I thought I'd help.'

She whacked him playfully on the arm. 'Trust you.'

'Here you go, darlin', we got you something as well.' Her dad handed her a large box. She sat on the floor, removed the lid and inside, wrapped in tissue paper, were lots of NC500 branded things. Coasters, postcards, a wallet and a T-shirt that said '*I cycled the NC500*' and a beautiful, framed map of the route.

Seeing the route again made tears sting her eyes. And that strange feeling of something like homesickness bubbled up again.

* * *

Lachy

Time was passing slowly in Zara's absence and whilst in the past this had never been a bad thing, now it was just a sad reminder of his loneliness. He had been out tending to the sheep and then to a local pub with Tosh and the rest of the buffoons he went to school with and as always Bess had dutifully sat by his side. She'd seemed sad too since Zara had gone.

The poor little collie really had adored her. He wasn't afraid to admit to himself that he'd felt the same. He bid his friends goodnight and walked back to the croft.

The answering machine light was flashing when he walked into the kitchen and his stomach lurched. He rarely got messages and he hoped, desperately, that it was from Zara. Just to hear her voice again...

He hit play: *'Lachlan, darling, it's me, Saskia. Where on earth are you at this hour of the night? Surely there can't be much to do up there in the middle of nowhere. Anyway, it's Mummy and Daddy's golden wedding anniversary and there's going to be a huge party. I haven't told them we've been taking a break and I need you to come. Mummy will be inconsolable if she thinks my plans of marriage aren't going ahead. And whilst we're on that subject, I've decided we can tell everyone the engagement is on. We can discuss the details when I see you. And I've been thinking... you can keep the little farm. But let's get someone in to run it so you can come home to your real job. Anyway. The party is at Mummy and Daddy's house. On the twelfth. I'll expect you on the eleventh and wear your tux, darling. You always look so delicious in your tux.'*

He slumped onto the chair at the table that Zara had favoured. Great. Saskia. *That's all I bloody need. How the hell do I get out of that?*

He checked his phone and realised it was far too late to call her back, so he'd try and think of an excuse and ring her when he was sober. Bess climbed onto her bed and Lachy poured some stale coffee from the jug that had been left warming. He wondered what Zara was doing now. He'd hoped she would at least text him to say she had arrived home safe, but she hadn't. He'd toyed with the idea of contacting the bike shop, but decided it would be too weird to explain the reasons for his call.

He thought about her passion for writing and the range of

emotions she had evoked from him when he had read her book. He wondered if she had dared to submit it to any literary agents yet. He could have offered help on that score, but knew she was too damned stubborn and in denial about her talent to accept it. So, of course, he had refrained.

He sighed and glanced over at Bess where she lay, head resting on her paws. 'Well, we're a gleeful pair, eh, lass? I'm guessing you miss her as much as I do. Why didn't we make an actual date to see her again? Why didn't we at least just ask her, eh? I knew that sleeping with her would be a bloody mistake. I knew I was bloody falling from the moment she yelled at me outside her tent.'

Bess walked over and sat before him. She nudged his hand with her head and he ran his fingers through her fur. 'And now I've got to go and play happy families with Cruella de Vil. Lucky me, eh?' He crouched down to make eye contact with his canine companion. 'Now, I know you don't like her. I remember you peeing on her designer shoes when she came to visit. But I promise you, I'll go to the party as a favour to an old friend and, after it's done, I'll tell her in no uncertain terms that I'm not getting back together with her. We were over a long time ago and I just don't love her. I don't think I ever did. And more to the point I don't think she ever loved me either. But I'll do this one last favour for her. And then that's it. You have my word, Bess.'

As if she understood completely, the dog licked his chin and gave him her paw.

* * *

Three weeks passed and life was almost back to normal for Zara. She had been spending more and more time with Josh and he'd been doing his best to make amends for his transgressions. There had been meals to fancy restaurants, nights out at the theatre and he'd cooked for her at her place, seeing as she refused to set foot in his again. He had even hinted at the idea they could move in together somewhere totally new. She was still thinking things through, but he was wearing her down. The only thing they hadn't done was sleep together. That prospect was taking a little more getting used to.

Although, Zara still couldn't dismiss the feeling that something was missing from her life. David Bowie's lyrics had taken up residence in her mind and the keyring that Lachy bought seemed to catch her eye often. Her next assignment was arranged and soon she would be leaving for the Maldives to check out *more* high-class honeymoon locations. The thought didn't grab her with eager enthusiasm as it would have once done, but she was looking forward to the distraction, nonetheless.

Marco had been seeing a lot of Toby and had announced at the pub the night before that they had agreed to be exclusive. It was good to see him happy with someone who epitomised a decent human being for once. Some of his former lovers had left a lot to be desired in that area. He had been messed about so much, leaving him with trust issues that had manifested in many one-night stands. She hoped this meant that things had changed for him.

London was still manic by its very nature but, instead of the fact exciting her as it always had in the past, she longed for the fresh air and open spaces of the Highlands. She had looked into hiring a motor home and travelling the North Coast 500 route again, but this time doing it in more luxurious accommodation. Her bid to get Noah to agree to her writing about the route from the opposite perspective to the original piece had fallen on deaf ears. Noah insisted he would *never* send her to Scotland again. It was his promise, much to her dismay.

Lachy haunted her dreams and her thoughts. What was he doing? How was Bess? Why hadn't he been in touch? It took her a while to realise that she had never actually given him her contact details. She'd lost his business card and all he had was the name of the magazine she was employed by, and he didn't seem the type to just turn up there. But a letter would have been nice. She had hoped, stupidly, that he missed her and might want to at least be friends.

The coming weekend had given her something to focus on. Her friends had rented a large seafront house at Ramsgate and they were leaving Friday morning and returning Monday evening. A long weekend and some fresh, sea air were just what the doctor ordered. The only downside was the fact that she was the only one not taking a significant other. Josh had been keen to go along but Zara wasn't quite ready to take that next step yet. The bags were packed, Marco and Toby had loaded Jake's car – it was the biggest – and Shelley was sitting on Zara's bed waiting for her to finish applying her make-up.

'Zara! Post!' Marco shouted from the hallway. 'Looks important.' He walked into the room and handed over the envelope. The return address was one in Inverness and her heart skipped a beat as she ripped it open.

'What is it? Is it from Farmer Hot Kilt?' Shelley asked with a lascivious grin.

'Give her a bloody chance, Shells,' Marco insisted, but then continued with, 'Is it though?'

Confusion washed over Zara as she read the words on the page. Nothing was sinking in. It must be a mistake. It couldn't be real.

'Zee, you've gone ever so pale. What's wrong?' Shelley

asked, her voice filled with concern as she moved towards the edge of the bed.

'I... erm... It's...' She shook her head as she handed the letter to Shelley.

Shelley cleared her throat. '"Dear Miss Bailey, we are delighted to inform you that your novel *New Beginnings* has been shortlisted in the Best Unpublished Newcomer category of the Original Fiction Association Literature Awards. This year the awards are to be hosted in Inverness. As you may already be aware, the first prize in this category is a four-book publishing deal and a twenty-thousand-pounds advance. The awards ceremony will be held at the Kingsman Hotel and Conference Centre, Inverness; further details are noted on the enclosed invite, and we look forward to seeing you there. Please confirm your attendance and guests to my secretary at the above address. Yours sincerely, Dominic McAllen. Chairman."' Shelley's voice became exponentially louder and higher pitched as she read.

'Fucking hell, Zee! You're going to be a famous author!' Marco and Shelley jumped round the room squealing as Toby and Jake looked on in bemusement.

Zara still couldn't understand it. How had this happened?

'I didn't realise you'd actually sent your book off anywhere! You bloody dark horse,' Shelley said as she hugged Zara tightly. 'I'm so proud of you. Still pissed off that you wouldn't let me read it. But so proud!'

'But... guys, I *didn't* send it off anywhere. I wrote a submission letter to accompany it but that was as far as I got. I hadn't even compiled a list of who I'd send it *to*, never mind being so presumptuous as to submit it to a competition!' She held her arms out and let them flop to her sides. 'How the hell has this happened?' She narrowed her gaze and pointed a finger back and forth between her two best friends. 'Did you—?'

'God, no!'

'Absolutely bloody not!'

They spoke in unison and wore an almost identical, incredulous expression.

Shelley looked to Marco and then back to Zara. 'I for one wouldn't invade your privacy that way, Zara. And I'm sure Marco's the same.'

Marco nodded emphatically. 'Absolutely. And anyway, I wouldn't want to send it off before reading it in case it's crap.' The whole room seemed to gasp simultaneously and Marco waved his hand dismissively. 'I don't mean it *is* crap, for fuck's sake. I simply mean that I love you too much to set you up for a fall like that.' He rested his balled fist on his hip. 'And whilst we're on the subject, I'm still mad at you for letting Hunky McKilt Pants read the damned thing before me.'

Shelley's eyes widened. 'Oooh! That's it! It's *him*. It's Kilty McSporran! He read it without your permission once – who's to say he wouldn't send it off without your permission too?'

Zara yelled, 'Would you two please *stop* with the offensive, stereotypical nicknames? After what we all went through at school, I honestly thought you'd both know better. And *no*, I don't think Lachy would do such a thing. Not after the reaction I had the first time he read the bloody book.'

The room fell silent and the group stood there, tilted heads and knowing looks on their faces.

'Wait, you all think it was Lachy? Seriously?'

Marco shrugged. 'Well, you did sleep with him very quickly so maybe he thought you'd moved to the next level?'

Zara scoffed. 'What the hell are you going on about, Marco? Is there an "I've shagged you so now I can send your manuscript off to competitions willy-nilly without your knowledge" level? Eh?'

Marco folded his arms across his chest sulkily. 'I was just saying.'

'The thing is, Zee, how well did you know him *really*?' Shelley asked softly.

Images of a naked, delicious Lachy gazing at her from his side of the bed sprang to her frontal lobe and she almost lost herself for a moment. Realising she hadn't answered her friend's question, she shook her head to try and eradicate the memories. 'I think I knew him well enough to not suspect him of doing this behind my back.'

Marco gasped and everyone turned to face him, waiting for the next gem of wisdom to fall from his lips. 'Did Josh know about the book?'

Zara thought back to one of their post-coital conversations. 'Yes. I mean, we talked about our hopes and dreams and stuff like that after he'd found my pink memory stick on my keyring. He asked what it was and I told him it was my book. And before you ask, no, I didn't let him read it. I just said that one day I dreamed of sitting somewhere with a lovely view and being free to be a fiction writer.' The group shared those knowing looks again and Zara shrugged. 'But why would he do it?' A light bulb flicked on in her mind. 'Unless...'

'Unless what?' Shelley asked.

'He's been doing everything in his power to make me take him back properly. He's been so sweet and thoughtful. Maybe this is his way of helping me get my dream come true?' She placed her hand over her heart as she realised it was actually a wonderful thing he'd done.

Marco scoffed. 'Well, I wouldn't bloody put it past him personally. Look what he did in Scotland with the posh hotel.

And he could've copied the memory stick without you realising when he called round to see you or something. I mean, it's always with you and you said yourself that he'd noticed it.'

The more she thought about it, the more confused Zara became. 'I think I'll message him. I think it's very kind but it's not good enough for awards and competitions. I'll have to withdraw it.'

Marco snatched the letter from Shelley's grasp and waved it in Zara's face. 'Not good enough? Look what's happened. You've been shortlisted in the Original Fiction Association Lit Awards, Zee. It's only one of the most prestigious awards in the UK for writers. It's obviously a bloody good book so don't be ridiculous. You can't withdraw it now. He may have just done you a huge favour.'

Marco was right, but Zara was too mixed up to admit it. She huffed like a sulky teenager and walked out of the room to retrieve her phone from its charging point in the lounge. At the very least she had to know who had done it.

32

Zara stared at her phone as if doing so would bring forth answers. When it didn't, she fired off a text to Josh.

> Hi Josh. Quick question. And please be honest. Did you happen to steal my novel and submit it to a competition on my behalf?

No reply came immediately as she had hoped it would, but she had been quite terse in her message so perhaps he thought she was angry with him. She sent a follow-on message.

> Just so you know, I'm not angry. I'm just a bit shocked. If it was you then thank you. That was a really sweet thing to do. I can't believe it's been shortlisted. I'll speak to you when I get home from Ramsgate. Maybe we could celebrate?

When they arrived at Ramsgate the sun was shining and there was only a light smattering of fluffy cloud overhead. There was a distinct chill to the air, however, that floated on the sea breeze and caused Zara to shiver. Summer would soon be over and she would be back to winter coats and knee boots. But today at least she had braved her summer attire and was planning on making the most of the beautiful day regardless of the slightly lower temperature.

The house was beautiful. Situated in the middle of a Georgian terrace, it had spectacular sea views and was within walking distance of everything the friends would need to make this a weekend to remember. Each bedroom had a king-sized bed and Zara joked that, unlike the others and their partners, *she* would be able to sleep diagonally across hers.

The décor in each room was light and fresh and the kitchen was kitted out with every gadget imaginable. Marco insisted on making use of one such piece of equipment – fresh Italian coffee for everyone – and of course he received no arguments.

As the group of friends sat in the small, terraced garden enjoying their coffee Zara's phone pinged.

> Hi Zara. I can't believe you guessed so easily. It was supposed to be a secret. I'm so excited that you were shortlisted but I had no doubt in my mind. Maybe now you'll see how much I really love you and that all I want is your happiness. I'd be honoured to escort you to the awards ceremony if you'll have me. Much love J xx

Zara smiled as she read the words over again. He really meant it when he said he'd do anything to win her back. Maybe she had been too hard on him. Maybe she could at least try to start trusting him again. And maybe even open her heart to him again. He hadn't mentioned Katie, or Caleb for that matter, and she knew he was trying hard to leave them out of any conversation that took place between them. She didn't want him to be unable to speak about his son and she'd need to let him know that. She resolved to contact him and maybe even go to his flat when she returned from the weekend away.

The friends spent a lovely afternoon walking on the beach and playing in the amusement arcades. It turned out Jake was a bit of a whizz on the penny falls and he bought them all ice cream with his winnings.

'The look on the cashier's face when you handed over that bucket of coins.'

'I know! If looks could kill, eh?'

As they walked along Shelley linked arms with Zara. 'It *was* Josh, then?'

Zara laughed. 'How'd you figure that out?'

Shelley smiled. 'I've known you for a long time, remember, and I know if it had been Lachy you'd be excited at the prospect of seeing him again. Your silence tells me Josh is on a mission and for some reason you're wondering if you should let him win you back.'

Zara sighed heavily. 'I see you and Jake together and now Marco and Toby and I want that for me. Am I crazy, Shells? Am I utterly loopy for wanting the possibility of happiness with someone?'

'Absolutely not. It's all that most people want. But you have to ask yourself if you'd be settling for second best. I know deep down you think Josh is still pining for Katie, so you need to be sure that he's 100 per cent sure too. Otherwise you'll be back to square one again. And even more heartbroken this time because you'll have let your guard down.'

Her words stung but she was right. Even though she knew it was ridiculous, Zara still liked Josh. And he clearly loved her or he wouldn't be going to so much effort.

'I know what you're thinking, Zee. And, yes, I think he does love you in his own way. But there's a huge difference between spending your life with someone you love and spending it with someone who sets your soul on fire.'

Marco appeared at her other side. 'What will you do about the awards?'

Zara shrugged. 'I don't know. My head and my heart are at odds about the whole thing. I'd love to go just to see if I really am good enough to be a writer. It'd be a fantastic experience. But I'm also terrified.'

Shelley stopped in her tracks and gasped. 'Zara, it's an omen. Look.'

Zara turned to see the shop that Shelley was pointing at. It was an evening-wear boutique. 'Come on. Let's go in and try some dresses on. If you're attending an awards ceremony you have to look the part.'

Zara was dragged into the shop by Shelley and Marco, who then proceeded to pull the most stunning gowns from the rails and hold them up against her. With only a small amount of reluctance she accompanied Shelley into the fitting rooms, where they both tried on several glamorous frocks. Then they paraded around doing a makeshift fashion show whilst Marco clapped, Jake rolled his eyes and Toby looked on in bewilderment.

Much to her own disbelief, Zara purchased the most stunning floor-length black dress. It had a sheer back, which was covered in art-deco-patterned lace and diamantés. Very classy and quite stunning. She felt like a princess. Shelley bought something a little more Shelley-ish and even hinted that she might wear her Doc Martens with it. But the buzz about the awards was really starting to grip her and she was ridiculously excited about the possibility she could actually win.

* * *

Back at the house she made a brief list of who she would like to take to the ceremony as her guests and decided she would contact the awards secretary as soon as she got back home.

'I do love you two. But, honestly, I can sort this out myself. First thing Tuesday I'm going to give the publisher a call and fess up that I didn't submit it.'

The rest of the weekend consisted of too much alcohol. Too much food and too many ridiculous games of drunken charades. It was the best time Zara had had in ages.

When they left the pretty house by the sea on Monday afternoon they were loaded down with ugly cuddly-toy prizes, far too many sticks of rock, a strip of photos from a photo booth on the seafront – who knew you could fit five adults in one of those things? – and lots of crazy memories of karaoke, including a scarily good duet of 'What Becomes of the Broken Hearted' by Marco and Toby.

Monday evening when she arrived home Josh was waiting on the steps inside the entrance to her building.

He stood as she approached him. 'Ah, here she is, my award winner in waiting.'

She couldn't help grinning. 'I might not actually win though.'

He stepped closer and slipped his arm round her waist. 'You've already won something.'

She frowned and tilted her head. 'What's that, then?'

'My heart,' he informed her and, regardless of how cheesy it was, she kissed him passionately until things got a little too heated for a public stairwell. He pulled away and gazed down at her. 'Zara, have you had enough time yet? Can we officially be an us again?'

This was it. The sixty-four-thousand-dollar question. After

what he had done for her, she couldn't fail to see that he was trying hard to make amends.

'I think... I think maybe we can.' She smiled.

His handsome grin confirmed he was both happy and relieved at her answer. 'Why don't I carry your bags upstairs and then... perhaps I could carry you to the bedroom?' His smile had gone and his eyes were hooded. There had been no word from Lachy, in spite of her wishing he would contact her, and so she figured she needed to close the door on that brief chapter of her life.

'Perhaps you could,' she whispered.

On hearing her words, he kissed her again, his hand sliding down to her bottom giving just a glimpse of what was to come.

33

Tuesday morning arrived and Zara sat in her office with the door closed. She tapped her fingers on her desk and waited for the display on her phone to show nine o'clock. Her heart was trying to escape through her blouse and her palms were sweaty. She was about to call and confirm her attendance at the most exciting event of her life. She didn't know whether to laugh or cry.

The telephone number was already programmed into her phone to save her fumbling to dial and when the time came she hit the call button, inhaling a deep breath that was meant to calm her racing pulse but did the opposite.

'Original Fiction Association, how may I direct your call?'

'Oh... erm... hello, is it possible to speak to Dominic McAllen, please?'

'I'm sorry but Mr McAllen doesn't take direct calls without a telephone appointment. Can I put you through to his secretary so you can arrange that?'

Zara cleared her throat. 'Oh, erm, yes, please.' She realised she must sound ridiculous. *Come on, Bailey, you can do this. Just be professional and calm.*

'Hold the line.' Click. A ballad she recognised by the band Sonic Idols played over the airwaves as she waited to be connected.

A voice snatched her from her daydream about the long-haired rock star she had hunted for in the Highlands. 'Hello, this is Sandy, secretary to Mr McAllen. How may I help you?'

'Oh, yes. Hello, my name is Zara Bailey and—'

'Ah yes, Miss Bailey, lovely to hear from you. Are you calling to confirm your attendance at the OFALA?'

She was stunned into silence for a moment that the secretary recognised her name. 'Oh... yes, that's right. Sorry, I'm still a bit shocked that my book was shortlisted.'

'Ah, well, believe it, Miss Bailey. We can't wait to meet you. The whole office was captivated by your book. *New Beginnings* is such a wonderful title *and* concept. We all just adored it.'

'That's wonderful to hear. Thank you. I honestly didn't think it was good enough. I would never have sent it in myself.'

'Oh, you didn't submit the book?'

Zara laughed. 'No, I wouldn't have had the courage. It was my erm... *friend*. He sent it in. I guess he has more faith in me than I have in myself.'

'Oh, I see.' There was a pause where the whirring of thinking cogs was almost audible. 'Well, there may be a slight problem, then. I'm afraid this now classes as a third-party submission.'

Zara frowned, not quite sure what that meant. 'Okay. Does that make much difference?'

The secretary sighed. 'I'm afraid it makes a big difference, Miss Bailey. The thing is... We don't accept third-party submissions. There has clearly been an oversight somewhere. Your own signature needs to be on the form.'

Shit. 'Oh, right. I see. Well, in that case could you forward me a form to my email address and I'll sign it and get it straight back to you?'

'I'm so sorry but that won't be possible. It would have to be sent as a new entry and the deadline for entries has now lapsed.'

Zara's heart sank. 'I see. And there's no way round it?'

'To be honest, no third-party submissions have ever slipped through the net to this point as the entry requirements are quite strict and very clear. I'm a little stumped.' She sighed heavily and it sounded like a gale-force wind in Zara's ear. 'Okay, I think I need to discuss this with Mr McAllen and come back to you. Is that okay, Miss Bailey?'

'Yes, that's fine. But please, *please* pass on my sincerest apologies to Mr McAllen. The last thing I wanted to do was waste anyone's time.' Her voice cracked and she closed her eyes. 'The fact that you all loved my book is a dream come true. And the fact that you were prepared to shortlist me for such a prestigious award is beyond amazing. And knowing that it could all be taken away from me is just heartbreaking. I'm so very sorry.'

'Leave it with me, Miss Bailey.' Sandy's voice was tinged with sympathy. 'I promise I'll be in touch as soon as possible. And, Miss Bailey, thank you for your honesty. It must have been a very difficult thing to hear. It's clear from speaking to you how much this all meant.'

Zara said goodbye and ended the call as tears spilled over from her eyes and she rested her head in her hands.

* * *

Every time her phone pinged with a message Zara jumped. But none of the messages were from Original Fiction Association. Her dream was slipping away and she was powerless to stop it. What made it worse was that it wasn't a dream she should even be having. Why hadn't Josh spoken to her about it first? Maybe he could have convinced her to submit it herself? Just before she was about to head off home her mobile rang and the name on screen showed it was the Original Fiction Association office.

Nervously, with shaking hands, she hit the 'answer call' button. 'Hello, Zara Bailey speaking.'

'Zara, hi, it's Dominic McAllen here. I'm sorry it's taken so long to come back to you. Let's just say it's been a hell of a hectic day.'

'Oh yes, I totally understand.'

'Now... I firstly wanted to say thank you for your honesty over the business with your book. I have to say I've not met many with your integrity, especially when something so big is at stake. How it slipped through the net has foxed us all, to be honest. I've a mind to fire someone over this once I find out how it happened. Anyway, I called a board meeting to discuss the matter and many people were on your side over the situation. Including myself.' Zara's stomach fluttered in anticipation and she tried not to let hope spark anew as he continued, 'And I hope that you now know how much talent you have. But – and I say this with an incredibly heavy heart, Zara – we can't bend the rules. So I'm afraid we can't accept your novel on to the shortlist.'

Her heart broke as she listened and silent tears trickled down her face. 'However, what I will say is, please do submit to the awards next year. I feel that you could have a very promising future. But it won't be from *this* round of awards, sadly. We're not accepting any further submissions just now as we prepare for the ceremony. The shortlist is to be made public at the start of September and the awards, as you know, take place in October, meaning this is a very busy time for the company. I know this isn't what you hoped to hear, Zara, and I have to say I'm so disappointed on your behalf. But I genuinely do mean this: you are a *very* talented writer, and I really do hope to hear from you in the future.'

She inhaled deeply and smiled – she was always taught that people could hear a smile over the phone. 'Thank you so much for your call, Mr McAllen. I really do appreciate your kind words. Goodbye.'

'Goodbye, Zara.'

34

It was at times of real anguish that you found out who your true friends were, and Zara knew she had the best. Over the next couple of days there were more flowers from Josh, wine, DVD nights, a trip to a comedy club and Marco dancing round the living room in his boxers complete with badly applied make-up. Everyone tried their best to lift Zara up after the devastating news. The memory stick had been placed in her underwear drawer, hidden out of sight, whilst she decided if she had the guts to try and find an agent or a publisher. She'd read online how difficult it could be and she wasn't one to handle rejection well, as she had discovered all too recently.

Even Noah had been rallying round to cheer her up. He'd offered to send her to his home country, Australia, so she could escape for a while. She'd graciously declined the very tempting prospect.

Friday arrived and Josh turned up for the evening. He was full of apologies again and was evidently worried that she would dump him.

'I mean, why couldn't they just slip it through anyway? I don't get it.' Josh sprawled on her bed as she got ready to go out – her friends had insisted on taking her out again, but she really questioned her toleration for more forced fun, preferring instead to stay home and listen to Florence and the Machine. But knowing full well that would only lead to thinking about little crofts in the Highlands, the handsome men who ran them and black and white border collie dogs.

'Because they have rules, Josh. Didn't you realise that when you completed the form?'

He frowned. 'What form?'

'The submission form for the competition.'

He cleared his throat. 'Oh, that form, durr. Silly me.' He rolled his eyes.

'I mean, what did you do – forge my signature?'

Before he could answer, Marco appeared in the doorway. 'Come on, Zara Bear. Time to go. You too, I suppose, Josh.' He gave her boyfriend a look of disdain and left.

'Ugh, I don't know what I ever did to him,' Josh huffed.

Zara turned and glared at him. It should've been blatantly obvious what he had done.

Seeing her expression, he cringed and jumped off the bed to put his arms round her. 'Sorry. Now come on, you look gorgeous.'

* * *

At the end of the night Josh went home, seeing as Zara's mood had descended with each alcoholic beverage that had passed her lips. She was relieved to have the bed to herself and intended to sleep in.

The next morning she awoke with a banging head and a mouth as dry as the bottom of a bird's cage. Marco had stayed at Toby's once again, so the flat was quiet and empty.

Flicking on some music, she decided to give herself one last day to be miserable and grumpy, but then she was going to snap the hell out of it before her friends totally gave up on her.

At lunchtime she sat at her desk with a falafel and hummus salad and flicked through her photos of the NC500 route once more. Her mobile rang and she answered without looking at the screen, presuming it was Marco or Shelley.

'Yup?' she asked with a mouthful of food.

'Oh, I may have called at a bad time. I was hoping to speak to Zara Bailey,' a woman with a posh accent said.

Zara swallowed and took a very quick gulp of water. 'This is she. Who's calling?'

'Ah, Miss Bailey. My name is Loretta Bateman of Bateman Welch Literary Agency.' Zara's eyes widened and she opened and closed her mouth, unable to speak. The voice came again. 'Miss Bailey? Is this a bad time?' Zara could now tell that the caller's accent was ever so slightly Scottish.

'Oh, gosh, no, not at all. I'm so sorry. H-how can I help you?'

'I think it's *I* that can help you. Or perhaps it's more a case of us helping each other.'

'I see. Go on.'

'Let's just say you have some *very* insistent fans and supporters in the book world and no doubt elsewhere. I was passed your manuscript and asked to read it as a matter of urgency. I'll be honest, I wasn't sure it was really going to be my thing, but I have to say I was highly impressed. *New Beginnings* is far more than the title might suggest. The emotion is very raw and believable. The lead character has real tenacity and a fire that I think people will relate to greatly. Now... I'm based in Inverness, not too far from the offices of the Original Fiction Association who I know you're familiar with, and I'm aware that's not exactly an *easy* place for you to access, but I was wondering if you might be interested in discussing representation by my agency.'

'Interested? In representation? By a literary agent?'

A laugh could be heard over the airwaves. 'Don't sound so surprised, Zara. You have a real talent for the written word *and* storytelling. I would very much like to represent you.'

Her heart rate picked up and she sat upright in her chair. 'Wow... I mean *yes*! Yes, that would be wonderful. I'd very much like to discuss that.'

'Excellent, excellent. So when do you think you'd be able to travel up? Or would it be better if I travel down to London?'

'I would *love* to come back to Inverness. I just need to book a hotel and travel and check with my boss. Can I come back to you? How soon were you thinking?'

'Hmm, in all honesty, with what I have planned for you, I'd very much like to do this as soon as possible. Monday?'

Yikes! 'M-Monday? Oh, right. Okay, can you leave it with me and I'll see what arrangements I can make.'

'Excellent. Obviously this won't be necessary all the time, but I do feel that an initial face-to-face meeting is a good idea. After that we can do most things by email and telephone. Come back to me as soon as you have details. Bye just now.' The line went dead and Zara stared at the phone. *Did that really just happen?*

She jumped up from her desk and yelled, 'Yes!' With a wide grin and equally wide eyes she glanced at the computer and at the door and at her phone. 'Shit, what do I do first?' Her mind was racing and her heart was doing a great impression of an erratic, haywire drum machine. She held up a decisive finger. 'I need to speak to Noah.'

* * *

Thankfully Noah now understood how important writing was to Zara *outside* work and his answer was a simple, 'Remember me when you have a bestseller.' He offered to pay for a flight so she could get there quicker. *Why the hell did I have to take the bloody train last time? Ugh, never mind that now.* She tried to refuse but he insisted. Next she called her parents, Josh, Marco and Shelley in turn. All had similar comments that someone from the Original Fiction Association really wanted her to be published.

Within an hour her flight was booked, along with a hotel room for an overnight stay in Inverness, so she contacted Loretta to confirm.

'That's wonderful news, Zara. I look forward to seeing you on Monday. I'll take you for afternoon tea at the Kingsman. That way you can check out the venue before the awards.'

Zara's stomach dropped a little. 'Oh, I'm afraid I was disqualified from the awards. If that was part of why you wanted to sign me, I'm afraid it's too late. It's a rather strange story but—'

'Okay, now I don't want to influence your decision about signing with my agency... Oh, who am I kidding? I totally do... But let's just say if you sign on the dotted line on Monday, I can get you reinstated as a shortlist candidate.'

The world must have tilted on its axis; did she just say what I think she said? 'But... but...'

'I know, it's wonderful, isn't it? Because the book has already been read by the panel and it was a mere technicality that disqualified it, we can put it through again. Dom was keen for that to happen.'

'Oh, my word. Was it Dom— erm *Mr* McAllen who contacted you on my behalf, then?'

'No, no, it was another fan. A very enthusiastic one, I might add.'

Sandy? It must have been Sandy. I must hug her when I meet her. 'Well, that's incredible. Thank you.'

'Zara, go and enjoy your weekend. I'll see you Monday. I know there are big things in your writing future.'

'See you Monday and thank you again, Loretta. So, *so* much.'

Later that evening her friends and family gathered at Zara's apartment. Marco opened the fizz and Zara's mum brought out a huge 'Congratulations!' cake.

Applause rang around her and she felt her cheeks flaming. 'Nothing's definite yet, guys, but I do appreciate this after the crap week I've had.'

'Ugh, bull poop, this award has your name already engraved on it, I can feel it,' her mum said as she placed the cake down on the dining table. 'Now get it cut. I think I may just have excelled myself with this one.'

She was right. The chocolate frosting smelled wonderful and the word *Congratulations!* was spelled out with white chocolate buttons and edible glitter. If this was what they did when she was *potentially* shortlisted and agented, what the heck would happen if she did win?

Josh was especially perky and making an extra-special effort with Zara's dad. Sadly he was receiving quite a frosty reception, but he was trying. She made a mental note to speak to her family and ask them to go easy on him. After all, she wanted him in her life, so they would have to get used to him being around.

The cake was divine and Zara felt loved. All was right with the world for however long it lasted, and she was going to grab the happiness she felt with two hands and hold on for as long as possible. Now all that was left to do was to see what Monday brought, but she dared to let a little spark of hope ignite again and it felt so good.

35

It was good to be back in Inverness. People were rushing round just like last time, but the atmosphere felt totally different from London. Not better. Just different. Zara made a mental note to pop into Highland Trax before her homebound flight and see if Patrick was around. It had been so lovely to see him at the reunion and he had said to stop by if she was in town. He'd no doubt be excited to hear what had happened and why she was in Inverness.

She met Loretta outside the Kingsman and when they walked in Loretta asked for her *usual* table. They were situated in a bay window with views out to the neatly kept gardens, where an abundance of colours made for a stunning outlook. With its Italian marble floors and thick, sumptuous drapes and modern chandeliers, the Kingsman was as plush as she had anticipated, and Zara was glad she had dressed in a smart designer suit for the occasion of meeting Loretta. Luckily the creases in her outfit gained on the flight had fallen out whilst she had been wandering round Inverness and enjoying the atmosphere again.

The afternoon tea arrived on two cake stands and was packed with tiny sandwiches, cakes and scones. Prosecco was placed down, too, and Zara had to pinch herself under the table to make sure she wasn't dreaming.

Loretta was a very elegant woman in her mid-forties and she reminded Zara a little of a modern-day Jane Russell. Her bright red lips were in contrast to her pale skin and dark wavy hair. Her own fitted suit dramatically matched her lips and her black stilettos complete with red soles made the already tall woman statuesque. She definitely belonged on a screen rather than behind a desk.

'So how does it all sound to you, Zara? Do you feel we could do your work justice as an agency?'

'I really do. I mean that. You represent some incredible authors and it would be an honour to be amongst them. Like I said, I don't want to do this for fame or millions of pounds. Although a living would be nice, obviously. But ultimately I just love to write but never expected I would be able to write anything other than articles and features.'

'Well, now you know it's a possibility. Although, I can't promise that fame *won't* happen. Once a book takes off you never know where it may lead. But you can accept and decline things as you feel it appropriate; so long as it's in line with any publishing contract we sign. And it seems to me that you have some wonderful experiences to draw from after your trip round the Highlands. It's a route that fascinates me, although I do think you're brave to have done it all on a bike and camping.'

'Brave or crazy, I haven't figured that one out yet.'

Once they had finished their afternoon tea Loretta pulled a pile of papers from her briefcase. 'Now, I don't want you to feel pressured at all. If you want to take these home and have your solicitor look over them, that's absolutely fine. Most people prefer to get a second opinion. But everything we've discussed is here: my commission, the specifications of the agreement, et cetera. So take the contract away and peruse it at your leisure. Then if you choose to sign, simply return it to me in the post, but scan the signature page and email it to me, then we can get the ball rolling.'

'I will. Thank you again. Before I leave, can I ask you something?'

Loretta held out her perfectly manicured hands. 'Fire away. What would you like to know?'

'How *did* you end up contacting me? Who was it that put my name forward? Was it Sandy from the Association HQ?'

'No. It wasn't Sandy, although I do know she adored your book as much as I did.'

'So who was it?'

Loretta smiled but shook her head. 'I... I'm not entirely sure they'd want me to tell you. Can we just leave it as a wonderful occurrence? Kismet perhaps?'

Zara dropped her gaze to her empty plate. 'Okay. It's just that I owe that person a lot. I'd really like to thank them.'

Loretta sighed deeply. 'Okay. Okay. It's a little convoluted. And this is why I mentioned kismet. Believe me, I couldn't have made this up. It's like a movie plot.' She laughed. 'I'm one of three sisters. We don't meet often due to schedules as we're all busy with our own businesses and such, but there was a family gathering some time ago now – my parents' fiftieth wedding anniversary, and we always make a point of attending *anything* our parents arrange. We each adore them. Anyway, they threw a party and my sisters and I were there. We got chatting and catching up and my baby sister, Sophie, was telling me about this friend of her fiancé's from school who had written a book. Apparently she had just finished cycling the North Coast 500.'

She raised her eyebrows and a chill travelled Zara's spine and she gasped.

'Anyway, my brother-in-law-to-be, Patrick, joined in the conversation and he was telling me about how it had turned out that this friend had hired one of *their* bikes for the trip. He knows I'm a literary agent, obviously, and was asking for advice on how to get a book out there. I think Paddy was planning to contact you with some tips, bless him. And *then*, unbelievably, my other sister, Saskia, the middle, overly dramatic one...' She rolled her eyes. 'Saskia was telling us how her fiancé had rescued a woman who fitted the same description when she was almost hit by a tractor. We all agreed what a small world it is.'

Zara's stomach plummeted to her shoes as the pieces of the puzzle began to fit into place. Loretta continued, waving her hand. 'We kind of got completely off track at that point, as you can imagine, but Lachlan contacted me the day after the party and said he hadn't wanted to interfere because you're a very strong-willed, independent woman who doesn't accept help easily, but that *he* had a copy of the book that Paddy had mentioned, your book, saved to his hard drive and that it was really, *really* good.' She cringed. 'I have to admit that I receive so many manuscripts professing to be excellent that I wasn't all that interested, but I didn't want to rain on his parade, as it were, so I agreed that he could email it to me.' Zara was doing her best to keep up, although the pain of finding out Lachy *hadn't* been single when she had slept with him knotted her insides and made her feel nauseated and she was struggling to think of anything else.

'Are you okay, Zara? You've gone very pale.'

Zara forced a smile and nodded. 'Sorry, yes. Too much cake, I think. Please go on.'

'I have to be completely honest that it sat on my desk untouched. So, imagine my shock when the day after *that* I was out to lunch with Dominic McAllen's wife – she loved the book too, by the way – and she mentioned you *again* and all the things that had occurred with the third-party submission problem, et cetera. It was like a lightning-bolt moment. This person's book was coming at me from every angle and I was sure it was fate telling me I had to do something. I asked more questions and when she realised I already had a copy of the book and I was intrigued, she asked me to read the book as soon as possible and see if I might like to represent you. So there you go. As I said, you have a *lot* of support. The book was the icing on the cake.'

'So your sister, Saskia, she's the current fiancée of Lachlan Grant.' It wasn't really a question. It was merely a clarification aloud that Lachy had lied to her. Just as Josh had. Men were clearly not to be trusted.

'That's right. Ugh, they've been together *years*. You should see how they look at each other. I wish he'd just marry the girl and do us all a favour. But, yes, bloody small world, isn't it? Lachlan's a lawyer, you know. A very good one too. The farm is purely inheritance and I believe he's selling it off to move back to the city. Between you and me I think that's partly because of Saskia's aversion to the outdoors. She isn't one for mud and sheep.' She laughed. 'But then again Saskia isn't one for much that doesn't have a designer label. Just don't tell Lachlan I said so.'

'There's no risk of that. It's highly unlikely I'll ever see him again.'

36

Back in the hotel room Zara's emotions were in turmoil. She was ecstatic that the contract for representation was only a signature away, meaning that, thanks to Loretta's connections, the competition shortlisting was back on. But disappointment and sadness came in waves too. *Why* had Lachy lied to her? Was it simply because what they had shared meant absolutely nothing more than some cheap thrill with a stranger? Was it that he wasn't ever expecting to see her again? Was it that his fiancée lived miles away and he fancied a quick shag? Was it all of the above?

She realised that it was stupid to feel so hurt by his lies when there had been no promises made; no agreements to take things any further and no future in their relationship. But nevertheless she had seen something in his eyes. She had felt a connection and thought he had felt it too. Was that why he hadn't been able to wave goodbye? Was it guilt for being unfaithful? Probably. At least that was something to make him bloody human.

As it was late and she hadn't felt hungry since the afternoon tea and the bizarre chain of events, she ordered a light snack from the room-service menu and flicked on the TV for background noise while she went over the contract once more. She couldn't hold this stuff against Loretta. It was nothing to do with her business and she seemed genuine and professional.

A knock at the room door indicated that her food had arrived so she went to answer it, pinning her hair up as she walked. Without paying much attention she opened the door and said, 'Could you just put it by the TV, please? I'll eat it there.'

'I *could* but I'm pretty sure these aren't edible flowers.'

Zara turned quickly to find Lachlan Grant standing there, that handsome face of his smiling as if everything were perfect and he weren't a complete and utter *shithead*. 'What the *hell* are you doing here?'

His smile quickly faded. 'I... I heard that you were in Inverness, through... erm *friends* and I thought I'd stop by and say hello... so... hello.' He laughed nervously as she glared at him but didn't speak. 'Look, the thing is, I haven't been able to stop thinking about you. I know what we had was meant to be a one-time thing but I can't accept that, Zara. I felt something other than just a simple attraction to you. When we... when we were in bed together it was... I've never felt that way before and I've been trying to pluck up the courage to contact you. But the way I felt was *so* intense – and a bit scary, if I'm honest – that I was afraid of being rejected. I mean, there was the huge possibility you didn't feel any of it and it was just my overactive imagination and a little dash of wishful thinking.'

He held up his free hand as the other still clutched the beautiful bouquet. 'And before you say no, I know we live in two completely different locations with totally different lives, but I don't want that to stop us from seeing if this could *be* something.' He stepped closer and she could smell the intoxicating scent of his cologne. The same cologne that he had been wearing on the day they had slept together. The day he had *lied* to her about being single.

But as she gazed up into his deep, chocolate-brown eyes sadness washed over her and tied her in knots. Why did he have to be such a bastard? He'd seemed so caring and funny and so bloody gorgeous. And this was like something from a romance movie and right about now she should be jumping into his arms telling him that, *yes*, she wanted to see where this could lead. That she hadn't been able to stop thinking about him either. Then they would tumble into bed together and seal their relationship the way it had started. But the truth remained. She was with Josh now and he was still with Saskia. He had been *engaged* to Saskia when they'd had sex and if he could be unfaithful to her living in the same country, he could certainly be that way when Zara lived so far away. He *was* a liar. A handsome, intelligent, sexy-as-hell liar. And they were ten a penny in London. She didn't have to come all the way up here to Scotland to find one.

He smiled again and looked at her with such hope. 'Do you think this could be something, too, Zara?' he whispered.

'It already *is* something, Lachy,' she said with a shaking voice. 'It's over.' She stepped back and closed the door before walking over to the bed and sitting down. All alone.

* * *

'Zara! Zee! Wake up! You're in *The Bookseller*!' Marco shouted from the hallway where he must have just collected the mail.

She yawned and rubbed at her eyes, wishing he could've just left her to sleep.

He burst into her room. 'Look! This is such a gorgeous photo of you. I'm glad they used this one. You looked way too serious in the other one.'

She sat up and took the magazine from him. The headline read:

Bateman Welch New Acquisition

Marco flopped onto her bed, took it back and read, '"Loretta Bateman at Bateman Welch is delighted to announce her latest acquisition for representation. Zara Bailey is a travel journalist who recently cycled the North Coast 500. Ms Bateman said of Miss Bailey: 'She has a raw talent for emotional and thought-provoking writing that will leave readers gripped and salivating for more.'" Ooh, *salivating*, Zee, I like that. She's right too. I bloody loved that bit on the beach where you didn't know what Evangeline was going to do. Would she report the murder or would she fall into Harrison's arms...?' he said dreamily.

She was relieved to have finally had the courage to allow her friends to read her book. Shelley had read it in one night and had telephoned her at two in the morning to shout at her for making her *ugly-cry*. Jake had taken the phone from Shelley and apologised that his girlfriend was inconsolable.

Shelley had snatched the phone back and said, 'If you don't win that bloody award, I'm going to bomb their offices, Zee.' Then she had paused and followed this with, 'Well, obviously not *bomb* them with a real bomb, but I'm very tempted to go and wipe snot on their cardigans. I've got plenty of it, thanks to your effing book. Which is bloody amazing, by the way.' She had then descended into more sobs.

'Hi, it's Jake again. I really am sorry about this. I told her to wait until morning but she refused. I'll get her to bed now.'

Zara cringed. 'Thanks, Jake, I'm sorry too.' Zara had tried her best not to laugh at Shelley's reaction but it had secretly made her so happy that the emotion had translated off the page for those in her life who meant the most.

Back in the present and Marco stood from her bed. 'I'll go make coffee.'

'Good plan. I need something strong to wake me up officially, seeing as you failed unofficially and I'm still half asleep.'

He walked to the door and turned. 'Look, I know it's only been a week but are you okay about the whole Lachy thing now?'

Zara shrugged. 'I have no choice, do I?'

'Did you not want to hear him out? I mean, there may have been an explanation. And he may be single now.'

'No, Marco. I'm with Josh now. And anyway, if Lachy was unfaithful with me behind his fiancée's back he could just as easily do the same to me. I'm not prepared to risk that.'

'But you'll accept that Josh did it?'

Marco's words stung and for a split second she wanted to slap him. But how could she when he was right? 'It's different, Marco. Josh and I weren't engaged. He hadn't even told me he loved me at that point.'

'That's hardly the point though, Zara. How do you know that Josh won't cheat again?'

Her eyes widened and she raised her hands. 'I can't believe we're having this conversation. It's different, that's it. End of. Get used to it,' she told him angrily.

Marco nodded and tried to smile. 'I just want you to be happy, you know, Zara Bear.'

Seeing the concern in his expression melted her a little and she reached out to touch his arm. 'I'm sorry, Marco, I know you do. But look at you and Toby. You two can be happy enough for the both of us for a while, eh?'

He gave her a sad smile and left her alone again. Alone to dwell on the fact that whilst one side of her life was coming together, the other side had fallen apart before the foundations had even been laid.

37

The journey from Inverness Airport had been filled with excited chatter from her friends. Josh had remained quiet, evidently sensing the attitude of mistrust radiating from Marco and Shelley, and Zara had been mesmerised by the view through the glass of the russet and gold of the trees that lined the roads. October in Inverness was beautiful, which, of course, meant autumn in Scourie would be even more spectacular. She shook her head and tried to think about different locations in the Highlands that would be just as beautiful.

Someone nudged her, dragging her back from the verge of melancholy. 'Do you have a speech prepared for the awards, Zee?' Shelley asked as the people-carrier taxi pulled up outside the hotel in Inverness. Zara opened the door and the chill of autumn entered the car and made everyone shiver.

'Oh, she doesn't need a speech, do you?' Marco interjected.

Shelley whacked him. 'Marco! You could at least sound confident that she *might* win, Jeez.'

Not for the first time, he whacked her back. 'Oy! *Actually* what I meant was she can just get up there and speak from her heart, *Shelley*.'

Shelley's cheeks flushed. 'Oh, I'm so sorry. I thought this was you hinting that the book's crap or something. I really was willing to fight you, you know.'

Marco burst into fits of laughter. 'I'd like to see you try. Toby would back me up, wouldn't you, Tobes?'

Toby snorted. 'Against Shelley? Are you mad?'

Jake laughed. 'Ooh, good answer, mate. Good answer.'

As they climbed from the cab Zara observed her friends and Josh with a contented smile. She was so happy that they had all decided to accompany her to the awards ceremony. Loretta had been incredible about getting tickets for everyone and she was pretty sure she had been allocated more than her fair share. Her parents were already in Inverness, having chosen to make a romantic break of the whole event, and would be joining them later and they would all walk to the Kingsman together.

Zara was under no illusions about winning the award. So she hadn't prepared a speech. She was just incredibly grateful to be there.

* * *

Zara slipped on the dress she had bought on her weekend away with her friends and stared at her reflection in the mirror. Her mum had tied her hair in a low chignon, slightly off to one side, and her dad had given her some beautiful diamanté earrings that she knew he hadn't chosen, but the fact that he had gone to the trouble of buying her something was so wonderful and sweet that she had cried.

Now, standing there, she hardly recognised the woman

looking back at her. How could this be happening? How could she, Zara Bailey, the travel writer, be attending such a glamorous awards ceremony? She was scared that if she pinched herself she'd wake up.

'Wow, look at you.' Josh whistled and she turned to see him in his tuxedo, looking every bit the dashingly handsome man.

'You don't look too bad yourself.'

He walked towards her and gently placed a kiss on her cheek. 'I hope you were in the bathroom so long because you were putting on some sexy underwear ready for later.'

She tilted her head to the side and said, seductively, 'Oh, now, that would be telling.'

38

The Kingsman was buzzing when Zara and her entourage arrived. A group of reporters snapped photos and there was a TV crew from Scottish Television broadcasting live as celebrities' cars pulled up surrounded by security. A huge crowd of people was gathered and Zara wondered why. It was a prestigious literary awards' ceremony but these things didn't usually attract such raucous crowds. A loud cheer roared and Zara's stomach knotted with anxiety as she looked back over her shoulder to find out what was going on. She watched as rock star, Nick Dacre, climbed out of a black car and waved to the gathered crowd. Her heart leapt.

Bloody hell, I'm going to be in the same room as Nick Dacre? It did nothing to calm her nerves.

She caught sight of herself in the mirrored exterior doors and had to do a double take. The long, fitted black gown she wore made her look incredibly sophisticated, even if she did say so herself. Once inside, her mum gripped her hand as they walked towards a set of double doors, flanked by security. They stepped through the doors into the room where the awards would be taking place and Zara gasped as she tried to absorb everything before her. Huge chandeliers hung from a ceiling draped with fabric. Round tables with the most wonderful floral centrepieces covered the full extent of the humongous room. Zara hadn't realised that the hotel was quite so big when she had visited it with Loretta. But it was massive. A smartly dressed blonde woman took their names and showed them to their table. Loretta and her husband were already there, and they greeted Zara with hugs before she introduced them to the people she had brought.

There were several awards to be presented and from the running order Zara's category was going to be one of the later ones of the evening. Great, longer to become a nervous wreck, she thought as she glanced round the room. There were various familiar-looking faces, but when her gaze fell on one particular face her heart almost jumped from her mouth.

'Oh my God, Shelley, it's Ruby Oatley. Ruby Oatley is sitting right over there.' Zara couldn't quite believe she was sitting in the same room as a rock star *and* her absolute favourite author in the world.

Shelley twisted in her seat to look in the same direction. They had shared a love of Ruby's books for many years. She slapped her leg. 'Oh, my word. We have to go say hi, Zee. We have to. I'd never forgive myself if we didn't,' she insisted. 'Ooh, ooh, maybe we could ask for a selfie.'

Zara cringed. 'Oh, I don't know. I'll probably make a total fool of myself.'

'No, you won't. Come on. I'll do the talking.' She grabbed Zara's hand and tugged her from her seat.

Once they reached Ruby's table Shelley tapped her on the shoulder. 'Excuse me. I'm sorry to intrude. But my friend and I have been huge fans of yours for years and we had to come and say hello.'

Ruby stood and smiled graciously. 'Oh, that's so lovely, thank you.'

'Yes, we're here tonight because Zara is shortlisted in the Best Unpublished Newcomer category, aren't you, Zara?'

Zara, transfixed on her favourite author, nodded and said, 'I write books now.' *What the hell did I say that for? Oh God, what an idiot. Idiot, sodding, arsing idiot.*

Ruby grinned and shook both of their hands. 'Well, good luck to you, Zara. Have a wonderful evening.' Just then a voice came over the sound system asking everyone to take their seats, so Shelley quickly dragged Zara back to their table.

'*I write books now?* I meet my favourite author in the whole world and all I can say is *I write books now*. Fuck me, I'm a total plank.'

Shelley giggled. 'Hey, just think, some utter loon might behave like that when they meet *you* one day.'

As they turned to walk back to their table someone stepped into their path.

'Zara, you look stunning.'

She lifted her face and her eyes were met with the sexy dark gaze of Lachlan Grant. He looked amazing in his dinner jacket. All clean-shaven and smelling delicious as usual. 'Lachy? What are you doing here?'

'I'll, erm, see you back at the table, Zee,' Shelley whispered before hurrying away.

He watched Shelley walk away and took a step closer. 'I... erm... I wanted to see you. God, I've missed you. I knew that you were shortlisted and, after the way things ended when I came to your hotel room that night, I wanted to speak to you. To find out why—'

Zara stiffened her spine. 'I have nothing to say to you.'

'Zara, please, just tell me—'

'Hey, gorgeous, is this guy bothering you?' Josh asked as he appeared beside her and slipped his arm possessively round her waist.

'No, Josh, it's fine, he's just going back to his table.'

Lachlan's gaze switched rapidly between Zara and Josh and he pointed. 'Is this... is this *the* Josh?' he asked with incredulity.

'Not that it's any of your business, but yes.'

His brow crumpled and he opened and closed his mouth several times before saying, 'Why the hell are you back with *him*? After what he did—'

Josh stepped forward. 'Hey, mate, I don't know what you think you're playing at but just do one, okay?'

Zara's heart pounded in her chest and she feared a fight would break out so she grabbed Josh and tugged him backwards. 'Look, Josh, I think things are about to start. We'd better go.' He nodded and gave Lachy one final, intimidating glare before walking back towards the table.

Once she had pushed Josh towards the table and he was out of earshot, she hissed at Lachy, 'I don't think *you* have any room to talk, Lachlan Grant. I know all about Saskia. And for your information Josh has made amends. He was the one to send my manuscript to the Original Fiction competition in the first place. Without him I wouldn't even be here tonight. Now I'm going back to my seat and I would thank you to stay away from me. I'm here to celebrate with the people I love, and I don't need any histrionics, thank you very much. So, please, just go back to your friends.'

A strikingly beautiful black-haired woman who bore a strong resemblance to Loretta appeared at his side and slipped her hand up his chest. 'Lachy, darling, are you coming back to the table?'

Saskia.

He turned to stare at the woman and removed her hand from his body. 'Do you *ever* listen, Saskia?' He turned his attention back to Zara and, with a pain-filled, sad shake of his head, he told her, 'Don't believe everything you're told. I thought you of all people, as a journalist, would already know that.' Then he turned and walked away.

Her lip began to tremble and her hands shook. What did he mean? Why did he look at her as if she had just broken his heart? She slowly walked back to her table as the lights went down. She took her seat and each member of her group wished her luck. Josh reached for her hand and gave it a squeeze. She forced a smile and feigned excitement. Whatever Lachlan had meant, it would have to wait for now. And maybe she'd never find out.

* * *

The atmosphere at the ceremony was incredible. So many talented writers were acknowledged for their contributions to contemporary literature and Zara couldn't quite believe *she* was in the same room as them. Ruby presented one of the awards and her speech about the winner was so heart-warming. Zara could only dream of being so eloquent.

'Next, ladies and gentlemen, we have the award for the Best Unpublished Newcomer,' the compère, a Scottish newsreader, announced. Applause rang round the room and each member of her group reached over and whispered good luck or squeezed her hand. Zara's heart was en route to her mouth now instead of trying to escape through her ribs. And she wasn't sure whether she wanted to cry or barf. Thankfully she managed to refrain from either.

'To present this award we have a man whose life has been a roller-coaster, to say the least. He has battled anxiety and some very tough decisions about his career. These days he's settled and made a life for himself in the Scottish Highlands. I would like to welcome to the stage, author of the tell-all autobiography *The Worst of Me*, ladies and gentlemen, Sonic Idols' Nick Dacre.' Zara's ears began to ring and she wasn't sure if it was the fans' screams in the auditorium or her own blood whooshing through her veins, but she stared at the stage as her favourite rock star walked up in a tuxedo, looking like sex on legs. She turned to her side and burst out laughing as Shelley sat there in stunned silence – a first for her – as she looked on.

The applause eventually died down and Nick began to speak. 'Thank you, thank you, everyone. It's great to be here tonight to present this award. Anyone, be it a musician, actor or an author, who puts themselves out there open for public scrutiny does so with such bravery. I know this from personal experience. And I know how it can backfire too. Yet people still choose to do it. Not because they're desperate for fame or fortune but simply because it's part of who they are. So much so, that without that element of themselves they wouldn't *be* themselves. I know this to be true. And so I'm full of admiration for this talented group of writers who are embarking upon this journey right now. I had the pleasure of reading these books after the votes had been cast and all I can say is I'm so glad I'm only presenting the award and not choosing who wins it. So, without further ado, the nominations for Best Unpublished Newcomer are... J. D. Bolton with *A Secret Kept*... Clara Higgson with *A Girl's Best Friend*... Zara Bailey for *New Beginnings*... Jack Danson for *He Came Back Alive*... D. S. Binns with *Somewhere*

Only We Know and Hallie McPherson with *Sunset Over Paradise...*'

He opened the envelope and leaned into the mic to say, 'Good luck, everyone, you're all awesome.' He pulled a gold card from the envelope and announced, 'And the winner is...' The pause seemed to last hours even though it was merely seconds, and an air of suspense filled the room as everyone held their breath. Zara almost lost feeling in her fingers from where they were being squeezed and it was hard to hold her excitement in. She was shortlisted in a major UK literary awards for the *first thing* she had ever written. If she won, it would be a dream come true, but the fact she was sitting there in that room as a contender was barely believable as it was.

39

Nick Dacre, lead singer of Zara's favourite band, was about to announce the winner of her category and she could barely breathe. He leaned in to the mic once more as if in slow motion and announced, 'D. S. Binns with *Somewhere Only We Know*!' The room erupted with applause and Zara was enveloped in a group hug of condolence, but in a way she was relieved. She wasn't sure she was ready to be thrust into the limelight in such a public domain. At least this way she could pursue her dream in her own time. And she would definitely be making time from that moment, she had decided.

'Are you okay, love?' her mum asked, holding her face so she would focus.

Zara nodded as best she could. 'I'm fine, Mum. I'm absolutely great. This entire evening has been a dream come true. It doesn't matter that I didn't win. Nick Dacre read *my* name out.' She grinned and her close group all laughed and hugged her harder.

'Well, it's good that you're taking something positive away at least,' Shelley said through watery eyes.

The winning author was giving an emotional speech on the stage and once again Zara was filled with relief. It would have been incredible to win, no doubt, but she wasn't one for speaking in front of masses of people, especially not when ugly-crying and with snot all over her face. No, this was a blessing in disguise.

Loretta came over and hugged her. 'I'm so proud to have you as a client, Zara. And I know for a fact that you have a big future ahead. Next year you'll be sitting here in the best author category, you'll see. Oh, and I know it's Sunday, but we have a breakfast meeting with Shonagh McAllen, Dominic's wife, in the morning.'

Zara pulled away and stared at Loretta. 'Why? Why would we have a breakfast meeting with Shonagh McAllen?'

Loretta grinned. 'Oh, well, she's an acquisitions editor at a major publishing house here in Scotland and let's just say there may be a *very* interesting and potentially lucrative offer on the table.'

Zara gasped. 'Really? But I thought—'

Loretta shrugged. 'They want you. What can I say?' She kissed her on both cheeks. 'Now relax and enjoy the evening. But don't enjoy it too much, okay? You need your wits about you tomorrow, Miss Bailey.'

Zara sat staring into space in a stunned stupor. So she didn't win the award but she was possibly being signed anyway? This couldn't be happening... could it?

* * *

At the end of the awards the bar was opened and everyone mingled, chatting and networking their way round the vast room. Loretta had gone and her mum and dad had left, too, with hugs and instructions to call them as soon as her meeting was over in the morning. Nick Dacre had come over to congratulate her on the shortlisting and she had to force herself not to fangirl all over him.

He fixed her with a sincere look. 'Honestly, Zara, my money was on your book. I absolutely loved Evangeline and so did my wife. We were rooting for her from the very beginning. I reckon *New Beginnings* will be on the shelves in bookshops in no time at all.'

Shelley interjected, 'Nick, this is really forward and possibly quite inappropriate, but can I take a photo of you with Zara, please? She's a huge fan... well, we all are.' Zara looked behind her to see Marco, Toby and Jake nodding like those little plastic dogs you find in cars.

Nick looked a little embarrassed as he grinned and lowered his eyes for a moment and Zara made a mental note to slap Shelley for this. But he lifted his face and slipped his arm round Zara's shoulder.

With a wide, handsome smile he said, 'A photo with my new favourite author? This will be one for my wall.' Zara's legs almost gave way. How the *hell* was *any* of this happening?

Shelley snapped several photos with her phone and said she'd email one to Nick's publicist. He *made* her promise.

Eventually Zara and her group of friends decided it was time to leave the ceremony and make their way back to their hotel.

As they walked towards the exit Marco asked eagerly, 'So who's up for a nightcap?'

Zara cuddled up to Josh. 'Not me, sorry, guys. I have a breakfast meeting with my literary agent, dontcha know?' She grinned like the Cheshire Cat and a resounding, *'Ooooh,'* came from her friends.

'Well you go ahead back to the hotel then. I think I can speak for the rest of us when I say the night is young?' Marco looked to the others for confirmation. Once he'd received it, he continued, 'A club it is then! Josh, you'd *better* let her sleep tonight,' he warned and Zara could tell he wasn't kidding around.

After hugs and kisses, her friends left to look for a venue in which to continue their fun. As she was about to exit with Josh she glanced round the room once more. There was no sign of Lachy so her chance to find out what he'd meant was gone. And she wasn't sure how she felt about that.

'Come on, we'll grab a taxi, eh? It's a bit chilly out there,' Josh informed her as he removed his jacket and wrapped it round her shoulders. She silently hoped that Marco and Shelley would forgive him soon as he was trying so hard to make amends.

As they climbed into a waiting cab a message pinged to her phone and she grabbed it from her bag, wondering if it might even be Lachy, but instead it was Loretta with the breakfast venue address.

Zara wished she had been able to speak to Lachy again. His cryptic words had thrown her and now that the event was over he was in the forefront of her mind yet again. *He* was the one who had boosted her confidence about the whole book business. *He* had been the first to read it and to love it. *He* had been the first to believe in her. And now she was questioning everything. What the hell had he meant? The clock on her phone said it was gone midnight and she was meeting Loretta at half nine in the morning. *Time to sleep... if that's at all possible.*

* * *

Back in the hotel she removed her make-up and her beautiful dress and as she put it back in the protective bag Josh slipped his arms round her waist. 'Hmm, I knew there'd be something worth unwrapping under there.' He began to kiss her neck and she closed her eyes. But his ringtone blared loudly from his jacket pocket flung on the back of a chair. He sighed. 'Ugh, who the hell is ringing me at this time of the morning?' He strutted off to retrieve the handset and stared at the screen. 'Shit, it's Katie. I better take it, it might be Caleb.'

His worried expression tugged at her and she nodded. He walked out of the room into the corridor to answer the call.

He'd been gone a while when she opened the door to see where he was. She could hear him speaking in a low voice, but he had walked round the corner at the end near the elevator. Curiosity got the better of her and she tiptoed to where he was. Holding her breath, she listened.

'No... no, Katie, I'll be home tomorrow, I promise. Don't cry.'

Oh, heck, Caleb must really be ill or something, she surmised, and she turned to walk away, berating herself for her lack of trust.

'Hey... hey, listen to me, Katie, okay? You *know* I love you.' Zara froze in her tracks. 'I'll *always* love you, but you said we were through, Katie, so what was I supposed to think?' A long pause ensued and Zara widened her eyes, covering her mouth so she didn't scream. 'Of course, I want you, babe. Don't be like that... Inverness... It's an awards thing. Yes, I'm with *her*. No... no, babe, please, it's only because she thinks I sent her stupid book into some competition. I was only with her because I was trying to get back at you... Yes, I know that was cruel and stupid. And I'm so, *so* sorry. But now I know the truth, eh? You, me and Caleb, baby, always. Okay? Always.'

Anger and sadness were desperate to leave Zara's body in raw, impassioned screams. But instead, holding her hands firmly over her mouth, she tiptoed back to the room and dead-bolted the door.

Zara crawled into bed and sobbed into her pillow. So it wasn't Josh who'd sent her manuscript to the awards. That must have been what Lachy meant. *It was him, not Josh. Oh God, and I was so awful to him.* Her body shook as she let out all her anguish. How could she have been so stupid? How could she have not seen through Josh and his lies? She contemplated contacting Shelley or Marco, but it was so late and if they were even back from clubbing their rooms were on a completely different floor so it felt unfair to bother them. Better she stayed alone. It was no more than she deserved after all. *Stupid, stupid Zara.*

Josh returned to the room and tried the door. When it wouldn't open, he banged on it. He called her mobile, banged some more. Then it all went quiet and the room phone rang. Security asked if she was okay and checked if they were to let the man at the front desk into the room. She informed them that under no circumstances should they let him in.

Josh appeared and hammered again. After around thirty minutes of pounding on the door she heard raised voices. Security had come to remove him. Eventually it fell silent and she cried herself to sleep.

* * *

The following morning the bags under her eyes had bags and she hopped into the shower, hoping that it would go some way to freshening her up. Once out and dried she checked her phone. Josh had been messaging her asking why she was ignoring him. The messages started out sweet but descended into swearing and insults. And as expected there were no messages from Lachy. But, when all was said and done, he'd still turned out to be a cheater. So maybe she was better off without him too. Even if it was him who'd sent the manuscript in and not Josh. Regardless of how sweet that was, he had still lied to her and cheated on his fiancée. She had to at least try to put it out of her mind. She had a potentially life-changing meeting to attend.

The butterflies were stampeding around her insides again as she dressed. She was thankful that she'd brought a 'just in case I win' outfit. The winner was to be interviewed on *Good Morning Scotland* before being whisked away to London for more publicity. Luckily now the outfit wouldn't go to waste. The smart shirt dress was fitted and elegant and definitely appropriate. She slipped on her designer stilettos to complete the look – dress to impress and all that – and set out to meet Loretta and Shonagh at the address from the text message.

The little brasserie-cum-bakery was wonderful. The pastries in the glass cabinet as she walked in were far too tempting. And she could feel her waistline expanding as she gazed longingly at the display. Something caught her attention and she turned to see Loretta smiling and waving from a table towards the back, so she made her way over to where her agent was sitting alone and her heart sank. Had Shonagh changed her mind?

Loretta stood and kissed her on both cheeks. 'I'm sorry I look so dishevelled. We've had a bit of family drama.' She looked anything but dishevelled.

'Oh dear. I hope it's nothing too serious.'

Loretta rolled her eyes as they both sat. 'Believe me, where my sister is concerned everything is dramatic.'

Zara's ears pricked up and she hoped Patrick was okay. 'Sophie?'

'Oh, good heavens, no. Sophie's happily planning her wedding to Patrick. No, this was *all* Saskia at two o'clock this morning.'

Zara wasn't about to pry, especially seeing as she knew about Saskia's connections to Lachy. The less heard about them, the better.

A waitress arrived and placed a cafetière, cups and cream on the table. 'Thank you, dear. I'll order the rest once the third member of our party arrives,' Loretta informed the young woman. Once the waitress had gone, she sighed as she poured coffee into the two cups. 'Honestly, there's no wonder she's single. I defy any man to take on such a little madam. You'd hardly believe she was a grown woman.'

Zara gulped. *Single?* 'Oh, man trouble?' Her interest was now piqued.

'You could say that. Although if you keep in touch with Lachy after your trip you probably know all about it.'

'I... erm... I don't keep in touch with him. I'm just so busy, you know...' She swallowed hard and willed her agent to continue.

'Well, I shouldn't gossip. She *is* my sister, after all, but... Oh, what the hell? It turns out that Saskia and Lachy broke up *months* ago. She hadn't told any of us for fear of embarrassment. Although why she felt it necessary to perpetuate the lie, I have no idea.'

Zara sat up straight. 'Months ago? Like, how many months

ago? Forgive my nosiness. Lachy never mentioned he was having relationship troubles when I was at his croft.'

'Oh, that's because to *him* it was all done and dusted by that point. He had moved home to nurse his father and had hinted that he would be staying indefinitely but Saskia was furious and demanded he sell the place. He refused, of course, and she broke up with him. Although in her mind it wasn't a proper break-up. She expected him to come running back to Inverness to beg her forgiveness. But why the hell would he do that? I mean, I love her, I have to really, but I wouldn't wish her mood swings on my worst enemy.'

Zara's heart hammered at her ribcage as she realised that poor Lachy had been completely innocent in the whole situation she had created in her mind. 'But... your parents' anniversary party...'

Loretta huffed with exasperation. 'Oh yes, that was a total shambles. She'd conned the poor man into accompanying her because she didn't want to break our parents' hearts with yet another failed relationship. Ridiculous. They know *exactly* what she's like. They would have totally understood. But he's such a good man he came anyway.'

Zara was stunned into silence.

'To ice the cake she turned up at the awards last night because she knew he had asked me for a ticket. She showed up just expecting him to welcome her with open arms. Anyway, he announced that he's head over heels in love with someone else and asked that she leave him alone to get on with his life. She had a total meltdown. The police were called and everything. She really is so very melodramatic. I really do like Lachy, and whoever this woman is that he's in love with, I wish them all the very best. He deserves happiness, the poor chap.' Loretta laughed and sipped her coffee. 'You could probably write a bloody book on all this.'

Rather distractedly Zara said, 'Yes, probably.'

'Ah, here's Shonagh now. Game face on, Zara.' Loretta gave an excited smile and stood to greet her friend.

They swapped air kisses and then Loretta announced, 'So, my lovely, this is the very brilliant Zara Bailey.'

Shonagh held out her hand and Zara shook it. 'Lovely to finally meet you, Zara.'

'And you too.'

'Now, what can I order for you, ladies? The pastries are to die for. And, Shonagh, would you like tea or coffee?' Loretta waved over the waitress.

'Coffee would be good, thanks.'

Loretta placed an order for more coffee and some breakfast pastries and when the waitress had gone Shonagh turned to Zara.

'Now, I just want to say that I appreciate you coming to meet me on a Sunday morning, especially after such a late night. But I wanted to make sure I got my offer of a publishing contract on the table before Loretta works her magic and you're snapped up by another lucky company.'

Zara shook her head in bewilderment. 'I still can't quite take all this in.'

Shonagh smiled warmly. 'Well, hopefully we can come to a mutual agreement and you'll be able to relax in the knowledge that your books will be safe with us. I'll give you plenty of time to discuss the offer with Loretta if you need it, and you may also discuss things with your solicitor if you prefer.'

'Sounds great. Thank you.'

* * *

Two hours later, full to the brim with *pain au chocolat* and cinnamon whirls yet somehow still floating on air, Zara hugged Loretta and promised to be in touch soon. She had already made the decision to sign on the dotted line, however, but didn't want to seem overly desperate to say yes right away. The offer of a three-book deal and a hefty advance had shaken her to the core and she needed time to let everything sink in.

When she got back to the hotel she gathered her friends and family and relayed the sordid details of Josh and his lies. There were gasps of horror and in turn each of them comforted her and expressed their honest opinions. Obviously Marco had hated him all along. Her dad was going to set the lads on him, Shelley was speechless, which was a first, and her mum cried. As always their unwavering support was immediate and she was hugged and congratulated on the exciting career developments. They were thrilled and so very happy for her.

She hugged her parents and said goodbye as they were going off sightseeing to make the most of their extra few days in the city. Once she was left with her friends, she asked if she could have a private word with Shelley and Marco. They shared worried glances but agreed to follow her to her room. Zara then relayed the conversations she'd had with Loretta and how it had come to light that Lachy hadn't cheated.

Her friends sat on the bed. 'Are you okay, Zee?' Shelley asked as Zara paced the room.

'No, I'm not okay. There's one thing missing from this whole scenario and I've been so stupid.'

'Lachy?' Marco asked.

'Lachy,' Zara confirmed.

'So, are you going to call him?' Marco asked.

Zara shook her head as sadness tugged at her heart. 'I have

no way to do that. He gave me a business card, but I lost it on my way back to Inverness.'

Marco looked sheepish all of a sudden. 'Erm... I might be able to solve that problem.'

Zara and Shelley turned to him in unison with, 'Oh?'

He cringed. 'I saw you speaking to him last night and I guessed it was him. I pretended to be interested in crofting and got his business card. You can have it if—'

Zara launched herself at him. 'Oh, my goodness, Marco, I love you so much. Thank you, thank you.'

Shelley scrunched her brow. 'But... why did you do that when last night you thought he'd cheated?'

He shrugged. 'Something just didn't add up. And I knew she'd lost his number. I had a feeling she'd end up regretting having no way to contact him.' He fumbled in his wallet and pulled out the card and handed it to Zara.

'Look, guys, I'm going to pack my stuff. I'll drop Lachy a message and ask him to call me. He once told me to text first, as he might be out on the quad if he's even left Inverness. I'm hoping he's still here though.'

Her friends hugged her tight and asked her to keep them posted before they left her room. Once alone she slumped onto the bed and began to compile an apology. She made several attempts to put her feelings into words, but each time deleted the inadequate ones. Eventually she came up with something she was fairly happy with, although it spanned several text messages.

Lachy, this is Zara Bailey. The strong independent woman with Silver Dickhead the bike. Aka, the stupid woman who believed someone who had a track record of being deceitful. I feel I owe you an explanation, so here goes.

After leaving the Highlands on completion of my bike ride, I heard something which led me to believe that you weren't single when I was at your croft, which meant that the special time we shared was tainted. I'm not someone who agrees with cheating and so to be with someone who appeared to be doing just that made me angry and disappointed; not only in you but in myself for being a victim of this twice.

When you showed up at my hotel that night I was only just in possession of what I thought were the facts of your relationship with Saskia, i.e., your engagement. Today I discovered the truth, however, which means I owe you a sincere apology. Today I've discovered that I was completely wrong. I should have listened to you when you showed up at my door. I should have let you in and given you a chance to tell me in your own words. I didn't and I'll regret that forever.

I know I've ruined whatever chance there was of us being anything, let alone friends, but I wanted you to know that you were right. I felt that connection between us too. It wasn't just lust. I felt something when I looked into your eyes that night that I've never felt before. And it's stayed with me ever since.

I've missed you like I miss home when I'm away, which I know probably sounds crazy but it's the truth. So yes, to answer the question you asked me that night, we could have been something. Something very special. And now that I've lost that chance I'm a little bit broken.

It turns out that you were the one who submitted my book to the competition and that you were instrumental in Loretta signing me. Josh said it was all him. That's why I forgave him. I know now that it was all lies. I hope that someday you can forgive me and look back and think of me with a small amount of fondness. But know that I will forever feel like I've missed out on the most wonderful relationship with a very special, caring, loving man.

I know you probably won't reply and I honestly don't blame you after how I acted. But I'm still at the Kingsman. If you haven't yet left Inverness perhaps we could meet? I want to tell you how sorry I am in person. I owe you that and so much more. I should've known better. With much love but more regret, Zara xx

She hit send on the last of many messages and stared at her phone. *Please reply, Lachy, please forgive me.* She packed her things away but kept her phone within earshot just in case. An hour later there was a knock at the door and Zara's heart skipped. She checked her reflection and inhaled deeply before opening it.

'Zara, don't slam the door in my face,' Josh said as he wedged his foot in the opening. 'Just let me in to talk. Please?' He looked terrible. His hair was untidy and he was still in last night's clothing. Although his once pristine tuxedo now looked as if it had been rolled around in the dirt.

'I have nothing to say to you.'

'I really don't get why you're being such a bitch. If it hadn't been for me you wouldn't even *be* here. I'm the one who helped you and now you're going to be making it big you think you can just dump me and move on? I won't let you, Zara. It's not fair.'

She started to laugh. She wasn't sure if it was genuine amusement at his naivety or if it was nerves, but she suddenly found him hilarious. 'You have no clue, do you?'

'No clue about what? One minute you were going to wait for me in bed and the next I go to answer a call about *my son* and you get all jealous and lock me out of the bloody room. Caleb was *ill*, Zara. His mother was frantic with worry. I had no idea you could be so heartless over a child's illness just because his mother and I share history. It speaks volumes about the kind of person you are, that's all I can say. I wonder if your agent knows what an ice queen you are.'

She snorted, unable to contain her incredulity. 'Josh, I *heard* your conversation. Caleb wasn't sick. Katie was jealous, that's why she was calling. She wanted you again as soon as she realised you and I were back together. A real case of wanting what you can't have. Your plan worked. Oh yes, I overheard you telling her about your plan too. You never loved me. You *used* me.'

His nostrils flared and his cheeks coloured. 'But... what about the competition...? *I* sent in your book. By rights I should be getting a cut of whatever you make. If it hadn't been for me—'

'What address did you send the book to, Josh? Hmm?'

'What? I don't know why you're asking me that. Just some address in Inverness, I can't remember.'

'Glasgow. The submissions were made to an address in Glasgow and then forwarded to the HQ in Inverness.'

He stepped back and scratched his head. 'Yeah, I meant Glasgow *obviously*. I sent it to Glasgow and they told me they'd forward it.' He scrunched his face and rolled his eyes, insinuating she was stupid.

'Wrong again. It *was* Inverness. You lied about submitting my... what did you call it? Oh yeah, my *stupid book*. It was Lachy. *He* sent the book and *he* put the agent in touch with me. So whatever claim you think you have it's all bullshit. Now piss off back to whatever rock you crawled out from because, looking at you, that's exactly what happened. Go back to your beloved Katie and see how long that lasts, eh? She can have you because I certainly don't want you, you lying, cheating bastard.' She slammed the door in his face, turned round and slid down the door until her bottom hit the floor.

Once she had calmed her racing heart and her breathing was back to normal, she checked her phone.

Still nothing.

A text came through from Shelley.

> Down in reception. Coming for a drink? Just seen your ex!

Zara grabbed her cases and headed down to the reception area where Marco, Shelley, Jake and Toby were waiting.

'Hey, honey. Are you okay?' Marco asked when she arrived. 'We've just seen Josh storming out of the hotel. He looked like shit. Still wearing last night's clothes too. Has he been up to see you?'

'He has. I gave him a very unpleasant piece of my mind and now, hopefully, he's skulking back to London.'

'Brilliant, well done you! He deserved that,' Marco said.

'Hey, has Lachy replied to your message yet?'

'No, Shells, he hasn't. But I can't just let things go. If something is worth having it's worth going to the ends of the earth for, right? I need to look into his eyes and know that it's over. I mean, I can't be in Scotland only a couple of hours away from his home and not go to see him, can I? He may reject me and I may get hurt, but at least I'll know for sure and won't spend my life wondering *what if*, will I?'

'So you're going to see him?' Marco asked.

Zara nodded. 'I'm going to hire a car and I'm going up there,' she said decisively. 'In Ruby Oates' books it's always the hero that goes to the heroine but I'm a modern woman. There's no rule to say I can't go to him and make things right, is there? I mean, men don't always have to be the go-getters, do they?' She looked to her friends for a response but they were all staring at her with a look of bewilderment. 'Oh, shit. Am I bonkers? Is this a stupid idea?' She slipped her hands into her hair and tugged at the strands.

Shelley huffed. 'If you want me to be honest – and I'm pretty sure you do – then, yes, I think you're bonkers.'

'Oh.' Deflated, Zara sat on the chair by the fireplace.

'But,' Shelley continued, 'people thought the bloke who invented the aeroplane was bonkers and the woman who discovered penicillin, people probably thought *she* was bonkers—'

'*He*. It was Alexander Fleming. He was a *man*,' Marco interjected with a smug expression.

Shelley scowled at him. 'I thought it was Marie Curie or someone.'

'Nope. She was radioactivity. Fleming was penicillin.' His grin got wider and Zara had to chew her lip so as not to laugh.

'Well, whatever. As I was saying, people do things all the time that other people think are bonkers. Take those bright yellow boots that Marco bought. Actually, that's a really bad example because absolutely *nothing* good came from that purchase but, anyway, if it gets you some closure or, best-case scenario, you get the man of your dreams, who gives a shit if it's bonkers? You get my point... hopefully.'

Zara widened her eyes. 'So I *should* go?'

Marco and Shelley glanced at each other and then shouted in unison, 'YOU SHOULD GO!'

40

After the completion of what felt like a gazillion documents, Zara stood in the reception area of the car-rental place waiting for a set of keys. Her stomach was swooshing like a washing machine and she wasn't sure if it was the over-indulgence on pastries or the fear over what she was about to do. It could all go drastically wrong. He could turn her away. Maybe she should call first? But then she ran the risk of him hanging up. At least if she turned up unannounced on his doorstep he was somewhat of a captive audience.

A man appeared and dangled a key chain in front of her. 'There you go, madam. Car's ready. It's the little silver compact round the corner and on the left.'

Another silver dickhead, eh? Is this a sign? She thanked the man and took the keys before walking round the outside of the building to the car.

It was tiny.

'God, it might as well be a bloody pushbike,' she grumbled to no one in particular. But reminded herself this had all been very last minute and it couldn't be helped that the matchbox car was the only one they had left.

She folded herself behind the steering wheel and grabbed her phone from her bag. She programmed the details into the satnav app to find the fastest route. She should be at the croft in just under two and a half hours. She plugged in her little portable speaker and rifled through her music to find the one song that would give her the courage to go. And as Florence and the Machine sang about Delilah, she pushed the button to start the engine and it purred to life like a little, feisty, silver-haired kitty.

Driving through the scenery in the afternoon sunlight was strange but wonderful. Just as she had anticipated the colours of autumn were visible and the leaves still remaining on the trees were every conceivable shade of burnt umber, sienna and ochre with a little crimson thrown in for good measure. Every so often a draught caused by her car whipped up the leaves in a kind of Mexican wave of colour, only for them to float gently down to the ground again.

The sun was beginning its descent and she was desperate to get to the croft before nightfall. The last thing she needed was to be stranded again. Especially if her arrival was unwelcome.

By the time she arrived at the croft the moon was up and the sky was a combination of light grey and orange. There was no sign of Lachy's car or the quad. She climbed out of Silver Dickhead Mark Two and walked to the door. With a little trepidation she knocked and waited but no one came. She could try the door and no doubt find it open, but that would be overstepping a mark. She wondered if perhaps Lachy had stayed in

Inverness or something. She knew he had friends there from his law-firm days. Or maybe he was with Saskia, trying to calm her down. Her mood descended rapidly at that thought and her lip trembled as she tried to eradicate the awful images of the two of them that her mind had conjured up.

She climbed back into the car and tugged up the collar of her thin jacket and wrapped it round herself as best she could as the temperature plummeted further. She would have to leave soon or she ran the risk of dying of hypothermia. And that wouldn't be the best thing for Lachy to come home to. She began to sing to keep herself awake and focused, in case he returned, but she must have dozed off as bright lights startled her awake and she twisted round in her seat to see headlights. She squinted and shielded her eyes but couldn't see who it was. Remembering how isolated she was, she gingerly climbed from the car, her limbs numb with cold, and hoped that whoever the driver of the car was he would take pity on her.

'Zara? Zara Bailey?' a confused voice asked.

'L-Lachy? Yes, it's m-me,' she said through chattering teeth as her body juddered.

Bess leapt from the car and ran towards her, making delighted little yipping noises. Zara bent to sink her face into the dog's fur. 'Hey, Bess, hey, girl. Hello... hello,' she repeated as the dog tried to get closer.

Lachy stomped towards her, breaking the beams of light with his silhouette. 'What on *earth* are you doing out here in the freezing cold in bloody stiletto shoes and a flimsy jacket, for goodness' sake?'

She stood and her lip trembled as she saw his face in the shafts of white light; his expression was one creased with anger.

She stammered, 'I h-had to come. I couldn't just l-leave

things. I'm so s-sorry. If you let me get a warm or m-maybe lend me a jumper I'll leave again. I shouldn't have come, sorry.'

'Your bloody face is blue. Jeez, woman, this is the Highlands, not one of your damned beach resorts. Come on inside.'

Tears escaped but thankfully he had gone to turn off the lights and engine, meaning he couldn't see her sadness. He shoved the front door open and she was reminded again that he never locked it. Considering his reaction, she should have waited inside all along.

He grabbed a hoodie from the hook by the door and tugged her arm. 'Here, put this on. Go sit by the fire and I'll light it.' His tone was sharp and terse. There was no forgiveness there. More tears came.

She did as instructed and suddenly felt a blanket wrapped round her. He then lowered himself to his knees and built a fire in the grate. 'Now stay there and I'll make some coffee,' he said before wandering over to the range.

Bess snuggled up to her and she buried her face in the dog's fur again. 'I've missed you, Bess. I've really missed you.' The dog licked the tears from her face and put her paw on her arm. *Such a sensitive soul.*

A few moments later Lachy returned and handed her a steaming mug. He sat down beside her as she wrapped her icy-cold fingers round the cup and felt the warmth seeping into her skin.

'Now, are you going to tell me what the hell you're doing here?' Lachy asked. Remembering their last encounter at the awards ceremony, she thought there was no wonder he was being so cold.

'I... I just wanted to see you. To talk to you. To explain. When you didn't respond to my text I decided I needed to come and demand that you listen to me.' Her voice trembled and more tears spilled over.

Lachy sighed and rubbed his hands over his face. 'Text? What text? *When* did you text me?'

'Earlier today, I texted to apologise for my awful behaviour.'

He heaved a heavy sigh. 'Right... I see. The thing is my phone got... erm... killed by Saskia after the awards ceremony. I delivered some unwelcome news to her and she snatched it from me and proceeded to stamp on it with her designer stiletto. It's wrecked. I've never seen your text, Zara. I'm sorry.'

Relief flooded her veins. 'So you don't know what happened, then?' He shook his head, his eyes now filled with sadness. With renewed hope she pointed at the entrance. 'Could you pass me my bag? I think I dropped it just inside the door. I'll show you the messages. I don't think I'm capable of saying it all out loud just now.'

He walked over to where she had dropped her bag and retrieved it. With one hand she fumbled around and pulled out her phone. She flicked through the messages and handed it to him.

He took it and stared at the screen. He smiled as he read the first line and glanced up at her with a shake of his head. But as he continued to read the long string of texts his eyes became glassy and he wiped at them, twisting away a little so she couldn't see.

41

When Lachy had finished reading the string of text messages he handed the phone back.

'So now you know,' she whispered.

'So now I know,' he agreed. A silence fell upon them and Zara's eyes gave way to more tears.

'Hey... come on... don't cry. It's fine. You weren't to know.'

She sniffed and wiped at her eyes. 'But it's all ruined.'

He tilted her chin and gazed into her eyes. 'It's only ruined if we let it be.'

She gasped. 'What... what do you mean?'

'I honestly have no idea how all this works, Zara. It's all completely new and ridiculously fast. But all I do know is how I felt when I kissed you that first time. Even before that, in fact, the first time I met you. No one has *ever* taken up space in my mind and my heart like you have. When you rejected me that night I arrived at your hotel, I was so confused. It broke my heart a little, I think. It's the only explanation I can come up with because I've been walking round like a bloody zombie ever since. Then I thought I would try again at the awards. But you were so cold towards me. And you were with *him*. Now, that really hurt. But then tonight, you show up here telling me that you regret what happened and... If I'd received your text message I can assure you I would have been straight back to Inverness. I would have come right to you. I didn't want to let you go the day you left for London and I still don't. And to clarify, I was single and still am. Saskia has her own issues and she won't be dragging me into them any more. I can promise you that. I was yours back then when we made love and I'll happily be yours now if you still want me?' His voice cracked as he rested his forehead on hers.

She nodded and laughed through her tears. 'I still want you.'

He pulled her into his lap and stroked her cheek but hesitated before his lips met hers. It seemed he was waiting for her to change her mind; his breath was short and staggered, his eyes pleading and filled with fear. It was her fault he was so reluctant, so she reached up and kissed him instead. Her hands slipped into his hair as she relished the feeling of his mouth on hers once again.

When the kiss ended she whispered, 'Lachy, take me to bed.'

He scooped her into his arms and carried her, effortlessly, up the stairs to his room. He placed her gently down and kissed her again, his desire for her almost palpable. Feeling a little warmer now her blood was rushing through her veins, she began to undress. She dropped the blanket and the other layers from her body until she was able to slip out of the shirt dress and kick it aside.

He watched as she removed each piece of clothing; hunger

and need visible in his tight jaw. Once she was down to her bra and panties he stood there for a moment devouring her with his gaze. Eventually something spurred him forward and he enveloped her once again, his mouth on hers with a passion that took the breath from her lungs.

'Oh God, I've missed you, Zara,' he mumbled as he nibbled at the soft skin of her neck. Her legs weakened and she moaned at the pleasure radiating through her. She tugged on his jacket and swiftly removed it from his body, and then at his sweater and swept that from his torso. She reached out and touched the flawless skin of his stomach and he inhaled sharply as her fingers reached his belt buckle.

Once Lachy was naked she pulled him backwards onto the bed. His fingers traced the outline of her breast under the lace of her bra and he leaned to kiss the mound of flesh it created above. He freed her from her lace panties and kissed her deeply as he reached round to unfasten the clasp that was keeping her breasts from his touch. Before too long they were skin on skin; heavy breaths the only soundtrack this time as he moved slowly inside her; her legs wrapped round him and her hands on every inch of skin she could reach.

He rested himself on his elbows and locked his gaze on her as his mouth tilted up into a heart-stopping smile. '*This* is where I belong,' he whispered, and she closed her eyes and arched her back, making the connection deeper still.

He moved faster, pulling her closer, and she grasped at him, whispering his name as pleasure heated her blood and she cried out. He followed soon after and peppered her face and neck with gentle kisses as she floated back to earth.

As he held her in his arms she stroked his chest and he smiled. 'I can't believe you're here, Zara. After everything that happened I never thought I'd see you again.' He tilted her chin and kissed her.

'Can we just agree it was all a misunderstanding, Lachy? And can we just forget about it?'

He tucked a strand of hair behind her ear. 'Absolutely. I'm so sorry you didn't win that award. I felt sure you would.'

'Did you really?'

He nodded. 'Really. It's funny because when I told Saskia I was head over heels in love with someone else I never expected any of this. Although, knowing that you were still in Scotland, I was so tempted to come to you again. I knew that Josh had told so many lies and I wanted to make you see that. But... I suppose there's only so many times a man can be rejected. So instead I came home and stayed busy to stop myself from coming back to try again.'

'I wish you had tried again.' She giggled. 'Then I wouldn't have had to drive Silver Dickhead Mark Two all the way up here and wait in the freezing cold.'

He laughed and tugged her on top of him. 'Would you be okay if I said I want you again? Right now?' His voice was a husky whisper.

Her heart leapt and her insides jellified. 'More than okay,' she breathed as he rolled her beneath him once more.

Zara awoke after midnight in Lachy's arms, their limbs tangled beneath the sheets and his firm naked body wrapped round her. She sighed and snuggled deeper into his embrace. *I'm finally home,* she thought. Then it dawned on her that she wasn't; that later the same day she would have to travel back to London. To her *real* home.

Without Lachy.

* * *

They sat at the table eating the scrambled eggs and toast that Lachy had whipped up as Bess lay on Zara's feet keeping them toasty warm. He kept looking across the table at her and smiling.

'What?' She felt her cheeks flaming.

'I don't think I've ever seen anyone more beautiful.'

'Hmm. With my messed-up bed hair and lack of make-up. You can't have a lot to compare me to.'

'You don't need to be compared to anyone,' he said in a gravelly voice that sent a tremble of desire to her core. 'You'd outshine them all.'

She went silent, placed her fork down and lowered her gaze. A lump of emotion had tightened her throat, making it tricky to swallow.

'Zara? Are you okay? Did I say the wrong thing?'

She lifted her chin and forced a smile. 'Not at all. I'll be fine... it's just...'

He stood from his chair and walked round to her side, kneeling down before her. 'Hey, come on, just say it. Are you having second thoughts about us?'

'Oh, goodness, no. That's not it at all. It's the opposite, if anything.'

He scrunched his brow. 'So what's wrong? You were so happy and now you look like you're on the verge of tears.'

'It's just that in a couple of hours I'm going to have to leave to take the car back to Inverness and then I'm going to have to get on a plane and go to London. Which means I won't be with you. I'll be over *six hundred* miles away. And we've only just reconnected. We have so much to learn about each other and I have no idea how we'll do that if we're at opposite ends of the country.'

'I know. It'll be hard for me too.' He reached up and stroked her cheek with the pad of his thumb. 'I don't know how I'll cope not seeing you, not holding you. And especially not waking up beside you. But we'll get through this. I'm in this for the long haul. I don't care how fast it's happened. I think when you know it's right you just know. And this... *us*... it's so right.'

She flung her arms round his neck and kissed him with all the passion she felt in the hope that he would still feel her on his lips when she left.

* * *

After a long, languorous shower together they dried and dressed. Zara borrowed a coat that swamped her and they took Bess to play on the beach. Every time the dog brought the ball back she dropped it at Zara's feet.

'I think she's more *your* dog than mine now,' Lachy huffed, feigning hurt. His comment was sweet but saddened her again as the time to leave loomed.

Later she checked in with Shelley and Marco to let them know she would be heading back in time for the later flight, and that she had called and changed her ticket but that they should go ahead and get their flight as planned. It was lovely that they had been so sure she would win the award that they had booked extra time off work, but she felt bad that she wasn't there with them.

'Just make the most of your last hour or so with Lachy, babe. We're absolutely fine. We've already had cocktails so it's just as well you're not flying with us.' Shelley laughed.

Finally the time Zara had been dreading arrived. Lachy walked her to the little silver car and pulled her into his arms. 'I'll call you tonight, okay?'

She nodded, unable to speak.

He tilted her chin and kissed her. 'Don't worry, Zara, we'll get to know each other. We'll talk as often as we can and I'll visit you in London. I'm not sure what Bess will make of the city but if she gets to see you, I'm sure she'll love it. She adores you as much as I do.' He pulled her to him again and stroked her hair. 'Just promise me you won't give up on us.'

She gazed up at him through tear-fogged eyes. 'I promise. Do you?'

'I promise with all my heart. Now go on or you'll miss your flight. Drive carefully and let me know when you're about to get on the plane.'

'I will. See you soon, Lachy.'

'As soon as I can possibly make it. Wild horses couldn't stop me.'

She turned to walk away and Bess yelped. She turned back and crouched and the dog came running to her and jumped up to lick her face.

'I'll be back soon, girl, don't worry. I promise.' She hurriedly walked to the car and climbed in before she could make any other decision. But her heart ached to be leaving Lachy and Bess again. She needed to come back soon.

Very soon.

Lachy

He'd never been a particularly emotional man. There had been exceptions, of course: his mother's funeral, his father's funeral, walking away from Zara's hotel room when she had rejected him, and that precise moment he had to watch Zara leave again. He'd only just got her back and now she had to go. There were words on the tip of his tongue but he dared not say them. *I love you, Zara. Don't go, Zara. Move here with me, Zara.* But of course they would have to stay unsaid. The last thing he wanted to do was scare her away. Especially not now she held his heart firmly in her grasp.

42

Being back in London was frustrating. Zara spoke on the phone with Lachy every single day, sometimes more than once. And they even connected via video call, which was marginally better. But nothing could compare with being in the same room as him, touching him, making love to him, kissing him. The homesickness she had felt before was now compounded and she knew that it was Lachy she was homesick for.

She was distracted at work and instead of being excited about her future trips abroad, she dreaded them for the extra miles they would put between her and the man she so desperately wanted to be with. The publishing contract had been signed and her first book was now with editors, which was all extremely exciting. And in every minute of spare time she had that didn't involve talking to Lachy, she was working on book two.

Things were increasingly serious between Toby and Marco and they had been talking about the possibility of moving in together, which meant that all too soon Zara would be alone again. Something she didn't relish the thought of, in spite of the fact she was ecstatically happy for her best friend.

An invite had arrived from Patrick and Sophie for their wedding, along with a side note that said she could bring a plus one. However, she was unsure how that would work with her plus one being the ex of the bride's sister. Wow, life was complicated.

Two months into her long-distance relationship with Lachy and she missed him more with each passing day, but at least Christmas was around the corner. Saturday afternoon and she was in her room on her laptop chatting to him by video call whilst Marco was out flat-hunting with Toby and their call was coming to an end.

'I'll see you next weekend for Christmas, okay?' he said with a huge smile on his face, even though she knew he missed her like crazy.

'I can't wait,' she told him.

'Look, Zara... I need to say something.'

Her heart leapt and she twisted her fingers in her lap, worried about his next words. 'Okay...'

'I love you. And I want you to move in with me.'

She gasped and he immediately covered his mouth with his hand. 'Shit, shit, I'm sorry. I take it back. Well, the bit about you moving in, not the bit about loving you, because if I'm honest I've been in love with you since day one. But... anyway... I love you. Let's leave it at that.'

She laughed at his rambling. 'I love you too. But—'

He held his hand up to halt her. 'Nope, don't say anything else. It was a ridiculous suggestion and I took it back anyway.'

She nodded. 'Okay. I'll see you next weekend. I love you, Lachy,' she repeated.

'I love you, my beautiful Zara.'

She ended the call and slumped back onto her bed with a huge grin on her face. 'He loves me!' she yelled into the empty room. 'He bloody loves me! Eeeeeeeeek!'

* * *

The Monday morning commute was chilly and the only thing that was nice about walking to the office from the station was seeing the Christmas lights. The twinkle of tinsel caught her eye and she had to stop and admire the extravagant window displays. She especially loved the bookshop windows; more so now her own book was out there and featured in those particular displays. It had only been out a week but the sales figures were incredible, so she'd been told. Her book launch was set for the week after Christmas in Inverness and she couldn't wait. Not only was she going to get to spend time with Lachy, but she was going home with him to spend a week there after the launch for Hogmanay. She was secretly hoping that she might get snowed in and have to stay longer – how romantic that would be. She couldn't wait to see Bess and the tree that Lachy had bought especially for her visit.

Noah poked his head round her office door. 'Zara, have you got a minute?'

'Sure, come on in.'

He walked in and closed the door behind him. 'We need to talk.'

'Oh? Is everything okay?'

He sat on the chair opposite her. 'Erm... yes, kind of. Well... the thing is... Here's the thing... I don't want you to be the luxury travel writer any more.'

Zara opened her mouth to speak but no words would come. She sat in open-mouthed silence for way too long until eventually she said, 'Are you firing me, Noah?' Panic set in. 'What did I do wrong? I don't get it. I thought I was doing well for the magazine.'

His eyes widened. 'Oh God, no, I'm not firing you. Not at all.'

Her eyes widened and she pushed herself up from the desk. 'Oh God, you don't want me to be the outdoors and adventures travel writer instead, do you? Because I know you loved what I did with the NC500 article, but it's really not my thing, Noah, and I—'

'Shit, I should have worded this better; I probably should have started with something more positive. Let me start over.' He stood and left the room. Zara sat back down at her desk, face scrunched in utter confusion.

Noah walked in again. 'Zara, have you got a minute?'

She gave him a look that she hoped expressed her incredulity. 'You know I have.'

'Right. Right.' He sat down in the chair opposite her again. 'Right.'

'You said that already.'

'I did. Okay. Look, it's like this... I want you to be my deputy editor.'

She gasped. 'Seriously?'

'Seriously. Now, the reasons behind this are purely selfish, so hear me out before you accept or decline. Oh, bugger, please don't decline.'

She grinned. 'I'm listening.'

Noah nodded. 'Good. Now, I'm very much aware that your book is taking off. It's flying off the shelves, by all accounts. I've bought copies for everyone I know.'

Still confused, Zara giggled nervously. 'Thank you, I think?'

'And I know that you're crazy about that farmer, Lachy. And

that he lives a gazillion miles away and there's a good chance, at some point in the not-so-distant future, you'll be leaving to move up there.'

'I never said I was—'

'Zara, I'm not daft. Long distance doesn't work. *Ever.* So one of you will have to make sacrifices. And obviously *he* can't bring his farm or croft or whatever it is down here to London. So... I want you to be my deputy so that I can keep you. And that you can work remotely for me from the Highlands whenever the time is right. If that's next week, so be it. If it's in two years, so be it. But the fact is you're the best writer I have. And I don't want to lose you. So instead of disappearing off for weeks at a time to far-flung places you can simply fly down to London once every couple of months for meetings and everything else can be done via the Internet. Video conference and such. What do you think?'

Her eyes remained wide and she was stunned into silence yet again.

He stood to leave. 'I'll leave it with you. Just think about it and let me know. But it's got to the point where I need a deputy. And I can't think of anyone better.'

'Th-thank you, Noah. I'll give it some serious thought.' But leaving London? Was that something she could do? She'd dreamed about it but only when she'd known it would never happen. Her family was here. Shelley and Marco were here. Almost her entire *life* was here.

* * *

Marco was staying at Toby's in the house he shared with some friends so that Zara and Lachy could have some quality time together over Christmas. She had told Marco about Noah's suggestion and about her doubts. He'd said she was the only one who could make such a big decision. Typical – when she didn't want his opinion he gave it freely.

She had bought a real Christmas tree and had decorated it in readiness, trying to make everything feel right, but knowing she had a difficult conversation ahead of her when Lachy arrived and she wasn't sure how he was going to take things.

The platform was freezing as she stood waiting for his train to pull in. He had travelled overnight with Bess and, from what she could gather from the texts he'd sent, the dog had been an absolute star. She had enjoyed the attention she'd received from the staff on board and had almost eaten her body weight in sneaky snacks.

When the train pulled into the station, she waited impatiently for them to disembark and when they did, she ran along to meet them. Bess barked and jumped around excitedly as Lachy pulled Zara into his arms and kissed her unabashedly as people walked by wheeling cases.

'This feels good,' he told her as he held her. 'I've missed you so much.'

'I've missed you too.'

'Come on, take me to your place so you can show me how much you've missed me, and by that I mean you can cook for me, woman.' He wiggled his eyebrows like some comedy character and she whacked his chest playfully.

'You'll have take-out pizza and be grateful. I have other plans for you, Mr Grant.'

His nostrils flared and his eyes darkened. 'That sounds better than food.'

* * *

Back at the apartment, Lachy dropped his bag on the living-room floor and took in his surroundings. 'This is a great wee place. Very modern.'

'I love it. It took a lot of work to get it like this, but I think it's paid off.'

'Aw, your tree's beautiful. Mine looks a bit haphazard. I think Bess could've done a better job of decorating it.'

'I bought a real one especially for you coming.'

He gasped in feigned horror. 'Don't tell me you usually have a fake one?'

She cringed. 'Afraid so. Getting that thing up here took two of us. It was like something off *You've Been Framed*.'

Bess ran around, her nose to the ground and tail wagging as she investigated every room. She was especially fascinated by the packages under the tree but eventually she lay down on the rug and dozed off.

Lachy laughed as he watched her. 'The staff on the train have worn her out. I'll have to take her for a walk later, with you not having a garden. But in the meantime, come here, you.' He tugged Zara's hand and pulled her into his arms.

'I can't believe you're here,' she sighed.

He ran his nose down hers and placed a gentle, loving kiss on her lips. 'Well, I am and I want to make the most of you while I have you.' He leaned and kissed her again, deeply and languorously this time. 'Now are you going to take me to bed?' he whispered into her ear.

She smiled and took his hand and pulled him into her room, closing the door behind them.

43

Later as they ate pizza and drank wine by the twinkling lights of the Christmas tree, Zara was deep in thought. She needed to speak to Lachy about the future and she anticipated it might be a difficult conversation.

'Earth to Zara.' He laughed as he ducked his head to make eye contact.

Shaking her head, she said, 'Oh, gosh, sorry, I drifted off for a moment.'

He frowned and a look of concern changed his expression. 'Where did you drift off to?'

She sighed deeply. 'Look, we need to talk.'

He straightened up and wiped his hands on a paper napkin. 'Oh, I see. Nothing good ever comes from a conversation that starts off like that.'

'It's not what you think. Well, I don't think it is.'

'Come on, out with it. I'm a big lad. Lay it on me.'

'Noah wants me to be his deputy editor.'

He squinted. 'And that's a bad thing because...?'

'He basically hinted that he thinks I'm going to disappear

off to the Highlands and live with you. And he doesn't want to lose me. But I've never said that I'd do that. I think he feels I'm maybe not in the right mindset to do the travel job any more because I'm too distracted by your absence.'

He swallowed hard. 'I see. So what are you saying?'

'I love my job. I love writing, but he's right. I *am* distracted by your absence. And therefore I'm not giving 100 per cent to my job. And you know me; I hate to give anything less than 100 per cent.'

Lachy lowered his gaze and his shoulders slumped. 'I see.'

'And long distance doesn't work. *Ever.* So Noah says.'

He lifted his chin and whispered, 'And what do *you* say?'

With a pounding heart she shrugged. 'I think I agree.'

He nodded silently and swallowed hard. 'Right... right. So... what you're trying to tell me is... even though we love each other... this... this weekend is our last?' The defeat in his voice almost broke her.

She frowned. 'That depends on *you*, Lachy.'

He closed his eyes and shook his head. 'I can't relocate to London, Zara. I'm so sorry. I would if I could but the croft, my land, I can't go back to being a big-city lawyer again. I just... I can't.' He opened his eyes again and fixed his watery gaze on her. 'I'd do *anything* to make this work. I just... I *can't* move to London. I'm so sorry.'

She closed her eyes and took a deep, calming breath as she searched for the courage she needed. 'No, I know that. So there's only one solution.'

Lachy sniffed and swiped at his eyes and his words came out in a rush. 'I want to say we can move past this. I want to *beg* you not to give up on us, Zara. But the last thing I want is for you to be unhappy. I couldn't do that to you.'

This wasn't exactly going how she'd planned.

She reached over and took his hands in hers. 'Lachy, *stop*, I need to ask you a question. And I need you to think about this because it's huge, okay?' He nodded silently, his lip trembling.

'Please can I move into the croft at Scourie with you?'

He inhaled sharply and the colour rapidly drained from his face. 'What?'

Oh, shit. That's not the reaction I wanted. 'I... I said please can I—?'

'No, no, I *heard* you... but you were breaking up with me.'

She shook her head vehemently. 'No! I wasn't! I was trying to pluck up the courage but... I didn't want to ask. The last time you mentioned it you immediately took it back, so I was worried you didn't want me to. So I was trying to get you to ask me by dropping hints. But instead you thought I was breaking up with you! None of this has gone—'

He grabbed her and pulled her into his lap and stopped her words with his mouth. When he pulled away, he smiled. 'I can't believe you just did that. Why didn't you just come right out with it? You're a strong, independent woman, aren't you?'

She rolled her eyes. 'Oh God, I really am *never* going to live that down, am I?'

He sighed as his shoulders relaxed and relief flooded his features. 'So... when can you move in?'

* * *

Christmas morning Zara awoke to the smell of bacon cooking and her stomach grumbled in anticipation. She climbed out of bed and wandered into the living room where Slade were informing everyone, in no uncertain terms, what day it was and the tree lights were twinkling away. Bess greeted her with a wet nose to her bare leg, which made her squeal. The dog thought this was some kind of a game and fetched her Santa toy.

'Bess, you *are* bonkers.' She wrestled with the collie for a while until Lachy brought through a plate of bacon sandwiches.

'Good morning, sexy,' he said as he planted a kiss on her head and the sandwiches on the coffee table.

'Good morning. Mmm, they smell delicious.'

'Tuck in before they go cold. The coffee's on.'

She grabbed a sandwich and took a huge bite. 'So today's the day you meet my folks,' she said through a mouthful of bacon.

Lachy laughed, his shoulders bouncing as he did. 'You do know that saying it with a mouthful doesn't make it any less scary, don't you?' Zara grinned. 'Anyway, should I expect your dad to punch me for taking his little girl away to Scotland?'

'Actually, no, they were surprisingly accepting of it all when I mentioned it. It was a relief. Dad's looking forward to coming up to visit. He says he wants you to set him to work.'

Lachy raised his eyebrows. 'Well, that can easily be arranged but he might regret it. You never know, they might just relocate themselves.'

'Funnily enough, Wills has applied to two universities in Scotland, so you never know.'

They finished their sandwiches and, of course, Bess got one of her own. As the collie lay munching happily on her breakfast Lachy pulled out a small box from under the tree.

'Now, this may come as a surprise to you but I brought this gift with me from Scotland, ready wrapped *before* we had our conversation about you moving north. I was super organised for once.' He handed it to Zara and she chewed on her lip. It was ring-box-sized. She tore off the paper and sure enough there was a little hinged box inside with a decorative bow on top. Her heart hammered at her ribs as she put her fingers on the lid and lifted it.

Inside was a little silver key. Zara took it out and looked up at Lachy with a question in her eyes.

'Remember when you left the croft after the accident and I gave you the keyring?' She nodded. 'I hoped, even way back then, that one day I'd be able to give you the key to go with it. And here we are. I knew as soon as you shouted at me outside your tent, when I found you illegally camped, that I'd fall for you. And it happened fast. And I knew from the moment I kissed you that I'd do everything I could to make you mine. It may have been a rocky road to get here, pardon the pun, but you've had my heart since the day I met you. And now you have the key to our home.'

Zara's lip began to tremble and she crawled into his lap and kissed him with every ounce of love she felt for him. She knew that the symbolism behind it meant that this was it for them. He might never lock the door to his home, but she knew that this was the key to his heart *and* to his life. And now they were hers.

* * *

One month later

The last of the boxes had been unpacked and Zara stood in the lounge at Scouriemore Croft as Lachy put the last of their photos up on the wall. It was really feeling like home since little bits of her furniture had arrived in her dad's van when they'd visited. The fire was blazing and there was an aroma of freshly made hot chocolate wafting in from the kitchen. Snow blanketed the ground outside and the sheep were safely in the barn now that winter had really set in. The freezer in the barn closest to the house was stocked to the brim and the fibre broadband was up and running, meaning she could have video calls with Noah, her agent or her publisher whenever she needed to.

The old antique desk by the window had been cleared of Lachy and his father's paperwork and her laptop sat there now, with book three open at chapter one. She would never get used to people wanting her autograph in their copies of her books, but at least she could escape to this beautiful croft when she wanted to shut out the world and spend time with Lachy and, of course, Bess too.

She sat down at her desk and peered out of the window at the beach below; the icy-cold water lapped at the shoreline and she knew that tomorrow, regardless of the cold, she would be down there, wrapped up like an Eskimo, with Bess, throwing her favourite ball. But for now her new best friend walked over and snuggled by her feet, just as she did every time Zara sat to write.

Lachy came over, wrapped his arms round her and kissed her temple tenderly. 'I'll go warm some stew on the range for dinner whilst you finish that chapter. Then later we can snuggle up and watch a movie before bed.'

'Mmm, sounds perfect,' she told him as she nuzzled into his embrace.

As she gazed out at the view before her, to the snow-capped mountains in the distance, she thought back over the past twelve months and all that had happened, from the NC500 that had brought her to Scotland in the first place, to the book that had changed her career dramatically and to meeting the love of her life. She knew she could have been forgiven for expecting to wake from a vivid dream to find none of it was real. But this was her life now. Her reality. And it couldn't have been more perfect.

Who could have predicted, when she finished her novel the previous summer, that the most incredible of *all* the new beginnings she would experience would be her very own?

EPILOGUE

TEN MONTHS LATER

Zara sat at the table in the prestigious Gladstone Library in London's Whitehall Place. Lachy clutched her hand and bounced his knee up and down.

'I think you're more nervous than I am,' she whispered.

Lachy squeezed her hand. 'I think I am. You look far too chilled out. What's going on?'

'Oh, I think the champers you had delivered to the hotel room this afternoon helped a little. And what happened *after* the champagne helped even more.' She nibbled her lip and gave him a knowing look.

He leaned forward and kissed her tenderly. 'I don't think it had the same effect on me. Maybe we should try again when we get back.'

'You're incorrigible, Mr Grant.'

'I certainly am where you're concerned, Miss Bailey.'

It was strange to be at the OFAL awards again. But it was even stranger to be in London for them. This year they were being hosted by London-based Bench Publishing. The setting for the ceremony was stunning. The shelved walls were filled, floor to ceiling, with books, some of them pretty ancient. The ceiling above was a painted, carved, relief plasterwork and in the centre of each panel was an ornate brass chandelier with opaque glass shades. The table centrepieces were tall candelabras with fresh flowers decorating the stands. It was a truly elegant affair.

The lights dimmed and a hush fell on the room. From what Zara had read of the nominees, the evening was set to be fantastic and very diverse. Zara was shortlisted in the overall Novel of the Year for her debut, *New Beginnings*, and only when the introduction music played did her nerves *really* kick in.

Her mum and dad grinned at her from across the table and Shelley, Jake, Marco and Toby held up crossed fingers as she glanced their way. She was, as always, grateful to them all for being there; especially Shelley, considering her pregnancy announcement the previous week and the fact that she was suffering from what was evidently *all-day* sickness. At least they hadn't had to travel far this time.

Award after award was announced and everyone applauded and cheered for both shortlist candidates and winners. The Best Unpublished Newcomer award was won by a young woman of nineteen and she trembled like a jelly whilst up on the stage. Zara wanted to go up and hug her.

The evening floated by and finally it was time for the Novel of the Year award. Zara's heart rate increased, Lachy's knee bounced faster and it looked as if the whole of her table were holding their breath. The list of books was a combination of the people she was shortlisted with the year before and a few other, more established authors. Her favourite author, Ruby Oates, was presenting the award and Shelley had said it was a sign. Zara didn't think she believed in signs, but the jury was still out.

Ruby stood on stage and chatted about her own journey as

a writer and Zara listened intently, fascinated, but she heard
Lachy chuntering, just above a whisper, for Ruby to get on with
announcing the winner. She stifled a giggle.

'So without further ado, ladies and gentlemen... I'm pleased
to announce that the Original Fiction Association Literature
Awards Novel of the Year goes to...' A thrumming vibration of
anticipation could be felt and Lachy's hold became tighter on
her hand. Her heart pounded and her stomach somersaulted.
There was an overly long dramatic pause... and then, 'Zara
Bailey for *New Beginnings!*'

Her table erupted, everyone was up on their feet, cheers
rang round the room, but Zara sat there stunned, staring
straight ahead, surrounded by people jumping and applauding
her.

Lachy crouched before her and cupped her face in his
palms. His smile was warm and so incredibly handsome and
for a moment she forgot why she was so nervous. 'Zara, my
love, you need to go and collect your award. You did it. You
won.' He kissed her and drew her from her trance-like state.
She stood, and as applause echoed round her she made her
way to the stage.

Once up there, Ruby kissed her on both cheeks and whispered, 'You look a little more shell-shocked than when I met
you last year. I've read the book and I have to say it's wonderful.'
Zara's eyes were wide. Not only had Ruby remembered her, but
she'd loved her book too. And Zara had thought last year's
awards were a dream come true. She took the crystal trophy
from Ruby and thanked her. When she lifted it a little she saw
her name engraved at the bottom on a silver plaque. *Bloody hell,
this is real.*

She realised a hush had settled over the room. They were
waiting for her to speak. *Oh, dammit... maybe I should've actually*

written something. If only she'd listened to everyone who had insisted she would win.

She cleared her throat. 'Ahem... thank you so, so much. This is a bit surreal. If someone had told me a year ago that I would be up on this stage collecting an award for a book *I'd* written, I'd have said they were delusional. But... here I am.' She paused and tried to look for Lachy, but the lights were too bright. 'Now... I hadn't prepared a speech... I think my family and friends have more faith in me than I do in myself, so I'll start by saying thank you to *them* for their undying love and support.' More applause and a whistle from her dad. 'And my wonderful publisher and agent, who put up with my neurotic emails filled with self-doubt. But there's one person, in particular, who I want to thank and that's my partner, Lachy. He grounds me; he lifts me up when I'm low. He keeps me fed and watered when I'm writing. And he reads every single thing I write and gives me his honest opinion.'

Emotion bubbled up from deep within her and she fought to keep her composure. 'I once told him I was a strong, independent woman, even though I was covered in mud and struggling at the time. I think I still am... although Lachy would probably just say I'm stubborn. But even a strong, independent woman needs someone to share her life with.' She placed her trophy on the podium. 'So... instead of a long, drawn-out speech I just have one question to ask.' She turned to face the direction of the table of her family and friends, hoping Lachy could see her. 'Lachlan Grant... will you marry me?'

The room erupted once more and, from somewhere, music began to play. A spotlight pointed to her table and her friends and parents were clapping, her mum and Shelley were sobbing, but Lachy wasn't there. Panic set in as her eyes darted round the room. She spotted Shelley gesturing and pointing for her to look to her right and when she did, her gaze fell on Lachy. He was kneeling on the stage a few feet away.

The applause died down and Zara looked at him with confusion. He grinned and wiped at his eyes. 'You kind of stole my thunder there, Bailey.'

She smiled down at him. 'What are you doing down there?'

'Well... As you were proposing to me over the microphone, I was sneaking up here to propose to you.' Laughter and applause rang round the room.

She gasped and covered her mouth with her hands as tears escaped and Lachy held aloft a small red velvet box. 'This one isn't a key, by the way,' he said so only she could hear. He opened the lid and inside was the most beautiful diamond ring Zara had ever seen.

'So my question to you is, will *you* marry *me*, Zara Bailey?'

'Yes, 100 per cent, yes!' She launched herself at him and kissed him as the audience stood and applauded the happy couple.

He whispered, 'I think we might need to buy a cabinet for your awards. In fact, I should probably tell you I have builders booked to start next week on the barn closest to the house. You're getting your own writing studio. Complete with your favourite view. I think every successful, strong, independent author needs one.'

'Oh, I love you, Lachlan Grant.'

'And I love you too, soon-to-be Mrs Zara Bailey-Grant.'

ACKNOWLEDGEMENTS

The inspiration for this book came from travels round the north coast of the stunning country I now call home and I, therefore, wish to thank the warm-hearted people who reside in the Scottish Highlands for their hospitality. You and the magical place you live in are the reasons I return every year.

I also want to thank the Proclaimers for their uplifting, foot stomping music that had a hand in getting my ideas flowing. The working title for this book was originally *500 Miles* – similar to their well-known song, and I lost count of how many times I listened to this and their other tracks throughout the writing process.

A squishy hug is going out to Caroline and Christine, my lovely friends, for being my beta readers during the writing of this story. As always you were honest and supportive and I love you very much for that.

Thanks to my marvellous editor, Caroline, and each member of the fantastic team at Boldwood for being utterly fabulous. From editors to cover designers, proofreaders, the marketing team and everyone else involved – I'm so grateful that I've had the opportunity to work with such a lovely and enthusiastic group of people.

I'm sending love and thanks to my agent, Lorella, and her team too. Thank you for working so hard for me and my books. I appreciate all you do.

I have a wonderful network of support around me made up

of both family and friends and I'm so incredibly thankful for having you all in my life. There are far too many for me to name individually but know that my heart is full because of you.

Finally I want to thank my readers. It still floors me that people actually read my books because they want to and I don't think that will ever really sink in. I never take reads or reviews for granted and appreciate every single one. Thank you from the bottom of my heart.

ABOUT THE AUTHOR

Lisa Hobman has written many brilliantly reviewed women's fiction titles – the first of which was shortlisted by the RNA for their debut novel award. In 2012 Lisa relocated her family from Yorkshire to a village in Scotland and this beautiful backdrop now inspires her uplifting and romantic stories.

Sign up to Lisa Hobman's mailing list for news, competitions and updates on future books.

Visit Lisa's website: www.lisajhobman.com

Follow Lisa on social media:

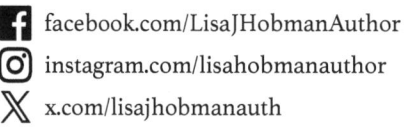

facebook.com/LisaJHobmanAuthor

instagram.com/lisahobmanauthor

x.com/lisajhobmanauth

ALSO BY LISA HOBMAN

The Skye Collection Series

Dreaming Under An Island Skye

Under An Italian Sky

Wishing Under a Starlit Skye

Together Under A Snowy Skye

The Highlands Series

Coming Home to the Highlands

Chasing a Highland Dream

A Highland Family Affair

Standalone Novels

Starting Over At Sunset Cottage

It Started with a Kiss

A Summer of New Beginnings

What Becomes of the Broken Hearted

Boldwood

Boldwood Books is an award-winning fiction publishing company seeking out the best stories from around the world.

Find out more at www.boldwoodbooks.com

Join our reader community for brilliant books, competitions and offers!

Follow us
@BoldwoodBooks
@TheBoldBookClub

Sign up to our weekly deals newsletter

https://bit.ly/BoldwoodBNewsletter

Printed in Dunstable, United Kingdom